ADVANCE PRAISE FOR

The Book Tour

"*The Book Tour* is a sensational debut that will leave readers begging Emily Ohanjanians for another novel to devour! I loved every page!"
—HANNAH BONAM-YOUNG, *New York Times* bestselling author of *People Watching*

"Reading Emily Ohanjanians's *The Book Tour* felt like sitting in a conversation with a close friend. It was at turns deliciously juicy and fun, with beautiful explorations of grief, the complexities of being a second-generation American, and muddling through how to live your life the way you truly want to. I adored Ana and Ryan's story and was completely caught up in Emily's perfect blend of wit and poignance. . . . A gorgeous debut!"
—JESSICA JOYCE, bestselling author of *You, with a View*

"Witty, warm, and wonderfully romantic, *The Book Tour* was an absolute delight from start to finish."
— JENN MCKINLAY, *New York Times* bestselling author of *Love at First Book*

"With a romance to root for and a witty, richly rendered peek into publishing, *The Book Tour* perfectly blends deft characterization with romcom delight. Ana and Ryan's story from between the covers to between the sheets is a tour de force and a book lover's dream."
—EMILY WIBBERLEY and AUSTIN SIEGEMUND-BROKA, authors of *The Roughest Draft*

"Steamy, swoony, and loads of fun, Emily Ohanjanians's debut, *The Book Tour*, is a triumph! I fell in love with fiery, capable Ana and serious, competent Ryan. Their love story, complete with nods to Ana's Armenian culture, a moving portrait of grief, and navigating first- and second-generation immigrant relationships, provided a nuanced and delightful read. Highly recommend—I can't wait to read whatever Ohanjanians writes next!"

—Uzma Jalaluddin, author of *Ayesha at Last*

"*The Book Tour* is a rewarding tale of friendship, family, and love. Sexy, straightlaced Ryan is sure to be your new favorite book boyfriend! Romance fans will adore this swoony, heartfelt rom-com."

—Lucy Lehane, author of *Thirsty*

"Moving, sexy, and witty, Emily Ohanjanians's *The Book Tour* is a rom-com lover's dream! Ana and Ryan's sizzling chemistry and emotional connection had me flying through the pages, and Ana's journey in learning to love herself and navigate her relationships with her family resonated deeply. Ohanjanians is a writer to watch!"

—Noreen Nanja, author of *The Summers Between Us*

"With a strong protagonist you'll root for, a sassy relationship you'll be cheering on, laugh-out-loud humor, and plenty of sexy heat, *The Book Tour* by Emily Ohanjanians is a spicy romance lover's dream."

—Holly Cassidy, author of *The Christmas Countdown*

"As smart as it is steamy, this debut rom-com is fun, fresh, and fast-paced, and the *sexiest* book I've read this year. Loved it!"

—Chantel Guertin, bestselling author of *It Happened One Christmas*

"Smart and laugh-out-loud funny, with spicy love scenes that will have you fanning yourself with one hand as you quickly turn pages with the other . . . an astonishing debut by Ohanjanians, who zips to the top of my list of auto-buy authors on her first time out . . . Don't sleep on this clever, deeply thoughtful novel. It's unputdownable."

—Noelle Salazar, *USA Today* bestselling author of *The Flight Girls*

The Book Tour

The Book Tour

a novel

EMILY OHANJANIANS

DELL

New York

Dell
An imprint of Random House
A division of Penguin Random House LLC
1745 Broadway, New York, NY 10019
randomhousebooks.com
randomhousebookclub.com
penguinrandomhouse.com

A Dell Trade Paperback Original

Copyright © 2026 by Emily Ohanjanians
Book club guide copyright © 2026 by Penguin Random House LLC

Penguin Random House values and supports copyright. Copyright fuels creativity, encourages diverse voices, promotes free speech, and creates a vibrant culture. Thank you for buying an authorized edition of this book and for complying with copyright laws by not reproducing, scanning, or distributing any part of it in any form without permission. You are supporting writers and allowing Penguin Random House to continue to publish books for every reader. Please note that no part of this book may be used or reproduced in any manner for the purpose of training artificial intelligence technologies or systems.

DELL and the D colophon are registered trademarks of
Penguin Random House LLC.
RANDOM HOUSE BOOK CLUB and colophon are trademarks of
Penguin Random House LLC.

ISBN 978-0-593-98475-8
Ebook ISBN 978-0-593-98476-5

Printed in the United States of America

1st Printing

BOOK TEAM: Production editor: Luke Epplin • Managing editor: Saige Francis • Production manager: Samuel Wetzler • Copy editor: Taylor McGowan • Proofreaders: Kathryn Jones, Deb Bader, Liz Carbonell

Book design by Alexis Flynn

Title-page art: Graficriver/Adobe Stock

The authorized representative in the EU for product safety and compliance is Penguin Random House Ireland, Morrison Chambers, 32 Nassau Street, Dublin D02 YH68, Ireland. https://eu-contact.penguin.ie.

To romance authors everywhere.
Your stories are everything.

The Book Tour

Chapter 1

Capable women are both overestimated and underestimated all our lives. A truth perhaps universally unacknowledged, but evident in some form or other at our every turn.

Our competence is either weaponized against us—*Why should I cook when your meals are so much better than mine, babe?* (Okay, words that have never been said to me since I can't cook to save my life, but the point stands)—or it's called into question. Because how competent could we really be without a hero swooping in to mansplain our area of expertise to us?

And if we're successful? Call in the haters. *You haven't earned it* or *Yeah, but the thing you're successful at is worthless* or *Why are podcasters publishing books? Stay in your lane, boo.*

Fine, maybe that last one is specific to me.

I'm buzzing with excitement for my book launch tonight when the push notification drops like a bomb on my phone. Among so many innocent ones—congratulations on my publication day, a request from Mom to call the gardener again because her hedges weren't cut short enough this morning, and various promos from Grubhub and Postmates—comes the full siren blare of *LitCrit* magazine's review of my book.

I shouldn't click through to read it. I promised Maral I wouldn't read any reviews she didn't personally send me after triaging first. My beloved cousin regularly saves me from my own clawing curiosity. Or tries to. (To be fair, it's a full-time job.)

But Mar's not here. She's in my kitchen, making us coffee before we begin recording the podcast, while I'm chewing my cuticles over my phone in the den that doubles as our recording studio. And hey, what she doesn't know won't hurt her.

It can hurt me, though.

> *So Proud of You* has become a top-charting podcast in recent years. Host Ana Movilian, who originally gained fame via her viral videos, interviews regular people and celebrity guests alike, a la *We Can Do Hard Things*, but with a focus on first- and second-generation immigrant experiences: their unique pressures, family expectations vs. their own dreams, and so on. Her sunny disposition is a hit with fans, and her brand of wholesome cheerleading includes spouting encouraging words many people never hear at home, which may explain her rabid online following but fails to shed light on why big publishing continues to favor influencers over real writers.

After skimming the next paragraph, which goes on to talk about how nothing is sacred anymore in the nonfiction space, celebrity books stealing shelf space in shops from more warranted offerings, and unnecessary fluff pieces like mine being less valuable than the paper on which they're printed, I close out of the tab like it's about to set fire to my phone.

I take a deep breath, willing away the unease that prickles under the surface of my skin. This is nothing new—I expected this. Fans may be excited about the book's release today, but since I made the deal two years ago there have been literary snobs who can't help shouting their abject distaste at "another book by some inane influencer" (that quote courtesy of *Talon* magazine).

They're lumping me in with a type: the Midwestern mom who gains a following making videos of countertop Tex-Mex concoctions and lands a six-figure cookbook deal, or the affable frat bro traveloguer whose memoir, bloated with pages and pages of photos off his Instagram grid, is shelved next to *Eat Pray Love*. Never mind that I worked my ass off—just as I do for everything else—writing a book I could be proud of. Never mind that my editor and publisher and most reviewers and tastemakers have lauded its quality. Never mind that the book is an extension of a brand that touches a deep chord for people, offering a sense of support and community they've never felt before (to the tune of four million followers across social channels, ahem, but who's counting).

Good luck shaking ya girl's confidence, *LitCrit*. Bad reviews aren't exactly hot takes—I've read my fair share by now. Hell, I've spent a lifetime ignoring haters or using them as motivation. No matter how hard a woman works or how earned her success is, some people—including, sometimes, her loved ones—will inevitably dismiss her wins. It's par for the course, and my skin's grown thicker than a reptile's. I practically have a magic wand when it comes to disappearing unwelcome emotions. Poof, they never even existed.

This is not going to spoil my big day.

As Maral's footsteps approach, I sit up straight, take a deep breath, and throw my shoulders back. Belatedly I realize I'm still clutching my phone and clatter it face down on the table just as she appears, holding two mugs, in the doorway.

She tilts her head disapprovingly. "You weren't reading reviews, were you?"

"No," I say, pasting on my winningest smile.

She takes in my bouncing leg under the table. "Ana," she admonishes.

"You look really pretty today." Major-league understatement. Even with a scowl on her face, Maral is a sight to behold, her dark waves cascading over one shoulder of the rose-colored dress she's already donned for the launch tonight.

She raises a dubious brow. "Uh-huh." Places a mug before me. "Simu Liu is all cued up. You ready to get started? Or do you need a minute?"

I sip the coffee, its dark-roast deliciosity powering through me. I imagine it washing away the prickliness the review left in its wake and flooding me with good vibes only. Poof.

Chin high, I slip on my headphones and adjust the mic. "I was born ready."

⋆♡⋆

"Thank you for spending this hour with us," I say into the mic ninety minutes later. "Shout-out to our sponsors, and my eternal gratitude to Maral as always for producing this episode, for being a co-host extraordinaire, and for generally being the best person on earth."

My cousin rolls her eyes at me even as her olive skin projects a blush like a sunrise. She hates it when I embarrass her publicly, which makes it all the more fun. She twirls her finger in the air. *Wrap it up.*

"There's my cue to shut the hell up," I say. "As you all know, this is our last episode before a brief hiatus because we're off on a publicity tour for my book over the next couple of weeks. Check out the link in my bio for event dates and tickets in a city near you! Thank you for listening. You're all wonderful people doing amazing things. I'm so proud of you."

I blow a kiss at the camera after my signature closing line—we started filming our recording sessions years ago, which boosted our profile considerably—and Mar stops the voice and video recordings.

"So you *can* stop talking," she says. "Editing this episode is going to take even longer than usual."

"Better hop to, only an hour before we have to leave."

She turns off the mics. "Our run times are getting unwieldy. Can you learn to stop asking so many off-script questions?"

I purse my lips. "Can you learn to stop booking such fascinating guests? I can't help it if I'm interested in what they have to say."

"Can we skip the thing where you try to refute me five or six times and just get to the thing where you realize I'm right? I don't have the energy for your . . . energy right now."

I heave an exaggerated sigh. "Fine, but just this once." She wouldn't be much of a brand manager if she wasn't so great at keeping me on track.

Maral taps her phone with a prettily manicured finger. "Shanthi says the setup for tonight is almost complete." She turns the screen to me and I'm greeted by my own giant smiling face on posterboard, erected on an easel by the door to the Rare Book Room. "That'll draw a crowd."

"Let's just hope it's a friendly crowd," I say, the *LitCrit* review slithering back into my mind before I banish it, sliding open the soundproof door so I can go get dressed.

"It's ticketed to max capacity," Maral calls after me. "It will be."

With events where every attendee has reserved a ticket, like at the Strand, where my book launch is taking place, we know that whoever is there *wants* to be there. So I have every reason to believe tonight will go off without a hitch. But some of the events on my upcoming tour are only partially ticketed, with additional space available for general admission, so it's possible we're in for some walk-in haters over the coming two weeks.

I'm grateful I even get the opportunity for a book tour, given how rare they are these days. My publisher is bankrolling part of it because I'm a public figure whose national speaking engagements prove that people will turn up in droves to see me, which translates to sales. My publicist, Meredith, has arranged for various interviews and bookstore events, and Woodsworth Press is sending her along to deal with setups, book and swag shipments, stock signings, and all the thankless grunt work she's assured me *will be a joy if it's in service of your book* (god love her, the liar). Maral and Shanthi are accompanying us on my dime, since Mar set up the rest of the speaking events at various conferences and symposiums along the route, and as my ace content manager, Shanthi has the dubious honor of recording my every public move for followers to enjoy.

I already did my makeup for the podcast and changing only takes a minute. I spend the balance of time before we have to leave finishing up a Q and A I was due to turn in to Meredith by end of day.

After pressing Send, a new email crops up. From the last name I expected to see in my inbox today.

```
Today, 4:47 p.m.
From: ryan.grant@woodsworth.com
To: ana@soproudofyou.com
Subject: Congratulations

Ana,

I wanted to wish you a happy release day. Your
book is going to touch a lot of people. Congratu-
lations on your achievement.

Best,
Ryan
```

"I'm so fucking sure," I mumble, scoffing at the sheer audacity. All at once, every bad review since the start of the book's publicity campaign comes rushing back to me in a montage of newsclips, many of them engineered by the man who's dared to sully my inbox.

Woodsworth Press's director of publicity, Ryan Grant.

When my agent, Nadia, and I were first meeting with publishers two years ago, many industry professionals were champing at the bit, lauding my as-yet-unwritten book as the next Big Thing. Most members of the team at Woodsworth felt this way. All except one—Ryan Grant.

To say Ryan was *markedly disinterested* in that first meeting would be an understatement. Sure, the weight of his unwavering gaze practically thickened the air when we first entered the boardroom, but his imperious posture, his bone structure, and the deep timbre of his voice were giving stern daddy. Not to mention the man looked like his smiling muscles had never been exercised a day in their lives—despite the rest of his body more than making up for that.

By the time we sat down with the full team to go through my book proposal, I could practically see the skepticism dripping from the man.

"So, it's not a memoir?" Ryan asked, leafing through the pages my agent had provided.

"No," Nadia said in her signature cool, husky voice. "It's more of a how-to."

"But do you use your own experiences as a framework?" he asked, his attention on me.

"I'll be using stories from people I've interviewed over the years," I said, "but the overall structure is more of a guide to becoming your own inner champion when you're not getting encouragement from external inputs like family."

A single dark brow rose. "But *you're* the brand. Readers will be disappointed not to see you in the pages."

"I'm giving voice to something my community has long been

hungry for—validation, encouragement. *That's* what people connect to." For good measure, I added, "I wouldn't be nearly as interesting subject matter."

Ryan held my gaze for a long moment, jade-green eyes twinkling in the light from the floor-to-ceiling windows. "That so?" he murmured. Then something shuttered over his expression, a deep frown overtaking it as he closed the booklet. As if to say, *I've read enough*.

It took everything in me not to scoff out loud. It's not like I *never* talk about myself publicly—of course I do. People know my parents moved here from Armenia when I was a toddler, they know Maral and I grew up together in Boston. They know I was a top student, class valedictorian, went to Harvard Med School. And they know I decided to leave in the middle of my residency to pursue *So Proud of You* full-time. They've never needed to know the *why* of any of it, and the show's gone gangbusters. Focusing on the guests has always been my MO—listeners enjoy seeing themselves reflected in other people's experiences.

"We *love* your idea." This came from Laura, the cheerful blond editor who took control of the ship before it could crash against the cliff face. "We've been big fans ever since that first viral video that put you on the map."

"Your YouTube channel got me through senior year at college," said Meredith, a publicist with a sweet sprinkling of freckles across her face. "And I actually think the fact that the whole thing started as a humble ode to your cousin means it's always felt super personal."

"We think we'd be the perfect partners to help broadcast your message to a wide readership," Laura said before launching a flashy slide deck full of marketing campaign ideas, cover mock-ups, and publicity plans. They were pulling out all the stops to try to woo me, but their publicity director's doubtful reaction still rankled.

When we reached a slide featuring the team's recent successes,

Laura's and Meredith's boasting motivational management tomes and celebrity cookbooks, I saw that, by contrast, Ryan's list featured a veritable who's who of scholarly superstars. Historians and political biographers and Pulitzer Prize–winning journalists. I had to fight not to roll my eyes. No wonder he was trying to poke holes in my idea—clearly it wasn't *highbrow* enough for his tastes. Someone like Ryan, with his career history of promoting Important Works, wouldn't *get* the self-help genre. Because someone who'd probably heard how smart and talented and capable and handsome he is every day of his life would never connect with a book about finding your inner champion when you've never had an external one.

Didn't matter, though. One naysayer doesn't spoil the bunch, and I loved the rest of the team. So, after a heated auction among various publishers, in the end I signed with Woodsworth (didn't hurt that they paid me a mint). I figured I'd be working primarily with Laura and Meredith anyway, but little did I know that Ryan would still be part of the picture.

"*Stop* looking at reviews," Maral says now, emerging from the den.

I startle. "I'm actually not!"

She points at my phone. "Your mom?" she asks, her tone low, knowing.

"No, happily it's been a whole two hours since her last directive."

"Did she acknowledge your book release, at least?"

I shake my head, trying to keep my tone even. "I don't think she knows it's today."

"Of course not," Mar says under her breath. Then, "So who inspired that face?" The look of consternation she mimes is more like constipation.

I clear my expression. "Remember that Woodsworth publicist who set up the interview with *Talon* magazine?"

Maral gasps. "The Storm Cloud?" she asks, referencing our nickname for Ryan. "He of shitty *Kirkus* review fame?"

"Among his several other missed swings," I say. "He just emailed to . . . congratulate me on my achievement?" My voice is laden with suspicion. I read aloud, "'Your book is going to touch a lot of people.'"

Distrust gleams in her eyes. "Huh."

"Weird, right?"

"Definitely weird. I thought you demanded he be taken off the campaign?"

"I didn't *demand*," I say. "I asked. Politely."

"Right. Park your steamroller, did you?"

"*Anyway.*" I wave my phone at her. "You don't think this is a bad omen, do you?"

"Of course not," she says.

But I'm not convinced. We call him "the Storm Cloud" for a reason. I love the entire team that helped bring my book to fruition, but Ryan is the exception. Laura insisted he'd be a boon for media outreach, given that his strong connections could get hits that would, in her words, *move the needle*.

I wanted to trust that she was right—that his deprecation in that first meeting and his aloofness in our every interaction thereafter wouldn't carry over into his media outreach—but Ryan's efforts might as well have thrown a lit match on a pile of butane-soaked advance copies. Almost without fail, the media hits he secured panned my work. Some in grander fashion than others. (The disdainful *Talon* feature, a real standout, released on a weekend when I was visiting Mom in Boston—a one-two punch I could have lived without.) Each hit was followed by a dip in preorders and abandoned coverage in other media publications. In six months, I wore out two pairs of running shoes from twice-daily circuits around Central Park in the effort to distract myself from the sense of doom. Luckily, Meredith's outreach balanced out his bungled attempts—the reviews she garnered were raves, and she even landed me a Reese's Book Club pick for the month, especially remarkable given the narrative angle is a departure from their usual nonfiction choices—and righted the train before it had the chance to derail. Minus the handful of bad reviews that continue to trickle in, which is normal for any book, buzz has been generally strong in the months since I (politely) insisted Ryan be taken off the campaign so he could stop jinxing its chance at success.

"Maybe the publishing staff are mandated to send congratulatory emails on release day?" Maral offers.

"He's the only one in my inbox."

"He's also the only one not coming to the launch, though." Maral holds my herringbone blazer aloft, and I slip my arms into it. "At least you won't have to see him."

"True. Good vibes only tonight." The last thing I want is him cursing the event with his presence. The farther away he stays from my book, the better. "Let's go crush this thing."

The bookstore is packed. I'm not surprised to find it bustling at five forty-five P.M. on a Tuesday—I've stopped in to the Strand at all hours on any given day of the week myself. There is no peace like browsing books, a strong black coffee in hand. Except maybe walking through my picturesque Upper West Side neighborhood during a snowfall, coffee in hand. Or running through Central Park at the crack of dawn, framed by beautiful towering skyscrapers, the promise of coffee close on the horizon.

Maybe coffee is the real key to peace.

The Rare Book Room, where events are hosted, is a reprieve compared to the commotion of the store, the scent of aged paper and bindings rich in the air. We're about an hour out from the official start of the event, but I had to arrive early to sign some stock for the store and for Woodsworth's marketing team, who are hosting giveaways on their socials. The room is a flurry of bookstore staff facing out copies on the shelves flanking the podium, caterers setting up the makeshift bar on a table by the windows, and a handful of junior Woodsworth employees laying out swag. Near the podium I spot Shanthi typing furiously on her phone while her face remains the picture of placidity—aka her default mode.

"Ana!" squeals Meredith as she wraps me in a hug, her red hair tickling my nose. "Happy pub day!"

Trailing behind her is Alison, the publicity assistant, who holds a phone up to capture my arrival.

"The place looks so glam—nice job, team," I say, taking in the high-top tables laden with tea lights and tasteful floral centerpieces. String lights hang from bookshelf after bookshelf of leather-bound books in burgundies and browns and golds. A dozen rows of chairs stretch out before the podium, and beyond them is a wide standing-room space for overflow.

"A lot of this was the bookstore, but the rest was all Alison," Meredith says, giving credit where credit is due. One of the many things I love about her.

"Alison, I'll be adding this to the chart I keep to track the number of ways in which I am forever indebted to you," I say.

Red spreads across the PA's face and down her neck. "Oh my gosh, it's honestly an honor." There's a small tremor in her voice that belies her capability. She's done so much for my book over the past year—getting copies out to influencers, arranging blog posts and online media tours, creating shareable advertising content, and so much more—that its sales will be owed in large part to her efforts.

Meredith ushers me to the podium, where Shanthi is tapping the microphone. She's arranged a light diffuser a few feet away, which will cast a glow that's flattering for the camera, if a bit glaring for the in-person audience. But while the room has space for up to a couple hundred people, the Instagram Live she'll be hosting of the event could be attended by thousands, if our broadcast of my keynote address at the Multicultural Women's International Conference last month was any indication.

I do some sound tests, whispering sibilants into the mic as a bookstore employee named Greg fiddles with the volume on the speakers, and Shanthi adjusts the light until she's satisfied with a shot she gets on her phone. Her expression doesn't change as she gives me a thumbs-up, which, for Shanthi, is about as emotive as it gets. She brings an unmatched level of cool to our team that balances out my inner (and outer) Tasmanian devil.

Alison is handing me books to sign when Nadia arrives in a flurry of color, her bright yellow blouse tucked into fitted emerald-green pants, red lips a bright pop against her fair skin and short black bob. She enters in medias res, as if she started her sentence on the way up the stairs.

"—been such a day, but you are the highlight!" She kisses me on each cheek, Armenian-style, like Maral and I taught her. "I'm so excited to celebrate your shining star."

My editor, Laura—a queen among women—comes over as well, and we all squee together as her bespectacled wife stands nobly at her side.

The room starts to swell with attendees and media. Alison fetches me a glass of water while Meredith walks me through the run of show, as if I haven't had it memorized since she emailed it to me last week.

It's showtime.

Greg from the Strand introduces the event: "We're honored to present Ana Movilian as she launches her debut book. *So Proud of You* is based on her wildly popular podcast, which in turn is based on her wildly popular viral videos."

Then Meredith introduces me: "It has been such a joy to help spread the word about this fabulous book—Ana is not only an immensely talented writer and content creator, but she's also an absolute gem of a human being whose mere presence lights up a room. Her confidence is inspiring—there is nothing in this world she can't do, and she believes the same is true for everyone. That's what her message is all about—celebrating others' amazing capabilities. This is the messaging we all need right now, and always."

My skin warms at her kind words. The room erupts in cheers, sending energy coursing through my veins and a broad smile spreading across my face as I step up to take the podium.

"Thank you, Greg and Meredith, for that generous introduction," I say. "And thank you to everyone for coming tonight. My journey to this moment is pretty well known. What started as an innocent pep talk recorded for my beloved cousin, Maral"—I gesture to Mar, who stands with Laura and Meredith near the bar—"as she struggled with educational expectations became my life's work. Too many of us face the challenges of our lives without the kind of encouragement we deserve. And many of us who are first- and second-generation Americans never hear the words that have become my motto, the title of my podcast, and now my book—"

Just then, I see a hint of movement at the back of the still room as someone enters quietly. For a moment I think I must be seeing things, because he wouldn't possibly show up to my launch, would he? After throwing wrenches in the publicity wheel and my (oh, who are we kidding) demanding he be taken off the campaign—right?

But there he stands, stern daddy in full effect.

Ryan Grant.

Chapter 2

"When I saw that first video, I had no idea it was going to affect me that way. No idea I'd been waiting to hear those words all my life, until I heard you say them and suddenly the floodgates opened."

The earnestness of the woman standing on the other side of the signing table is touching. It never gets old, no matter how many people express this sentiment. No matter how many cities I speak in, how many events I attend, how many guests I interview for the podcast, how many case studies I delved into for the book. It will never get old to see people moved by the message in that first video I made almost six years ago.

It was intended to be a quick pick-me-up for Maral, and neither of us could have known how that video would change the course of our lives.

Mar had been in the second year of her urban planning master's on the heels of a punishing environmental engineering undergrad, working on her thesis and at the end of her rope. She texted me lamentations of the highest order. what's the actual worst that would happen if i dropped out? and when my parents disown me, can i come live with you? and i can work at the hospital's coffee kiosk. you'd get free coffee every morning. (if you say no, i'll know you've been abducted and the response is moot... oh and also will call Liam Neeson or at least the police.)

I could relate somewhat—it's not like my own eight years of postsecondary education had been a walk in the park. It may have looked that way from the outside—my parents sure loved telling people I could have slept through college and still graduated at the top of my class. But high achievers are only high achievers because they work their asses off, and I had felt my fair share of frustration through school.

Empathizing with my cousin after a particularly depressing slew of messages, I ducked into the break room at my residency hospital and held my phone up to my face, pressing Record and starting with, "You can do this. You are a badass, a queen, a goddess of the highest order. You've worked hard your entire life and deserve literally every good thing the world has to offer. If I could lay it at your feet, I would, but you gotta go get that shit. You've earned it. No matter what happens, I'm so, so proud of you." Nothing I said in the rest of the three-minute video I sent her was new—I've lauded Maral's capability, work ethic, intelligence, and myriad other strengths since time immemorial and encouraged her through countless academic challenges—but she credits the video for getting not only her through the rocky middle of her thesis, but her roommate, Emaan, through a tough cellular neurophysiology exam. When Mar saw fit to post the video on YouTube ("Maybe it'll help a few other people too"), it seemed to resonate so deeply with strangers that it was shared far and wide, garnering over thirty million views in its first year.

Mar asked me for a new video every time she was facing a particularly brutal exam or paper, and because people appeared to enjoy the messaging—which was always some evolution of the original—we uploaded each of them to YouTube. Mar created a channel for the content, which transcended the college crowd quickly, garnering fans of all ages and from all walks of life. Till then I'd only been a casual YouTube user—mostly to look up rudimentary DIY home repairs whenever my parents' Dorchester bungalow needed upkeep, or the odd recipe that I had valiant hopes for but unfailingly butchered. But seemingly overnight, the channel amassed a shocking number of subscribers, which led to Instagram and TikTok accounts that did the same, which led to Maral and I starting the podcast, which was followed by speaking events, a book deal, and, fingers crossed, even bigger things to come. Whirlwind after whirlwind, all in service of people who desperately need the encouraging words no one else has ever said to them.

I finish signing the book and hand it back to the woman, whose eyes gleam as she thanks me and wishes me well on my tour. My phone buzzes, Mom's name scrolling across the screen. I worry my bottom lip for a second before swiping to answer.

"Hi," I say quietly so attendees can't hear. "Everything okay?"

"When you and Maral are home next week I need you to move the couch so I can vacuum underneath. It is zuzveli."

For the thousandth time I wonder when she'll stop referring to Boston as *home* when Mar and I haven't lived there in five years. "Maral is staying with friends while we're in town, but I can do it, don't worry. And it's not next week, it's in two weeks." Boston is our last tour stop.

She sighs. "Have you called the gardener yet? If he doesn't complete the job, you shouldn't pay him the full amount."

"Not yet." I catch the eye of someone waiting in the middle of the signing line and smile. "I've been a little busy today."

"Always so busy. It's not like you are a doctor anymore."

I count to five before answering—a trick Maral taught me since my mouth often doesn't get the memo that it needs to consult my brain before doing its thing. "I was never a practicing doctor, Mayrik." I hold my breath for another second before saying, "My book released today."

There's a pause on the other end of the line. "Is that what's in the package you sent me?"

"Yes."

She makes a sound that's somewhere between acknowledgment and dismissal. "The courier kept ringing and ringing the bell while I was watching Drew Barrymore. I thought it was an emergency."

Nope, just the fruits of my labor. I'm practically drawing blood with the way I'm chomping on my tongue. "I have to go. I'll call you tomorrow, okay? And I'll see you in two weeks."

"Oh. Okay, Anahid jan." Then, more buoyantly, "I will have nazook ready for you."

My shoulders release from around my ears at her mention of my favorite Armenian pastry. Feeding me is her love language—this is her trying. I smile. "I'll bring my appetite."

I drop my phone into my bag as the next person in line steps up, gently placing a copy of my book on the table. Standing on the other side is the one person I've kept an eye out for while hoping we wouldn't have to interact all night.

"Great to see you again, Ana," Ryan says. His ramrod posture makes it so he's literally looking down his nose at me. Typical.

"Surprising to see you again, Ryan," I say.

"I wouldn't miss your launch."

It certainly wouldn't miss you. "I didn't expect you, given you aren't working on the book anymore."

"This event is for fans, not just people working on the book," he says. He raises a brow at his copy, which remains untouched, so distracted am I by his implication that he's a fan. As if. "This *is* where we get our books signed, right? I wasn't sure if you were the author because there's just no indication anywhere . . ." He makes a show of turning in a slow circle, indicating the room splattered with images of my face.

"That's the kinda razzmatazz that sells influencer books, I guess. I know it's not your standard fare," I say.

"No, the books I work on are usually not Reese picks." He bows a little. "Congratulations, by the way. I haven't had a chance to tell you that since the news broke."

That twinkle in his eyes. I almost forgot it, my memories painting him as wooden, dead-eyed, in all his standoffishness. But there it is, adding a golden glint to the green of his irises. Decidedly humanizing.

"I got your email," I say. "That was plenty."

His expression remains neutral but I see his Adam's apple bob. Shit—I didn't intend to sound unkind, but my tendency to blurt out words without filtering them is one of the reasons Maral says I should be an indoor cat. I know Ryan didn't willfully try to harm my book. At least, I hope he didn't—he wouldn't be much of an ambassador if he shot his employer's product in the foot. But his grumbly curmudgeon energy in every interaction we've had over our two-year acquaintance, mostly terse emails and clipped calls, has telegraphed his distaste for it. I wanted tonight to be all positivity. Which means he and his opposite-of-the-Midas-touch vibes are non grata.

"I met your cousin," he says. "Is the rest of your family here too?"

I pull his copy toward me. "They're not local," I say. Although even if Mom lived down the street and I sent a car to bring her here specifically, it's a toss-up whether she'd come. Vartouhi Movilian is not really a crowd person. Or a reader. Or supportive of my career in general.

Dad might have come, though.

The thought comes at me, unbidden, like a boxing glove. All at once I feel knocked out, heavy in my chair.

I suck in a breath and point my Sharpie at the title page. "Who can I make this out to?"

"Me," he says.

My eyes flash to his. "Why?"

"Is that a trick question?"

"I'm just surprised," I say. *That you'd want me to sign a book you clearly have no regard for.* "That you'd buy a copy. Given you work for the publisher."

"The bookstore requires proof of purchase if we want to get it signed."

"And you just *had* to get it signed?" I ask.

His eyes are steady on me. "Yes," he says. "I just had to get it signed."

My brows knit together. *What is this guy's deal?*

Whatever. Another sale is another sale. What do I care how he spends his money?

I scrawl my name on the title page before handing the book back to him. "Hope you enjoy it more than *Kirkus* did." Clearly my mouth can't resist the digs.

"Most people enjoy books more than *Kirkus* does. And I already have." He taps the hardcover on the table. "See you soon, Ana," he says, and heads off to join the rest of the Woodsworth folks by the bar.

See you never, Ryan.

What does he mean *I already have*? He could, and I assumed *did*, pitch *So Proud of You* without having read it—the proposal he practically dismissed was thorough enough for him to know its general deal. Not that his pitching was award-worthy, given that the media outlets he reached all pooh-poohed it.

Like that *Talon* magazine interview he set up.

He positioned it as a huge coup when he first told me about it—exposure to *Talon*'s circulation of 1.1 million readers meant potentially garnering a new audience, and the journalist was Ryan's buddy from college. *Daniel Fox.* His very name brings bile to my throat. While he was supposed to write a glowing feature on my rising star after my book deal was announced, instead he took a derisive spin, ultimately lambasting me as a trite internet personality who had no business getting a book deal at all. I'd tried to quash my suspicions during the interview, when he asked leading questions with a permanent smirk on his face. Tried to ignore the discovery in my pre-interview internet stalking that he was a creative writing major turned journalist and thus may have Opinions that would bias his take. Ultimately, I wanted to trust Laura's assertion that Ryan's instincts would pay off. Trust that my work would speak for itself. But certain people will never take you seriously—trolls, Daniel Foxes, Ryan Grants. The lesson is to surround yourself with people who will. And try to convince yourself they're the ones who know what they're talking about.

Over an hour later, when the line thins to an end, the room is still filled with guests holding dwindling glasses of wine, grease-stained napkins that previously held canapés, and copies of my book tucked into their armpits or branded totes. I should mingle, and I will, but what I really want is—

"Here," Maral says, handing me a sweaty glass of clear liquid, a curl of lemon rind floating among the ice cubes.

Bless her. She knows me so well.

I take a sip of the vodka soda. "Boyid mernem," I whisper. An Armenian expression that translates literally to *I'll die for your height* but somehow means *I love you*. Aggressive devotion is an endearing quirk in our culture.

"Full house," she says, clinking her own glass of white wine against mine. "Cheers, Ayn. You did good."

High praise from Mar—she's not usually so effusive.

"This is all Meredith and Alison," I say.

She points to the dwindling display of books on the table. "You did write that thing, right? I seem to remember you working twenty-hour days for several months instead of your usual sixteen."

"Yeah, my workout regime really took a nosedive during that stretch."

She purses her lips. "You dictated the first draft into your phone from your Peloton."

"Movement helps with creativity," I say. "If only Siri knew how to separate my voice from Ally Love's, that might not have ended up being *more* work to edit afterward."

"Speaking of editing," she says, checking her phone, "I'm going to head out in a minute—the last episode still needs to be spliced and Simu just uploaded better audio from his end of the interview to Dropbox. Shanthi's got his video, so she'll be able to post clips as a Reel tonight too. She says she's not sleeping anyway."

If there's anyone who works more hours than I do, it's Shanthi. I've told her to take a page from Mar's book (she only works twelve-hour days—something about boundaries, whatever those are), but she's clearly cut from the same cloth as me.

"But first," Mar says, turning covertly toward the group of Woodsworthians still by the bar. Laura, Meredith, and Ryan are clustered together, body language casual as they converse. Well, Laura and Meredith are casual. Ryan always looks like he forgot to take the hanger out of his jacket. "I'm still wiping my jaw off the floor from when the Storm Cloud showed up in the middle of your speech. Nice recovery, by the way."

I shake my head. "An email *and* an in-person showing. What if that's a double bad sign? Bad things come in twos."

"That's threes."

"*Fuck.*"

She tsks. "Take it down a notch. So he's here—it's not like he's working on your book. He can't taint something he can't touch."

I exhale. "You're right."

"I was surprised he introduced himself to me. Like, why make the connection at all, you know? But maybe he's a fan of the podcast."

"If he's ever listened to a single episode of the podcast, I will go camping for a week straight."

She gasps, knowing that's the big guns. "Hey, he showed up tonight. Life's full of surprises. Better order a tent."

Although most of our interactions have been via email or teleconference, I've also met Ryan in person several times. Maral might normally have come to one or two of those with Nadia and me, given that she's my brand manager and the keeper—and maker—of my schedule, but as luck would have it, she had conflicts. She was visiting her parents in L.A. the week we did the photo shoot for my cover—which Ryan didn't even need to be at, let alone spend scrutinizing my every pose like Don Draper minus the cigarette for two hours straight. On the day we had the prepub meeting with the Woodsworth marketing and publicity teams, she was ironing out the contract for Mindy Kaling's appearance on the podcast (which paid off—it's still one of our most streamed episodes, and one of my personal faves). I recorded our discussion about the long-lead campaign and annotated the audio file with copious ideas that came to me during and after, then sent her an email or twenty over the next few days as more ideas bustled in, to which she replied, *I'll never miss a meeting again.*

Maral's eyes travel up and down the length of Ryan. "He's not what I expected."

"Less cumulonimbus, more human man?"

"That. And . . ." She tilts her head. "He's hot. The way you described him, I imagined a dowdy old-world professor type. Spectacles perched on the end of his nose. But he looks . . ." She swirls her wine. "Like someone you'd have on rotation."

"Ha." She means the short list of men I call upon to serve my physical needs from time to time. Okay, fairly frequently. (What can I say? I have a lot of physical needs.) The prerequisites are that they be unattached, good in bed, and as uninterested in a relationship as I am. No questions asked as to why. Unsurprisingly, there are quite a few takers. "He wishes."

I sip my drink, trying to assess Ryan with unbiased eyes. Sure, he's handsome. But publishing as an industry is notoriously short on men, and everyone knows that when men are in short supply, the few options become more attractive by default. He may be a publishing ten, but he's a New York seven. Whereas Jacob—the latest addition to my *rotation*, as Mar put it—is a solid ten all around.

My eyes trail from Ryan's rich brown hair to his five o'clock shadow, the darkness of which makes the jade green of his eyes all the more vibrant, not to mention the soft pink of his lips (why am I looking at his lips). He's wearing a charcoal-colored button-down shirt that pulls a little across the breadth of his back, and dark jeans that look like they were measured and manufactured to mold to his exact shape.

He looks strong . . . substantial. Like a tree, rooted to the earth. Immovable. Steady.

Okay, maybe he's a New York eight.

Or maybe I've just gone too long without having my physical needs served.

"Need a napkin for that drool?" Mar says, tone mirthful.

I snap to. "What? Shut up."

"You look like you haven't had dinner and he's a juicy kebab."

"You're gross," I sputter.

"Whatever you were just imagining doing to him is grosser."

"I wasn't imagining anything."

"Then why are you getting so worked up?"

"I'm not," I lie. Damn, I must be hard up if my mind is wandering as far as *Ryan Grant*. How long has it been since I last had sex? It's been a busy couple of weeks. I'll have to consult my Rolodex (aka the contacts in my phone grouped under *hookups*) posthaste.

"Right," she says, eyeing me. "'Cause far be it from you to have feelings of any kind."

I roll my eyes. "Don't you have a podcast to edit?"

She finishes her drink, setting the glass on a high-top. "Mingle, have a good time. I'll see you in the morning. Pancakes on me before we head to the airport." She double-kisses me before heading off to say her goodbyes.

I wander around the room, chatting with people and finishing my drink, then make my way over to where Nadia and Meredith are having an animated conversation.

"So, success?" Nadia asks me as I approach.

"I would say so." I sling an arm around Meredith's shoulders. "Thanks to this brilliant human."

Meredith goes scarlet under her freckles, which never fails to charm me. "Does she ever stop with the compliments?"

"No," Nadia says solemnly. "It's one of her worst qualities."

I smile, squeezing Meredith. "I can't wait to spend the next two weeks embarrassing you with praise before the entire country."

I feel her stiffen. She and Nadia share a wide-eyed stare.

"What did I say?" I ask.

"Um," Meredith says quietly. "Nadia?"

Nadia waves her hand. "We can talk about it later."

"Talk about what?" I ask.

"Just some news," she says, too quickly. "You and I can go for a drink after the launch and I'll tell you—"

"*What* news?"

"Sweetie, let's just enjoy the rest of your—"

"Nadia Vivian Chan, so help me god," I growl. "You know there is no chance I am going to be thinking about anything but the fact that there's something you two know that I don't know for the rest of the night unless you tell me *right now*."

There's no pulling wool over my eyes, no matter how temporarily. Nadia is all too aware of this—I'm not exactly what you'd call *low-maintenance*. She and Meredith share another glance, this one sheepish.

"Well," Meredith says, her voice a little brittle, "it's my news, really. I told Nadia this morning but we didn't want to ruin your day."

"*Ruin my day?*" I say, aghast. "What the hell is going on?"

"It's actually great news. For me." Meredith's smile is a rictus. "I, um. Got a new job. Senior publicist, at Burton Publishing."

Oh. Wow. "The educational publisher?"

"Yeah," she says.

She told me early on—when I insisted on taking her out to lunch so we could get to know each other better—that she'd wanted to be a teacher when she first left school. A friend of her family's is some muckety-muck at Woodsworth and offered her a publicity assistant role right after she graduated five years ago. Being up to her eyeballs in student debt, she took it. While she enjoyed it—and is amazing at it, frankly—she hoped she'd eventually be able to parlay her experience into an educational publishing job. Best of both worlds.

Now here she is, dream fulfilled.

A rush of happiness washes through me, and I can't help hurling myself at her in a full bear hug. "Oh my god—congratulations!"

Her eyes are glistening when I pull away. And then, I go stock-still.

Wait.

She's my publicist. I need her. How could she have gotten a new job when she's in the middle of *this* job?

"I know, the timing is shit," she rushes to explain. "But I've been at the same level for a few years and Woodsworth has put a freeze on promotions so I've been looking for a while. I need a higher salary, I don't want to live with three roommates in a one-bedroom anymore, and I just happened to get an offer from Burton last week. Actually, *So Proud of You* made my portfolio that much more impressive. They specifically said that."

"Glad I could help," I say weakly.

"I'm sorry. The role is too good to pass up." She's watching me anxiously. "I just handed in my resignation. My last day is next Friday."

Next Friday. "We're in L.A. next Friday. What, are you going to fly home in the middle of my *All Day* interview?"

Meredith swallows. "No . . ."

"Are you going to stay on for the full tour?" I ask, my brow knotted. "I admire the dedication, but will you get paid beyond your last day?"

Nadia puts her hand on my arm. "Hon."

"I, um." Meredith coughs. "I can't go on the tour."

I need another drink. This is worse than I thought.

"So. Okay." My voice sounds low, hollow. "I guess we don't *need* someone from Woodsworth. But Maral's only arranged some of the speaking events, we still need someone to do all the bookstore event logistics." My mind is spinning through all the details that could go wrong that absolutely can't go wrong. This tour *has* to go well—my reputation, my career, my *future* depends on it. "We don't know anything about the store reps you've been in contact with or their expected shipments or—"

"Oh, don't worry," Meredith says quickly, as if glad to be called upon to deliver some good news at last. "We've got that all sorted—someone's coming in my place."

I suck in air through my teeth. "You know I love Alison, but she's still pretty green—"

"It's not Alison," she says. "It's someone way more experienced, senior to me, even. And luckily he knows everything about your campaign because he worked with me on it." Her eyes flick to Nadia, who nods for her to go on.

No. *No.* Not the Storm Cloud. *Please don't say*—

"Ryan is going to come on the tour with you."

Chapter 3

JFK is a zoo and I love it. Not counting the toxic vibes emanating from disgruntled travelers and beleaguered airport staff, this is exactly the kind of energy I thrive in. The excitement—the *promise*—of escape, of exploring new horizons. 10/10, highly recommend.

Maral, with her single weekender slung over a shoulder, helps me wheel my three swollen suitcases to the bag check. Shanthi texted us this morning that she was going to get to the airport early, try to use the Wi-Fi for some last-minute launch posts, and meet us at the gate. Now I wonder if she just wanted to get out of porter duty.

Usually my speaking events are one-offs and we're only away for a night or two at the most. We used to do day trips in the early days too, but Maral has stopped booking those as a humble protest against air travel. If it were up to her, we'd take a cross-country train for this tour, preferably electric.

But that would mean being stuck for even longer with harbinger of doom Ryan Grant. Hard pass.

My heart sinks again at the reminder that Meredith isn't coming with us. She's the reason my book has gotten so much positive buzz, securing favorable coverage in outlets like *Refinery29*, *Marie Claire*, and *People*, where my videos and podcast had been mentioned (positively) in the past. She's also the one who got an advance copy into the hands of a Hello Sunshine scout, which is how we landed the Reese pick. Meredith has been a guardian angel for my book, her multiple emails a day always a bright spot. In short, I love her.

And as much as I'm feeling sorry for myself over losing her and being stuck with a tour publicist whose commitment to my book is questionable at best, I am so, so happy for her. She got a better, more fulfilling job. One that recognizes her value, that will allow her to live life on her own terms. She wanted it. She strove for it. She earned it. She's a fucking boss and deserves every good thing.

After we clear security, I pull up UrbanStems on my phone and place an order to be delivered to her at the office, the nicest arrangement they have, and scroll through the card options for a combo apology/congratulations one. They make those, right?

My phone blips with a message from Nadia: Have a TV update—is now a good time?

I gasp, tugging on Maral's sleeve, showing her the screen. "Oh my god."

I dial Nadia and put the call on speakerphone—I know it's obnoxious in a public place, but dreams are coming true here, people, so just deal with it.

"We have interest," Nadia says by way of answering.

My legs have a mind of their own, making me jump up and down in the middle of the airport concourse. "Who?" I ask.

"Craig Waters. Based in L.A. His daughter's a fan of the podcast, and he thinks you'd make a great host for a talk show he's producing."

Somehow I stop myself from screaming at full volume. It's happening—it's all coming together.

Mom's voice looms, as it tends to do, at the edges of my consciousness. Her response when I told her I was leaving my residency to focus on the podcast full-time rooted itself in my mind.

If you were on television, that would be one thing. Like Oprah, or Drew Barrymore. But dropping out of medicine to, what, talk to people through their phones?

When the podcast took off, I talked to Nadia about the possibility of parlaying it into a TV show. Specifically in L.A., where Mom's expressed interest in moving to since Maral's parents relocated there a few years ago. Nadia's been casually scouting in Hollywood for me, with nothing really solid to show for it yet. But finally, with the podcast's fifth year charting in the top ten and buzz building for my book, my name is recognizable enough that she got a bite.

I've already envisioned the whole thing: I've got a roster of ideas for episodes, guests, themed shows, and special events. In my mind the set is artfully decorated with lemon-yellow chairs on a blue stage, plants and bookshelves in the background, maybe a skyline. (Maral insists it has to be L.A., but my mind's eye can only picture NYC for some reason. That is *the* skyline, after all.) I'll buy a house a tight twenty-minute drive from the studio, with a nanny suite—or pool house—for Mom, and a neighboring property for Mar. Close to her parents' place in Glendale. We'll find Mar a house with lots of trees on the property to combat the smog, maybe install solar panels on the roof. California's way ahead on energy-efficient housing—she'll love it. I'll love it. We'll all love it.

Finally, I can start to repair the giant crater that was blown into our world six years ago, fill it with my family's contentment once and for all, seal it up. Every last one of us, happy. I'll make sure of it.

"So what are the next steps?" I ask Nadia.

"We secure a meeting with Waters and his team. I'll aim for next Friday, when you're in L.A., so you can meet in person."

"What can I do?" I ask, restless energy vibrating through me.

"Go on your book tour and sparkle like you naturally do. I know Shanthi will be sharing clips from events and interviews on your socials—Waters follows you, so he'll be inundated with proof of your charisma." Her husky laugh is tinny through the speaker. "Leave the rest to me—I'll update you as soon as I have more to share."

I exhale. "Okay." Leave it to her—cool. I can do that. It may be wholly foreign to me, but I can leave all my hopes and dreams in the hands of someone else. Easy peasy, tummy queasy.

After we hang up, Maral hits a Hudson News for some granola bars since we'll be flying through lunch and our short-haul flight to Chicago won't serve any food. (I offered to make her something for the flight before we left my apartment, but she looked at me like I'd offered to skin a rat on a plate, exclaiming, "What have I ever done to you?") I crane my neck in search of coffee and spot a Starbucks just beyond our gate. I'll drop my bag and hit it up, stat.

Shanthi sits cross-legged on the floor, her phone charger plugged into an outlet on the pillar she leans against, her thumbs flying over the screen. This is her default setting—lucky for me, because *SPOY*'s online presence has benefited heartily from her dedication.

She casts a quick glance at my overstuffed carry-on as we approach. "Did you leave anything at home?"

"Only her dignity," Mar says.

"You can never be too prepared," I say.

At the edge of my vision, Ryan approaches the gate. For someone whose vibe is so forbidding, his gait is surprisingly graceful. Like me, he doesn't dress down for travel and has the nerve to look decent, clad in business casual. He's so buttoned-up, I doubt he even owns a pair of sweats.

Unbidden, my mind conjures an image of Ryan in sweats and, much to my annoyance, it's not unappealing. Not even a little.

He's wheeling a compact hard-shelled suitcase and scowling at his phone. "Good morning," he says when he reaches us, as if the words taste bad in his mouth. He's clearly no happier to be on this tour than I am that he's coming.

"You look cheery," I say. "Looking forward to spending the next two weeks with us, I'm sure."

Finally, he raises his eyes, and I fight the urge to fidget under his keen appraisal. "Is it that obvious?" he deadpans.

"What's wrong?" asks Maral, nodding at his phone.

"There's been a change of plans for tomorrow's event."

"Change of plans?" Shanthi asks from the floor.

He seems to notice she's there for the first time. "Ryan Grant," he introduces himself.

"This is Shanthi Prasad," I say, because manners above all, "my content manager."

"Nice to meet you," he says. "I've been impressed with your work—you've taken Ana's socials to significantly greater heights since you started, what was it, a year ago?"

Who is this person, so reticent in his interactions with me, throwing around accolades now like free condoms at a college orientation? And how does he know when she started? Sure, we did a quick post introducing her as the woman behind the woman when she first took over, but he'd have to follow my accounts—or at least check them—to have seen that. And I know for a fact that Ryan doesn't even have a personal social media account (I checked—it's polite to follow people I meet in a professional capacity).

"Change of plans," Shanthi repeats, not acknowledging the compliment. Classic Shanthi—even I can't break through with my litanies of praise.

His cheeks puff out on an exhale. "More like a notice that we'll have to change our plans."

"Explain."

"The dry cleaner that shares a wall with Prologue Bookstore had a fire last night. The smoke damage has affected every business in the building—they have to close the premises for the rest of the week at least."

Prologue is meant to be hosting tomorrow's event—a reading and Q and A followed by a signing. We've pre-sold over a hundred tickets already, and general admission is being offered at the door. *Was going* to be offered.

"We're trying to find a new space," Ryan says. "Alison is making calls as we speak, and will hopefully have something for us before we board. At the latest, soon after we land."

Shanthi nods. "I'll be on standby to spread the word," she says, seemingly unfazed by the news.

I, however, am fazed as hell. *Of course.* Ryan steps in as the on-tour publicist and before we even board the first flight, the opening event is compromised? Storm Cloud in full effect. I try to catch Maral's eye so I can visually scream, *See? bad things!,* but she's buried in her own phone.

Ryan finishes typing and pockets his device. "I'm going to grab a coffee before we board. What can I get for everyone?"

Maral's and Shanthi's orders were locked and loaded, judging by the speed with which they shoot them out. But I'm too wary of letting this guy ingratiate himself to me.

"Nothing for me," I say.

Maral pops her head up, finally making eye contact. She knows I've been seeking out coffee like Gollum hunts his precious since before we arrived at the airport. She also knows I wouldn't settle for just any express market swill.

"Are you sure? Starbucks dark roast?" he says, as if he knows exactly what will entice me. "You can smell the sweet smoky goodness from here."

My mouth waters even as I clock that he's repeating verbatim words I've used to profess my love for its aroma on the podcast. That would mean Ryan has listened to at least one episode, when my bet would've been that he's listened to exactly zero.

But this revelation has nothing on my tenacity. "All coffeed out for today."

He shrugs and heads toward the kiosk.

"In my entire life, I've never heard you say the words *all coffeed out*," Maral says.

"Madam," I say, "don't think I didn't notice you swoon when he offered to get you any beverage your heart desires."

She sets her weekender on the floor. "I don't get people tripping over themselves to fulfill my desires every day like you do. Especially not men who look like him."

"What exactly is doing it for you?" I ask. "Is it the black cloak? Or the scythe?"

"Maybe the way he fills out that blazer," she says. "Shanth, you agree, right?"

"Yeah, he's hot," Shanthi says impassively.

"You're not even attracted to men," I say.

She shrugs. "I can still appreciate the goods."

"Did you two miss the fact that tomorrow's event got fucked the second he stepped in as publicist?" I ask.

"Did he set fire to the dry cleaner?" Shanthi asks, not looking up from her phone.

Mar gasps dramatically. "Of course, it's the only answer. He must have flown to Chicago after your launch last night, committed arson, and then flown back to New York so we'd be none the wiser and he could fly back to Chicago with us this morning. Diabolical. The carbon emissions *alone*."

I glare at her. "You of all people know how hard we've worked to make this tour a success."

"And it will be," Maral says, in the voice she uses to mollify me when I get worked up. "The event is not fucked—they'll find a new spot and it'll go great. I know the shitty coverage freaked you out—"

I begin to sputter a rebuttal, and she holds up a palm to silence me.

"—but it's far outweighed by the well-deserved praise the book has received. You got a starred review in *Booklist* and *Publishers Weekly*—do you know how incredible that is? The book is solid, you killed it. Preorders were strong. All the tour events have been arranged by Meredith and me, and he's just here for logistical execution, which it sounds like he's on top of. You know he's not *trying* to sabotage the book."

I exhale. God, I hate it when she's reasonable. But it doesn't change the fact that he just doesn't get the book, or care to. I don't want to promote something I worked so hard on with someone who looks down on it—there are enough haters out there without having one inside the house.

"Maybe you'll warm up to him by the end of the flight," Maral says.

"Unlikely," I say, "since you and I are spending the flight going over the interview questions I'll be—"

"Nah," says Maral. "I'm going to sit with Shanthi, and you're going to sit with Ryan."

"What?" The plane is an Embraer, with two seats on either side of the aisle, which means we have to couple up. "Why?"

"So you can make nice."

"I'm always nice." There is no need to *socialize*. He is on this trip in a strictly professional capacity, his only function being to make sure things go smoothly. Although whether he's capable of doing that remains to be seen.

She purses her lips, unconvinced. "If you're going to be this stubborn for the next two weeks, you're going to be even more insufferable than usual. The last thing you want to do is sabotage the tour yourself by assuming he's going to ruin it."

To my dismay, yet again she has a point. I don't want to do anything that could threaten this tour. I realize I'm clenching my jaw and try to relax my muscles.

Make nice it is.

Storm clouds do pass, after all. The sun always comes out eventually.

♡

If Ryan is surprised by the seating arrangements, he shows no sign of it. He placed my carry-on in the overhead compartment, lifting it as though it were filled with feathers, before settling into the aisle seat next to me. He's since been typing witheringly into his phone—probably dealing with publishing crises of various proportions, including tomorrow's event venue—ignoring the announcement to set devices to airplane mode.

I can't help feeling smug that, if the plane explodes because of Ryan (and whatever the reason is behind airplane mode), Maral will be proven wrong for once.

I regard the advance review copy of a book sitting next to the Starbucks cup on his tray. The author is a famous astrophysicist. Must Ryan be so predictable?

"Looks like a fun read," I say.

He glances from his phone to the ARC. "That's for work. It releases next year—I have to pitch it over the next few weeks."

"I suppose your old buddy Daniel Fox would love to feature an astrophysicist in *Talon*. Such a worthy profession." I'm grateful Mar is too far away to overhear us lest she chastise me for the dig.

"He probably would," he affirms. "Dr. Conrad's world-renowned—"

Confirmation bias has me itching to roll my eyes.

"—but I don't pitch to Daniel anymore," he finishes.

I stop short. "Really? I imagine he'd fawn all over a science darling writing about astronomical phenomena for the highly educated layman."

The corner of his mouth quirks—the first sign of a non-scowl I've ever seen on his face. "Did you finagle an ARC from Meredith?" he asks.

"No, but I've read enough of this kind of book to know its deal."

He puts his phone down on the tray table. "I would have thought you'd go for a different kind of book."

Oh, I'll bet. "Let me guess. *Untamed* or *We Were Dreamers*?" Surely all celebrities-turned-authors are on his shit list.

"I was thinking more *When Breath Becomes Air* or *Women in White Coats*."

So he remembers my bio. I suppose it was his job to pitch *me* for a while there too. It's not like it's a secret, anyway, the fact that I went to med school. "Believe it or not, I don't only read books that reflect my education. Do you only read about publicity?"

"Believe it or not, I didn't study publicity."

Inwardly I gasp. *But you're such a pro. Nary a misstep to be seen.*

He moves his phone and book to his lap as he stows his tray table. The screen keeps lighting up, notification after notification filling the space. Emails with all-caps subject lines and exclamation points galore, and a few texts from someone named Celine. The last one is three heart emojis.

Huh. Ryan has a girlfriend.

I guess it's not *totally* preposterous. He's attractive enough. Assuming *Celine* doesn't mind going out with a starched shirt.

"You're supposed to turn that off," I say, nodding at his device.

He locks eyes with me for a moment too long before he taps open his contacts. "That reminds me, we should exchange numbers in case we need to communicate on the road."

"We have each other's emails."

"I'm willing to bet you get a million email notifications a day. Texts will sift to the top, priority-wise."

I *do* get a shitload of emails and historically am not the greatest at keeping up with them, which is why Maral triages my inbox regularly. And there *are* many logistical reasons we'll need to stay in touch these next couple of weeks.

A second after I recite my number, my phone blips with an incoming text. *What the—* Above the unfamiliar number and message preview reading It's Ryan, the airplane symbol is missing from the corner of the screen. Oops.

"You're supposed to turn that off," Ryan says. His voice is deep, barely above a whisper, and it slinks up the sides of my neck.

I tamp down the shivery sensation as we both tap our screens offline.

"So what *did* you study?" I ask, unable to stop my curiosity, even about Ryan.

He hesitates. "Creative writing," he says finally.

I suppress a smirk. I guess that's how he and Daniel became acquainted—two Guy in Your MFAs sadboying all over each other. "What's the deal, then—those who can't do, publicize?"

He stares at the back of the seat before him. "Something like that."

I catch the tension in his tone and guilt gnaws at me for how glibly I phrased my question. I pivot toward conciliatory. "It's not easy."

"What?" he asks over the roar of air pressure as the plane ascends.

"Writing," I say. "I remember thinking, *How hard can this be?* But turns out—really hard."

Writing a book hadn't been on my radar until Nadia suggested it as a way to broaden my brand, but as soon as she did, ideas flooded my mind. I was confident I could pull it off—challenging tasks have never scared me away—and was so excited to distill the messaging from *So Proud of You* into a new format, offer a different audience a way to access it, that I stayed up all night putting the proposal together. We started shopping it the following week.

When it came time to write the actual manuscript, though, it wasn't quite so smooth. I'd envisioned pulling more from my podcast transcripts and social posts, editing and recasting them as needed to fit within the framework of the larger narrative, but I wound up feeling like I was working from the ground up rather than the top down. Hitting walls in every direction. The first draft felt like a beast that took every ounce of my brainpower to tame.

"Well, seems like you got the hang of it," he says.

I tend to get the hang of things. Bust your ass 24/7 your whole life and that can happen. But if I had a dollar for every comment I've entertained about the effortlessness of my achievements, I could buy the airplane we're flying in. "Doesn't mean it was easy," I mutter.

His eyes find mine. "I didn't mean to imply that it was. Writing is brain-busting, no matter how capable the person doing it."

Wait. Did he just . . . express compunction? I didn't know men were capable of doing that. In my experience, they only double down when you refute them.

"A contract and deadlines provide prime inspiration," I say.

That trace of a smile tics on his lips and, fuck me, something happens in my belly—like a guitar string being plucked. "Something tells me you're in no need of a muse."

"What does that mean?"

He shrugs. "Just that you seem very driven."

Credit to him for the euphemism. *Driven* has other implications, and I've been called every barbarous word out there. "I get it," I say. "Overbearing type-A ballbuster, steamrolls her way into places she has no business—"

"No," he says. "Drive is an admirable quality. It can take a person further than talent or skill." He pauses for a moment. "I guess that's why it's called *drive*."

I gasp. "Ew, was that the daddest dad joke of all time?"

He cringes. "Unintentionally, yes?"

I don't know anything about his personal life, but I could have sworn he doesn't have children. There's no ring on his finger, not that that's a prerequisite. "You better keep those gems to yourself, Grant. You do not need to be handing me ammo on a silver platter."

He nods, his lips pressed together. "Noted."

My eyes can't help roaming over his jaw, his cheekbones, the line of his shadowed neck. His dark hair is thick. It would be easy to imagine the feel of it between one's fingers. So easy.

If one were to imagine it. Which I'm not.

If there is one redeeming aspect of the Storm Cloud coming on tour, it's that he is . . . not hard to look at. Hard *not* to look at. At least these next two weeks will be adorned with some nice eye candy, which will incite zero complaints from me.

It's also not lost on me that he sort of paid me a compliment. Good to know he's committing to the cheerleading aspect of the gig.

When the light on the console indicates we're at cruising altitude, I lower my tray table and open my laptop. *Entertainment Weekly* is running a feature about me online next week, and I want to get a jump on their interview questions.

A flight attendant arrives at our row in short order, napkin in hand. "Anything to drink?"

Distracted, I blurt, "Coffee, please," then mentally kick myself. For one thing, airplane coffee is barf, and for another, now I've outed my childish refusal of Ryan's offer at the airport. It's like the scent wafting from his latte embedded itself in my subconscious. I was powerless against it.

He watches as I take the small paper cup from her, declining cream and sugar. Ryan raises a hand to indicate he's fine, his eyes not straying once from my burning face.

I avoid eye contact as I take a sip from the cup, and the flavor of the lukewarm liquid—somehow simultaneously burnt and insipid—causes me to gag involuntarily. I school my features, unwilling to let the revulsion show.

Ryan's attention is rapt on me. *Go back to your astrophysics book, perv.*

"Good coffee?" he asks, his voice low. Taunting.

"Mmhmm," I murmur, feigning absorption in my laptop screen.

"*Smells* good. Not quite sweet, but definitely smoky. Almost charred." Finally, he drags his gaze away, raising his own cup to his lips to take a long swig of his latte. "Wonder if they grind the beans fresh on the plane."

Chapter 4

Being on the road has many positives. Exploring new ground, meeting new people, the general excitement of change. And hotels. Maral would say the high-thread-count sheets or fancy aromatherapy toiletry sets or plush robes are the best part, but I'm not exactly a *relaxer*. For me, who has sprung awake with energy to burn since I was in diapers, a well-appointed hotel gym is manna. The vast array of equipment is a pleasant shake-up from the stationary bike, free weights, and resistance bands I exhaust on a daily basis in my apartment.

The time difference between Chicago and New York is only an hour, but my body can't help its commitment to rising before the sun. Just as my mom can't help her commitment to sending Good Morning memes. She and Maral's mom, Sosi, text them to us every day at the crack of dawn—garishly cutesy greeting-card-esque images with the words good morning emblazoned across them. Today's, for instance, is an AI-style illustration of a doe-eyed kitten holding a bouquet of sparkling roses. I respond to Mom with a simple text wishing her good morning back, short and sweet given we were on and off the phone for over an hour yesterday.

After we arrived at the hotel from the airport yesterday afternoon, Mar, Shanthi, and I gathered in my room to get some work done. (We get our own rooms when we travel because a. we're adults and b. to quote my sweet cousin, *We get quite enough of you during waking hours, thank you very much.*) But I spent a fair bit of time dealing with Mom's gardener, followed by her bank, correcting their system glitch that keeps sending her mortgage and credit card bills to her instead of me. I called Mom to fill her in on each development along the way, Maral ushering me into the hallway when my cell yell—necessary to be heard over Mom's TV blaring in the background—started to give her a headache. By the time I was done, Ryan had sent a message confirming the new bookstore for the event today, saying he was headed over to take care of logistics, and the three of us spent the remainder of the afternoon spreading the word to ticket holders about the change of venue.

"See?" Maral said in the elevator when we broke to grab some dinner—Shanthi had said she wanted to try a Chicago-style hot dog and our grumbling tummies wholeheartedly jumped on board. "It's all coming together. No storm in the forecast."

"Do you ever get tired of I-told-you-so-ing me?" I muttered, even though my relief was a living thing.

"No," she said.

Now I hop out of bed, wasting no time digging through suitcase number two for running shorts and a cropped racerback tank. Teeth brushed and sneakers on, I'm out the door less than ten minutes after I open my eyes.

Being a (super-)early-morning person—though Maral calls me a *relentlessly all-day person*—means I'm usually solo in a hotel fitness center. But when I arrive at the mirror-walled room filled with treadmills, spin bikes, ellipticals, rowers, and various strength training machines, someone is already there, running at an impressive speed on a treadmill that faces the window overlooking a still-dark North Michigan Avenue and Navy Pier beyond.

It's only after I enter through the glass doors and catch a glimpse of the runner's thick, dark hair, damp at the base of his neck, that I recognize it's Ryan.

His confident stride and the slick sheen of his skin indicate he's been at this a while. His even breaths, despite the significant speed and incline, betray his level of fitness. I don't want to notice how his threadbare gray T-shirt clings to the perspiration on his back. Definitely don't want to notice that that back is corded with muscle, lats and deltoids that make me wonder what other movements would cause those muscles to flex. What other activities might showcase his strength. His vitality. His endurance.

His thighs and calves are shaped like an athlete's, pounding that belt like it's wronged him. A determination in his tread that says he's not just working out, he's working *something* out.

"What did that machine ever do to you?" I ask.

Ryan's pace falters, and he braces himself on the handrails, lifts his feet to rest on the sides of the running belt, and turns to me.

"Good mor—" he starts to say, but doesn't finish. His eyes flick away from mine for a breath of a second, lighting on my bare midriff and legs. He clears his throat.

I feel the corner of my lip lift. So. I'm not the only one checking someone out around here. *Well, get a load, Grant. These aren't even the shortest shorts I own.*

"Good mor to you too," I say, climbing onto a treadmill a couple stations over. "I see I'm not the only early riser among us."

He starts running again, his gait less stompy. "Didn't sleep great."

I power up the machine to start at a light run. "Travel can throw people off." Sleeping in a different bed, those tight hotel corners, the unfamiliar surroundings. I try to imagine the kind of creature comforts Ryan might rely on at home, but other than stacks of Nobel-worthy ARCs and an ironing board to press his one hundred identical gray shirts, I come up blank.

"What about you?" he asks. "Nerves?"

"Nerves?" I say, as if it's a foreign word.

"Big deal, a book tour. Lots of authors get anxious."

I increase my pace, not sharing that the only thing making me anxious is the last-minute publicist change-up. "I'm so used to putting myself out there, these events are pretty 101."

"Music to a publicist's ears," he says. "Meredith was glad she didn't have to broach media training with you."

She said as much to me too. Apparently it can be a process, getting authors up to speed on how to present themselves best in interviews, talk about their book in short, snappy sound bites, and stay on message even when interviewers sometimes don't. But I've always been comfortable with public speaking (Mar credits my level-eleven extroversion for this), and doing so much of it over the years has given me enough experience that I could probably become a media trainer myself.

"She's been a dream to work with," I say. I've been trying to keep my snark in check since the flight yesterday, but I realize belatedly that that may come across as a gibe if he reads comparison into the sentiment. "I'm going to miss her," I add, hoping that expressing something personal may soften my previous words.

"Meredith's one of the best in the business, and your book was a big coup for her," he says, decreasing the pace on his machine. "But career decisions are a trade-off. We have to go with the option that will meet our greatest needs."

It sounds like he's speaking from experience, and I wonder what needs Woodsworth satisfies for him. If he studied creative writing, how fulfilling is it to promote other people's creative output? And yet, I can relate. I went to med school and was so close to becoming a practicing doctor—a career path that would satisfy the most important people in my life, offer financial security, and do some good in the world—only to abandon ship when my most pressing needs demanded I pursue something else instead. Which at the time was less about *So Proud of You* itself and more about my desperate, clawing need for self-preservation when it felt like the ground was crumbling beneath my feet.

Ryan's treadmill stops and he wipes it down, ever efficient in his movements. He seems to be avoiding looking in my direction, but I do no such thing. I blame the fact that I haven't had sex in a few weeks, but if his shirt clinging to his back was a sight, the way it hugs his pecs and taut stomach is a goddamn spectacle. I only just started my run and already I'm panting.

I throat-punch my libido. Ryan's head doesn't need any more inflating, even if he's unaware that my thoughts are an air pump. What's he trying to prove with that body, anyway? What does a publicist need so many muscles for?

"Excuse me?" he says, finally glancing my way.

My jaw clenches. I said that last part out loud, didn't I? Shit. Fate won't stop till she's buried me under twenty metric tons of embarrassment, using my own inability to stop myself from blurting my every thought as a shovel.

He's still waiting, and for once I'm not quick on my feet in coming up with a believable cover-up for my inopportune blurtage. Horniness is clouding my brain.

"I didn't say anything," I say instead. Like a smooth criminal.

He adjusts the weight on the chest press. Slowly, deliberately, as though to rub it in. "My mistake."

He pushes the handles of the machine forward, his shoulders, biceps, and chest contracting in sharp relief beneath his shirt. I've already worked up a sweat, but fresh heat tingles like pins and needles up my thighs. Have I ever even seen his forearms before? No. I definitely would have noticed those veins and sinews. Or are they only emphasized by the light of the sunrise, glinting over the horizon of Lake Michigan?

"If my muscles offend you," he says, pressing the handles forward again on an exhale, "maybe you shouldn't stare at them."

I scoff. "Don't flatter yourself." I stare straight ahead. Maybe if I glare at the sun long enough, I won't be able to see anything anymore.

"I'm not the one flattering me," he says, a bit under his breath, but I hear it. And was that a smile in his tone? Is his face even capable?

I pause my machine and turn his way just in time to see him glance quickly back up at my eyes. The classic move of someone who doesn't want to get caught looking where he shouldn't be. Oh, but I caught those darkened eyes circling my legs, my stomach, my shoulders. The various expanses of bare skin starting to glisten with sweat.

"Now who's staring?" I say, quirking a brow. My tone is flirty, but his face falls immediately.

"Shit," he says, rattling his head. "I don't know what came over me—I'm sorry."

I know what came over him. I look *amazing* in these shorts. "It's okay—"

"No, it's not." He rises from the bench and wipes it down quickly. "I crossed professional boundaries. It won't happen again."

The air is thick with tension, and my instinct is to say something to dispel it, convince him it's fine, I was only kidding. Because I *was* only kidding. I'm used to people checking me out and I honestly don't care if he does (especially not when I was checking him out too).

In fact, to put it more accurately, I kind of like it. A lot. Not that I'd tell him that.

At least now I know he's not a robot. Beyond the indecency of that T-shirt clinging to his torso, it's gratifying—in a way I don't care to give too much thought to—that, for a few seconds there, he wasn't the rigid, aloof Ryan Grant. He was decidedly . . . *not* aloof. Not with that heat flaring in his eyes, something wild overcoming the impassivity in them for just a moment.

He's snapped back to factory settings, though, his movements speedy as he bids me goodbye and passes me on the way to the exit, gone before I can think of what to say. But not before I get a waft of his scent—warm skin and freshly washed clothes, with an overlay of sweat that, ridiculously, prompts a clench in my nether regions.

The room seems awfully quiet after he vacates it, the tension lingering and sending restless energy through me. *Just forget it.* Easier said than done. I blast my M.I.A. playlist and level up my workout, adding sprint intervals to my run, followed by high knees, jump squats, and the most punishing burpees I can manage, forcing the release of endorphins, trying and not quite succeeding to banish the insistent hum deep inside my body. Now who's working *something* out?

I rush back to my room, beelining for one of my suitcases. Garments go flying as I dig through it, until finally I pull out the small pouch I packed with various electronic accoutrements— an extra power bank, a multi-pronged charger, noise-canceling headphones—and find what I'm looking for: a small travel vibrator.

I don't allow myself to think. I just strip off my drenched clothes and put it to use.

Despite having explored Chicago extensively during past visits for speaking events, I've never been to Elevate Books. It's near Lincoln Park, a scenic neighborhood with tree-lined streets boasting homes tucked behind wrought-iron fencing. Its plethora of architectural styles showcases the city's evolution over time—redbrick Victorians next to opulent French-style limestone behemoths next to old factories converted to modern loft-style condos. The bookstore, tucked between an antiques gallery and an empty storefront on a major thoroughfare, looks like it's lived here for a century. Its clientele does too.

Maral, Shanthi, and I greet Ryan when we enter the shop, and the first thing I notice is how obvious it is that they're accommodating us at the last minute. Whereas the Strand had displays of my book on breakout tables and endcaps, and huge posters with my face all over them throughout the store, Elevate doesn't have a single copy of my book by the entrance.

It's not like I expected a fully dedicated display or anything, but I know for a fact that Ryan spent a large chunk of the morning personally relocating shipments of books, placards, and swag from Prologue. So I know he's not to blame. The store could have put a stack of books on a table. Maybe a poster at the entrance. You'd think a live event would be a draw, something they'd want to capitalize on to sell more books.

But it isn't long before I realize what a colossal miscalculation that is at this store.

I try not to walk downwind of Ryan's scent as he leads us to the clearing in the center of the shop where they've (he's?) set up a podium, rows of chairs, and a table with my books arranged in a fanned display.

Passersby cast curious glances at the setup and at our group, which definitely stands out in this store of rumpled, tweed-jacketed, burlap tote–carrying patrons. My favorite white Armani suit, with its clean lines and lapel-less jacket, screams *outsider*. At least Shanthi is casual, in flared jeans and a Henley. Maral's sharp outfit and long, styled, mermaid-like hair aren't helping us fade into the scenery, and Ryan could not command more attention if he stood on a table and banged two pots together. He's dressed in a crisp shirt and blue jacket over dark jeans, which, coupled with his commanding posture, definitely draws the eye.

Or does it just draw *my* eye?

I have purposely banished from my mind the events of this morning. As someone with an overactive libido, there's no telling what will set me off. I can't be held responsible for what gets me going, and an objectively attractive man in the throes of exertion, setting off powerful pheromones in all his sweaty glory, would be prime material for most anyone attracted to men. Never mind that the oxygenated blood pounding through my own veins made me a prime target for horniness.

Him checking me out didn't help. I did not imagine the thirst in his eyes.

Who's to say he didn't go back to his room and do the same thing?

Don't think about that. Don't think about Ryan doing anything of the sort. Definitely *don't picture it. No, I said don't!*

While many of the people seating themselves in the audience must be ticket holders who received our alert that the venue had changed, some seem to be wandering over from browsing book displays, curious to see what the shake-up in what is likely otherwise a quiet showroom is all about. Some are toting books they've gathered for purchase—a quick peek at a couple of stacks reveals a dense volume on theology, a coffee-table book about illuminated manuscripts, a fat spine that just reads *Lincoln*.

Oh boy.

Ryan announces five minutes to start time into the mic, and Shanthi gets shots of the seats filling, which she'll likely post in fast motion as a Reel. I bounce lightly on the balls of my feet, which Maral recognizes as a sign that I'm hyping myself up. She's been watching the room the same as I have—she knows what I'm thinking.

"Whatever's sprinting on that hamster wheel up there, stop it," she says, pointing to my head. "Most of the people here sought you out. They want to hear your reading, your answers to their questions, and get their books signed."

I blow out a breath. "And the others?" I ask.

"They thought they were just shopping for books, but lucky for them, they get to have their minds blown and become superfans of a brand they'd never heard of but now realize they can't live without."

"I'm going to rock their worlds," I say, confident.

"That's the spirit."

"By this evening, we'll have a bunch of new followers."

"Think of the backlist podcasts they'll get to enjoy."

"They haven't even heard the Jameela Jamil interview."

Maral finger-guns me. "That was a good one."

"That was a *great* one."

She nods. "I'm envious of these people. They're in for a treat."

I squeeze her triceps. She knows just what to say to send me back to my resting state of positivity.

Instead of a bookstore employee, Ryan steps back up to the mic to introduce the event. Try as I might to trust his professionalism, to believe that he'll present the book enthusiastically, I can't help the frisson of doubt that creeps in.

"Thanks to everyone for joining us this afternoon," he begins. "We didn't expect to be holding this event here today, but we're grateful to Elevate for accommodating us, as well as to those of you who still found us when we changed venues at the last minute."

Okay, so far, so good. Ticket holders seem pleased to have their amenability acknowledged.

"Many people know Ana Movilian from the viral video now dubbed *You can do this*, which has been viewed over a hundred and eighty million times. Or you may be one of the four million people who follow her on Instagram or TikTok, or one of the countless podcast listeners she's amassed over the past few years. I have the privilege of knowing her as the supremely talented author of this game-changing book." He holds up a copy, the glossed type of the title shining under the overhead lights. "The message of *So Proud of You* began as a harkening to children of immigrants, like Ana herself, but its appeal is universal. For anybody raised in a household where expectations were high but encouragement was low. Where they may have been loved but were never told as much in words. Where the burden of hope from older generations was placed on the shoulders of singular descendants, yet the acknowledgment they deserved for reaching these impossible standards was always just out of reach. This book offers the inspiring message that so many of us could use but have never received, teaching us to be our own best champions."

I realize I'm not breathing, and consciously inhale through my nose. Did Ryan Grant really just say all those wonderful things about my book? The book whose proposal he criticized, whose campaign he partially torpedoed?

The floor beneath my feet feels like it's shifting. Have I had it all wrong? Does Ryan actually . . . *respect* what I do?

Or is he just doing what any good publicist would do, and committing to the gig?

After reciting my brief bio, Ryan invites the crowd to welcome me to the stage. As we pass each other on my way to the podium, he gives me a nod that looks affable, as though we're friendly colleagues. But it takes him a few extra seconds to peel his gaze from mine, raising more than one question in my mind—ones I'll never be able to ask.

Most people applaud but there are a distinct few who don't. Not uncommon, in my experience. Some people just aren't demonstrative. It's nothing personal.

The reading goes smoothly—I chose a crowd-pleasing passage from chapter four, an inspiring anecdote from a Pakistani financial analyst who broke the cycle of comparing his successes against others'—and I talk a bit about the most memorable interviews I did in the process of researching for the book.

Shanthi's phone stays trained on me the entire time. I'm so used to being on display that it's second nature to keep the delicate balance of professional and approachable in my expression. Ryan watches intently, and when the Q and A portion begins, he stands sentry by my side as people begin to line up in front of the audience.

"Hi, Ana," says the first person, a diminutive woman with dark curls, wearing jeans and an olive-green T-shirt, a copy of the book clutched in her white-knuckled hands. This woman is a ticket holder, I'd put my money on it. "I just want to say thank you for your podcast. It's been a real help for me and my brother in dealing with our dad. He . . ." She swallows. "He doesn't really understand that life here is different than back home. He moved us to America so we could have more opportunities, but he expects us to pursue a career of his choosing. My question is, how did you convince your parents to let you choose your own path?"

If I had to list the top five questions I get when we put out AMA calls, this one would be among them. It's so common for parents to dictate the direction their kids' lives take—and not just immigrant parents. Living most of your life in one cultural context and raising your kids in a completely different one, yet expecting the rules of your old world to apply (impossibly) to theirs, is tough to reconcile. First- and second-generation kids have to assume different, often oppositional, roles at the same time. Having one foot in their family's culture, and the other in this North American one. Belonging to both and to neither.

Mar and I count ourselves fortunate that our parents were generally easygoing about a lot of things when we were growing up. They enrolled us in local public schools, encouraged us to befriend American kids. They understood it was important for us to integrate with the culture surrounding us.

Sure, there were things that set us apart. Our friends brought ham-and-cheese sandwiches to school and plugged their noses at our lahmejouns and boregs (their loss). We spent Saturdays in Armenian school while other kids went to gymnastics or soccer. There was the time my friend Kaitlin rooted through our fridge during a study session and exclaimed that zero percent of the yogurt containers contained yogurt. (Why buy Tupperware when groceries come in perfectly good food storage containers?)

But having met so many children of immigrants over the years, I've realized we had it easy in so many ways. We didn't face overt racism or macroaggressions or threats of deportation, for one thing, but we were also lucky as far as the weight of familial expectations went. I pushed myself much harder than my parents ever pushed me, striving for achievement after achievement through my entire school career. Being a top student was my priority, my identity. My way of trying to brighten Mom and Dad's days, of proving to them that everything they'd sacrificed was worth it.

Have I felt Mom's disappointment since leaving medicine? Sure. But she doesn't understand that it wasn't so much a choice on my part as a need, absolute and stemming from deep down in my soul after the bomb that detonated my entire world. Medicine was entangled in so many complex emotions and memories that my residency felt like jumping back into the steaming detritus every day. I *had* to take an alternate road, one that would pull me out of the wreckage, provide me air to breathe. Whether or not it was the right choice was beside the point.

"It's not easy," I answer. "And I know there is potentially a lot at stake. But big life choices can be a trade-off. One path may please your father but lead you astray in terms of what you want for yourself, whereas another can fulfill your soul but disappoint him. You are never going to change the way your father thinks—all you can do is change the way you respond to him. It's your life, and you have to choose what will meet your greatest needs."

The woman smiles and heads back to her seat. From behind me, I feel the palpable energy of Ryan's gaze as he recognizes his own words from this morning. He shouldn't be surprised I took them to heart. I'm an equal-opportunity sponge when it comes to absorbing wisdom.

The next person up is a sixtyish white man with ruddy cheeks, in a worn corduroy jacket and a newsboy cap. "Your book is based on a—a video, I believe?" he says, squinting disbelievingly in my general direction but not quite meeting my eyes.

"Well, no," I say. "It's based on the experience of—"

"I don't understand when books became so meaningless," he interjects. "In my day, you had to have something of value to contribute to the world to get a book published. Now any pretty face can post some video of themselves talking about god knows what and get paid to write a 'book' that pollutes fine shops like this."

The way he said *book*, like it had air quotes around it, does not escape me. And I doubt this *fine shop* would stock mine unless under duress.

I bite the inside of my cheek. "This book is not about the video, as I said, it's about the experience of being raised—"

"What's next, will that British toddler or his finger-biting brother write a book?"

I'd actually read that is my first thought, followed quickly by *Who does this guy think he is?* My hackles are up, my mind swimming with images of derisive review headlines; of Daniel Fox sneering at me from across a table, a recorder propped between us; of Ryan slamming my proposal shut on Woodsworth's boardroom table.

Ryan leans across me to speak into the mic. "Sir, if you don't have something of value to contribute, I suggest you step aside and allow the next person to ask their question."

"Now, hold on just a minute," the man barks. "This is a public event. I am a paying customer at this store, and I've seen the likes of Frederic Gold and Irving Dunham here. Authors whose books *mattered*, whose books made a difference to society—"

I stiffen, my fight response ignited even as a voice at the edges of my subconscious whispers doubt into my mind, willing me to withdraw. A voice I silence, rallying to shut this doucheface down.

But Ryan beats me to it.

"Ms. Movilian's book released only two days ago," he says, his tone measured, "but the hundreds of reader reviews already pouring in disprove your claim that it doesn't matter or make a difference to society. This book has touched readers from all walks of life, has been described as a beacon for a demographic of Americans whose inner struggles have been fought alone until *So Proud of You* drew them into the open. Her work makes people feel less alone in a lonely world, empowers them to take emotional control of their lives, gives them hope where it's becoming increasingly difficult to find. If that doesn't matter, I don't know what does."

It's as if Ryan's words have sucked all the noise out of the room, reducing the entire bookstore to a single frequency, a faint throbbing sound like bass through a distant subwoofer.

I don't quite hear what the man grumbles as he relinquishes the microphone to return to his seat, or leave the store, who even cares. My heart is still racing, adrenaline coursing through my body. I hold tight to the sides of the podium to stop my fingers from trembling. I barely hear the next person's question, which Ryan helpfully repeats from less than a foot away, where he's remained, close, the tickle of his breath against my ear the only sensation I feel.

Chapter 5

The cursor blinks a staccato rhythm on the laptop screen. As it has been for the twenty minutes since I sat at the hotel room desk, willing inspiration to strike. But the dang document remains blank. Which is not great, considering Alison is expecting my essay for *Parade* tomorrow, I haven't written a single word yet, and I normally do my best work while riding the buzz after an event.

Getting up in front of a crowd, feeding off their energy, usually gives me the kind of high that carries me through hours of creative output, inspiring ideas and clarifying execution like the best drug money can buy. But if events are drugs, this afternoon's was a dud batch.

The Elevate reading wasn't a flop, not at all. In fact, it was, overall, a success. If that snob wanted to throw me off my game, he'd have to try a lot harder than that. I'm used to being underestimated. It happens a lot when you're a woman, when your "exotic" looks (read: dark hair and eyes, olive skin, hooked nose) can mean that people don't take you seriously. When condescending journalists or book reviewers portray you as a hack. Or when you forgo an illustrious career path in favor of becoming an internet personality and your family reacts like you've chosen to suck dick for nickels. When you're confident enough in yourself, you learn to brush it off, to rally. After all, there are far worse things people have to endure in this world. Maral's and my parents reminded us of this at every turn growing up, as earthquakes and political unrest and threats of further genocide caused undue suffering to people in our homeland while we got to live this ridiculously privileged life in America. As our parents left behind everything and everyone they knew to build a life of more opportunity for us.

Do you know how lucky you are? Maral and I repeat our parents' oft-used refrain whenever we face champagne problems now. And an event that didn't go *perfectly* is nothing.

But that doesn't stop the low-frequency doubt from reverberating in my deepest recesses. Picking out truths in the lies. *Something of value. Meaningless.* The man's voice morphing into Mom's when I told her I was quitting my residency. *Dropping out of medicine to, what, talk to people through their phones?* The disbelief, the disparagement, echoing in my mind, dampening the ideas that usually ping off one another like rainbow-colored gumballs. Not even the audiobook of my favorite Gloria Steinem biography has helped, and that's usually a slam dunk for revving the old engine. But the cursor on the screen continues to taunt me.

Upon returning to the hotel, we retreated to our four separate rooms. Maral could tell I needed downtime. She's no stranger to me withdrawing when I'm not at my best. She knew all I wanted tonight was to enclose myself in my room, peel off my suit and "confidence underwear"—what we call bra-and-panty sets that are senselessly expensive, sexy as fuck, and make us feel so powerful they may as well be armor—and change into sweats and my threadbare Harvard T-shirt. Habits akin to a power-down switch. She didn't even ask about getting dinner or doing any Chicago-y stuff before we leave tomorrow. Just assured me that it was a successful event and that the coming ones will only get better, then squeezed my hand when the elevator reached her floor and headed toward her room.

Ryan doesn't know me, however, and paused for an inordinate number of seconds before stepping off the elevator at his floor, eyes speaking when his mouth didn't. But I wasn't about to answer with anything but a curt "good night."

Now, in the heavy quiet of my room, his words from the Q and A come flooding back.

Her work makes people feel less alone in a lonely world, empowers them to take emotional control of their lives, gives them hope where it's becoming increasingly difficult to find. If that doesn't matter, I don't know what does.

Is it possible that he actually thinks my book is worthy? That I'm not just some trifling internet personality? I lean back in my chair, hitching my knee up against the desk, trying to reconcile this possibility with what I've believed of Ryan all along.

Not only did he subvert my concerns about bad luck, but he actually resolved the only thing that went wrong all night.

What he said was one thing. The fact that he said it was a whole nother.

I don't need anyone to fight my battles for me. I have an arsenal of mental weaponry that I've unsheathed countless times over the course of my life. You don't go down an educational path populated by extremely privileged people without learning a thing or two about how to elbow out space for yourself. I would have wrecked that gremlin—charmingly, of course . . . there was still an audience to endear myself to—but then, there Ryan was. Defending me.

Well. Defending my book, anyway.

It should have rankled. Who was he to think I needed some knight in shining Nordstrom to ride in and save the day?

But what might otherwise have infuriated me . . . didn't. In fact, it felt nice. Like having someone else in my corner hadn't diminished my strength, only reinforced it.

A soft knock comes from the door. I briefly consider pretending

I'm not here—I *did* hang the DO NOT DISTURB sign on the knob when I got back. But Mar would only disturb me if it's important.

When I throw open the door, however, it's not Maral on the threshold.

It's Ryan.

He's the most dressed-down I've ever seen him outside the gym, in a heather-gray Henley and worn jeans. Nowhere near rumpled, but not quite as prim as usual. Semi-casual looks a little too good on him.

"Oh," I say, not even registering that I should hide my surprise.

He's silent, his eyes flickering from mine for the briefest of seconds to take in my clothes, which are so casual they may as well be pj's—the worn tee feels entirely too snug against my unsupported chest—before he quickly casts them away from me.

"Hi," he says, clearing his throat. "I—I wanted to see how you were feeling."

"Fine," I say.

He nods, very interested in the doorjamb. "Good. I'm glad. I wasn't sure if . . . Is Maral here? Or Shanthi?"

"Nope, just me." I remember my manners. "Um, do you want to come in?"

He hesitates, still not looking at me, tension radiating from him as he considers my question thoroughly. As though I asked, *Hey, you want the nuclear codes?* instead of just politely inviting him into my room so he doesn't have to stand in the hallway.

Finally, he nods. "Thanks. I thought, uh. I thought maybe you'd . . . want their company."

"Why?" I ask.

The door closes behind him and he finally makes eye contact. "They're familiar. People you're comfortable talking to."

"Talking to about what?"

"About . . . well, anything you want to talk about." Red blooms above his neckline. "Do you need anything?"

"*Yes,*" I say. "If you could write a thousand words about overcoming bias, I would be ever grateful."

He gives me a pleading look. "I meant more like, do you want me to grab you some dinner?"

Ah, back to work, then. "Thank you, Mr. Grant, but your author management services are no longer needed this evening."

"I'm not asking as a publicist. I'm asking as a . . ." He trails off.

I smirk. "I would very much like you to finish that sentence."

"As a friend," he says.

"A *friend.*" I give a low whistle. "Watch out, Ryan, you wouldn't want to cross those strict professional boundaries you're so fond of."

He frowns. "Consider it a temporary thing."

"Like temporary insanity?" I ask.

"Oh no, the insanity is permanent."

I laugh, and a smile tucks itself into the corner of his mouth. It looks stupidly good on him.

"I hear Chicago makes what's basically a cake but with pizza ingredients," he says.

"Have you never had deep-dish pizza?" I am incredulous—it's a rite of passage in this city.

He shakes his head. "Never been here before."

And he's not out there exploring? "You should go get some right now, then walk the Magnificent Mile, the Navy Pier, see if the Art Institute is open. It's a shame to waste your last evening here."

"I could say the same to you."

"I've been to Chicago half a dozen times, and anyway, I'm . . ." I consider how much to share about why I don't exactly feel like gallivanting around the city right now and decide on nothing. "I'm busy with this essay," I finish.

He nods. Doesn't do what I thought he'd do—cut his losses, tell himself he did his job trying to keep the talent happy, even if she was unreceptive—but instead slides his hands into his pockets and stands in the center of my hotel room as if he's rooted to its checkered carpet.

He takes in the suitcases open on luggage racks and the floor, clothes and papers strewn on various surfaces, a book and reading glasses atop the disheveled bed. My mother would be mortified at someone seeing my room in this state, but it doesn't occur to me to mind. Maybe today's events have numbed me to basic decency. Or maybe it's because he offered to get me dinner—as a friend. Which he said we are.

Are we?

On their circuit, his eyes scan over the nightstand, and all at once I realize I definitely shouldn't have invited Ryan into my untidy room. Because right there, for anyone with working eyes to see, is my vibrator.

Fuck.

"*So,*" I say, my voice much too loud. All the better to distract him with. "Um. Thank you, for, you know, arranging the change in venue for today. Went off without a hitch."

Did he see it? If he did, does he even know what it is? It's not like it's a honking dildo. It's just a small finger-slip device, a cheerful lilac purple, barely noticeable. It could be anything!

It takes him a moment to turn back to me, though. His eyes are stolid as usual, but his pulse is noticeably beating double-time at his jugular. *Fuck.*

"Just doing my job," he says.

Did I imagine that hoarseness in his tone?

I decide to act like he didn't see anything. What's he going to do, *ask* me about it? I could deny it, anyway, play it off like he's mistaken, it's something else entirely. A high-end thimblette for turning the pages of my book. Yeah.

I halt my spiraling thoughts. What the hell. This is my room. I'm a grown-ass woman who can pleasure herself all she wants.

He doesn't have to know what I was thinking about this morning while doing said pleasuring.

"I guess it's a good thing you came after all," I say. Christ. Did I have to say *came*? Put me to bed, I'm done.

"Glad to be of service. I had some making up to do."

This brings me up short. It's the first time he's addressed the elephant in the room. But hey, I'm here for it. "Well, your chivalry today is a good start. Rescheduling events and calling out douche canoes at Q and A's certainly add points in your favor."

"Well, I think if we'd found a better venue, the . . . *douche canoe* would likely have been moot. That was not our target demographic."

"Don't worry, the points don't cancel each other out or anything. That's not how the math works."

"There's math involved, is there?"

I nod, serious. "Complex calculations. I don't expect you to understand."

His lips quirk again, showing the barest hint of a smile—tiny but mighty, if my heart rate has anything to say about it—before he sobers. "Listen, what that guy said. You know that's about him. Not about you. Right?"

Is he trying to console me? Does he think I need consoling? "Of course," I chirp. "You can't exhale in this world without breathing on a guy like him. It's no sweat."

He opens his mouth, closes it again. Then says, "I know you could have handled yourself. Formidably. He just made me so—" He unfurls his hands from fists, shakes them out. "I didn't mean to speak for you. I hope I didn't overstep."

If only he knew. *You didn't overstep. Having you speak in my honor was like throwing a warm blanket over my shoulders on a cold day. Wrapping it tight, rubbing the feeling back into my arms.*

"It's fine," I say.

He shakes his head. "It was unacceptable, the way he disparaged your work, in public, at an event intended to celebrate it. I'm sorry that happened to you."

My heartbeat drums in my ears. Not only do Ryan's words paint a completely different picture than the one I had of what he thinks about my book, but the empathy he seems to show so effortlessly is even more unexpected—that has to be why my chest suddenly feels like there's a monkey playing a tambourine inside it. *I'm sorry that happened to you.* Such a simple statement, containing so much.

Has he experienced something similar? Had his work disparaged publicly? Now I feel guilty for asking to have him taken off my book's campaign. That can't have been a good look for him at Woodsworth, an author shouting that she doesn't want to work with him.

I realize I know nothing about this person standing in my room, next to my unmade bed. A surprisingly intimate scene for two relative strangers. But it doesn't matter. Even if I did know him, it's not like he'd know me any better than the rest of the world does. That door is sealed up tight. Has been for years. Because I'll never forget how it ended the last time I opened it: with my heart swirling down a drain.

And that was with Nathan—the person who was meant to love me the most. There's no chance I'm about to open it to some rando.

I wave a hand through the air. "I've already forgotten it."

He studies me for a long moment, as though unsure whether to buy what I'm selling.

"And I appreciated your kind words," I say. "Even if they took me by surprise."

"How do you mean?" he asks.

"Just . . . I'm glad you liked the book, in the end."

"In the end?"

I shift on my feet. "You didn't seem thrilled with the proposal. At that first meeting."

His furrowed brow clears, and his face falls. "If I gave the impression that I didn't believe in the idea, forgive me. I did—I do. Your book is excellent, Ana." My name on his deep voice makes a slow, liquid heat drip from my stomach down to my toes. "I think it's going to make a difference in people's lives. But I've told you that already."

My chest deflates on a release of air.

He believes in it.

Relief washes through me like water through a parched throat. Not because I care what Ryan thinks so much as I want the on-tour publicist to be an actual champion of the work. Knowing he isn't begrudgingly shilling what he considers a subpar product feels like unbuckling weights from my ankles.

A smile sneaks across my lips. "Well, now I believe you."

"Good." His eyes dip to my mouth for the briefest of breaths and he clears his throat again, stands up even straighter, if that's possible. "The early sales data says it will reach a lot of people."

It's all about hitting those sales targets. "And if it flops, I'll just resign in disgrace."

"What's your fallback plan?" he asks, grave.

I sigh. "I guess I'll go be a doctor."

He exhales what sounds like a laugh. "Sometimes it's hard to believe you went to med school."

"Because I'm just a pretty face?"

"Of course not. Not that you're not—" He holds up his hand, shakes his head. Tries again. "Because you're so good at what you do."

My heart rate ramps up again.

"But," he continues, "I'm willing to bet you're good at anything you do."

The slow, languorous honey in my veins obscures my thoughts. Which must be why I say what I say next. "Want to call my mom and tell her that?"

His eyes are warm, intent. "Does she not think you're good at what you do?"

I take a breath. Did I just unseal the door? How did Ryan of all people cause me to?

"She doesn't really understand my work," I say, leaning a hip against the bureau. "She's from a different generation, a different world altogether. To her, the internet is for Facebook propaganda and Armenian political news. She doesn't really read, let alone English books. So my work is just . . . outside her purview. Medicine, she understands. It's global and goes back as far as humankind. So yeah, she'd have rather I'd stuck with that."

He nods. "Why didn't you?"

"You mean why did I focus on creating the brand that got me a mid-six-figure book deal from your publisher?" I bat my eyelashes at him.

The amused glint in his eyes is slight, but it's there. "I mean, becoming a doctor is no small feat. Med school is competitive and challenging. And you were almost at the finish line. You were, what, in your second year of residency when you changed course?"

"Stalk me much?"

"Anyone who listens to your podcast knows that."

My chin drops. "You've listened to my podcast?"

"Of course I have."

Although I suspected it already, the confirmation is still startling. Maybe it shouldn't be—he was working on my book, after all. Any publicist worth their paycheck would do their research, listen to a few episodes to get a sense of the brand and its market. But still, it's just so unexpected of the Ryan I thought I had a handle on.

"We started the podcast while I was still in my residency, and things kind of snowballed," I say. It was a few months after the first video went viral. The potential audience for *SPOY*'s messaging seemed huge, given the response on YouTube, so we set up a makeshift studio in Maral's tiny apartment in Boston and rode the wave. "Within a year, my following had ballooned, we were offered sponsorships and paid ads, I signed with Nadia, I was doing tons of speaking events . . . it kind of took over my life. I didn't have time to do both."

"How did you choose?"

My father died, collapsing my entire world and crushing my ambition for medicine in the rubble.

"The immediate positive feedback from *So Proud of You* showed me that there's more than one way to help people," I say. "I liked the community it created. And I wanted to see where I could take it."

It's not the full story, but it's not untrue. The podcast, the community we built, was a ray of light in the eternal darkness of that time.

He takes me at my word. "And Maral felt the same."

Mar's path was an altered version of mine. The same year we started the podcast, she started an entry-level job as an environmental engineer at a Boston urban planning firm after finishing her master's. She's kind of a weirdo in that she likes to have a bit of downtime every now and again, and working two basically full-time jobs was not her idea of fun. Finally, she decided—with some gentle, not-at-all-overbearing coaxing from me—that it was worth exclusively working on *SPOY,* to see out its potential. She even agreed to move to New York, despite our parents' protests. I was making enough by then to pay her well, and she's always been fiscally responsible.

"Yes," I say, "so if you want to tell her parents she's awesome at what she does too, you'd be doing us both a solid."

"Not fans there, either?"

"I mean, would your parents have been cool with paying for your education, only to have you park it in favor of something you don't even need a high school diploma to do?"

"I wouldn't know," he says. "My mom could never have afforded higher education. She'd probably have been happy if I didn't have to pay off so much student debt."

Shit. "I shouldn't have assumed. I'll check my privilege."

"Nothing to apologize for."

"Well," I say, "I didn't exactly apologize."

He smiles—his first full, unguarded smile. Goddamn, it's a sight. "No, I guess you didn't."

I bite my lower lip.

"Anyway," he says, looking at his shoes, "I'd have thought you were a scholarship darling."

"Well, Maral's parents paid through the nose." She'd gotten a little help from MIT, but not the full tuition. Her parents were in a better position to help financially than mine would have been—her dad was an engineer himself, had moved to the States for grad school, and was the reason my parents got a timely sponsorship to immigrate here themselves, so he made a decent living. Mine would never have been able to send me to college, let alone med school, let *alone* at Harvard. "But you're not wrong. I got a full ride."

"Why am I not surprised?" His tone is tender somehow, and he's looking at me like he's trying to puzzle me out.

"What about you?" I ask. "How did you go from writing to publicity?"

He puffs out a breath. "Publicity paid the bills."

"Did you want to be a writer?" I ask.

"It was an interest."

"Was?"

He hesitates a moment before amending, "*Is* an interest."

The plot of Ryan's life story thickens. "Why didn't you pursue that?"

"Oh, um. I need to eat. And live somewhere?"

I laugh. "You want to achieve both of those things, in New York? Amateur."

He nods. "It was a pipe dream."

"Is it hard, spreading the word about other people's books full-time instead of working on your own?"

"Not in the way you might think. I sought a career in publishing because books have always been meaningful to me. If my efforts get more of them into more hands, all the better. And Woodsworth is a good employer."

"They meet your greatest needs?" I ask, raising a brow.

He gives a single slow nod. "They do." There's something in his voice that's almost . . . resigned?

Questions pile up in my mind like grains of sand in an hourglass, but I do an admirable job of tamping down my natural tendency to railroad him and choose just one. "What are you writing now?"

He seems genuinely surprised at the question. "Why do you assume I'm writing something now?"

"Just because it's not your job doesn't mean you aren't doing it on your own time. Writers are always writing something. They can't not. It's a compulsion." I know this from research, having interviewed countless people who don't have their parents' blessing to pursue artistic endeavors but can't stop themselves from expressing themselves creatively, even if it's not in a professional capacity.

He watches me as I speak, eyes twinkling. "It's . . . commercial sci-fi," he says finally.

"About . . ."

"About two people separated in the multiverse. Trying to find each other again." You'd think I had him by the throat, the way the words come out strangled.

"Like, a love story?"

He pauses for a beat. "It's still rough," he says by way of an answer.

"When can I read it?" I ask.

He scratches his eyebrow, red creeping farther up his neck. "It's—I'm—it's not fit for consumption."

A laugh bubbles out of me. "I'm kidding. I won't make you share it." I wink. "Yet."

He's flustered—I've flustered him. The delight blooming in my chest is pure sunshine.

"Do you think you'll submit to Woodsworth when it's done?" I ask.

"Ah," he hedges, "it's a little premature to even think about publishing it. And also, no. That would be a conflict of interest."

Of course. Those professional boundaries. "I've been my own boss for so long that I forget about the red tape of corporate bureaucracy."

"Yeah. The red tape can be . . ." His eyes flash to mine. "Limiting."

The words sound loaded, but there are other publishers—lots of them. Tons of ways to get his book out into the world. If it's good.

Somehow, I can't imagine Ryan writing anything bad.

"Well, I believe in you," I say.

He looks surprised. "High praise if I've managed to impress the famed Ana Movilian."

I squint. "The word *impress* is a . . . choice."

"Are you"—his brows rise—"so proud of me?"

"Okay."

"I see the appeal of your whole deal even more now—"

"All right."

"—that it applies directly to me."

"Yep."

There are sparks in his eyes, as if fireworks are going off inside his head. It brings a whole new dimension to his vibe, his serious demeanor made . . . not quite playful, but a step in its direction. Somehow, it makes him even more handsome. I'm very aware once again that he's in my hotel room, that the door is closed, that I'm commando under my clothes. That there is a sex toy not ten feet from us, and that the sum total of all these things is causing my nipples to stiffen.

I cross my arms over my chest. If he notices, he has the class not to show it.

"Well, I'll leave you to your . . ." He regards the mess around him. "Essay."

We say our good nights. As the door snicks shut behind him, it heralds a sudden breakthrough. Ideas flood my brain for how to tackle the essay topic, creative juices flowing, as though the conversation with Ryan turned on a tap. I race to the desk and start typing riotously on my laptop. I don't stop for a good twenty minutes, banging out a solid first draft that I then begin to fine-tune. The momentum drowns out any hint of the distant sting that's pestered me since Elevate. Inspiration, check. Energy restored.

Chapter 6

"It is like *ghrr ghrr ghrr*," Mom says in Armenian, imitating the gurgling noises her washing machine is making.

I pause my packing to do a quick Google search for plumbers in her area and make an appointment online. "Someone will be there tomorrow to fix it."

"Aren't you coming home this weekend?"

"Next weekend," I remind her. Again. "And I don't know the first thing about repairing a washing machine."

"If you can operate on a human body, you can fix an appliance," she says.

"I've never operated on a human body." I didn't even specialize in surgery, not that that matters.

She sighs. "And I suppose you never will."

I count to five. "I'll help with anything else you need when I'm in town," I say, keeping my voice steady. "Sorry, Mayrik, I have to catch a flight." I'm due to meet everyone in the hotel's lobby in ten minutes to catch the shuttle to O'Hare Airport.

"Okay, janikus. Travel safe." Her parting words land warmly in my heart, rooting themselves there.

Before I pack my laptop in its travel case, I check my inbox one more time and emit a squeal like a piglet: The email I've been waiting for has finally landed.

```
Today, 9:18 A.M.
From: nadia.chan@veritytalent.com
To: ana@soproudofyou.com; maral@soproudofyou.com
Subject: We're on!

Waters's office finally confirmed last night—we're on
for next Friday in L.A. Meeting with Craig and his
team re: vision for the show. I'll fly out & meet
you two beforehand. Excitiiing!

N
```

In the lobby, Ryan's at the checkout desk while Shanthi's already seated in the shuttle parked in the porte cochere. I spot Maral looking at her phone just outside the hotel entrance and crush her to me in a bear hug. My smile threatens to split my face in two, and I'm dismayed by her tempered one. She's not nearly as excited as I expected her to be.

"What's wrong?" I ask.

"Nothing," she says, affecting cheer.

She's always been more subdued than me, but that's not saying much given that I've been described as, quote, *a fireworks display of ebullience*. Her elation is just more subtle. Despite the fact that this is the first step toward the best thing that could possibly happen to us.

"Mar," I say, holding her by the shoulders. "If this goes well, we can achieve a pinnacle for *So Proud of You,* and *finally* make our parents happy."

She smiles unconvincingly. "I know. It's great!"

She's clutching her phone in her hand, and I can see on the screen that she has her email open.

"What happened—did you get a follow-up from Nadia or something?" I check my own notifications, but I don't see anything from my agent. Sometimes Nadia's in touch directly with Maral to arrange meeting details I don't need to be involved in. "Did they cancel already? Are they going in a different direction?" And then a terrible thought occurs to me. "They didn't get wind of yesterday's event, did they? Is there any video online from the Q and A? I told Shanthi not to post any—"

"Hey." She blackens her screen and cups my elbows. "Take it down a few levels, please. It's nothing like that. Anyway, I don't think some loser's standards for literature will even register on Craig Waters's radar."

"You never know—Hollywood is extremely fickle."

"Ana, breathe." I do as instructed, inhaling the scent of her leave-in conditioner and exhaling. "It's all good. We're going to meet with Waters next Friday, and soon you're going to be hosting your own TV show."

A spark ignites in my chest. I imagine making the call to Mom, imagine her reaction to the prospect of moving to a city with a concentration of Armenians so high it feels like the motherland. Of living near her sister- and brother-in-law again. Near *me* again, so I can figure out how to fix her washing machine myself and project-manage her home from the inside rather than from a distance. I won't have to bear her lamentations about my living so far away anymore, nor about my choice of career—those will finally, blessedly, begin to peter off. *If you were on television, that would be one thing.* And I will be. Like Oprah, at whose altar she worshipped when I was a kid, or Drew, whom she watches religiously now. She partakes in TV, she understands TV—it's a media source as familiar to boomers as the concept of medicine. She'll feel just as proud to see me on her screen as she would to call me Dr. Movilian. And her gratification will make being in her presence day to day bearable again. More than that—it'll be enjoyable. Finally.

Knowing Maral will be by my side every step of the way only makes it sweeter. I may be the host but there would be no show without her. This beautiful freaking mermaid I get to live my life alongside. How lucky can a person get?

"*We're* going to get a TV show," I say. "And we'll get to live in the same city as our family again. Win-win!"

She nods, her chest expanding on a breath. "Win-win."

The light drizzle that was falling upon our arrival in Seattle becomes progressively heavier over the weekend. If this were our first stop on the tour, I might have made a crack about Ryan having brought the storm with him, but I'm past that now. I'm nothing if not growing every day.

By late Saturday afternoon, when we gather in the hotel's atrium to head to the First Women conference, Maral is making relentless fun of the fact that I brought three full suitcases and not a single raincoat resides within them.

"You knew we were coming to the Pacific Northwest. Rain is a given."

"I'm an optimist?" I say, but I grimace. My green silk suit is unlikely to survive even a bolt from the Uber into the conference center.

"We'll see if you're still one when you look like a drowned rat in front of a thousand people," she says.

I shrug. "A lack of vanity puts people at ease."

"Let me get a few shots of you before you become hideous," Shanthi says, and I pose by a tall monstera while she snaps away.

Ryan joins us with four long black umbrellas tucked under his arm. "Courtesy of the hotel," he says, handing them out.

"Our hero," says Maral, covertly elbowing me.

Since the event at Elevate on Thursday evening, and our conversation in my hotel room thereafter, Ryan seems to have warmed a touch. He's not quite so forbidding a presence anymore. In fact, he's not forbidding at all. Still laced-up, sure—he is who he is, I guess—but now I know there's a human behind all those knots.

Take this chivalry, for instance. These could be patio umbrellas, they're so huge, keeping not only my hair and makeup dry en route to the conference center, but my entire outfit as well.

The hall is buzzing with entrepreneurs, thought leaders, and professionals. I know before we even check in that this is my crowd—a lot of people recognize me, asking for selfies and expressing their anticipation for my talk. I can practically feel the energy from their positive reinforcement entering my bloodstream, sparking renewed excitement for my keynote. This is going to be a good one. I'm grateful to Mar for getting me on the docket when she learned it would coincide with the time frame of the tour.

Woodsworth arranged to have copies of my book available at the pop-up bookseller station in the concourse, which is where Ryan heads immediately to check stock and displays.

Once we find the conference organizer, Devi, she leads us to a staging area, where Shanthi records me meeting and greeting some of the other panelists and exchanges handles so she can tag them in our stories. I'll give the keynote during the cocktail hour, after which we're invited to stay for the banquet dinner and attend evening networking events as we please.

It's hard to tell if it hits different just because I'm riding the high from Nadia's email, but on the heels of the not-great vibes at Thursday's Chicago event, my talk might be the best I've ever given. Top five for sure. Cocktail-hour engagements can be tough. People are getting buzzed and chatty; they have spent minds and unspent energy after a long day of meetings. But the crowd is rapt, almost every eye on me despite the catering staff milling about with trays of hors d'oeuvres.

I've added a few updated anecdotes to my talk and some subtle suggestions that my book, with more in-depth stories of the same ilk, is available for purchase. Afterward, the applause and cheering resound in the banquet hall, and through the multiple doors at the back I see a line start to form at the bookseller in the concourse.

Maral smiles broadly, standing to the left of the stage next to Ryan, both of them clapping. I swear I see a look flash in Ryan's eyes that's reminiscent of our bump-in at Chicago's hotel gym, when I caught him staring at my bare skin. *Heat* would be the most apt term to describe it . . . before a curtain seems to close over his expression.

Still, it serves to catapult my whirring pulse that much higher.

We spend the dinner hour chatting and networking with conference-goers, my heart like a snowball gaining momentum and heft as it barrels downhill. Connecting with like-minded people is better than any drug.

Once the crowd begins to thin, people heading off to various after-dinner events or calling it a night, the four of us regroup and Maral pulls up her Uber app to take us back to the hotel.

"No," I whine, "I don't want to go back yet."

"Do you want to hit up one of the networking sessions?" she asks, holding up the brochure Devi handed her.

"Nah," I say. I'm too antsy, pumped with post-show adrenaline and wanting to keep the party going. "Let's go drinking!"

Shanthi raises her hand for a high five and I slap it hard. Maral's irises gleam—she's in too. I turn puppy eyes to Ryan and watch him fold in a matter of seconds.

The rain is pouring in sheets as we race to our waiting Uber, which Shanthi has directed to a bar in Belltown. At a different time of day, the drive would afford us a choice view of Pike Place

Market and the Spheres, but as it stands, the darkness and deluge will obscure the sights Seattle has to offer.

Shanthi and Maral pile into the back seat and Ryan goes to open the front passenger door. The driver yells something we can't make out over the sound of the downpour. He waves at the front seat, which is piled high with insulated restaurant delivery bags.

"Sorry!" he calls. That much we hear.

"Are we ridesharing with *food*?" I ask.

"I'll call another car," Ryan says.

"It's fine, we can all fit in the back!" Maral shouts.

The car's a Civic, not exactly a double-wide—I don't think Mr. Boundary will appreciate being smushed between us. But it's a short drive, just a few city blocks, and every second of indecision while the rain batters the pavement means our shoes and pant legs get even more soaked than they already are.

Ryan motions for me to get in first, and I return the gesture.

"You get in first," Maral says to Ryan. "Ana's smaller, she'll be able to squeeze in more easily."

I glare daggers at my cousin. I'd like to squeeze her small head in a vise.

"I don't think—" Ryan begins.

"Or you can stand in the rain and ruin those dry-clean-only clothes," Shanthi says.

He looks to me and I raise my eyebrows as if to say, *It's up to you*. He presses his lips together and, as Maral yells for us to hurry, folds himself gracefully into the backseat, closing his umbrella and dropping it into the footwell along with the others. I do the same but I'm nowhere near as elegant, given that there's almost no seat left and I have to practically climb on top of him.

If anyone had asked me a few days ago whether I ever envisioned so much as touching Ryan Grant, I'd have laughed. Never in a million years did I think I'd be perching half an ass cheek on his lap.

I'm careful to balance most of my weight on the door console so I'm sitting as gingerly as possible on the very edge of his thigh, which is rock-solid with muscle beneath the soft flesh of my butt. The driver apologizes again, saying it's a busy night and gesturing vaguely at the windshield getting pummeled by rain.

The car feels so unbelievably small, every sound amplified within its confines. The shush of my pants against Ryan's as I adjust my position. His audible swallow. When the driver pulls a sharp corner and I fly fully into his lap, my back against his chest (again, no goddamn give whatsoever), his harsh exhale rings so loud it fills all my mental space.

"Sorry," I murmur.

"Don't be." His voice sounds strained. It takes some maneuvering to peek at his face in my peripheral vision, to see if I can read his expression, but his eyes are clenched shut. I feel bad that he's uncomfortable, but the guilt becomes hazy when his warm breath rustles strands of my hair against my neck and a shiver courses through me. Hazier still when another turn almost sends me flying off him before large, warm hands splay across my rib cage for the splittest of seconds to secure me, keep me right where I am, before they curl into fists at his sides.

Maral and Shanthi are cool as anything, discussing impressions garnered from the conference like nothing untoward is happening back here. Meanwhile, I am trying to steady my breathing, engulfed in Eau de Ryan. I haven't had a sip of alcohol yet, but I already feel intoxicated.

Blessedly, the car pulls up to the bar a few minutes later. You'd think all the HIIT workouts I do would mean I'm somewhat agile, but climbing off someone's lap from the back of a sports sedan tests that theory. I have the brief impression of hands at my waist again, giving me a gentle boost, and need to brace myself against the car for balance when I'm finally standing.

Ryan emerges behind me, sweeping an umbrella over the both

of us, obscuring his expression momentarily. Am I imagining things or does his breathing seem deeper and . . . measured? I know I'm not imagining what I glimpse in his eyes before he schools it away, or the quivery, melty sensation it inspires in my belly.

As soon as we're inside, I beeline to the bar and order four draft pints. We walk our drinks to a high-top table, me downing a sizable gulp on the way.

Maral raises her glass into the air. "A toast—"

"Yes!" I say. "To all of you, the finest team a girl could ask for."

I don't miss the annoyed expression on Mar's face at my interruption. "And to Ana," she insists on finishing, "who killed it today."

Everyone clinks to that, and I mouth *boyid mernem* at her.

Conversation flows smoothly. When we first brought Shanthi on, Mar and I were amazed at how seamlessly she fit into our dynamic. Although her family is Sri Lankan and not Armenian, we've had similar experiences with being raised in relatively progressive immigrant households. Being almost ten years my junior, she was still living with her parents on Long Island when we first met, but has since moved into a studio in Brooklyn. We all work mostly remote from our own places, but there's no small amount of travel involved in the gig, and we mesh well as we schlep around the country.

Ryan, gradually emerging from his taciturn shell, is drawn into the conversation tonight. Maral and Shanthi are full of questions about famous authors he's worked with, and he's irritatingly respectful in his answers. Shanthi orders another round in the hopes of getting him to loosen his lips, but he remains steadfast in his integrity.

"What's the fun of drinking with someone who doesn't want to gossip?" Shanthi asks.

Ryan shrugs. "A couple of beers aren't worth jeopardizing my job."

"How many beers will it take, then?" asks Maral.

He smiles. It takes me a moment to realize I'm holding my breath. Or just forgetting to breathe. It's not fair how the movement of a mere seventeen tiny muscles can transform his face from broody and handsome to dazzling and handsome. "It'd take something a lot more enticing than alcohol," he says, throwing an almost imperceptible glance my way.

"Bet we can find some coke in this bar," Shanthi says.

"*Jeopardize your job* is kind of dramatic," Maral puts in. "You think we're going to tell anyone at Woodsworth what you say about people who've probably had worse juice spilled about them on social media?"

"So go ask social media," he says. "I wouldn't cross that line even if you weren't public figures with devices glued to your palms." He nods at Shanthi, who, sure enough, is typing into her phone as we speak.

"I'm not a public figure," she says. "Although I might seem like one to someone who has zero online presence."

"I'm online," he says.

"You're not on Instagram," I say, and everyone turns to me.

"Yes, I am," he says.

What? "You don't follow me."

"Of course I do."

I tap into the app, pull up my followers, and search for his name. "Nope."

He takes the device from me and types something different into the search field: *aintlovegrant*. The icon shows a man about twenty feet from the camera, standing on a residential sidewalk, brownstones extending behind him like books arranged on a shelf. He's wearing a cap and sunglasses.

"*This* is you?" I ask, incredulous. "How on earth would I know?"

"Are you meant to know?" he asks.

"You're a publicist!" I tap his profile open. "There aren't even any posts on your account. How does Woodsworth let you get away with this?"

He shrugs. "They've never cared."

Shanthi makes a sound of disgust. "Is it because you're old? They let you get away with whatever?"

His brows draw together. "I'm only thirty-six."

Two years older than me. Yet I can't help thinking that Ryan seems so much older than other men the same age. More mature.

I press the blue Follow button, then pull down the menu to add him to my favorites. "In case you ever decide to post anything," I say.

The glint of satisfaction in his eyes borders on cockiness, and it does something to my insides. The lower region, specifically.

"So you have an account," Maral says. "Doesn't really count if you're unsearchable." She gives him a once-over. "What kind of secrets you hiding, Grant?"

As if on cue, his phone rings, and he pulls it from his pocket. The name *Celine* scrolls across the screen and he excuses himself to take the call.

"Is it just me, or does he get cuter when he's questioned?" Mar asks.

"It's not just you," Shanthi says.

I take a sip of my drink, and then another. Obviously they find him attractive—any person with a hypothalamus in their brain would find Ryan attractive—but hearing them voice it aloud pulls back a curtain inside me that would do best to remain closed. Giving credence to something I might otherwise be able to pretend doesn't exist. A secret between me and my vibrator.

Mar is eyeing me. "For the horniest woman I know, you're awfully quiet on this subject."

Caught out, I pause a moment too long before responding, "I don't think it's relevant."

"Relevant?"

"Yeah, I mean, we're working together. I'm pretty sure he's on the phone with his girlfriend right now. There's no way anything could happen."

"*Happen?*" She and Shanthi exchange an amused look. "Whoa. I was just saying he's cute—not that any of us would ever hook up with him."

"Right." The word whooshes out of me. "I know." I drink again.

She squints. "Unless you've thought about this already."

"I've thought about hooking up with Ryan as much as I've thought about hooking up with Shanthi, which is to say, not ever even once. No offense, Shanthi."

"None taken," she says flatly. "You're not my type."

"Oh," I say, frowning. Now I need to know more about this. "Not into charismatic dynamos?"

She waggles her head from side to side. "You're a little . . . *much.* No offense."

Offense! Definite offense. Although it's not the first or even tenth time I've heard this assessment—often put less kindly.

"Anyway, this isn't about me," I say.

"No, it's about Ryan, and your crush on him," Mar teases.

"Can you stop? You're embarrassing yourself."

"More like I'm embarrassing you."

I glare at her. "You should never drink."

"Excuse me!" She stops a passing server. "Can we get another round, please? This evening is getting interesting."

I drop my head into my hands. "Okay. Yes, sure, he's cute. But we're *professionals* and there are boundaries and it's not right for us to shit where we eat, so to speak."

"First of all, gross analogy. Second, nobody's shitting anywhere," Maral says. "Commenting on someone's looks—positively, no less—is a far cry from ripping his clothes off."

I try not to let my brain conjure the image of ripping Ryan's clothes off... and fail. I push my pint glass away. I need to *reduce* dopamine production, and drinking isn't helping.

"And I'd have thought," she continues, "that for someone who compartmentalizes her sex life like a bento box, it would be no big deal for you to do that."

"Well, maybe it *is* a big deal."

Maral's face exposes her surprise—and delight—like a showcase. I suddenly realize the error of my words, which could be construed as being more significant than they are.

"I mean," I clarify, "that it would be wrong to cross that professional line. With him."

"Don't worry about that," Shanthi says. "A couple beers won't make him *jeopardize his career*."

It's like the universe is taunting me, because just then the server delivers our next round. I order a glass of water.

Ryan returns then, seeming unsurprised to see a third beer sitting next to his half-drunk second one. "Sorry about that," he says.

Maral nods knowingly. "Girlfriend?"

I could kick her. I settle for a glower that could melt her skin off instead.

Ryan wipes at a small puddle of condensation on the table. "No," he says simply, and she raises her brows at me, mouthing, *No girlfriend.*

So what if she's not his girlfriend? There's clearly something going on between him and the jovial woman in his phone. Given all the heart emojis she texts him, maybe she *wants* to be his girlfriend, but he's keeping things casual. Not that I'm judging—*casual* is exactly the term I'd use to describe my own relationships. *Relationships* being a stretch as far as descriptors go. Sexual acquaintances? Fuck buddies? Is that what Ryan and Celine are? Does Ryan have a lot of those?

Where are Maral's inappropriate questions when I need them?

I drink my water, trying not to envision his hopping sex life, or marvel at how the bar's moody reddish lighting accentuates his jawline, or remember the way his body felt under mine earlier in the car.

Meanwhile, Maral yawns dramatically and checks the time as though she's in a middle-school stage production. "Damn, it's late. We should get back and finish that Reel," she says to Shanthi.

"Yep," Shanthi says, rising. "Time difference is kicking my ass. Does your body just get less and less tolerant of external influences as you age?"

Maral flips her hair. "I wouldn't know. You'll have to ask our village elders here."

Ryan nods, deadpan. "It's all downhill." He reaches into his pocket. "I'll order a car—"

"No need," Maral says quickly. "We'll just see you in the morning."

Noting Ryan's caught-in-headlights expression, I pipe up. "We don't need to stay—"

"You both still have drinks to finish," Mar insists. "Unwind, celebrate, enjoy."

Ryan's eyes find mine as Maral and Shanthi bid us a hasty good night, leaving so quickly you'd think a bomb was seconds away from detonating in here.

Which suddenly feels accurate, as Ryan and I are left alone.

Chapter 7

Being with Ryan, alone, in an establishment designed to soften people's sharp edges, is maybe not the best idea. Not when my senses have been heightened by alcohol. Not so soon after I was draped over his body in an enclosed space. Not when I've envisioned him using that body in unspeakable ways while pleasuring myself. Not when I as good as outed my attraction to him to Maral and Shanthi, and they clearly left us here together as an ill-conceived setup.

Not when I just found out he doesn't have a girlfriend.

Yet here we are.

I can do this—I can remain professional and friendly. Professionally friendly. Friendlyly professional. So what if he looks like that? So what if his scent is packed with pheromones specifically calibrated to make my belly feel heavy with want? So what if I keep wondering what it would take to crack the ice that confines him and see just how unrestrained he can get . . .

I'm just hard up. But I've got my little friend back at the hotel, and as soon as we're back there, I'll take matters into my own hands.

Alone.

Even if I imagine I'm not.

He's talking—he's midsentence, in fact. *Get in the game, Ana.*

"Hrm?" I ask, real professional-like.

"I said, we sold out of all the books Meredith had shipped to the conference."

"Excellent," I say, eating a sesame stick from the bar mix on the table. It's probably crawling with microorganisms, but the sustenance may help sober me up.

"Maybe we should hire Maral as a consultant."

"No doubt she'd kill it. I saw a book on climate change in your spring catalog—she'd be an ace at placing that."

"Right," he says, "she's an environmental engineer."

I nod, licking salt off my bottom lip. Ryan looks away quickly, zeroing in on his beer glass.

"Does she work the kind of long hours you do?" he asks.

I shake my head. "Nobody works the hours I do. Except maybe book publicists."

"Ha."

"I'm serious, actually. Meredith and Alison are the quickest email responders I've ever met."

He nods. "There's a saying: It's PR, not ER. But I don't think it's gotten through to the people who do it."

"Have you ever considered a less demanding job? You know, to give you more time for your other pursuits. I believe something about the multiverse, and a love story?"

He pins me with his eyes. "I'm kind of . . . tethered to Woodsworth at the moment."

"Why?"

"Various commitments," he says vaguely.

I recall his saying that this job meets his greatest needs. "So what is writing for you if not your greatest need?"

He thinks about it. "Writing is . . . who I am."

"Existential," I say.

"It taps into the part of me that feels the most real," he qualifies.

"There are no airs, no expectations or restrictions. I don't feel hemmed in—I can just be myself. It's the only thing I do that's just for me."

"You're not published yet," I say. "Once it's out there, it's for everyone else."

"True. Although who knows if I'll ever cross that bridge."

"You will," I say, somehow sure of it, and am rewarded with another of his smiles. *Breathe*, I remind myself. "So being your true self isn't your greatest need?"

He sighs. "Is it anyone's? Most of us live in service of others. Your podcast is evidence of that—how many of your guests talk about the pressure of familial duty versus their own desires?"

"How many podcast episodes have we had?" Because basically every single guest I've interviewed has touched on this to some extent.

"Three hundred and thirty-seven," he says immediately. "And, spoiler, the theme runs through every single one."

My head snaps back at the exact figure. "How do you know that?"

"I told you I've listened to your podcast."

"You didn't tell me you've listened to every episode." In a million years, I wouldn't have guessed . . . Thank goodness Maral's not here to hear this and gleefully hold me to my camping promise.

"It's very relatable," he says simply, sipping his beer.

I'm trying to make sense of this. Trying to slow my mind enough to snatch one of its million thoughts and questions.

My confusion must be evident because he asks, "What?"

"I just . . ." I trail off. "I'm trying to figure you out."

He's still for a beat. "I'm a mystery wrapped in an enigma."

"You are, though." I lean forward, elbows on the sticky table. "When we first met, I could swear you had zero respect for what I do. Not just because you seemed totally disinterested in my book proposal, but it was like you had a wall up against me in all our interactions."

He stares at me, unblinking. "I can promise you that was not disinterest."

A shiver courses through me. I think back, trying to identify whether I could have misread his behavior that completely. Whether that was just Ryan being Ryan—serious, reserved, pensive.

He releases a breath. "It's true that I hadn't listened to more than a couple episodes of *So Proud of You* before our first meeting. But they were so good, and then I met you—" His eyes do that thing again—blazing momentarily before he regains his composure. He pulls his pint glass close to his chest. "I kept listening because it compelled me. I read your manuscript for the same reason."

My heart skips a beat, then several more. "You didn't think I was a trite internet personality."

His eyelids drift shut for just a moment before his gaze finds mine again. "Ana, my opinion of you could not be further from that. You are . . . a force. In the best possible way. Which is why I thought you should include more of yourself in the book."

The floor seems to open up beneath me, my fingertips gripping at the edge of a cliff. "Your media hits made it seem like you were phoning it in."

He grimaces. "I wasn't. Your message is important, and it's one that deserves to be spread far and wide. That's what I was trying to do—reach outlets that may not otherwise have covered your book. Like *Talon*—I thought, with its circulation being what it is, that tapping Daniel would help broaden your book's reach. We were friendly in college and he'd written glowing pieces about a couple of authors I'd pitched him before, and I was sure he'd be as taken with *So Proud of You* as I am. It seemed like a slam dunk. I had no idea he'd spin his piece that way . . . I felt absolutely sick when I read what he wrote." He shakes his head. "Needless to say, I haven't been in touch with him since—well, other than the scathing email I sent telling him exactly what I thought of him after his *article* was published." He meets my eyes. "I'm sorry about how that went down. And that a lot of the other hits missed their mark. I wish I could control how every outlet covered your book, but that's free media for you. It was shit luck, but I swear I just wanted to get your book in front of more readers."

The air has left my body. And not just because I didn't think Ryan could talk that much all at once. I make a conscious effort to inhale. "And then I went and had you fired," I say faintly.

His brow draws down. "Well, *fired* is not the word I'd choose. I still have my job."

"But I had you taken off my book." I cringe inwardly and maybe a little outwardly.

"You had every right," he says.

I sigh. "If it helps, your hits were not the only misses. The bad reviews didn't exactly stop after you stepped off the campaign."

"I know it can hurt to read bad reviews," he says. And I'm surprised at how comforting it is to hear those words said aloud. "Like you said, once it's out there, it's everyone else's, and everyone's a critic, especially these days." He sips his beer. "But look at the response you had tonight—you couldn't take a step in that conference center without being stopped by someone raving about how you changed their life. That's got to feel good. Screw the bad press. Only four days in the market and your book is already a success story."

Tonight did feel good. Right now feels pretty good too.

I raise my glass and he clinks his against it. "I guess I don't have to fall back on being a doctor just yet."

"Sorry to Mrs. Movilian," he says.

A smile tugs at my lips. "You can tell her that in person when we hit Boston."

"I look forward to it," he says.

The image of Ryan meeting my mother is comical in its incongruity. Like Mr. Darcy meeting Lucille Bluth. I think she'd like him—her only hang-up would be that he's odar. Not Armenian. When you come from people whose population was half wiped off the face of the earth by genocide, who have been persecuted, killed, and chased from their land for generations, many consider it dire to keep the pure lineage alive by any means necessary—namely by making sure your kids procreate with other Armenians. Not that I'm procreating with anybody, let alone Ryan.

My parents never forbade me from dating non-Armenians. They liked Nathan, the only serious boyfriend I ever had, and his ancestry was as British as it gets, evident in his blond, blue-eyed, fair and freckled looks. We met in med school, where he was on his way to becoming a doctor, like me. He sang music into my grandchild-hungry parents' ears about wanting a big family one day and settling in Boston near both our families. He talked a big game . . . but turns out that's all it was: talk. Because the minute things got real—the minute he saw the side of me I know now to never bare again—he was gone.

You can't win 'em all.

Which is why I don't even try anymore. If you don't open your heart, it can't be hurt.

It's so much easier and more gratifying to have all the fun and sex without the heartache of commitment. It's made life a lot simpler.

Take Ryan, for instance. If we didn't have this . . . professional acquaintanceship, I would just let myself take a big ol' bite out of this pheromone sandwich between us. Enjoy the way his dilated pupils are drinking me in, alcohol seeming to have loosened their usual tether. Rub myself against him in any way I could, like a cat in heat.

"You okay?" he asks, awakening me from my reverie.

"Aherm," I say, taking another sip of the beer I meant to stop drinking but is somehow almost gone. "I think I need to call it a night."

"I'll get the bill," he says without hesitation.

Five minutes later, we emerge onto the wet street just as the monorail whirs by on the track above us. The rain has calmed to a light mist that carries the salty aroma of fish up from the marina a few blocks away. Good—all the better to block out Ryan's scent so I can keep my head about me.

I'm grateful for the short drive back to our hotel, and ungrateful that the Uber has enough room for us to sit on opposite sides of the back seat.

When we get into the elevator, Ryan pushes only one button.

"You're on the fourteenth floor too?" I ask.

"No, but I'll make sure you get back to your room okay."

A smile creeps across my face, the mirrored elevator multiplying it a hundred times. "You know I live alone, in New York City. No white knight to escort me safely home there."

"You have my number now," he says.

It feels like a mic drop. Is he inviting me to call him, beyond his capacity as my publicist? Boundaries be damned.

Okay, Ryan. Let's fucking go.

"So your chivalry extends to my calling you next time I'm walking home from the subway in the middle of the night?" I ask.

Concern crosses his expression. "Please tell me you don't walk around alone in the middle of the night."

I shake my head. "But I might start if it means you'll come to my rescue." My limbs are soft, hazy. I don't know what comes over me (yes, I do: three pints on the heels of being pressed against a body that should be accompanied by the *2001: A Space Odyssey* theme song), but my index finger is tracing a slow path from his shoulder down his arm. "Gotta use those muscles for something."

He goes still as a statue, watching the movement carefully, the look in his eyes an evolution of the one I've seen a few times now—heated, hungry . . . dark. His breathing has become heavy, his chest visibly expanding and contracting as his gaze remains glued to my hand.

And that's when I put the final nail in the coffin.

"Shame to waste them on being a gentleman," I say.

His eyes snap to mine, pupils blown so big they swallow his irises. "Ana," he says, a warning in his tone that only serves to embolden me.

"Ryan," I say, a challenge. A dare. An invitation.

A war plays out on his features—keep things civil, or annihilate those boundaries he's so horny for? He steps closer, despite himself. He's had a few drinks tonight too, and who's he kidding: He wants this just as much as I do.

I rise to my toes, lean in. Feel his ragged breath rush out against my open mouth. Brush my lips tentatively against his. And then, I'm kissing Ryan Grant in an elevator.

He returns my kiss softly, hesitantly. Then I slip my tongue into his mouth and it sets something inside him loose, his kiss becoming insistent, rebuttals and reason giving way. He gathers me close, stroking his tongue deep, claiming this kiss as what it is—the heady culmination of an attraction we couldn't have kept under wraps if our lives depended on it. His hands grip my waist, snake up my sides, my back, tangling in my hair as if he's trying to touch as much of me as humanly possible.

He kisses like a god. Or a devil. Whichever is better, because holy hell, I can't get enough.

I'm vaguely aware of a bell chiming as the elevator reaches my floor. He spins us out into the hallway, never removing his lips from mine or his hands from my skin. His long strides push me backward and my ass bumps up onto something—a console table flush against the wall—his tongue sweeping and curling against mine in a way that makes me relish the potential of what else it can do.

He crowds up against me, my legs splaying readily open to welcome him. A low, rumbling groan emerges from deep inside him as he presses his substantial erection against me. My pussy clenches with want, heated and wet as hell already. I can't help the whimper in my throat, nor my hands as they paw at his chest, those arms, his back, taut and hard as granite. I pull him closer, my fingers entwined in the fabric of his shirt, which I want to rip off right here, right now, damn any other hotel guests who happen upon us.

He removes his lips from mine long enough to press ravenous kisses along my jaw, my neck. He dips his tongue into my ear and the erogenous sensation is so powerful, it's as if he's touched my sensitized clit. I hear a low moan and realize belatedly it's coming from me.

"God, please," I pant. We have to fuck. Now. "Let's get in my room, I want to—"

But my voice seems to shift the air, somehow. He's pulled back, his breathing hard and unsteady, his pulse jackhammering in his throat in time with my own. He stares at my lips, his eyes blown dark, wide but dazed, as if he's waking up from some fever dream.

"What?" I say. "What's wrong?"

"We—" His voice is hoarse. He unwinds his fingers from the roots of my hair. "Fuck, I'm so sorry, Ana."

"I'm not. My room is twenty feet away, we're almost home free."

He swallows hard, winded, like he's just run a marathon. "No, I'm—I can't. We can't do this."

"*What?*" I say, maybe a little too abrasively. "Why?"

"This is a bad idea."

"You're wrong. This might actually be the best idea." My fingers are still in his shirt, and I tug at him so his crotch surges against mine, circling my hips a little so we both feel the friction—the promise of what could be. He shudders, a choked groan vibrating deep in his chest. His eyelids droop, reminding me of how he looked in the car earlier this evening—eyes clenched shut as my body pressed against his. I thought he was frustrated. More like *sexually* frustrated.

He gently pries my hands off and steps fully back. "We're drunk."

I shake my head, even though he's right. "It doesn't matter. I'd want you sober too."

He looks positively pained, glancing again at my lips, his eyes drifting shut for just a second. "It's not right. We have over a week left on this tour. I'm working on your book. It's a huge conflict of interest." He scrubs a hand through his hair. "I should have controlled myself. I couldn't—you're—" He blows out a breath, shaking his head. He tries to be subtle about adjusting himself, but hiding what he's packing is an impossible task.

At least he's hot and bothered. But then, so am I. My legs are so weak, I don't trust myself to climb off the console.

And, much as it's honorable for him to protect our workquaintanceship, he has no idea who he's dealing with.

"We can be discreet," I say. "I'm not going to get in my feelings about it or anything. We're just two consenting adults who would be making each other feel good for the night. Back to regularly scheduled programming in the morning."

He studies me, his chest still rising and falling. There's something in his expression now that wasn't there before. Regret at not allowing himself to close the deal, most likely.

Well, join the club, buddy.

He rubs his forehead. "Does anyone ever say no to you?"

"No," I say.

His palm drags down his face. "Never could have imagined I would, either."

Chapter 8

"So plan to spend the whole day after the Craig Waters meeting in Glendale, stuffing your face with boregs."

Maral's voice carries from the bathroom, where she's adding soft waves to her long hair with my curling iron—she packs light, but sure makes use of the accoutrements I bring—as she tells me about her parents' call first thing this morning.

"There are much worse ways to spend an afternoon," I say, mouth already watering at the prospect of my horkoor's home-cooked delicacies. One of the many wonderful things about Armenian culture is the food, something I miss now that we live so far from our parents, given that I'm incapable of replicating even the simplest recipe. You can find food from any culture in New York, but restaurants don't make it like moms do. "They know we're only there for the day, right?"

She puffs a humorless laugh. "You think that makes any difference? They'll take literally every minute they can get."

"And I'll take every morsel of Sosi's cooking I can get." Maral's mom's boregs are second to none, not that I'd ever tell my own mom that.

"Speaking of food, greasy spoon for breakfast?"

"You know it," I say, my stomach rumbling in anticipation of pancakes.

"Get up, then. Our train leaves in a couple hours. Why are you still in bed, anyway? I don't think I've ever seen you lie down for so long when the sun's up." She pokes her head out of the bathroom. "Jet lag getting to you in your old age?"

She loves to make fun of me for being three years older than her, and it's getting less funny with time. I found a single gray hair a couple of years ago and she had a *field day*. "Maybe it's because you force-fed me beer."

She nods sagely. "Alcohol tolerance deteriorates with age too."

"Right along with cousin tolerance."

I'm only mildly hungover this morning, which is impressive given how little sleep I got. I couldn't find a comfortable position, my body wound up and in desperate need of release. Even after I went a round with my little purple friend, the tension didn't ease, my mind replaying Ryan's kiss like the horniest GIF of all time. My skin warming at the memory of his touch. Of his lips, soft but hungry as they devoured mine. Of the determined swirl of his tongue in my mouth, promising delights my pussy was not willing to forget anytime soon.

Goddamn, when that ice cracks, he warms *up*. The only rigid thing about him all the more impressive for its rigidity . . .

I bury my face in the pillow to muffle my groan. I'm so hard up, desperate to finish what we started last night, and absolutely beside myself that we won't be able to.

We can't do this.

It's not right.

Then why did it feel so fucking right?

I know the only reason I'm this wound up is that we didn't close the deal. If Ryan hadn't stopped things from going any further, we would have had a good fuck—okay, an *amazing* fuck . . . likely a hall-of-famer, if that kiss was any indication—and I'd have slept like a baby last night. Right as Seattle rain this morning.

It's not that I don't understand why he stopped things from going any further. Yes, we were drunk—though I would have been just as eager without a drop of alcohol in me—and yes, it would be a conflict of interest. He doesn't want to compromise his job, which I can't fault him for.

Even though he doesn't even *want* this job. Not really. He said it himself, in not so many words. It pays the bills, but what he really wants to do is write. Surely he could find some other way to earn a living while pursuing the thing that makes him feel the most like himself . . .

Yeah, Ana. He's going to quit his job so he can fuck you, strings-free. Get over yourself.

I'm normally a reasonable person when I'm not in goddamn heat.

If only he understood that sex, for me, is not some monumental act. That I don't get attached. That we could enjoy each other's bodies and not get weird about it afterward. No weirder than we're liable to be today after that kiss . . .

A soft knock sounds from the door.

"Doesn't housekeeping know we're checking out this morning?" Maral says, emerging from the bathroom to answer it. "Hey." She sounds surprised. "Aren't we meeting at nine?"

I can't see the doorway from the bed, but I can guess who's there by her question. Her tone with Shanthi is much more familiar, and Maral wouldn't be quite so surprised to discover her knocking at my door.

Shit. I jump out of the bed, not wanting Ryan to see me in a position that might cue the unmet potential of last night, but realize too late that the thin camisole and boy shorts I slept in are no better. What Maral is thinking, inviting him inside without checking that I'm decent first, I have no idea. When she turns and sees me in my state of undress, she seems to remember herself, her eyes flying wide as she throws me the closest thing she can find. Unfortunately, it's my blazer from last night. I can't decide if it would look stupider to stand there in skivvies and a blazer or to just let the partial nudity ride.

Before I can decide, Ryan is in the room, a coffee in one hand and a small paper bag in the other. His eyes find mine, then flicker to my barely-clothed body, heating instantly. My nipples salute him, at full attention, which seems to be their resting state when he's around. He casts his eyes up to the ceiling, like a plea.

"Sorry," he says, turning around for long enough that Maral can hand me the complimentary robe from the closet. "I texted, but didn't hear back."

I silenced my phone last night, knowing Mom would be Good Morning–memeing me at the crack of East Coast dawn.

I try to keep my tone light, as if nothing is amiss. "It's fine," I say. "We're all adults here. Well, Maral's maturity is questionable."

He sets the cup and bag on the dresser. "I brought you coffee and a muffin," he says, then adds more quietly, "and some Advil."

Something inside me swells and recedes, an ocean wave lapping softly at a sunbaked shore. "That was really nice of you. The coffee smells delicious," I say.

He nods. "I found the nearest airplane and had them make it fresh for you."

I laugh, and am rewarded with a heart-stopping smile.

Maral's eyes move from him to me, then back to him. There are a thousand questions tucked behind her glossed lips, but she's too polite to ask them. She'll wait till about one nanosecond after he's gone and then fire them at me like a machine gun.

"We're going to get some breakfast before the train," she tells him. "You should join us."

Maybe she plans to ambush me later, then.

"Thanks, but I'm going to catch up on a few things. I'll meet you in the lobby at nine."

I try to ignore the notch in my throat, which is not disappointment. It can't be. I shouldn't be surprised that he wants to keep his distance. All the better to avoid any potential weirdness—or maybe further temptation? Although he did come to my room with thoughtful morning-after offerings...

My heart squeezes at his instinct to nurse me. To take care of me. Something nobody's ever done.

But he's just going above and beyond—author care at its best. Doing his job. The job he's so hell-bent on not jeopardizing.

I kick myself for being uncharitable. Of course he won't risk his career for the sake of a fuck. He's a responsible, considerate, quality person. Only a shortsighted idiot would throw away a long-term career for a night's worth of fun. No matter how fun that night would be.

Don't think about the fact that he looks like a certified snack in that sweater and smells like freshly showered heaven.

I just have to come to terms with the fact that things between Ryan and me are professional. Maybe a little friendly too, but that's it. The line has been drawn in the sand.

I'll have to work out my sexual frustration alone for the time being, until I can find someone to do it with. There's a chance I could meet someone on tour. It's happened before—the fact that there's a clear end in sight, with no possibility of commitment, makes travel trysts that much more enticing (it's why I always travel with condoms). And I'll text Jacob, line him up to come over the night I get home from tour. Or maybe Malcolm's available. Plenty of options.

Not that I can remember ever being as turned on as I've been in the eight hours since Ryan's lips first touched mine. I've only ever slept with men I've been attracted to, and I'll only keep a man on the roster if the sex is good, but I can't recall ever feeling like I'll explode if I can't rip someone's clothes off in the next second. Or *still* feeling that way the next day.

"Suit yourself," Maral says, leading him back to the door. He follows with a final glance at me, an expression on his face that I can't quite parse.

When the latch clicks shut behind him, Mar whirls on me. "Tea. Spill. Now."

"You don't waste time," I say, shedding the robe and clothes from my overheating skin.

Maral follows me into the bathroom, sitting on the closed lid of the toilet as I turn on the shower.

"Don't test me," she says, indignant. "I'm this close to killing you for not telling me the second I walked in here. Did you guys fuck?"

"Jesus, Mar." I pin my hair up before stepping into the cool stream.

"Don't dodge—did you?"

I scrub at my face. "No. We kissed, but he stopped it going any further."

She makes an incredulous sound. "So what did it for you—the cloak or the scythe?"

I sigh. "I've come a long way these past few days." As if she didn't know—she's partly to blame, or thank, for what happened last night.

As I lather, I fill her in on our conversation at the bar, explaining that Ryan was only trying to do right by the book. That he felt it deserved recognition, and was trying to get as many eyes on it as possible. That he was disappointed in the coverage he secured. That he told off Daniel Fox.

"Aww," Mar says, "and you thanked him by shoving your tongue down his throat."

The memory of Ryan's tongue swirling against mine makes me sway. I steady myself against the tiles. "That happened in the elevator, actually."

"Forced proximity," she says, nodding knowingly.

I finish rinsing and shut off the water. "And then when I suggested going to my room, he jolted away from me like I was an exposed power line."

"What did he say?" she asks, handing me a towel.

"That we were drunk, not thinking clearly. That it's a conflict of interest."

She waggles her head. "He's not wrong."

"But I can compartmentalize."

She raises a brow. "Not everyone shares your skill set for stifling emotions."

"You can't stifle something that doesn't exist," I say, dabbing on moisturizer.

She's silent for a long moment, avoiding eye contact in the mirror. "Maybe he can't compartmentalize. I think he likes you."

"No, he doesn't," I say.

"Ana, dudes don't bring you hangover cures first thing in the morning if they haven't caught feelings."

"His job is to keep me happy," I insist, heading back into the room to dress. "And he probably feels like he has to double down now after rejecting me. Like I'll report him to Woodsworth or something unless he plies me with coffee and pastries."

Maral unwraps the muffin Ryan brought me, taking a hearty bite. I grab the coffee cup before she can get her mitts on it, sipping and feeling renewed warmth at Ryan's gesture, not to mention his impeccable taste in coffee. It's dark and strong, from a local roaster, judging by the emblem on the cup. He remembered that I take it black, a small fact that nevertheless makes my throat feel funny.

"I've noticed the way he looks at you when he thinks nobody's watching," Mar says. "He's not as buttoned-up as he appears. His face says everything."

"Well, his mouth said no when you invited him to breakfast."

"Because I'd be third-wheeling you guys something fierce." She frowns, chewing. "I'll have to keep that in mind for the rest of this trip. Keep out of the way more. I'll let Shanth know too."

"You absolutely will not. It was one drunken kiss, and nothing else is going to happen."

She rolls her eyes overtly as she takes another bite. "He better have some rock-solid resolve, then. He's dealing with the most tenacious person in the history of the world. Does he know you don't take no for an answer?"

"I do if a guy rejects me."

"Which has happened exactly zero times in your life."

I stare at her for a beat. "It's happened once."

She licks a crumb off her bottom lip, her face falling. "This is not the same. Ryan is a grown-ass man, unlike that loser piece of garbage who dropped you when you needed him most. Ryan's got his shit together. He can handle a real human woman."

My eyes burn, a sensation I resolutely banish as I slip on my shoes. Nathan seemed like he could too. He was the quintessential Good Boyfriend in every way. Perfectly loving and supportive through our relationship as we finished our last year of med school and embarked on residencies at the same time. He gave me all the fun, love, and sex I'd always wanted out of a relationship. He charmed my parents, promised the picture-perfect kind of forever they'd always wanted for me, and meant to follow through.

If only things had stayed so perfect.

If only Dad hadn't died, tearing down the tentpole that propped up the fabric of my life, causing everything to come crashing down around me. The impossibility of working at the hospital day after day. Mom's total collapse. The heartache I had to keep bottled up every day, lest I upset the cart and make things worse for her and thus myself. The grief that took Nathan by complete surprise when I let it loose in his presence, seeking comfort, solace, but instead getting shocked denial, silence, neglect, and, eventually, retreat.

You've changed. You're not who I thought you were. I don't think I can do this anymore.

The coffee churns like acid in my stomach. I throw the cup in the garbage.

There's no way I'll put myself in that position again.

Not that that's an option here, anyway. Ryan and I work together, and that precludes anything else.

"He won't be *handling* anything," I say. "It would have been a one-night thing, and now it's going to be a no-night thing."

I grab my bag, turning up the ringer on my phone. Which is when I see the texts Ryan sent me this morning.

> Didn't see you at the gym. Feeling okay?
>
> Hope you slept well.
>
> Would make one of us.
>
> I have a large dark roast with your name on it. Can I drop by?

The last message is time-stamped almost two hours after the first three. I wince, envisioning him waiting for me to respond, getting no answer. Then I envision him tossing and turning in bed, same as I was, and think how easily we could have remedied that. How eagerly I would have done so—climbed him like a bronco and eased his distress.

Professional, I chide myself. *You have to keep it professional.*

"It's not the end of the world if I have to wait a couple more weeks for sex," I say, more to myself than to Maral. Willing myself to believe it.

"Tell that to your vibrator. Don't think I didn't notice it living on your nightstand."

I throw on my jacket and open the door. "Say what you will, but that old girl has never let me down."

The train ride to Portland is not as scenic as I envisioned. Mostly stretches of industrial buildings, rural residences, and some farmland, where I was hoping for craggy oceanfront-abutting cliffsides, *Big Little Lies*–style. Maral rolled her eyes when I said as much, telling me to look at a map for once in my life. Then she started detailing the qualities of the western lilies whizzing by outside the windows, lamenting that they're endangered by commercial and residential development and explaining how environmentally friendly urban planning measures could mitigate its habitat loss— which is about when I inserted my earbuds and powered up my laptop. She huffed a breath and moved to a seat across the aisle.

Sunday morning seems to be an uncommon travel time for this route. The train car is practically empty. Shanthi and Ryan opted to stretch out in their own respective areas, whereas Maral and I planned to go over a few podcast-related items together before I chased her away.

Even though trains bring out my best work—something about the lulling movement induces creativity—I can't seem to concentrate. I've been stuck on the same response to one of the questions Alison forwarded from *Vanity Fair* for the last half hour. I'm all too aware of how few words Ryan has said to me since we met him in the lobby after breakfast. He just loaded our suitcases into the shuttle and climbed in, directing the driver to the Amtrak station. Since then, he's been focused on his phone or getting our tickets or finding the right platform.

He hasn't even responded to my text. I sent him a Sorry I missed these! The coffee was a lifesaver en route to the diner, and he just thumbs-upped it.

It's unlike me to itch for someone to acknowledge me. I haven't wanted anything from a man beyond good sex, followed by an almost immediate kiss goodbye at my front door, in years. Things are so much easier when there are no expectations. When you can let your body enjoy the spoils of temptation without having to curate which parts of your mind or heart to share the rest of the time. It's easy to share only the fun parts when a relationship is all about sex.

And it appears that when that physical need remains unfulfilled, my brain goes into overdrive. Which is saying something.

Just as I'm about to give up on work, Ryan rises from his seat, walking down the aisle in my direction. Why my stupid heart speeds up, I will not consider. He's probably just going to the bathroom.

But he stops at my row, standing silent for a moment. Like he doesn't know how to speak. He points at his head, indicating my earbuds. I forgot I had them in, even though my sound's been on all this time. I pull one out.

"Hey," he says.

"Hi," I respond.

He opens and closes his mouth once, then twice. Finally, he lets out a breath. "What are you working on?"

"*Vanity Fair* piece," I say.

If he notices my mostly blank screen, he doesn't mention it. "Is it weird that I've done some of my best writing on trains?" he says.

Of all the things. "Not weird at all," I say. "Me too."

The sun peeks through the clouds, highlighting gold flecks in his irises. Again, he seems at a loss for what to say. "What music are you listening to?" he asks.

My face warms. "It's a biography of Ruth Bader Ginsburg."

He smiles, as if to say, *Should have known,* and my heart turns to mashed potatoes. Jesus, that smile.

"One of the audiobooks I relisten to when I'm in need of inspiration," I say.

He nods, his eyes not straying from mine. "Feeling uninspired?"

"Just . . . having trouble concentrating."

His breathing is even, measured, but I can see that telltale sign in the pulse in his throat—he's not feeling quite so measured inside. "Yeah. Me too."

Is he tormented by the same memories I am? The feel of my body in his hands, yielding to his masterful touch? My mouth opening for his, hot and needful?

I don't know how to broach the subject gracefully, in a way that won't make me wish for the earth to swallow me up. Neither must he, given his stop-starts. But I know I don't want him to continue his path down the aisle, and neither must he, given the way he's lingering. I remove my bag from the seat at my side, a silent invitation.

His eyes don't leave mine, and after a beat, he lowers himself into the seat. The corner of his lip lifts into a barely there grin, which I return. He puts his palm out, nodding at the earbud I removed. I hand it to him, and he inserts it into his ear.

We listen in silence, both gazing out the window for a few minutes. When I turn back to my computer, struck by an idea for a response to one of the interview questions, I catch Maral watching us from across the aisle. And smiling.

Chapter 9

The reading at Powell's is attended by over a hundred people. The audience is engaged and chatty in a good way, and many people get several copies of the book signed, citing gifts for friends and family who are huge fans but live elsewhere or were otherwise unable to attend.

I ride the high all through Monday morning, when we travel to San Francisco (by plane this time—sorry, Mar and planet Earth), and into the reading at City Lights Bookstore that evening as well. The staff and patrons, many of whom have already read the book, are so welcoming and excited to meet me that I appreciate anew all the work Meredith put into finding the perfect stores to host us.

Ryan seems to be overcompensating for our boundary-crossing by going into hyperdrive work mode. I guess I can let him off the hook given that he's killing at his job, verifying that bookstores have received the expected shipments of stock and promotional signage and making sure everything is set up properly and such.

We haven't had a moment alone together to address (or awkwardly avoid, as it were) what happened between us on Saturday, and I can't tell whether that's by happenstance or due to deliberate engineering on his part. I've pulled up his contact more times than

I care to admit, chewing my lip over whether to send him a message. But ultimately I always decide against it, not sure what to say or how to say it or if there's even a point in saying anything if it's not professional in nature.

He's been on his phone a lot more since we got to San Francisco. I thought maybe there was a problem with the event or the stock signings I'm booked to do at a local distribution center, but in one of my less proud moments I caught—okay, snuck—a glimpse of his screen and saw a text chain a mile long, rife with emojis. Then I peeked at the contact name at the top: *Celine*.

The gurgle in my gut is definitely not attributable to the fact that he's texting with a woman who uses that many hearts and smileys and cartwheels and samba dancers. I would have pegged Ryan as a man who'd be drawn to a more serious type. A Kevin to his Captain Holt. But then, he's clearly not serious enough about Celine—whatever their situationship—to avoid kissing another woman. Maybe his fling choices are cheerful sprites who temper his inner grouch by fawning all over him with heart eyes.

As we wrap up the signing, Mar, Shanthi, and I regroup to go for dinner. Shanthi invites Ryan, but he says he already has dinner plans for the evening. *With who?* I want to yelp, but congratulate myself on not blurting out the inappropriate question. It's none of my business. But tell that to the organ going haywire in my skull. Maybe Celine lives here in San Francisco, or maybe he's got a *second* lady friend here in town—maybe he has hundreds! Girls in every port.

It's none of my business, it's none of my business, it's none of my goddamn business.

Fisherman's Wharf is only a twenty-minute walk from the bookstore, and we wind our way through the briny salt air, peeking into harbor-themed tourist shops and buying some pre-dinner beignets from a stand Shanthi points out. While the mid-September weather is cool, adrenaline from the event compounded by feelings I'm trying in vain to ignore keep me almost uncomfortably warm.

Maral can tell something is off, but thankfully Shanthi's presence keeps her from probing. We eat seafood at a restaurant overlooking the twinkling lights of the Ferris wheel by Pier 41 and spend the remainder of the evening wandering the Marina District, taking in the Wave Organ, then the Palace of Fine Arts. Its magnificent lagoon-enclosed rotunda transports us into another world entirely, albeit temporarily. I enjoy the distraction of snapping photos for the feed while it lasts, before we call it a night and head back to the hotel.

Knowing I'll be spending the morning with Ryan for the stock signings, I devise a plan to inquire about his dinner in the chillest way possible so as not to reveal how desperate I am for details. Mar would tell you *chill* is not in my repertoire, but I'm determined to debut it tomorrow.

Any fledgling chill I may have had goes out the window when I receive a text from Ryan first thing in the morning:

> I won't be able to accompany you to the stock signings today. The car will pick you up at 9 to take you to the warehouse. Jim Harding is the site manager who will get you set up. All very straightforward. Shouldn't take more than a couple hours.

I swallow hard, rereading the text far more times than necessary. It's so businessy that it makes my stomach feel hollow.

Who texts first thing in the morning after a surprise dinner the night before to beg off their plans for the day? Their *work* for the day. Someone who got laid is who. Someone planning to get laid again. Or at least enjoy a cozy morning with their lover. Coffee and croissants and curling up, tucking cool feet under each other's thighs and sighing wistfully into each other's satisfied faces.

So he's got a side dish in San Francisco. Who cares? I could probably find one by just walking out into the street. God knows there are plenty of takers in New York, and this is the land of sexless tech bros—there are dudes in Patagonias who'd line up around the block for a piece of this.

What ownership do I have over Ryan, after all? None whatsoever. As Maral said, he's a grown-ass man. He can do whatever, and whomever, he likes.

I chastise my roiling stomach and text back, Cool. Have a great day! then start to get dressed.

Shanthi accompanies me to the warehouse, which is in an industrial neighborhood on the outskirts of the city. The route is pleasantly scenic despite being freeway-heavy, with whole districts of the city perched on hillsides both distant and near, bright houses popping against the browns and greens of the landscape.

When we arrive, Shanthi photographs me standing in front of the hundreds of books piled on skids, stickies tucked into their title pages so I can flip to them quickly for signing. I'm led to a large table laid out with Sharpies and water bottles. There are also two cups of dark roast coffee waiting for us, which is a surprisingly thoughtful touch.

"You know the way to my heart," I tell Jim, the affable warehouse manager acting as our guide.

As I finish scrawling my name on each title page, Jim—who only breaks from gushing about his grandchildren to gush about his wife—slaps the cover with a SIGNED BY THE AUTHOR sticker. Shanthi takes a long video of me signing about twenty books, which she'll post at 5x playback speed so it looks like I'm moving in fast motion.

When I'm finally done, Jim leads us to our waiting car in a parting that rivals an Armenian goodbye for drawn-outness. We thank him for his help, and soon we're speeding back along the freeway to our hotel in the city, enveloped once more in the scenic hillsides.

I check my phone and see a few new text notifications. My horkoor Sosi's daily Good Morning meme from L.A., rivaling Mom's from earlier this morning in garishness; a couple from Nadia asking how things are going; and one from Maral in our group chat with Shanthi, suggesting we all grab burritos after the stock signing then check out the Golden Gate Bridge.

Nothing more from Ryan.

Shaking the cobwebs from my mind, I type out a response to Nadia to say things are great and that I'm looking forward to seeing her at the meeting with Craig Waters's team on Friday. Only three days away, it shines like a floodlight on the nearing horizon.

I can feel myself vibrating with unspent energy, and I will the car to get us back as quickly as the laws of motion will allow. I am not capable of sitting still for very long in general, and certainly not when my insides feel like someone filled them with Pop Rocks.

"You in for the bridge?" asks Shanthi, referencing Mar's text.

"Nah," I say, "I need to go for a run."

"Didn't you hit the gym this morning?"

What does that have to do with anything? "Call it self-preservation. Nobody wants to be around Mar after she's eaten a burrito," I say. Beans don't agree with her, and that disagreement doesn't agree with anyone within a twenty-foot radius of her.

I feel Shanthi eyeing me, my legs jittering impatiently, but the second-best thing about Shanthi is that she will never pry. (The best is that every piece of content she touches turns to gold.)

When the car finally delivers us to the hotel, I rush to my room, throw on workout clothes, and bolt back out into the cool, sunny air. I don't even stretch, just turn left toward where the road inclines and hoof it.

The wind whips my short ponytail behind me as I pound the city sidewalks, dodging people and dogs and strollers. I realize belatedly that I should have brought my earbuds, put on some music, a podcast, or an audiobook, anything to drown out my spiraling thoughts about a man who has no right to take up so much of my headspace.

I duck into Salesforce Park, a tree-lined walkway snaking between skyscrapers that gives a similar enough impression to the High Line in New York that it makes me momentarily homesick for my beloved metropolis. I banish the sentiment by conquering the steep hills from Union Square to Nob Hill, punishing my quads and calves till I can't think of anything but the burn. I know I'm going to pay for this tomorrow, but right now it's a must.

After an hour, my legs are on fire as I slow to a walk, catching my breath. I wish we'd booked some kind of promo activity for this evening, which otherwise stretches before me, way too empty. Maybe I can catch up with Maral and Shanthi at the bridge, or do some other touristy thing that will occupy my body and mind.

My phone rings and I all but drop it in my haste to see who's calling—Mom. I worry my lip for a moment, the fire in my muscles growing more acute, before sending her to voicemail. I can't trust myself to be solicitous right now, nor to magic-wand the emotions threatening to surface as expertly as I'd like. I'll call her later when my armor is stronger.

A couple of blocks from the hotel, I round a corner and see a man who's a dead ringer for Ryan walking side by side with a tall, lithe blond woman. They're each carrying a coffee and laughing over some shared joke I'm too far away to hear. I'm sure it's not Ryan for that reason alone—I've never seen him so physically at ease, almost . . . *joyful*. I don't even think that state exists in *his* repertoire.

But as he turns my way, our eyes lock, and even from twenty feet away I feel the weight of his gaze right down to my toes.

Yup. That's Ryan.

And he's with a beautiful young woman who is . . . beautiful and young. Like, *really* young. She doesn't look like a teenager or anything, but early twenties at the most.

I steady my breathing. That's fine. Who he chooses to date is totally his prerogative. Even if she looks like she's on a ticking clock to be dumped by Leo DiCaprio.

Just smile, say hello, and pass them by. Let them continue their date in peace. Then go back to your room, wash this hog sweat off yourself, crawl into a hole, and disappear forever.

But they have the audacity to *stop*, the clearly hilarious joke lingering in Ryan's smile. I wish it would stop being so devastating, but no such luck.

"Ana," he says.

"Hi-lo," I say inelegantly. "Hi, hello. That was supposed to be both. Of those. But came out as a fun li'l mash-up." *Stop talking.*

He looks good. Really good. His dark hair shines gold in the sun, his eyes lit up. A relaxed set to his normally rigid shoulders. Fresh and rested and happy.

Which only reminds me that I'm sweating balls. I'm not normally self-conscious about how I look, but can't help feeling like a swamp creature next to his ethereal date. "I went for a run," I say needlessly.

"Oh, these hills are killer!" says the divine being. "When I first moved here I could never run outside. The only plus side is that it never snows or gets icy. Which is amazing!"

"That is amazing," I say, clocking that she's also friendly. "I don't need any help breaking my neck. My clumsiness makes a valiant enough effort."

She laughs loudly, palming Ryan's triceps as if to draw him into the joke. The move shows such a casual comfort with his body that an arctic ripple crawls down my esophagus. He returns her joviality with an indulgent smile, and then looks back to me.

His gaze travels to my neck, where stray hairs that have fallen out of my ponytail cling to my skin. His throat bobs, and he stands up straighter.

A beat passes before his date finally says, "Well, if he's not going to do the honors, I guess I'll introduce myself! I'm Celine."

And there it is. The woman of emoji fame.

"Ana," I say, shaking her outstretched palm, realizing too late that mine's a clammy fish. "Shit, sorry."

"Oh my god, don't worry about it! I'm actually a high-key fan. I'd say I rival him, but that might be impossible." She smiles coyly at Ryan. "My roommates and I play your videos to fire up before exams."

A college student. I should have known. I meet so many of them that you'd think I could recognize their shared identifiers a mile away. Jeans, hoodie, Chucks, a sling bag. Long straight hair, natural dewy blush on her smooth, luminous skin.

"Hope you're passing," I say. "Otherwise, I recommend Beyoncé."

Another laugh bubbles out of her, a sweet tinkling sound that makes her that much more endearing. I totally understand what Ryan sees in her—she's a beam of light, the kind of person who just feels good to be around.

"I'm so excited that you have a book out now too. I asked Ry to bring me a copy, but he totally flaked." She smacks his shoulder playfully.

Ry, who has been as silent as a sentry, finally speaks. "I'll send you one as soon as I get back to the office."

Celine rolls her eyes at me, like, *Can you believe this guy?* "I'm so glad he was able to come on the tour with you, otherwise it would have been Thanksgiving before we saw each other!"

Thanksgiving. They celebrate holidays together? I feel sick.

"It was nice to meet you," I say, my manners making an appearance at last. "I'm going to . . . go."

"Wait!" Celine cries, looking anxiously at *Ry*. "Um, we're about to go for lunch. Please—we'd love for you to join us."

I can't think of a less appetizing way to spend lunch than to third-wheel with this angel and the man who's had me tangled in horned knots for days. And even though he shot her a look as soon as she said it, I can't believe Ryan didn't immediately shut down Celine's request. Is he a total psycho? Kissing me one night, meeting up with her days later, and then having the nerve to be cool with us all just sitting down for lunch together? *Barf.*

"No," I say, "I couldn't—"

"Oh!" she says. "I know you probably want to shower and change. I should have said, we don't mind waiting! Take however long you need. We'll just pop up to Ry's room in the meantime."

Double barf.

"*No,*" I blurt. "I insist. You two go—enjoy your date."

A guffaw bursts out of her, loud enough to ring in my ears. She can barely catch her breath, bending over at the waist and clutching her stomach.

"*Date,*" Celine wheezes, as if the word is the funniest thing she's ever heard. "Ew!"

I look from her to Ryan, alarmed, and see a dusting of pink on his cheeks. His expression shifts, from a dawning understanding to something that looks almost like anger.

"Ana," he says, "Celine's my sister."

Chapter 10

I didn't exactly have a leg to stand on after that, so I agreed to join them for lunch.

His sister. Celine is Ryan's fucking *sister*.

I wish Ryan had said as much when Maral asked him if it was his girlfriend blowing up his phone. Or told me he had to miss the stock signing this morning because he had to meet up with his *sister*. Could have saved me from climbing the fucking walls.

Did he not want us to know he has a family? Is it also a conflict of interest for me to know he's a human with a life outside of work?

If I was hoping for an opportunity to dig, I'm out of luck, because from the moment I meet them downstairs after I've showered and changed until we're seated at a local sandwich shop that she describes as *out of this world,* Celine doesn't stop talking. She's majoring in environmental engineering at UC Berkeley, "like your cousin!" She barely takes a breath as she tells me all about her classes this year (lots of math and science courses that sound very familiar), the dilapidated student housing that she and her three roommates have rented for the year and how it compares to the dorm they lived in for their first two years (much shittier), and her favorite spots for cheap eats in the city (including this shop, where we just placed our orders—she insisted I try the Reuben, and who am I to argue with my de facto tour guide).

Ryan watches on good-humoredly, leaning back in his chair, returning a smile or making an appropriate noise when she turns to him in the midst of her monologue. But she's mostly laser-focused on me, rambling at a pace that betrays her excitement, asking questions and not letting me finish my answers before interrupting with a follow-up or launching into some new story of her own.

She reminds me of me.

"How long have you lived in New York?" Celine asks around a mouthful of Reuben. "I miss it. I miss how crowded it is and how many different kinds of people you see every day. Where I live, it's all students and app developers. I miss seeing people dressed in nice clothes! There's so much good fashion in New York. Here it's all fleece vests, bo-o-ring."

It's true. You see exceptional fashion everywhere you look in Manhattan. Even the dogs—sometimes *especially* the dogs—are dressed to the nines.

"I moved there about five years ago," I say.

"Is it hard to be away from your family?"

I choose my words carefully. "My mom definitely wishes we still lived in the same city."

"Tell me about it. Ry doesn't bring it up but I know he wishes the same." She bumps his shoulder with hers. "Although it's nice being able to make a mess once in a while. You should see his place—it looks like a serial killer's." She takes a big bite of her sandwich. "So why'd you move?"

"Celine, can you at least pretend to be polite?" Ryan says.

"No, but seriously," she goes on, "your work is mostly virtual or requires travel. You could do that from anywhere. If I didn't have to be on campus, I'd never have moved so far away."

I sip my water, washing down the sandwich bread that seems to swell in my throat. It's a question I've answered countless times, and this is the calmest way it's been asked of me. As in, not by an inconsolable middle-aged Armenian woman begging me to explain how I could ruin her life this way. I've come up with every answer under the sun—always careful to avoid the full truth.

"It's more central, for traveling," I respond circumspectly. "And I love it there."

It's the partial truth, at least. I had visited New York before, but upon moving there, it felt like emerging into the sun after a bleak, endless night. Boston had been home for twenty-five years, but that last year after Dad died changed the face of the city for me. Its familiarity tainted by grief. By the crushing weight of absence. By the heartache of having to carry it alone.

New York offered new life. The vastness, the opportunities, the mix of every different kind of person you could ever hope to meet, the constant frenetic energy of millions of people pulsating through the veins of this grand metropolis. Finally being able to breathe. To feel something other than loneliness.

"Why didn't your mom move with you?" Celine asks, and Ryan gives her an exasperated look.

Mom did raise the possibility. She doesn't have anything keeping her in Boston, since Mar's parents relocated to L.A. a few years after she and I moved to New York. Mom suggested potentially moving to New York herself, but I gently discouraged it, evading her queries and citing that she wouldn't be any better off near Mar and me when we're so busy and traveling all the time. That was also a partial truth—I couldn't exactly tell her that I needed space. That her grief was swallowing my soul, and her endless groaning about my leaving medicine was crushing my ability to keep the necessary smile on my face.

She finally relented, and has since made a handful of murmurings about joining Maral's parents in L.A. I've urged her to do it, but she's concerned about being so much farther away from me than she already is, knowing I'd visit even less with that much distance between us. Hence my plan for us to all settle in L.A. together. New ground, with reliable buffers, so that I'm not bearing the weight of her needs alone. She'll have family there, her sister- and brother-in-law, and friends—other Armenians who've immigrated over the years, joining the largest concentration of the American diaspora. She'll have me again, and I'll be able to tolerate her presence for longer than a few minutes at a time because she'll finally be satisfied with my career choice once I'm lighting up her TV screen.

And I won't have to visit Boston ever again.

"It's something I'm trying to solve," I say. "Figuring out a plan for us to live near each other again."

Celine smiles. "The hardest thing about going to school across the country is being far away from my family—especially this guy." She punches Ryan's arm. "Pretty tough lesson that not everyone will bend over backward to fulfill my every need. You set the bar too high—now I'm ruined forever."

"Be honest. You just miss my cooking," Ryan teases, but he gives her a smile so warm that something dissolves behind my sternum. It's clear from his expression that he misses the hell out of her too. I can't even imagine living far away from Maral, only seeing her on holidays and summer vacations. It just doesn't compute, how you can be anywhere but in close proximity to your *person*.

Then I clue in to what he said. "You cook?" I ask him.

He turns his grin on me. "Yeah." His eyes flicker over my face. "I cook."

The domestic image my mind conjures is too pleasing. Ryan moving efficiently around a kitchen, focused on a task, creating something from scratch, nourishing his loved ones. Doesn't hurt that in my vision he's wearing a pair of gray sweats that leaves very little to the imagination.

"You?" he asks.

I shake my head. "I char. But I look cute perched on a counter, glass of wine in hand, chatting with the person cooking."

He regards me closely, throat working on a slow swallow. He reaches for his water.

Celine grips my forearm. "Ry makes the *best* pancakes you'll ever have in your life. They're the ideal combination of airy and fluffy but also, like, substantial? My favorites are the ones with blueberries, but the plain ones are good too . . ."

She keeps speaking but I can't hear her anymore, practically tasting the heaven she described on my tongue. Is it possible? Could this man who kisses like a wet dream also make the best version of my favorite food? I need to stop learning things about him—the positive attributes are going to short-circuit my brain.

"Will you move back to New York when you graduate?" I ask, picking up the second half of my sandwich.

"Yeah, I mean, I hope so!" she says. "It depends on job prospects and stuff. I have one more year after this one, and I have to start building my network."

"I'll introduce you to Maral," I say. "She hasn't worked in the field in a while, and only ever in Boston, but I'm sure she has contacts elsewhere on the East Coast."

"Really?" she squeals. "Oh wow, that would be amazing!"

Ryan's eyes meet mine as he mouths *thank you*. I would have done it anyway, but his appreciation is a nice bonus.

I text Mar to see when she'll be back from touristing this afternoon, and see she's already sent me four messages. burritos a bad call with a squiggly-mouthed emoji. A selfie of her and Shanthi with the beautiful red arches of the bridge behind them, followed by you're missing out, then, fifteen minutes later, shanth wants to go on a "bay adventure" whatever that is. involves a boat. maybe meet a sexy sea captain. meet us at the fillmore tonite?

"She and my content manager are going to check out who's

playing at the Fillmore later this evening. We can meet her there?" I suggest.

Celine's face falls. "Oh, boo. I have a WOTF meeting tonight." The unintelligible word sounds like something between a sneeze and a dog's bark. Her features brighten again, and she gasps. "Oh my god, will you come?" she practically shrieks.

"WOTF?" I ask.

"Women of the Future! It started as a women in STEM group a few years back, but it's grown to become a much bigger association. Now basically any enterprising women on campus can join. I'm on the board. The meetings are pretty big, we're holding them in lecture halls this year. It would be the *hugest* coup in the *world* if you would speak—"

"Whoa," Ryan interjects. "Boundaries, Celine. You can't just ask Ana to speak at your school."

Celine looks crestfallen. "I thought you didn't have firm plans tonight," she says to me.

"Still," Ryan says. "Ana gets paid a lot of money to speak at universities. You're putting her in an awkward position to have to turn you down."

"Oh," she breathes, rattling her head. "I didn't think of that." After a beat, she squints one eye. "But if you don't have plans, and you wanted to—"

"*Celine*," Ryan warns.

Before I know what I'm doing, I drape my hand over his, hoping to calm his tirade but only sending sparks of electricity through my skin. I remove it immediately, but his gaze remains glued to the place where I touched him.

"Of course I'll speak at your WOTF meeting," I say.

"Ana," he says, "you don't have to—"

"I'd love to. Truly." I smile at him. "I mean, these women are the *whole future*."

There is no word for the sound Celine emits as she leaps out of her chair, sending it flying backward. She hugs me while I'm still seated, blathering gratitude and endless praise.

Ryan still looks grumpy.

"This isn't a conflict of interest, is it?" I ask, smirking. "My speaking at your sister's school?"

Pink creeps across his face even as he narrows his eyes with good humor. "I suppose we can make an exception."

"Phew." I smile.

Celine wraps her slim arms around his broad shoulders, and he softens into the hug. Seeing her bring out this more . . . unfettered, laid-back side of him makes me feel like I'm being let in on some kind of secret. She throws me a wink he doesn't see. "He'll do anything for me," she coos. "Always has."

She excuses herself to go call her fellow board members and let them know about the change to the agenda for the evening.

When she's gone, Ryan turns soft eyes to me. "You really didn't have to say yes."

"I know." I shrug.

He shakes his head. "She's tenacious."

"That's the best kind of person."

The skin around his eyes crinkles. "I couldn't agree more."

The Berkeley campus is just outside the city proper and takes forty-five minutes to get to by train. The three of us agreed to meet in the lobby before heading to the station, but when I arrive, Ryan is waiting alone.

"Celine had to head back early for a seminar," he says. "She'll meet us at the student union."

Oh. Okay. This will mark the first time we've been alone together since the kiss. No big, right? Here's my chance to introduce my chill.

Chill as lava.

Settling next to each other on the train makes me think of when he shared my earbud on the way to Portland. It's becoming habit, sitting next to Ryan in a moving vehicle. No matter that his scent makes me want to do lewd things to his body, his very presence is starting to feel . . . expected. Comfortable. Welcome.

As elevated freeways and low-rise buildings whip by outside the window, I finally say, "You know, you may be taking the whole professional boundaries thing a bit too seriously. You could have told me your sister lives here and you wanted to spend time with her."

He doesn't make eye contact, looking sheepish. "I didn't want it to seem like I had an agenda for coming on the tour, other than serving your book."

"I would never have thought that." It truly would not have occurred to me. Mar and I are planning to see family on this trip. If Shanthi's family lived en route, I would hope she'd do the same. "Family is everything—of course you should see your sister when you're in the same town."

He nods. "Thanks. I didn't want to miss the stock signing, but it was the last time we'd be able to see each other while I'm here."

I wave him off. "I'm relieved, actually. I thought you were avoiding me."

"Avoiding you?"

I take a breath. "I thought maybe you regretted . . . Seattle. You've been a bit distant the past couple of days."

"I—" He scratches the back of his neck. "I've been feeling guilty for making such a creep move. I meant to apologize the morning after, when I brought you coffee, but Maral was there and you were dressed . . ." He clears his throat, and my nipples peak under my jacket at the memory of him seeing me in a thin camisole and panties. "I didn't want to make you uncomfortable. I figured keeping my distance would be the best bet. Easier to stay in line that way."

Something hot ignites in my belly. He's not exactly saying *I can't be around you without wanting to rip your clothes off,* but he's not *not* saying that, either. "For the record, you didn't make the move—I did. Even if you had, I wouldn't call it creepy. Except when I thought Celine was your date."

Realization dawns. "You thought she was my girlfriend." He leans forward, his voice quiet. "Do you think I would kiss you if I had a girlfriend?"

One of my shoulders rises in a half shrug. "Maybe you had some kind of arrangement. Or maybe you two were casual. Or, hell, maybe you're a cheater."

"None of the above," he says, his eyes intense. "Ever."

I fidget with the hem of my jacket. "Well, I wouldn't know. There are all kinds of relationships these days."

"I'm out of the loop. Haven't had a relationship in a long time."

"I don't have them at all."

He regards me for a beat too long. "Why not?"

"Not worth the heartache," I say before I can think better of it. "Anyway, I'm glad I was wrong. And Celine is an utter delight."

He's silent for a moment, inquisitive eyes roaming my face, then nods. "Thanks for indulging her. She was, uh, very excited to meet you."

For some reason, this touches me. I don't know why it would matter that Celine thinks highly of me. But it does.

"You must miss her, living so far away," I say.

He heaves a breath. "I do. It's hard to go from sharing the same space for so many years to her being almost three thousand miles away."

"You lived together until she went to college?" I ask, surprised.

"Part-time. She stayed with me in the city on weekends, but during the week my work hours were too long. She'd spend too many hours alone, so she mostly lived in Queens with my mom."

This doesn't clarify the picture. "Most high schoolers live with their parents anyway, don't they?"

"They do." He hesitates for a moment, as if searching for words. "Our situation is a bit different."

"How so?"

"Celine's my half sister. We share a father, although *share* is a generous term for it. He left my mother when I was a baby."

"Shit," I say. "That's awful."

"We'd hear from him every few years—a Christmas card or a call if he happened to be passing through and remembered we lived in the neighborhood. Then, when I was sixteen, we got word that he'd had another kid. Well, gotten a woman pregnant, anyway. He didn't exactly stick around for her, either."

His voice doesn't carry the level of accusation or vitriol you'd expect from someone whose father abandoned him and the person he cares most about in the world. Maybe that's just Ryan being Ryan, buttoning himself up. Maybe that whole shtick helps to keep unwanted emotions from spilling out.

Maybe we're not so different in that regard.

"It was important to me to be in Celine's life," he says. "It's weird—even though neither of us knew our dad, really, I felt a connection to her. Every time she saw me, her little face would light up. Her chubby arms reaching for me, making grabby hands until I picked her up. I swear, there is no acceptance like an infant making you feel like the most important person in the world." He smiles faintly. "Luckily, her mom, Devon, was okay with me coming over, helping however I could, even if it was just watching the baby while she slept or went out. But it was pretty clear she was struggling from the beginning. She couldn't keep a job, didn't have any family to help. Didn't seem particularly maternal, which is not a knock on her. She was in a tough position. One day, she just . . . up and left."

Oh wow. My heart aches for Celine, abandoned by both parents at such a young age.

"Celine was almost two years old when she went into foster care. I turned eighteen a few months later and applied to take legal guardianship. I wasn't exactly ready to be a full-time single parent, though, so my mom agreed to be my co-applicant."

"Jesus," I say before I can stop myself. My mind is abuzz, reforming the image of the life I assumed Ryan had, trying to absorb the sheer amount of responsibility he took on at such a young age. Becoming the father his own father wasn't. "And your mom was okay with adopting your dad's other kid?"

"She had feelings about it, obviously. It wasn't easy for her, emotionally or practically. It took some convincing—she didn't have the same level of emotional connection to Celine that I did, being that they weren't related. But we were granted a visit as part of the potential guardianship process, and when we arrived, Celine ran straight into my arms, squealing my name with the biggest smile on her face, and, well, Mom's not made of stone. That sealed the deal."

"Still, she was basically an empty nester by then, right?" I say. "She probably thought she was done raising kids, and then had a toddler running around again."

He focuses on the middle distance, as if remembering those days. "It was a lot. I had just started college, and she didn't want me to give it up. I was still living at home, commuting to NYU. I had some scholarships, but money was sparse. I contributed what I could from part-time jobs. Mom had a day job as a receptionist at a dental clinic, and I changed my schedule so I could take classes at night. That way, we traded off being home with Celine until she started preschool a couple years later."

"What about your social life? Friends, parties . . . dating?"

He meets my eyes. "Not much time or bandwidth for those things."

"And you weren't bitter about that?"

He considers his answer. "I'm pragmatic by nature. My circumstances made it so I always had to operate within restrictions, and once Celine came into my life, it was only natural to put her needs first. Stricter boundaries just came with the territory."

Serving Celine's needs is one thing, but I can't help thinking that his adherence to boundaries is more about controlling—or blocking out—his own needs. Because they competed with hers?

"Worth it, though. You've met Celine," he says, eyes glimmering with pride, with devotion. "Was it hectic for a while? Sure. But for better or worse, Mom had had training, raising me on her own."

"But you hadn't."

"I mean, yes and no. She worked long hours when I was growing up, trying to make ends meet. I'd learned how to do things for myself. And I took odd jobs as soon as I could, to help out."

My brain lights up at the thought of little Ryan running a lemonade stand or throwing rolled-up newspapers onto doorsteps from a Schwinn. "What kind of jobs?"

"Tutoring, dog-walking, babysitting." He smirks. "Real glamorous stuff."

I smile. "Hey, don't knock childhood glamor jobs. I did all those same things."

I try to think of how I can meet him halfway in this conversation. I never adopted a child as a teenager, but I feel I can relate on some level, at least.

"My dad worked long hours too," I say. "He was the clerk at a corner store. His shifts lasted all day. He'd open the store first thing in the morning and close late at night."

He turns toward me, settling back against the train wall. "What was his job in Armenia?"

"His family owned a coffee shop, and he worked there. It was kind of a hybrid corner store and coffee house—they sold ground beans as well as dried fruits and nuts, other pantry items. And they had a couple of tables set up inside and out where they served coffee to in-store patrons. I've seen a few pictures."

"So your love of coffee goes back generations."

I put a hand over my heart. "It's our legacy."

"Did your mom work?" he asks.

"Her mom died when she was pretty young, so she looked after her dad and helped to raise her younger siblings, mostly. When my parents got married, she helped with the shop. After they immigrated here, she took some odd jobs, trading on the skills she had. She baked pastries for the local deli. She could sew, so she made adjustments for a local seamstress when they were backed up. That kind of thing. She could do those things from home, so she and my aunt could trade off being home with Maral and me."

I stick to practical details because I'd rather swallow thumbtacks than put a dour spin on what's otherwise a story of resilience and starting over—the kind of story people like to hear. From the kind of Ana people like to see. So I keep it light. Don't tell him how Mom retreated for long periods in those early years in Boston, and was never quite the same after immigrating. That the transition from the rural Armenian village she'd called home her entire life to a Western urban metropolis was not easy on her. She went from being surrounded by family, siblings and cousins, a language she knew, and a role she embodied to her core to living in a city where she only knew her sister-in-law's family, had to learn a whole new language, find space, and weather microaggressions in an entirely foreign culture. Had to raise her child within it when she was still trying to figure it out for herself. It took a toll on her.

And not just on her.

"How long did you all live together?" Ryan asks.

"I was twelve when we moved into the house my mom still lives in now. But till then, we all shared an apartment. Mar's parents had come over on my uncle's student visa a couple years before us and applied for citizenship. After the Soviet Union collapsed, they were able to sponsor our immigration."

"How old were you?"

"Three."

"If you were born there, does that make you first-generation?"

"Technically, yes. But because I was so young when we moved,

I identify more as second-gen. I remember almost nothing from my life there."

I have a couple of vague images from life in Armenia, where I was born. A wooden matryoshka doll in my grandmother's house. The deep maroons and olive greens of a low-pile area rug. The hazy bumps of mountains on the distant horizon. My mother's smile.

"How come you never talk about this stuff?" he says.

"What do you mean?"

"I mean, you've written a whole book and recorded three hundred and thirty-seven episodes of a podcast about people's experiences as children of immigrants, which you are too. Yet you rarely talk about your own life."

My pulse ramps up a little as I remember our first meeting. His insistence that readers would be disappointed in a book that didn't focus on my story, such that it is. "*So Proud of You* isn't about me. It never has been. Readers and listeners appreciate the focus being on our guests."

He's eyeing me, as though he suspects that's another partial truth. Then he straightens in his seat, saying under his breath, "Guess I was just hungry for details."

My heart hammers. I'm pretty sure I heard what I just heard, but before I can process it, he goes on.

"No wonder you and Maral are so close, having lived together."

I nod, re-entering the moment. "We shared a room in the apartment our families rented. She couldn't pronounce Anahid, so for the longest time she called me Aynay. Still does sometimes." My smile turns wicked. "I used to terrorize her."

He huffs a sound that could be a laugh. "You, a terror? But you're so measured and easygoing." The mirth in his tone is unmistakable.

I narrow my eyes. "Believe it or not, I am practically zen now compared to when I was a kid."

"I would pay good money to see footage of young Ana."

I whistle. "I wouldn't even register on the screen, just a puff of smoke as I zinged around the room."

He's watching me, his indulgent expression mirroring the look he gave Celine earlier today. I don't let myself linger on the comparison too long. On how it's making my chest feel gooey.

"One time I folded myself into the bottom drawer of the dresser in our room," I say. "Mar was playing peacefully by herself for, like, half an hour, lulled into a sense of solitude. She came to get something out of the drawer and I jumped out. I've never heard anyone scream that loud. And it's the only time I've ever been punched in the face."

His mouth drops open. "She punched you?"

"It was a fear response, unintentional. I would have pegged her for flight over fight, but shows what I know." I point to the faded scar on my chin from where my skin split.

He examines it closely. "Huh. I guess you're not perfect after all," he says, a mock wistfulness in his tone.

"Far from it." If only he knew.

"I'm glad you lived to tell the tale."

"Well, it was the first and only time she physically assaulted me," I say. "Although I have been a lot kinder since then."

"Think she'd corroborate that?"

"Memory is fallible," I say.

"Hard to believe memories of you wouldn't stay vivid forever," he says, his gaze dropping to my lips for a moment before he turns abruptly toward the window.

This time there's no doubt in my mind—I heard it. And I know precisely which memory of me is playing vividly in his mind.

I also know that, as much as Ryan is playing the good boy, acting all professional and trying to put our kiss out of his mind, it's haunting him just as much as it is me.

Chapter 11

The lecture hall is packed. Every seat claimed, people sitting on the steps and standing at the back of the room, jackets slung over their arms and backpacks at their feet.

Celine says the association meetings are usually well attended, but that this is the busiest she's ever seen it. "We spread the word that you were coming, and ta-da!"

She explains the run of show—they'll go through a few agenda items and then I'm up. She introduces me to the WOTF president, Amani, whose gushing is slightly more restrained than Celine's was upon meeting me. After she thanks me four times for coming tonight, she directs Ryan and me to sit in the taped-off chairs at the front of the room so the session can get started.

Colleges might just be my favorite venues for speaking events. There's such vitality in young people whose minds are being opened to the breadth of the world, the possibilities it contains. Feeling their energy renews my sense of purpose. This is what it's all about—what it was all about when I sent that first video to Maral, a grad student dealing with outsized expectations from both the institution and herself. Pushed there for better or worse by parents who worked so hard to give her that opportunity to prove herself.

I texted Maral earlier that I couldn't meet her and Shanthi this evening because I was doing an impromptu talk at the Berkeley campus, and I see her response now when I pull out my phone: cool. I swipe away the notification and open the video camera, handing it to Ryan so he can record me for socials.

Amani holds court like a true boss—her bright pink hijab may as well be a crown. By the time she invites me to the podium, I'm so enamored of the WOTF meeting in session that it takes the room erupting in applause to shake me out of it.

"Hello, women of the future!" I say into the mic. Their appreciation reaches a higher pitch, a few whoops ringing throughout the room.

I launch into my usual college speech, making appropriate amendments for the size of the crowd and the specific organization. It's finely honed at this point, but no matter how many times I do this, it makes me swell with gratification.

Even though there isn't a formal Q and A session tacked on to the end of my speaking time, I hang around and chat with the students. As a line forms down the aisle, Ryan disappears through the double doors and returns minutes later, two bottles of water in one hand and my phone in the other. He delivers the items to me, apologizing to the student I'm speaking with for the interruption before asking me if I'm comfortable, if I need anything else. A chair, perhaps, or something else to drink or eat. I decline, and he stands aside—but not too far.

It takes an hour and a half before the auditorium is almost empty, with only a handful of stragglers hanging back. Amani and a few others excuse themselves to meet assignment deadlines after thanking me profusely for bringing such excitement to their usual Tuesday night meeting. Celine and a couple of people who I assume are on the board of WOTF are the last ones clustered together near the door.

"There's a student mixer tonight," Celine says. "They've sourced a couple of kegs—drinks are on us!"

Ryan raises a censorious brow at her, clearly unimpressed with her underage drinking, before his gaze drifts to me. "We should be getting back..."

"No! Hang out a bit," Celine says, making some kind of eyes at him. "Ana deserves to unwind after doing us this solid."

His scowl is next-level. "Celine..."

"Ryan," she says in an admonishing tone of her own. More quietly, she adds, "Let yourself enjoy something. For once?"

"I'm down," I say, and they both turn to me. Maybe I'm speaking out of turn—there's clearly some subtextual communication happening between them—but someone needs to be the deciding vote. And while a college kegger is not my idea of the *most* fun Ryan and I could have together, there's no need to examine why I'm so eager to spend more of the evening with him when there's no sex involved.

Celine beams. Ryan's muscles seem to relax and his frown melts away, which a week ago I would have thought was as good as a smile for this sourpuss. Boy, was I wrong.

"Okay, then," he says. "Hope you like foam."

The beer is not only foamy but room temperature.

Ryan and I each nurse a solo cup as we stand at a makeshift bar in the residence hall common room, chatting over the din of music with various students who either introduce themselves self-assuredly or have to be coaxed to join the conversation. Some people clear out a central circle in which to dance while others mill among friends, and soon enough Ryan and I are left alone.

"Subpar alcohol is one thing I don't miss about college," I say.

"Couldn't beat free back then, though," he says, thunking my cup with his.

An absent smile spreads across my face. "I crashed every faculty reception I could find to stuff myself with the free hors d'oeuvres."

"I took a cooking class as an elective because it meant taking leftovers home for dinner."

"I babysat for one of my professors and pilfered her kids' Lunchables."

He sips his foam, grimaces. "Free is no longer as motivating when you have disposable income. Why are we here, again?"

"Because your sister invited us. She wanted you to enjoy yourself *for once*." I quirk a brow at him. "Gotta make up for lost time, given you didn't go to parties in college."

"Doesn't seem like I missed much." He scans our surroundings, the painted cinder-block walls with tape remnants from years of posters being hung and removed. "I overheard some kids talking about midterm exams and my trauma response was immediate."

"Okay, unpopular opinion time." I raise a hand. "I loved exams."

His face is all skepticism. "No, you didn't."

I hold up both palms now in surrender. "There's a reason Maral says I'm the biggest nerd to ever nerd."

He eyes me suspiciously. "What part did you love? The pressure, the sleeplessness, the heart palpitations?"

I laugh. "I loved learning new things all the time. I loved studying, knowing the effort would yield a payoff. Loved having knowledge at the forefront of my mind—being asked a question and having the answer, right there, like a quick draw. I loved proving myself. Loved the feeling of value it gave me. Loved being evaluated on my hard work."

"Evaluated favorably, I assume," he says.

I flip my hair. "Naturally."

A curve forms at the corner of his lips. I want to dip my tongue into it.

"The pressure didn't get to you?" he asks.

"Not that pressure."

He stays silent, waiting for me to continue. Patient, intent. So attentive.

I try to figure out how to explain it in a way that won't expose something I'm not willing to. "My parents came here with almost nothing," I say. "They weren't educated, but they worked all their lives to provide a life for me. I started working at a young age to contribute, in the hopes of relieving some of the pressure on them to make ends meet." I draw circles on the rim of my cup. "I felt guilty striving for something that seemed . . . superfluous. Even if, eventually, I was able to contribute more."

A line forms in the center of his brow. "Parents want better for their kids than what they had. Including a higher standard of education."

"I know they wanted better for me than what they had—they sure loved telling people I got into med school. But the more I followed the path toward *better*, the further away from them it seemed to take me."

He's silent for a long moment. "That must have been tough."

I wait for him to throw in a chaser—*But look at you now*, or *They'll come around*—effectively dismissing what he surely sees as misplaced and fruitless guilt. That was Nathan's go-to the handful of times I expressed these feelings to him. But it never comes. Ryan just lets the acknowledgment hang in the air. It's at once an immense comfort and so unsettling that I feel the urge to dispel it myself.

"People face a lot worse." I shrug. "It's fine."

His thumb strokes the side of his cup as he considers me. "You did an interview early in the podcast with a guy from eastern Europe. Yuri something. He had all these financial expectations on him as the eldest in a family of five siblings."

"I remember Yuri. He worked three part-time jobs to help provide for his family, had to drop out of high school eventually just so they could scrape by. Never mind going to college."

He nods. "He said he regretted not pursuing an education. That he never realized his potential—that his potential simply wasn't a consideration in the context of his life. Serving his family meant denying himself."

No wonder Ryan found *So Proud of You* relatable. He may not share the first- or second-gen traits, may not have weathered the lack of parental praise that so many kids do, but he certainly felt an immense weight of responsibility.

The reason he hasn't been able to pursue his dream is that he was too busy being, in effect, a father to Celine. From the age of eighteen, he had to provide for her. And even before that, he was helping his single mom make ends meet. I imagine a young Ryan sitting at a kitchen table in an apartment in Queens, bills spread out beside his homework. Conscientious and dependable, even as a boy.

"What would you do differently if not for Celine?" I ask.

He exhales long and slow. "Write more, for one. Work somewhere that allows me more time to dedicate to it. Allows me to pursue . . . competing interests." The dark fringe of his lashes flutter slightly as his eyes meet mine, and my heartbeat raps at the implication of his words.

"You make it sound like Celine and Woodsworth are inextricably tied."

"They sort of are." He seems to weigh his words. Then, as if they're being dragged from him by force, he says, "Woodsworth has a program. They cover half of your dependents' tuition fees as long as you're employed with the company."

My mouth drops open. "Wow. That's . . . generous."

"Very," he says. "It's been a game-changer. It means she won't have to consider paying off giant debts when she weighs employment prospects after she graduates. It'll give her more freedom."

Something funny happens in my chest as I listen to Ryan talk about his sister's future, knowing everything he's done to set her up for success . . . for happiness. Knowing how hard he works to provide her with open pathways while restricting his own.

"What about your freedom?" I ask.

"It's just . . . never been a priority."

"You mean you haven't made it a priority." Because his most pressing needs have always been his sister's needs. Before my brain catches up, my hand is draped over Ryan's forearm. "Celine's lucky to have you as her big brother."

My skin prickles where it's touching him, and his gaze pins me in place, the raucous room going silent. The golden flecks framing his pupils gleam like the rays of the sun, the entire solar system revolving around them. Warm and vibrant. Central.

I wish it didn't send heat radiating through me. Because he's golden-handcuffed to the company, needs to walk the straight and narrow, to do everything in his power to not jeopardize his job until Celine graduates.

Not create a conflict of interest that could risk it all.

Even if he wants to.

I drain the remainder of my drink, and he does the same.

The night air is cool as we wander from the train station back to the hotel, the streets illuminated by bright signage and hanging red lanterns throughout Chinatown. I ask question after question about Celine's childhood, and he doesn't seem put off by the rapid-fire interrogation. On the contrary: He regales me with stories. The time she put a cannellini bean up her nostril and had to be rushed to the hospital. When she choked on half a strawberry, prompting Ryan to enroll in a CPR class. Or the daddy-daughter middle school dance he took her to. I imagine young, hot Ryan among all the middle-aged dad bods—the spectacle that would have been for a gymnasium full of pubescent girls.

He's a captivating storyteller and credits her for it. She would insist he invent original bedtime stories every night, which she called "mind stories." When she showed particular affinity for one, he would run with the positive feedback and write it. Inventive tales of otherworldly characters and events. The few times he submitted them for college classes, they garnered high grades.

"Now we know your sci-fi author origin story," I say.

"Blame Celine's unquenchable thirst for interdimensional travel."

"Does she write too?" I ask.

"Nah, she was always more interested in science, nature... She wanted to live in the woods as a kid. Her ideal weekend was going camping."

"Oh god."

"My thought exactly," he says. "She begged and begged me to take her."

I've never understood camping. I like being outdoors—on that first warm day of spring, just try to keep me inside—but pitching a tent miles away from civilization and the nearest coffee shop? I can't make food on a stove, let alone over a fire, and going to the bathroom over a dirt hole buzzing with flies is about the least appealing thing I can imagine. "How'd you get out of it?"

"I didn't. You should see her when she really wants something. There's no saying no."

"Then she earned your compliance," I say, smug, even though I have nothing to do with Celine's strength of character. But something tells me Ryan wouldn't say no, anyway.

"If it means she's going to save the world's forests," he says, "I consider it an investment in climate action."

"She and Maral should partner up," I say. "Urban planning and infrastructure reform with an emphasis on nature conservation." I imagine them working together, becoming a world-renowned team for creating strategies for sustainable urban spread, and feel an inexplicable swell of pride at the fantasy. It's been so long since Maral worked in the field, so long since I envisioned her as anything other than the kick-ass brand manager so vital to *SPOY* now.

"Is Maral's goal to go back to urban planning?" he asks.

"God, no—we've built something really special. She's as committed to it as I am."

He nods. "I wondered, given her interest in climate action. But then you'd lose the ace up your sleeve."

"She wouldn't leave me in the lurch," I say, a sly grin curving my lips. "I have too much dirt on her."

"I have a feeling Maral's dirt is sterile."

"Says the most fastidious person in the world," I say. "I seem to remember the term *serial killer* being used to describe you."

"Easy to appear fastidious to a sloven."

I gasp, stopping in the middle of the sidewalk. "Was that a *burn*? Did you just burn me?"

"If the mess fits," he says, eyes glittering under the streetlights.

"Savage. That's the last time I invite you into my room."

"I hope not," he says, the last word clipped as he clamps his mouth shut.

Mine drops open unceremoniously.

Did he just?

He did.

"As I live and breathe—" I say.

"That was—"

"Did Ryan Grant just—"

"—uncalled for—"

"—cross professional boundaries?"

He exhales like a deflating balloon. "I shouldn't have said that. It just slipped out."

Maybe I'm rubbing off on him. I'd love to know what else would just *slip out* if he didn't keep such a taut leash on himself. "I didn't mind." No use lying. I look both ways down the quiet street we've veered onto, making sure we're alone. Take a step closer, reach for his hand. "I liked it."

He stiffens, his Adam's apple rising on a thick swallow.

I pull my hand away—I'm overstepping, he only said that opportunistically, he didn't mean it—but he reaches out and grabs it back, curling his fingers tight around mine.

The contact sends ripples of electricity up both our arms—I know he's feeling the same thing I am. There's no chance his eyelids have flown to half-mast because my touch doesn't affect him just as much as his affects me.

His gaze rises to meet mine, remaining hooded, dark. He grips my hand more firmly, drawing me nearer despite himself, my body only a few inches from his. This close—at any distance, really—he radiates something that tugs deep in my belly. And lower.

How can his hand feel so right in mine?

"Ana," he says, but nothing else.

His breath comes out in a rush when I tip my head back and my lips part, ready for a kiss he's reluctant, yet visibly hungry, to give me.

"We . . . can't," he whispers, hesitating on the second word, showing his lack of conviction.

"But you want to," I say. He hasn't let me go.

"That doesn't matter. I—" He licks his lips and I want to die from what it does to me. "We're drunk."

"Don't do that," I say.

"Don't do what?"

"We had one beer that was mostly foam, almost two hours ago."

My free hand traces a path from his shoulder down over his hard pec and the flat ridges of his abdomen, drawing a shudder from him.

"I would never jeopardize your job," I say. "I know now how important it is. Celine's tuition and—I would never mess it up for you. We can be discreet. Nobody at Woodsworth would ever know." My fingers reach his belt, lingering on the leather. "Don't you get tired of denying yourself?"

He exhales shakily. "You have no idea."

"Then just take what you want for once."

He searches my eyes, his brow gathered. "We're on this tour together for another week. What if things get . . . uncomfortable? I don't want to put you in that position."

"I can think of a few positions we'd both very much enjoy being in, and none of them would be uncomfortable." I snake my hand around his waist, up the hard muscles of his back, pulling him closer, aware that he doesn't resist in the least. "All I want is to enjoy each other's bodies."

Frown lines form grooves in his forehead. "Is that really all you want?"

There's something in his voice. Disbelief . . . pleading? As if the answer to that question is important. As if he *needs* to know.

He's worried I'll catch feelings, cling, get hurt when we have to go back to being strictly colleagues. I have to convince him that the last thing he needs to worry about with me is emotional entanglement. That this is 100 percent physical. That I have no feelings whatsoever. Other than horniness.

In other words, convince him of the truth.

Because that *is* the truth.

"Yes," I say. "I'm not in the market for a relationship. That's totally off the table. This would just be sex."

He's breathing deeply, brow gathered, eyes searching mine. "Just sex."

Just hearing him say *sex* is enough to send heat cascading up my thighs. "That's what I want."

A beat passes. "Ana, I don't know if I can—"

"You remember that kiss," I interrupt. "You know how good it would be."

A thick swallow. Fingers twitching at his sides.

I close the remaining few inches between us, the tips of my breasts grazing his heaving chest. "Do you want me, Ryan?"

His heavy-lidded eyes drop to my mouth. "God, yes."

"Then get out of your head," I say, a breath away, "and enjoy me."

I bring my lips to his, uncharacteristically tentative, in case he wants to stop me—but it's abundantly clear he wants the exact opposite as he opens his mouth greedily for my kiss.

Chapter 12

The moment our tongues collide, I realize what a colossal mistake it was to kiss Ryan. Not the kiss itself—because *god*, is that the least wrong thing I've ever done—but where it's happening. Outside, in public (indiscreet AF, even if the street is empty), and two blocks plus a nine-story elevator ride away from my hotel room.

His mouth betrays a need that's been stifled for much longer than a few days. There is no teasing, no artful exploration—Ryan kisses like a man starved, and I am the feast. His fingers rake into my hair, fisting it gently at the roots so he can maneuver my face to get his fill.

I clutch the lapel of his jacket, and he hauls me so tight against him, it's as if he wants to pull me inside him, snuff out every molecule of air separating us. This kiss went from zero to a hundred in point-five seconds, and we're too far away from a place private enough to get naked enough for all the filthy things I want to do to this man.

I break the kiss. His face follows mine for a moment, leaning forward as I inch back, reluctant to disconnect.

His dazed eyes land on my swollen lips. "God, Ana, your mouth," he rasps.

"Let me show you what else it can do," I say, pulling him on unsteady feet toward the hotel, hoping we won't run across anyone who could report him for indecent exposure, the way his erection is surging against the crotch of his jeans.

Interminable minutes later, we finally crash through the door to my room. I reach for him immediately, rising on my tiptoes and diving for his mouth, but he stops me.

No. Please . . . I just got past those defenses—

"Don't move," he says, laying a kiss on the back of my hand, which feels oddly romantic.

He steps into the bathroom, turns on the faucet, and washes his hands thoroughly, methodically. Fastidiously.

"Please don't tell me you're going to serial-kill me," I say.

He smiles, sending a pulse through to my pussy. "No. But I'm going to touch you. A lot."

The knowledge that he's cleaning the city grime from the train, the campus, and countless surfaces off his hands as a show of respect for my body's most intimate places makes me heady.

He approaches me, a panther stalking his prey. Except no prey wants to be caught the way I desperately need to be right now.

He cups my jaw before his lips land back on mine, and it's . . . everything. Hot, and wet, and winding. A thought flitters into my mind that his lips belong here, on mine, working their magic on me, but it's too vague to fully grasp. Besides, fanciful thoughts like that don't belong anywhere near a casual hookup.

I push the jacket off his shoulders, and it drops to the floor with a soft shush. I lift the hem of his sweater, and he breaks our kiss long enough to oblige, pulling it up over his taut stomach and broad chest and off those insane shoulders. The view beneath is so spectacular that I don't know what to focus on—the defined deltoids, pecs, or ridged abs dusted with a hairway that leads straight to heaven.

"Are you kidding me with this body?" I ask, smoothing my palms over his skin, feeling him flex under my touch.

"Guess the muscles do serve a purpose," he says. "All the better to please you."

His expression is ravenous as he takes my mouth once more. I barely register my own jacket being pushed off my shoulders, his tongue is doing such spectacular things to mine. Sparks ignite on my skin when his fingertips sneak beneath my shirt.

"Can I—" He swallows. "Undress you?"

"Yes," I say, helping him with the buttons of my blouse. He watches, glassy-eyed, as I expose the skin underneath. He opens the lapels, guiding them over my shoulders and down my arms slowly, taking in every single movement.

Where I expect him to dive back in for another kiss, he surprises me by keeping an arm's length of distance between us. My shirt now discarded, I'm standing before him in a sheer black bra, pencil-thin pants, and heels. He stands back, an incredulous look on his face as he takes in the sight of me.

"I don't know if I'll survive seeing you any less clothed than this."

My lips quirk. "But what a way to go."

I step out of my heels and unbutton my fly. I turn, peeling the pants over my ass, giving him the full view. My panties are sheer too, and his chest rises and falls heavily as I lean forward, pushing the pants down my legs before kicking them off. Rising back up, I arch my back to emphasize both my booty and my breasts, and the effect is palpable. The usual composure in his eyes vanquished by something reckless. Wild.

He's done watching.

He advances on me, his kiss ferocious, frantic, like I'm stolen goods and he doesn't know how long he'll get to enjoy me before I'm repossessed. His hands are impatient, squeezing my ass none too gently, groaning, and my clit throbs in response. I practically climb him, gripping his shoulders, throwing my legs around his waist, and he holds me up, grinding his still-clothed erection into the notch between my legs. I'm impossibly turned on, circling my hips to get more friction there, to press his hardness right against my most sensitive spot. If I didn't want to fuck him for real, I'd dry-hump him to death.

"Jesus, Ana," he rasps. "Keep doing that and I'll be done any second. I feel like I've been hard since you had your ass in my lap in that Uber in Seattle—I'm ready to blow."

He walks us to the bed and lays me down as I reel from his words. Remembering that squishy rideshare, his clenched eyes, my hormone-induced dizziness. Knowing now how turned on he was heightens my own arousal.

He presses kisses to my mouth, my jaw, my neck, my sternum. He pauses at my chest, rising slightly to take in my puckered nipples, visible through the sheer fabric. "Beautiful," he murmurs, leaning down to lick the nub through the fabric.

"Let me take off my bra—" I say, cut off by my own moan when his lips close around the stiff peak. The sensation causes a jolt of pleasure straight down to my core.

"I imagined what they'd look like," he whispers against my skin as he moves across my chest, giving the other nipple the same attention. "Since Chicago, when you answered the door in that threadbare T-shirt with no bra underneath. Since Seattle, that tight goddamn camisole you sleep in. Couldn't believe I got to see you that way."

The memories assail me: the way his eyes shot away from me on both occasions. Learning he's been dreaming of my tits all this time—maintaining that prim exterior for the sake of propriety while inside he burned for me—sends a fresh rush of wetness through my folds.

He leans back, kneeling between my splayed legs, looking down at me. I unclasp my bra, trailing it down my arms and throwing it aside. Keeping my eyes on his, needing to take in every nuance of his reaction, realizing just how much it's contributing to the eroticism of this moment.

During hookups, I normally aim to take my own pleasure first and foremost. That's kind of the whole point. But right now, watching his pleasure as he sees me nude for the first time, knowing we haven't even gotten to the sex yet, seems to be rewriting a significant aspect of my sexual identity.

He stares. Takes his time tracing the lines of my body with his eyes. "You're so beautiful," he says, softly. "So fucking beautiful, Ana."

He trails a finger down my torso, stopping briefly to gently pinch my nipple, causing me to clench around lamentable emptiness. He notices me squirming, and a gleam kindles in his eyes.

"Needy, are you?" he asks.

"Yes," I breathe. "I've been hard up for days."

He leans down, kisses the swell of my belly. "Days, huh," he says sympathetically, trailing his tongue down my skin, kissing my open thighs. "Let me see what hard up looks like on you, baby."

The gruff *baby* on his voice, deeper than usual and thick with desire, threatens to undo me before he even hooks his fingers into my panties to pull them off, his eyes glued to that spot between my legs.

He leans forward, lashes fanning against his cheekbones as he inhales. "Jesus, fuck," he groans, and presses a kiss to my clit—soft, tender, like it's a precious thing worth cherishing. "I take it back. You are perfect. Everywhere." I clench again and his eyes lose focus. "I'm going to take care of you. I hope you're ready."

"Please," I whimper, senseless with need.

He swipes his tongue through my slit, a slow taste that draws a growl of appreciation from deep in his chest. He teases the lips of my sex for a few seconds, indulging in their feel, their flavor, before homing in on the sensitive bundle of nerves at the apex. Treating it with precise, rhythmic flutters of his tongue. A gentle insistence that spreads bliss out in concentric circles from the center of my body to the tips of my extremities. Shimmering through my veins, my bones, my skin.

His attention is unwavering, consistent, only increasing in pressure and speed as the tension in my muscles builds. As if the movements of his mouth are directly governed by the responses of my body, connected by invisible marionette strings. Something inside me knows he won't stop until he gets me there—and maybe not even then.

My fingers find their way into his hair of their own volition, tugging gently, commending his efforts. He clutches my hips in response, moaning as if *I'm* the one giving *him* pleasure, when it's the unwavering pace and friction of his tongue making my breath come in short, choppy pants as the pressure builds to a breaking point.

"Oh my god, Ryan, don't stop, please don't stop," I ramble, my legs starting to quake.

His palm trails from my hip to my pelvis, pressing down to keep me still, and I realize belatedly that my hips are writhing, seeking more of the tongue he's so generously lavishing me with. I can't stop—my body on its own trajectory, unimpeded by rational thought. The sight of his solid forearm, roped with veins and muscles that strain as he holds me in place for his singular purpose, hurtles me over the edge.

My climax rolls through my body in a crescendo that swells as he only continues his skillful ministrations. My hips will no longer be caged, rising off the mattress as I cry out in a broken sob. But I vaguely notice his arm is no longer holding me, anyway—he's moved it down to slip two thick fingers inside me. I'm still mid-orgasm, it's impossible to feel anything better, but when he hooks his fingers, pressing firmly against my G-spot, I explode anew.

I gasp, a crackling sound, my body twisting despite being attached to Ryan's fingers and face, his pace continuous but gentling, letting me ride down the wave. I'm shaking all over, still spasming, so full of sensation that I don't notice he's pulled away until he's back again a second later, eyes feral, mesmerized by the orgasm tearing through me. If he's proud of himself, he should be. A-plus, Ryan. Gold star. 10/10, no notes.

Somewhere in the midst of this maniacal evaluation, I hear a low, vaguely familiar hum. I've barely resumed breathing when I feel Ryan thumbing my sensitized clit again, testing me out. It's too much—it should be too much, right? I shouldn't be circling my hips, seeking his hand yet again. *Insatiable, you thirsty beast.* But that's exactly what I do, and I'm rewarded with the identity of that humming sound as I feel a sudden sting against my clit.

Not a sting—a vibration. My vibrator. On Ryan's thumb, buzzing against my tender flesh and making my wide eyes fly to his.

He's watching me raptly, pupils blown so big his eyes are practically black—the devil himself.

"I thought I'd die when I saw this in your room," he says, his voice a low abrasion. "Imagining you making yourself come made me nearly climb out of my skin. Pictured using it on you myself. But nothing I pictured could compare to the real thing."

If I could think straight, I'd realize this confirms my suspicion that he spied it on my nightstand back in . . . where was it? On Earth somewhere, anyway. A place I've long since vacated as his expert touch has catapulted me into the clouds.

Impossibly, pressure starts to build again.

"Wanted to know how you'd taste, how you'd feel as you came apart on my tongue." He taps the vibrator against my clit as he inserts a finger again, teasing that spot inside me and causing my head to thrash against the mattress. "Fucking dreamed of making you scream."

His words are what do it more than anything. This time the orgasm is so fierce, tearing through me so acutely that my back arches right off the bed. I cry out as my body bolts upright, bucking my hips against his hand, riding it hard even as it feels almost like too much. He leans forward, fluttering his tongue over my nipple before pinching it between his lips, doubling the onslaught of sensation and ripping the air right out of my lungs.

How? How is it possible to come three times in such close succession? If my brain could compute anything right now, I'd try to puzzle it out, but that equation will have to wait for its solution. Right now the organ in my head is busy perishing, causing my mouth to spout nonsense about Ryan's skilled hands, his wasted talents, how I can't believe he's capable of this and been keeping it secret, how he should do this for a living instead.

Ryan seems to sense that I'm depleted—for now. He turns off the vibrator and gathers my slumped body into his arms, my heated skin against his. His scent is made stronger by his arousal, and my mouth seeks his in a deep kiss that tastes like the masterful things he just did to me.

I crawl onto his lap, feeling the rough chafe of his jeans against my inflamed flesh. The fact that he's still wearing any clothes—particularly ones that restrict his sizeable erection—after everything he's done to me feels cruel and unfair.

"Oh, Ryan." I pout. "This is simply unacceptable."

I reach between our bodies, cupping him through his jeans, earning a shaky exhale.

"You give me three orgasms before I even get to see your dick?" I tsk.

He's breathing roughly as I unbutton his jeans and drag down his zipper. But suddenly my progress is halted, his hand stilling mine.

"I don't have a condom," he says. "I didn't bring any on the trip."

Because he didn't expect to get his bones jumped. Never imagined we'd be obliterating boundaries in such grand fashion.

"My mouth is pretty talented too," I say.

A noise escapes him that's either a choke or a sob. "You don't have to do that."

"I know I don't. But you'd like me to. Wouldn't you?"

It's like there are cactus needles in his throat, judging by the pained look on his face when he swallows. "That doesn't matter."

"Of course it does."

The tortured look in his eyes causes clouds to gather behind my rib cage. I swallow down the emotion that has no business rising in my chest.

While he's supposedly been dreaming of watching me come, I've been riding my vibrator for days, imagining his glorious erection. No chance it's not coming out to play.

Plus, making sure he gets his due will help to reinforce that this is just a hookup. Mutually beneficial. Casual. Meaningless. Never to be thought of again after tonight.

Forget the fact that the image of Ryan worshipping my clit, spellbound by my orgasms, will be impossible to evict from my mind anytime soon. Hard to believe it'll ever vacate the premises.

If that memory's going to live rent-free in my head, though, may as well add to it. In for a dime and everything.

"Well, I'm about to blow your mind too," I say. "Because I came prepared."

I reach for the small toiletry case on my nightstand, pulling out a short strip of condoms and tearing one off. There's an unmistakable tremor in his muscles as I push him onto his back, kneeling between his legs to pull his jeans off.

The dick print against his briefs is delectably vulgar. I pull the material down and his cock springs free. Saliva floods my mouth.

Jackpot.

Christ. If his mouth and hands alone weren't capable of plunging me over the edge of oblivion, this gorgeous instrument would definitely do it. It's long, thick, twined with veins, the skin on the purpling head so taut that there's no way he'll last long.

The urge to taste him is so strong I can't not. I lick up the underside, flicking the sensitive ridge just below the head before capping my lips over the dome and swirling my tongue around it.

His eyes roll back in his head and he groans, "*God.*"

I hold him by the base and take him deep, keeping my tongue in constant motion when I pull back to the head, adding stimulation to the most sensitive parts. He punches his hips forward, seeking more of my mouth, but a moment later he's pushing me away by the shoulders, panting, "Please, please stop."

"Pretty sure you were enjoying that."

"Understatement of the century," he says. "But I desperately want to fuck you, Ana. Can I?"

Why not both? But he is looking *very* close, and if tonight is a one-off, he should get what he wants out of it. "I thought you'd never ask," I say.

He rips open the condom packet and rolls it down his length. His gaze is riveted to mine as I straddle his hips, an earnestness in his expression that seems to reach inside me, sending fissures through vital organs and filling my belly with something I can't name. So I focus instead on where our bodies meet, guiding the crown of his shaft to my entrance and feeling his whole body stiffen in anticipation.

The feel of him gliding inside me, inch by inch, rivals the considerable pleasure he's already given me tonight. Not only because I love being filled—and holy hell, his cock is spectacular, hitting all the right spots and forcing me to focus on breathing through the sensations—but because I'm giving him the same immeasurable pleasure in turn. His powerful thighs rigid with tension, abs clenched, hands impatient on my skin.

When he's fully seated inside me, I circle my hips and start to rise again, but his fingers dig into my waist, holding me still.

"Go slow," he rasps, his body radiating like it's nuclear.

"Yes, sir," I say.

I lower again carefully, the friction exquisite. I'm so wet that, despite his size, my body is eager to accommodate him. I lean back slightly, balancing myself on his thighs, pleasure cascading through me and causing my whole body to undulate as I ride him. I'm on full display and he's captivated, eyes burning with intensity as he watches. It turns me on so much that it's impossible not to speed the rolling wave of my hips.

"You're the sexiest thing I've ever seen." He rises to kiss me, hands clutching at the roots of my hair. "Riding cock like a fucking goddess," he whispers against my lips. "Of course you'd be a dream in bed. How could you be anything else."

His quiet praise winds me even tighter, and I grind my hips forward, chasing the sensation building yet again low in my belly.

"You feel amazing," I pant, clenching around him. Sucking him deeper.

He growls into my skin. "If I could last, I'd fuck you as hard as I want to, make you scream from it. Would you like that?" I nod, his stubble scratching against my cheek. "Yeah, I thought so," he drawls, sucking on the base of my throat. He punches his hips upward, showing me what he means, eliciting a hoarse exclamation from me. "But it's been a while, and you're so fucking hot, I'm dying. Next time."

Next time. I shut my eyes, ignoring the trip wire those words plant in my mind. The dangerous potential in them.

My pace has increased, there's no help for it, and he's meeting me halfway with his own thrusts, the coiling pressure an exquisite torture, he the most magnificent tormentor in history. He angles his hips to hit the spot he's getting to know so well, driving into me once, twice, before stars explode behind my eyelids. A choked cry escapes me and he gathers me close, holding me against his broad chest, firm, protective, like at any second I could be snatched away. He pounds his hips up, his control lost, making strangled noises as he follows me over the edge. His body shudders against mine as he rasps my name like a curse. Like a prayer.

The daze takes so long to subside that I don't realize until minutes—maybe many minutes—later that his hands are stroking my back in soothing circles, his lips pressing gentle kisses on my shoulder, my cheek, my temple as he whispers more praise into my skin. It doesn't even occur to me to stop him.

Chapter 13

I wake to a bright room, blinking at the sun trickling through the curtains. I haven't slept past sunrise in as long as I can remember. I consider that I should have set my alarm, despite the fact that my body naturally wakes me early. But rational thought was nowhere near my addled mind before I fell asleep last night.

Your senses being completely annihilated by the hottest sex of your life can have that effect.

Last night was *the hottest sex of my life*. I need to let that sink in for a minute: the fact that I had the hottest sex of my fucking life with a man I work with. A man I'll have to be professional with on an ongoing basis.

Which is something I can totally do. I am well versed in non-committal sex. It's in the bag.

Never mind that afterward, he laid me down, whispering sweet nothings and scattering gentle kisses on my sensitive skin. Pulled the covers over me when goosebumps rose on my arms and thighs, smoothing the material delicately with his strong hands. Went to the bathroom to dispose of the condom and came back with a glass of water for me. Never mind the tender, thoughtful Ryan that rose to the surface like a buoy on stormy waters.

He's not the first man to treat me that way after fucking my brains out. Just because I can't remember anyone else off the top of my head doesn't mean they haven't existed. I *did* just get my brains fucked out, after all.

I move to get up and feel warm fingers close around my hand. Ryan's.

I'm so used to waking up alone that I completely forgot we didn't get around to saying goodbye last night. Instead, we lay in bed for a while, talking, and kissing, and touching, and then Ryan rolled me onto my back and pressed his ready member against me again, and well. I wasn't exactly going to ask him to leave.

I peek at his profile. The prominent line of his nose, the pout of his lips. The shadow along his jaw, the fan of his lashes. So peaceful. Relaxed in a way I've never seen him.

He's still sleeping. Does he even realize that he's grasping my hand? Or is it something he's doing unconsciously?

It feels . . . nice.

Too nice.

I start to rise again, but I'm stopped when I hear him rumble, "Stay."

So he is awake.

"We should get up," I say.

"I have a better idea," he says. His voice is deeper from sleep, radiating from him like a cat's purr. "We stay here."

That does not sound unappealing. "What time do we need to get to the studio for filming?" I have an interview with *San Fran Live* this morning.

"Not till ten." He looks at the bedside clock. "We have plenty of time. My alarm'll go off when we need to get up." He pulls me closer by the waist, and I don't resist.

"You set your alarm last night?" I ask.

"I set it in the morning."

"Yesterday?"

"Yeah," he says, like it's obvious.

"You set your alarm for the next morning, the previous morning?"

"Yeah," he says again. "Right after it goes off, I set it for the next day."

I am bewildered. "Why?"

"Because it's efficient. A task completed. And no chance I'll forget."

There is something so Ryan about this maniacally responsible practice that it makes my legs feel heavy, rooted to the mattress. "That is serial killer behavior."

"If we'd left it up to you, we might have slept in."

"Nah, Maral will be knocking on my door within an hour. She comes to my room every morning."

"You know your phone has an alarm on it," he says.

"It's not a live wake-up call, I'm always up. It's just a routine, how we start our days while traveling. And often at home. After my workout, she comes over and we talk while I shower and dress."

"Damn," he says. "Is that an open position? How do I apply?"

My pulse gallops as he pulls me in for a kiss. Morning breath be damned, the soft heat of his mouth right now rivals coffee for the best thing to wake up to. Just like every other kiss we've shared, it intensifies at warp speed, as though the world is ending and we'll never get another chance at human contact again. The answering tug between my legs is acute. He responds automatically, as though his brain is connected to my body by a circuit, sensing what I need and zeroing in on fulfilling it. He kisses down my chest, my belly, and disappears beneath the sheets. I sweep the white material away so I can watch him in action, working such masterful magic on me that it takes only a handful of seconds for me to plummet to my little death.

"Christ, you're a dream," he says, kissing the insides of my still-trembling thighs. "So responsive. I want to go down on you all day, make you come until you can't see straight."

As if to underscore his words, he gives my clit a dreamy French kiss. I'm still so sensitive from my climax that I gasp at even the gentlest contact.

"Maybe you're just really good at giving head," I breathe. "How are you still single, exactly?"

His gaze remains locked on mine for a long moment. "Maybe I've been waiting for you."

I lick my suddenly dry lips. My heart refuses to slow down, even though my orgasm has passed. That's the kind of sentiment that sends this barreling away from the discreet, one-time, no-strings thing it has to be, and neither of us can have that.

In an effort to shift the atmosphere, I pull him up for an open-mouthed kiss, tasting myself on his tongue. I snake a hand down and grasp his cock, giving it a long stroke, and he shudders against me.

"I'm pretty competitive," I say, pushing him onto his back and inching down his body. "Can't let you show me up."

"Ana," he says, voice hoarse as he twigs my intention, "it's not a compet—"

I give his head a gentle lick, and his breath leaves him in a short burst, his hands fisting in the tousled sheets. When I close my lips around the smooth dome, his hips move in a slow roll that rivals a Magic Mike dancer, and it's such a turn-on that I feel my own want building yet again.

After the number of orgasms he's given me in the last nine hours, I'm amazed at how quickly I rev. He's a drug, addicting me, stringing me out.

The thought should cause warning bells to go off, but at the moment my brain seems only willing to process sensations, which are numerous and varied and overwhelming. The taste of him, the feeling of power and pride as he takes his pleasure from my mouth, his voice rasping a litany of filth and praise as his eyes consume me with such rapture I have to look away. His body tightens and he warns me that he's close, tells me to stop, presumably so he doesn't finish in my mouth, but I only milk him harder. The muscles of his abdomen clench as he growls glorious nonsense about my eyes, my mouth, my legs, and my ass, his climax ripping through him so fiercely that I know this image will replay in my mind all day—or much longer, if I'm honest.

He's still rippling with tremors when he drags me to him for a kiss so deep, so searching, that I forget myself, twining my arms around his neck and giving myself over to the uproar behind my sternum. A sensation both delightful and torturous, suggesting that, despite my best intentions, this may not be as easy to give up as I thought.

Decked out in citrus colors, *San Fran Live*'s brightly lit studio teems with crew members rushing this way and that. A producer named Brit greets us as we arrive and leads us to a green room offering various craft service options. Shanthi beelines for the pastries as Brit takes me through the run of show, explaining when I'll be called out to the sound stage for my segment. She praises me for knowing the basics of on-camera interviews, calling me an "old hand"—a term I might have preferred she edit—and offers to answer any questions I may have. Being an *old hand*, I don't.

There's a screen mounted to the wall on which we can watch the show before my segment is scheduled to film. I try to focus on the content of the interviews with a famous tennis player, a dog trainer to the stars, and a nutritionist launching her own line of premade smoothies-in-a-jar, knowing that viewers get a slight dopamine hit when guests mention something from an earlier segment in their interview. And I want to make as strong an impression as possible. I've done lots of TV spots before, but given our meeting with Craig Waters is in just a couple of days, this might be a clip that his people would weigh more heavily in their considerations of whether or not I'm fit to host my own show.

But focusing is not exactly my forte this morning. You'd think I'd be loose as a goose after last night. And this morning. My muscles are thrumming with the memory of Ryan's body, though, the prowess with which he wields it, and my mind is wrestling with the fact that I ever could have considered him straitlaced. Having him in such close proximity and tamping down the post-carnal vibe between us in the presence of Maral and Shanthi is only winding me tighter.

Ryan had returned to his room by the time Mar showed up at my door a couple of hours ago. It was a mercy. I was going to tell her about what happened between us, of course, but I'd preferred to avoid bashful greetings and awkward goodbyes if she happened upon us. There had been nothing awkward about the way Ryan said goodbye, as if he wasn't going to see me an hour later when the *San Fran Live* car came to pick us up. Nothing awkward about the deep, slow, winding kiss that shot sparks down my spine, causing me to arch against him and draw a rumbling groan from his chest.

We couldn't have done *that* in front of Maral.

For her part, she wasn't so much surprised when I told her as she was smug: "The way you two have been devouring each other with your eyes, it was bound to happen sooner or later." But she followed it with an appraising look and asked, "How do you feel?"

I beamed, post-orgasm glow probably emanating from my pores. "Like a million fucks."

She rolled her eyes. "But I mean, you know. The whole working-together thing."

"Fine," I said. "It was just one time."

"Are you sure?" Her tone seemed to be hedging something else—a different question.

"Well, it was multiple times, but one night. And morning."

Okay, maybe I wasn't fully done with Ryan. How could I be, given what he was capable of? What was the harm in continuing this one-night thing for the duration of this trip? Make it a one-trip thing. It made logical sense that until we got back to New York, we were "off campus," so to speak. Who cared if we did it once or a few times? What happens on book tour stays on book tour. Until we were back home and back to real life, we could enjoy this discreet physical diversion as we pleased.

I broached this with Maral. We were side by side in my bathroom, applying our makeup, and her reflection stared at me thoughtfully.

"What?" I said.

"Nothing," she said, putting her liquid eyeliner back in her toiletry case.

"Do you think it's a bad idea?" I asked. I genuinely wanted to know what she thought. It may be my modus operandi to steamroll ahead with whatever I want to do, but Maral is an insightful genius and I always want to know what she thinks.

"On the contrary," she said. "He's nice and seems to care about you. I think a relationship with him would be good for you."

Whoa. "That's not— *Relationship* is a stretch. You know I'm not interested in anything more than a limited-time sexathon."

She assessed my reflection as I leaned into the mirror, dropping my chin *Scream*-style to apply mascara. "Are you sure that's all he's interested in?"

"Of course," I said. "His job is too important—he can't do anything to threaten it. I told you about his sister's tuition issue."

"You did. But being beholden to family doesn't negate how a person feels. Life is bigger than what we owe people."

Her tone had an unexpected weight to it. I lowered the mascara wand, giving her my full attention.

"I just think you guys have a lot in common," she said, beautiful brown eyes imploring me, making my chest feel heavy.

"Yeah," I said steadily, "one of which is that we know this is a casual thing."

She opened and closed her mouth, then paused. "I've dated a lot of guys. I can tell when someone's in it for a good time and not a long time. Ryan . . . doesn't seem like that. Everything about him screams *serious*, and he seems to really like you. All I'm saying is, don't be so quick to dismiss the possibility of more."

I thought back on Ryan growling into my skin last night, telling me he'd been dreaming of getting me naked since I greeted him bralessly in my hotel room in Chicago. Clearly he's attracted to me, just as I am to him. But that's all it is: attraction. We're two healthy, sexually charged people who happen to have electric chemistry. Yeah, he respects me, and we do good conversation, and he wants to know about my life as it relates to *So Proud of You*'s themes, but that just means he's a curious, attentive person—it does *not* mean he wants a relationship with me. Hell, Woodsworth alone is a huge, glaring obstacle in the way of that possibility.

To say nothing of it being an absolute no for me, either way.

Still, Mar's words come back to me now as I watch Ryan frown and swipe at his phone in the green room chair across from me. Sensing my stare, he raises his gaze to meet mine, his expression softening like a peony in bloom.

The possibility of more.

Images flash through my mind like a reel. Toothbrushes side by side on the bathroom vanity. Breakfast side by side at the kitchen island. Sharing a too-small throw blanket on the couch, soft curves yielding against hard muscle. Mistaking each other's reading glasses for our own. Christmas with his family, Soorp Dznoont with mine. His big spoon to my little. Sharing plans and hopes and dreams. Bearing witness to good times and bad. Being known. The shine in his eyes gradually dimming. Withdrawal. Deep sighs. Silence.

You're not who I thought you were. I don't think I can do this anymore.

Nathan's fatal words come at me in a rush of memory, and my hands are suddenly clammy, fingers trembling as I wipe them on the wool of my pants. This is the opposite of focusing.

I recenter myself, homing in on the TV screen, where the nutritionist is blending a slice of mango with about a bushel of kale and some kind of radioactive-orange powder in a Vitamix. Her skin is luminous, and I make a note to add the jarred smoothies to my rotation. Can't burn a smoothie, right? Though if anyone could, it's me.

When Brit comes to escort me to the studio for my segment, Shanthi falls in step behind us to record my walk through the backstage area for a behind-the-scenes post, trailed by Maral and Ryan. They stay by the cameras as I'm led to stand behind a curtain from which I'll emerge when I'm introduced by the hosts.

They do a short introduction, showing a clip of my first viral video—which is often the prelude for my televised interviews—and elevator-pitching my book, before I'm invited out onto the set.

The interview itself goes swimmingly. Predictably, as soon as I'm on, everything else goes out of my mind and I'm sharply focused on the hosts as their spotlight-worthy smiles ask me the questions I've already prepared answers for (Maral received them a few days ago from the show's producers). Our rapport is effortless and, if I hadn't written the book myself, I'd be hooked into buying a copy.

When one of my answers garners a particularly hearty laugh from the crowd and I turn to acknowledge them, I feel a heady rush as I look out onto the studio audience. Thinking this could be a regular occurrence very soon, assuming all goes to plan and the meeting in L.A. is successful. This interview will only help—I'm killing it.

Afterward, Brit leads me offstage, where I'm de-micced and handed a network-themed tote bag with various swag items inside. Maral informs me that Shanthi's back in the green room and she's off to grab coffee with Celine—I put them in touch and, today being our last full day in San Francisco, they're taking the opportunity to meet up and talk all things environmental engineering.

Before she leaves, she shoots me a knowing look, raising one perfectly threaded brow toward Ryan.

For his part, Ryan's wearing a smile that could rival the show hosts', it's so bright. Who would have thought this man, a total curmudgeon up until this week, could transform so completely? It's so dazzling, I feel like I'm floating.

"You were amazing," he says.

I shrug one shoulder mock-coyly as we head back toward the green room. "I just pictured you naked."

He looks like he could eat me with a spoon. "I have great news," he says quietly. He pulls me into a nook piled high with clear bins of what looks like extension cords and lighting equipment. His phone screen glows with an email from Meredith, the bolded subject reading *BIG NEWS!!!! CONFIDENTIAL!!!!*

I see my email address in the "To" field alongside his, Laura's, and Nadia's, but I haven't checked my inbox in a couple of hours. I skim the body of the email, which is pretty to-the-point.

So Proud of You is a New York Times bestseller!!!!
  Congratulations!!!!!!!!

Then there are about five lines filled with emojis ranging from champagne bottles and clinking glasses to cartwheels to confetti. Then a line saying that the list won't be public till this afternoon and to keep it to ourselves till then. Followed by two more lines of emojis.

Holy fuck.

"Unbelievable," I say. It's the only thing I can say.

"Believe it," Ryan says. "You did it. Congratulations."

The floor feels like rubber. The overwhelm is real. Postcoital hormones coupled with a TV spot sure to garner Craig Waters's attention *and* my book hitting the bestseller list? I steady myself with a hand on Ryan's forearm, and I don't know if it's elation or the solidness of him beneath my fingers that makes me do it, but I sway forward and kiss him hard on the lips. He reacts immediately, his mouth opening, tongue swooping in like a conqueror. His arm wraps around my lower back, keeping me upright and slightly bowed back, and in the headiness of the moment I forget that, while we are tucked into a recess in the wall, we're still in a public place.

I pull back, dizzy. We're both breathing hard, and from the glimmer in his darkened eyes, I know his thoughts are identical to mine: that if we didn't have to be at a regional radio station in an hour for my next interview, we'd find the nearest private space—office, bathroom, janitorial closet—and tear into each other.

He exhales sharply, dropping his arms to his sides. "Let's get through this next interview. Then we're going to celebrate."

"Oh yeah?" I coo. "What did you have in mind?"

"Dinner. Dancing. Champagne cruise around the bay. Anything you want."

"Hmm. None of that is very discreet," I say. "And what I want can't be done in public. At least, not without breaking several indecency laws."

Amusement twinkles in his eyes. "What kind of man would I be if the only thing I gave you to celebrate this achievement was some dick?"

My inner walls clench at that word on his lips. "Your dick is not just *some* dick."

His lashes obscure his irises, amusement supplanted by desire. "Oh no?" he breathes.

"No, it's . . . pretty special." *As special as it gets.*

"You sure treat it that way." His gaze roams down my body. "It's never been so spoiled."

I bite my lip, and his eyes zing to my mouth as though pulled by a string. "Let me spoil it again tonight."

He swallows hard. "There is no world in which I'll turn that offer down. But, Ana . . ." He pauses, his expression grave, like he's about to drop a truth bomb that could blow the solid ground beneath us wide open.

He takes my hand, calling up the memory of him reaching for me under the blankets in his sleep. Like his body was moving on autopilot, the gesture inevitable. Essential.

Everything about him screams serious, *and he seems to really like you.*

My pulse speeds up, the tag in my collar suddenly itchy against my skin, words rushing up my throat to stop whatever it is he's about to say.

"Incoming, six o'clock," I blurt, casting a pointed look over Ryan's shoulder at a tech hand approaching this not-so-hidden nook, an interruption so blessedly timed it's as if the universe is conspiring to save me.

Ryan registers the crew member as he passes us and drops my hand. Presses his lips together, gesturing silently for me to precede him down the hallway.

My palm tingles all the way back to the green room.

Chapter 14

The bestseller list goes public that afternoon, and my phone blows up. Social media notifications curtain the screen as I answer calls from friends and associates. Laura is over the moon, and Meredith exclaims that this is the best way to celebrate her last week at Woodsworth. I wish we could celebrate together in person, but that will have to wait till I'm back in the city and can shower her with the adulation she so thoroughly deserves.

Nadia is a blur when she video-calls me while dancing around her agency with her assistant, Quinn, and an hour later, a bottle of champagne and a glaringly yellow flower arrangement is delivered to my hotel room with many *xoxo*s on the notecard. Maral pops the cork and sloshes uneven pours into four plastic tumblers from the coffee bar, which we all cheers heartily together.

The sense of satisfaction hits deep. After all that hard work, all those sleepless nights poring over draft after draft, *So Proud of You* has achieved a designation that, for better or worse, validates its existence within the publishing sphere. Whether or not the book meets Mom's standards of success, whether or not literary snobs believe in its value, it has reached people—the people for whom it was written. The whole point of this venture was to help a huge community of individuals feel a sense of validation and empowerment, to make them feel less alone in a world that often denies them. If this book can make them feel some modicum of acceptance, of pride, for who they are and what they do, then the more copies that get into people's hands, the better.

We polish off the champagne, and Shanthi declares that we should keep the party going, brooking no arguments from Maral, Ryan, or me. We get as far as the hotel bar, where she orders a round of shots and another bottle of bubbly. Our cheerful, too-loud-for-the-space banter keeps getting waylaid by my phone's chirps and rings, and eventually Maral slides it out of my hands, effectively taking over its management. I'm flying so high that I practically launch it at her before demanding, politely, that the bartender play strictly Beyoncé power jams for the rest of the night and yanking everyone to a space I claim as a dance floor. Including some hapless patrons who, if you ask me, are only too happy to get caught up in our celebrations.

We are midway through botching the lyrics to "Run the World (Girls)"—not knowing the verses doesn't stop us from shrieking them at full volume—when I notice Mar pulling off to the side to check my phone. Her eyes go wide, a smile blooming across her face.

My pulse leaps. Is it Nadia? Did Waters hear the news? Maybe he's decided we don't need to even have a meeting—he's greenlighting the show!

I squint—*oh wait*. That's her phone. Nadia would likely send any news to both of us . . . but doubt niggles at me. Mar's smile is *big*. Bigger than it's ever been when we've discussed the show.

Come to think of it, she's been on her phone a lot lately, more than usual. And that morning we left Chicago, she was being cagey about me seeing her screen.

She never keeps things from me. What's going on?

Could Maral have . . . a secret boyfriend?

The room spins a little. I steady myself with a hand against a nearby pillar.

Is it possible? She tells me about all her dating escapades, but could she be seeing someone seriously and keeping me in the dark? Obviously yay for her if she's with someone who makes her smile like that. Literally nothing in this world—not even ten TV shows—would mean more to me than Maral being happy.

But why wouldn't she tell me?

I force myself to inhale and exhale slowly three times. My heart rate obeys the command to calm down, and I dance my way over to her, leaning slightly behind her so I can sneak a peek at her screen—but it's black now. She tucks it into her pocket and turns to me, the smile still plastered across her face.

She's so radiant that tears prick my eyes.

"Boyid mernem," I say, earnestness dripping from my buzzed voice.

Her brow furrows in question, but then she responds in kind, "Yes ko boyid mernem." She pulls me into a tight hug. "I knew it. I *knew* this book was going to take the world by storm. There's nothing you can't do."

A tear breaches the dam of my eyelashes, tumbling down my cheek. I whisk it away. "You know—" I exhale. "You're the most important person in the world to me. You know that, right?"

When I pull back, her expression is wary. Caught?

"I know," she hedges.

"And you can tell me anything."

She shifts from one foot to the other. Her eyes won't meet mine when she says, "Then you should know . . . your singing is way off-key."

"That's not news." I've never been able to carry a tune.

"Okay. Ryan hasn't stopped ogling you the entire night."

It takes every ounce of effort that exists within my body not to turn to see if she's right. She's a sneaky devil, turning the tables on me. "Speaking of . . . guys." *Smooth segue, Ana.* "Anybody on your radar these days?" I ask, feigning innocence as I peruse the dance floor.

She shakes her head wistfully. "We can't all have dreamy publicists drooling after us."

I huff a laugh. "I don't know if that's how I'd characterize it."

"That's exactly how I'd characterize it."

Not meaning to—totally unwittingly, I swear—I catch a glimpse of Ryan. Not drooling, exactly, but there's something definitely akin to salivation in his expression. His irises are dark, his mouth set in a firm line. A mouth whose skills I've become pleasantly familiar with . . .

Want spreads through me like a gnarled root.

"Damn. I don't even want to know what he's imagining doing to you tonight," she says. "You better hydrate."

If I could last, I'd fuck you as hard as I want to, make you scream from it.

I order a water and down half the glass. When I turn back, Mar's off dancing again, yelling along about working hard till she owns it. I wonder briefly if her pushing me so hard toward Ryan is intended as a distraction from whatever it is she's trying to hide. But her joy is so infectious that I decide to let it go for now and join in, linking our fingers and twirling her into a dip.

We sing and dance and drink and eat into the evening, and I daresay this little hotel bar on an unassuming street is the hoppingest place in town.

I stick to water for the remainder of the evening and my buzz wears off considerably with food in my belly. Which is a good thing, because I do not want Ryan turning down my advances for a reason as stupid as integrity. I want the least gentlemanly version of Ryan that exists tonight.

When the bar starts to quiet down, Shanthi packs it in, and Maral jumps up from the table alongside her—Queen Wingwoman in action. She hands me back my phone, telling me with a wink that she's silenced my notifications. We agree to meet in the lobby tomorrow, which I read as her covert way of saying she won't come to my room for our usual morning routine, since I'll likely be occupied.

As soon as the elevator doors close behind them, I slide my hand under the table and onto Ryan's knee. "Damn," I say. "There goes my fantasy."

"Fantasy," he says, intrigued. "Do tell."

"I envisioned us carrying out some kind of clandestine operation to evade discovery. You know, you slipping me your key card under the table, telling me when to meet you in your room."

He's watching my lips. "If you want to role-play, I'm down."

"You say that now. Wait till the ball gag and zapper come out."

He smiles tenderly. "I can't wait to learn all about your kinks. Tell me over dinner?"

My stomach drops. Not at the implication that he'll do anything I want in bed, although I'm pretty sure he knows I won't ask to electro-stimulate him. But because he's . . . asking me out? Like . . . on a date?

A prickle crawls from my chest up my neck, bristling the hair at the base of my scalp.

Much as I want to deny Maral's assertion that Ryan may have more-than-casual feelings, the evidence is mounting against me. His tenderness during sex, that expression on his face at the studio this morning, asking me out-out rather than just back to his room. I can't deny something that's staring me right in the eye.

I should be touched. The tingly sensation unfurling in my chest suggests I *am* touched. That this man, whose interest any woman would be lucky to have, wants more from me than just sex.

But I also know where *more* leads. *More* may start with benign warmth in your chest, but it morphs, overheats, becomes a malignant fire that burns all your carefully erected defenses to the ground. Leaves you grappling in the ashes.

It's safer to keep things strictly about sex. No, not just safer. Necessary. There are practicalities to consider, after all—how exactly is more even possible when he works for my publisher? Has he forgotten that teeny tiny complication? I certainly haven't—it's a get-out-of-jail-free card. A lifeline.

I square my shoulders. I can right this train, keep it on the correct track. The only track. I just have to stay focused, and keep him focused. Should be easy enough—he's already drinking in my every move like I'm an oasis in the desert.

"The only thing I want in my mouth is you," I say. My pinky brushes the evidence of his arousal. "And it seems like you want that too."

"I'd have to be dead not to want that," he breathes.

Good. Yes. "I believe you also promised to make me scream from it." I affect a pout. "Are you the kind of person who reneges on promises, Ryan? Because I don't think I can abide such a lack of honor."

His voice drops dangerously low. "I'm a man of my word. And I'll deliver, believe me."

Hot. Damn. "Then what are we waiting for?"

The arousal emanating off him is so fiery that the air practically refracts from it. But there is something else going on behind his eyes. Some kind of war he's fighting in the privacy of his mind. Even though there's no point to it. Not within the reality of this situation. He has to know that.

Finally, resignation seems to eclipse the fight.

He removes a key card from his wallet and slides it across the table to me. "Room 704," he says gruffly. "Five minutes."

Relief and satisfaction pour through me like warm honey. He rises from the table, heading to the elevator. I almost regret starting this little ruse because the sight of his strong back makes me want to climb him right this minute. I've never been one for delayed gratification. I comfort myself with the image of him opening his door to me in a few minutes, his pants tented. Or better yet, nonexistent.

I tuck the key card away and chew on a couple of mints from the hostess station during my struggle to wait five minutes, springing into action the second the time is up.

When the elevator dings open on Ryan's floor, I startle at the sight of him loitering in the hall outside his room.

"Lost?" I ask.

Ryan leans against his doorjamb. "I forgot I only have one key card. Didn't expect to need another."

I purse my lips. This could also be fun. "Well, entrance shall be granted to thee, if thy key you can find on me." I twirl slowly to display the many potential spots his key could be hiding on my body.

Ryan glances behind him and over my shoulder, making sure we're alone. Then he stands back, assessing me. From my heels up my legs and belly to my mid-cut neckline.

"I'd like to search every inch of you," he says. "But the way I want to do it, we should definitely not be in public."

"Then you better find your key quick."

I sidle up to him, turning slightly so that my ass brushes against the hard front of his pants. His hands fly to my hips, gripping me just shy of too hard. My high-waisted pants don't have pockets, but that doesn't stop his fingers from roaming from back to front all the same, moving dangerously close to where I'm wet already and wanting. He lingers for a moment and presses an open-mouthed kiss to the side of my neck.

"I know one of your kinks," he says. "Torture."

I grind my ass into the bulge of his crotch. "You like it."

"No, Ana," he breathes. "I fucking love it."

He reaches under my blouse, the skin-to-skin contact sending shocks through my core. (Who needs a zapper? Ryan's hands are electric enough.) He runs his fingers along the band and straps of my bra before moving to cup my breasts over the fabric, teasing my nipples between his fingers. I arch back against him.

"Christ," he groans.

"Won't find Him in there, either."

"Wouldn't be so sure," he says, working his way down my torso. "Your body is the closest I've come to seeing God."

He feels around my waistline, hesitating only a moment before skating his hand down the front of my pants and into my underwear. When he finds my drenched pussy, he seems to be in no hurry to keep looking for the key.

He slides wet fingers over my clit, drawing my breath out in a whoosh, and rubs it slowly, deliberately, working me expertly toward orgasm. I'm so hot, it doesn't take much, but just as I'm about to come, he pulls his hand out of my pants entirely. From the corner of my eye I see him put his fingers in his mouth.

I steady myself against the doorframe. "Who h-has the torture kink?" I ask unevenly.

"Looks like we were made for each other," he says.

I try to ignore how . . . *significant* that sounds, focusing instead on his glazed expression as he drops to his knees, feeling each thigh, then down my calves. My blood is effervescent, rushing to every spot he touches like it's made of metal and his hands are magnets.

Finally, when he tucks his fingers inside the cuff of my pants, he knows he's hit pay dirt. He pulls the key out from where it rests against my ankle.

"Thank god," he says shakily, tapping it against the door as he rises. He swings it wide and gestures for me to precede him into the room.

We don't get far—the moment the door closes behind us, he's

pressing me against it roughly, his lips on mine punishing. He breaks away long enough to splay hot kisses down my neck, along my collarbone. When he dips his tongue deep inside my ear, like he did after that first time we kissed, I again feel a jolt right through to my clit. My knees give out from the sheer overwhelming pleasure, and he catches me before I collapse. He lifts me up against the door, pushing into the V of my legs, every inch of his torso against mine, as though he's trying to vacuum-seal our bodies together.

He's sucking a spot below my ear that causes the most pathetic whimpering sounds to escape my mouth. I'm all body and earthly delights and no self-consciousness whatsoever.

How is this man so skilled at teasing every erogenous zone that exists on a woman's body? He must have had lots of sex in his life.

Something whirls in my stomach, an undertow dragging me under.

I banish that thought from my mind. He can have as much sex as he wants, with anyone he wants. If I'm the beneficiary of the skills he hones during his trysts, lucky me. *Just appreciate it, Ana.* Needless quease begone.

"I believe I was promised a hard fuck," I pant.

His teeth scrape along my neck. "Impatient, are you?"

"I'd say I've been pretty patient—waited for it all day," I confess, past the point of self-preservation. So what if he knows? It's not like he feels any differently, judging by the evidence driving against me.

"Waited for me to fuck you hard," he says, as if the words taste delicious in his mouth. "To give your greedy pussy the treatment it craves."

Of their own volition, my muscles clench. He feels it right where his own need is concentrated most, his eyes closing unsteadily. I can barely breathe, let alone respond, loving that this taciturn man has such a mouth on him.

Still holding me up with strong hands under my ass, he walks farther into the room, which I vaguely note looks like he just arrived, nary a personal item scattered anywhere. Even his suitcase is tucked away, fulfilling my expectation of him so thoroughly, so reliably, it makes my throat swell.

I dismiss the thought, climbing down and undressing as quickly as humanly possible. My clothes crumple on the floor at my feet, the only thing out of place in his pristine room. Ryan is riveted, cataloging my every move.

"Get on the bed," he says. His voice is low, the command firm.

I sit, my breasts swaying, and his eyes flash to them as he falls to his knees before me. He pushes my legs open, exhales a harsh breath when a crude sound emanates from my wet labia parting. "*Fuck*," he growls, descending as if by rote—as if he can't possibly see the evidence of my desire without diving for it, living to satisfy it.

And satisfy it he does. His light edging from the hallway comes to fruition as he goes to work on my pussy like it's his literal job. The flat of his tongue delivering consistently, with single-minded dedication.

"Ryan," I gasp. "Don't stop—I'm going to come."

He groans in response, making out with my clit like it's the love of his life, sucking on it, his fingers stroking inside me zealously until the sensations are so overwhelming I don't know which part of him is pushing me over the edge—I just know I'm flying like a winged creature in a clear blue sky.

He doesn't stop, seems like he'd keep going indefinitely if I didn't tug him up my body, fumbling at his clothes as they abrade my over-sensitized skin.

He makes quick work of his shirt, jeans, and briefs while I reach for a condom from my purse. He climbs back over me, moving like a jungle cat, the undulation of his muscles turning me into a Neanderthal, so basic in my mindless attraction to the display of sheer strength.

He takes the small square packet from my hand, ripping it with trembling hands and rolling the condom on in record time. "I've been thinking about you all day."

"We've been together all day," I say.

He notches the tip of his erection inside me, eyelids fluttering shut at how fucking right it feels. Or am I projecting? "We've been *working* all day. But my thoughts have been"—he slides deeper—"very NSFW."

I gasp at his entry, my pussy fastening tight around him. Like it's been waiting for this—for him—to feel complete. Exactly as it should be.

"Goddamn," he rasps, snaking his arms around me, gathering me so close that my breasts crush against his chest. "You feel so perfect. I want to fuck you forever, baby."

His words tie my throat up in knots. My heart beats so hard against my sternum, I'm sure he can feel it against his own. I'm very aware of my legs wound around his hips, holding him so fixedly to my body that he can barely pull out before driving back into me again. Very aware that he seems reluctant to pull out at all, as though any space between us has personally wronged him and he's seeking revenge by eliminating it entirely.

Very aware of the words *baby* and *forever* lingering in the air like smoke from a burning fuse.

I unwind my legs, drawing my knees up. Giving him better access.

Relinquishing attachment.

He made a promise, and Ryan is a man of his word.

"Hard," I say.

He rises up on his elbows, the sound of his lips de-suctioning from my neck audible in the quiet room, and looks down at me, a question in his eyes. Is he surprised I'm cashing in on what I was promised?

Or does he know I'm responding to the words he just uttered?

I school my face into a sultry pout, my eyes heavy-lidded. Trying another tack, I implore him again. "Please will you fuck me hard, sir?"

His gaze narrows, studying me intently. Then, a quirk in his lips shows he's willing to play along. For now.

"At your command," he says, drawing back and thrusting with such force it takes me a second to get a breath.

I asked for it but wasn't prepared. Even digging my heels into the mattress and bracing one hand against the headboard is no defense against the onslaught of Ryan's cock. He pounds into me with such delicious roughness that I'm driven up the bed, his mouth everywhere—on my lips, my neck, my shoulders and breasts, like he can't get enough. Like he wants to imprint the taste of me on his tongue.

Forever, baby.

The sensations come from every angle. The friction in my pussy and against my clit; the suction on my skin; the bounce of the mattress under my back; the weight of Ryan's body on top of mine, pinning me with a force so solid, so certain, that it causes something squishy and undefined to crowd my chest.

"*Ryan.*" His name catches in my throat.

He stops immediately. "Too much?"

"No, it's . . . it's not that," I say. *Why did I even say anything?*

I feel so safe, somehow, coveted, his body wrapped around mine like armor. I have to remind myself that this is temporary. That I don't want it to be anything else.

He doesn't move, concern gathering in his forehead. "Are you okay? Ana, I'm sorry, I—"

He starts to pull out but I yank him back, my nails digging into his ass. God, there is no fucking give, even there. "No, I want it," I say. There's no part of me that wants him to stop, or slow down, or go easy on me. If anything, I want him to do the opposite—pound me so rough I can't walk straight, can't think about anything beyond how to get air into my lungs. "I want you to go even harder."

He watches me for a moment, breathing deeply. Understanding seems to spread across his features as all tenderness evaporates from his face, replaced by that old forbidding frown.

He pulls out brusquely, kneeling up. I feel so empty suddenly, hollowed out, devoid of the very thing I need. Just as I'm about to protest, to plead, to beg for him to fill me again—to tell him I don't know what's happening inside my head, but I do know there's no world in which he doesn't belong inside me—he flips me over onto my stomach. I barely register the change in position before he pulls my hips up, tucks a pillow beneath them, and drives into me from behind, so deep his firm stomach smacks against the swell of my ass.

"This how you want it?" he rasps in my ear. "So hard you can't think past it? Can't feel anything but the pound of my cock inside you."

My chest tightens, my eyes stinging even as pleasure practically blinds them. And he doesn't let up, pumping into me mercilessly, hitting my G-spot dead-on and stealing every thought from my mind. A man of his word.

"I'll fuck you however you want, Ana, you know that by now. My cock can't stand down if I'm anywhere near your orbit, and I'll serve it up to you any way you wish."

I clench around him, his words causing the involuntary response, and his groan vibrates against my back. His arms wind around my torso, gathering me close. Pressure builds in my core as my head clouds with delicious images of Ryan yielding to my desire whenever I want. A misty, senseless thought bubble forms—*you can have him forever*—before dissolving like a contrail in the sky.

"I'll make you come until your legs give out." His breath is hot on my neck, a shadowy undertone to his hoarse voice. "Even if that's all you want from me."

His hand snakes down to rub my swollen clit, the sensation combining with the storm on my G-spot to bring on an orgasm that's more wallop than wave. The impact is so shattering that a scream rips from my throat, muffled in the mattress as I clutch futilely at the sheets. He crushes me to him as he shudders through his own release, as though he needs every inch of my skin against his to be able to come, as though our bodies can snuff out the words that hang both said and unsaid in the air.

Chapter 15

The soft rustle of sheets. Diffuse light seeping through sheer white curtains. The scent of hotel soap, brought to life on Ryan's skin, both provocative and comforting.

It's this recognition that stirs me awake.

"Good morning," he says from the other side of the bed.

"What time is it?" I ask, my voice sleep-logged.

"Early," he says. "Not even six."

He looks tired. His vibe is . . . different than usual. Wary.

"Couldn't sleep?" I ask.

His hair rustles against the pillow as he shakes his head.

"Off your usual routines," I posit.

A beat passes. "You could say that."

I rub my eyes. "Don't publicists tour around promoting books all the time?"

"Not as much as you'd think." He hedges. "And that's not the most unusual thing about this past week."

Behind him, the room is spotless. Because it's Ryan's room, and Ryan is orderly, neat. Everything in its place.

Except for my clothes, strewn haphazardly across the carpet.

I am the odd thing out here.

"Don't usually have casual sex with your authors?" I ask, trying for lightness. Even batting my lashes in the effort.

"Don't have casual sex at all," he says softly.

Maral called it, as usual. And despite the fact that he should be in the museum of impossible things (a man from New York City, with that masterpiece of a body, who could *pull* but chooses not to?), I can't help but admit it tracks. Ryan is serious, mature, loyal. He gave up his young adulthood to raise a child who wasn't even his own. He devotes himself fully to everything he does—it makes sense that he'd do the same with relationships.

It's such a vulnerable thing to admit, yet he's unselfconscious about it. Probably because he's a fucking god in bed. "You could have fooled me," I say. "How are you so good?"

His lips tug at the corners. "I've been dreaming of making you come for . . . a long time."

I huff a laugh. Don't know if I'd characterize the nine days we've been on tour so far—more specifically, since that morning in Chicago when I first caught him drinking in the sight of my legs—as a *long* time. But then again, any length of time spent full of unmet desire can feel like forever.

"I'll admit," I say, "*Ryan Grant, sex god*, was not on my bingo card for this year."

"What was my descriptor instead?"

I make a show of thinking about it. "*Ryan Grant, stuffed shirt*."

A soft chuckle. "Ouch."

I raise one shoulder. "That's the price for your aloofness."

"Maybe my aloofness was by design," he says. "I couldn't exactly tell you what I really thought. Not if I didn't want to send you running for the hills."

"Oh god. Do I want to know?"

Despite the dim light in the room, there's still that twinkle in his eye. "At that first meeting, you breezed into the boardroom like you owned the place. Confident, empowered. Magnetic. Full of so much life that you were practically lit from within."

His words reflect a version of me that's well worn—the version people are drawn to, that's fun and makes them feel good and beams light into every room I'm in. Brightness and positivity personified, complete with jazz hands. It does come naturally, most of the time. But it's not the full picture.

The full picture is one nobody ever sees—also by design.

I'm surprised to hear that's how Ryan saw me, though, given the vibe he gave off in that first meeting. But then, I've seen how quickly he draws the blinds on himself around me. Has his standoffishness been a mask all along?

"Then I started listening to your podcast," he goes on, "and discovered how thoughtful and engaged you are in your interactions. People are comfortable sharing their stories because you make them feel like they're the most important and interesting stories in the world. You make people feel seen, made *me* feel seen in a way I hadn't before. The pressure, the loneliness, put into words and validated. Yet you so rarely shared about yourself, and all I wanted was to know you. The you that's inside this perfect exterior."

His kind words about my podcast, and me as its host, touch an unexpected chord. But his reiteration that he wishes I would share more about myself feels different—higher-stakes, somehow—now that we've been intimate. My skin heats uncomfortably. The sheets tangled over my body feel like weighted blankets, heavy and constricting.

"I haven't exactly been in a position to express myself freely, but now, given *this* . . ." He takes my hand, and my heart starts beating double-time, trepidation swirling in my belly. "Ana, I—"

As though sent by the heavens, a foreign ringing sound blares through the room. I breathe a quiet sigh of relief, willing my pulse to calm down, as Ryan reluctantly reaches for the landline on the nightstand.

"Hello?" he says into the receiver. "Yeah, she's here." He hands me the phone.

"*Where have you been?*" Maral asks on the other end. "Actually, never mind," she rushes to say, "I know where you've been. *Why haven't you answered your phone?*"

My purse lies strewn on the dresser across from the bed. "You silenced it yesterday."

"Fuck me." Her exhale hisses from the speaker. "Okay, don't look at it. Go to your room immediately. Shanthi and I will meet you there."

"What's wrong? Are you okay?" I say, worried and instinctively walking toward my phone.

"I'm fine, but stop," she says, knowing exactly what I'm doing. "Let me tell you before you—"

But it's too late. I've already seen my lock screen, the comment notifications piling up in real time like bricks being laid for a wall.

> Jeez, get a room! Isn't SFL a family show?

> that's her publicist! i was at the reading she did at powells and he intro'd her

> hope ur independntly wealthy bro coz ur about to get fiiiired

My brow knits as I read one nonsensical comment after another across social platforms. I tap on one randomly and see the post it's attached to—a fan has tagged me, and who knows what they've said because my eyes immediately freeze on the image they've captioned.

It's Ryan and me, in the *San Fran Live* studio corridor, bins and equipment piled high next to us, when he showed me the email from Meredith with the *NYT* news yesterday. When I kissed him. When we thought no one was watching.

Someone captured the kiss in all its glory. Despite the as-yet-undefined problem hanging in the air, I can't help marveling at just how *glorious* the kiss looks. The way Ryan leans into it with his whole body, the way my hands grip his lapels, the sliver of tongue shining through our open mouths. *Damn.*

But this *damn* is on the internet, apparently, for all the world to see.

"Shit, shit, *shit*," I say.

"I know," Maral sighs.

My hands are shaking. "How far does this go?"

"Not totally clear yet."

"Is there *any* chance Woodsworth hasn't seen it?"

"Unlikely," she says solemnly. "The whole team follows you, and you're tagged all over the place."

Notifications keep popping up at the top of my screen—didn't peg her for a slut; Wonder if that's how she got her book deal?—and my eyes clench shut.

I try to calm my frantic mind, ease the nails-on-chalkboard feeling in my gut at the injustice of being painted with the wrong brush. At not being able to defend myself against mischaracterization. At not being able to defend Ryan against the shitstorm that's going to come for him because of this. Because of *me*.

Ryan stands next to me, so substantial and gorgeous it makes me want to cry. He's clearly heard my end of the conversation. I raise my phone to show him, then watch as his face loses every ounce of color.

"*Shit*," he says, cradling the device in his hands.

"I know," I say.

"It's limited to social media, at least," Maral is saying on the landline. "It's not like it's headline news or anything. Maybe he can head it off at the pass."

"Maybe," I breathe as Ryan's skin goes from white to slightly green. "Should we put out a statement or something on *SPOY*?"

"No," I hear Shanthi yell on the other end. Oh god, Shanthi

knows. Obviously—if randos know, she would too. But still, it feels shitty that she found out from a source other than me, when she's been adjacent to us all along.

"That will only make things worse," Mar says.

"So, what?" I ask. "Just let it ride?"

"It's rage bait," she says, her tone soothing—as though anything about the words *rage bait* is soothing. "Engaging only substantiates it."

It goes against everything in me not to stand up for myself as I'm vilified for being a woman who has a sex life. After spending my whole life working my ass off, being depicted by even random internet trolls as someone who didn't earn her success is a dropkick in the teeth.

But there's a more practical and much more pressing problem at hand. Involving the man to my left, who's becoming progressively grimmer as he doomscrolls my phone.

The job he didn't want to jeopardize? It's in jeopardy now.

Thankfully we are past the crest of notifications, being in California—the East Coast had already had its heyday by the time we caught wind of the uproar—and they peter off over the course of the morning. For not the first time, I'm glad my mom is not tuned in online. She doesn't know anything about my personal life (nobody does, which makes this all the more mortifying) and I'd like to keep it that way. The last thing I need is to give Mom fodder for diatribes about how kissing random odars is not going to lead to my marriage and her grandchildren. But her Good Morning meme came in like clockwork, followed closely by a two-minute voicemail complaining about the neighbors' dogs who keep defecating on her lawn, confirming that she's none the wiser.

I left Ryan to call his boss and weather the fallout in private. I offered to face Woodsworth with him. To tell his employer that there's nothing untoward here, that I'm totally complicit—the instigator, in fact. But he said there was no chance he was going to put me in that position, then kissed the back of my hand before leading me to the door.

My heart is still living in my throat.

I know just how important his job at Woodsworth is for his entire family, given that the company bankrolls a large portion of his sister's significant tuition. If he gets fired for breaching the first rule of publicist–author relations—thou shalt not bed thy client—it is going to be a nightmare for them financially. The guilt may well eat me alive.

Shanthi, for her part, has shown zero opinion on this whole thing. She just denounced gossip-hungry trolls—dropping F-bombs galore—when she and Maral gathered in my room and has since focused her attention on giving me only non-negative updates.

Somehow, I have not lost any followers—in fact, I've gained some. People scouring my posts for Easter eggs about my sexual proclivities, I imagine. Gawpers gonna gawp.

I'm considering turning off my phone entirely when a name I recognize fills the screen.

"Nadia," I say as I pick up.

"Ana, my god," she says. "Are you okay?"

I feel a sting in my nose at the concern in her husky tone—a telltale sign I'm about to tear up, which only adds to the absurdity of this whole morning. "I'm fine."

"Don't look at any of that vile shit."

Easier said, etc. "Yes, ma'am."

"Hell, who is anyone else to judge? God knows if they were hotel-hopping across the country with that daddy, they wouldn't be able to resist him, either."

A watery laugh escapes me. As if just any woman in Ryan's proximity would be powerless against his sexuality. As if he and I came together simply because I was near him. It's impossible to imagine that Ryan and I could ever not have connected, whether we were in proximity or not. How could attraction that potent, sex that good, be possible and just never materialize?

"I just wish everyone was so understanding," Nadia adds ominously.

A cavern opens in my belly. I've seen a lot of unsympathetic people spouting off this morning, but it sounds like she's referring to something specific. "What happened?" I ask.

Maral's face is grave as she perches beside me on the edge of the bed. I put the phone on speaker.

"I'm here too," Mar says. "So's Shanthi."

"Hi, girls," Nadia says, all friendly. "Listen, this is not the level of setback you think it is—"

"Just tell me," I say a little too stridently.

"Craig Waters has postponed the meeting tomorrow."

The cavern in my stomach fills with scorpions, and I fold in half. "Postponed," I say, as if testing the word in my mouth. We're in L.A. for only one full day—we have to leave Saturday to make it to Boston for the next event. We can come back, though. After the tour wraps, I can fly back out. No problemo. "Till when?"

She hesitates for only a beat, which is an age in Nadia time. "Indefinitely," she says.

Fuck.

"So it's not postponed, it's canceled," I say, tone petulant.

"*Postponed* was the word they used. It's possible they'll be willing to pick the conversation back up again when this blows over."

How long will that take, though? And by the time this *blows over*, who's to say that Waters won't have moved on to some shiny new potential host? Hollywood is fickle, and I'm under no illusions that my glitter won't wear off quickly. If it isn't permanently tarnished already.

Kill me.

Nadia sighs. "They're concerned about their image—they want to project wholesomeness."

"I can be wholesome," I say.

"They follow your socials—they've seen the tags. They're not interested in any kind of sexual controversy."

The scorpions have run amok, lesioning my insides. I melt back onto the bed, throwing an arm over my eyes.

The worst part is: I get it. As someone whose whole career is predicated on being *seen* online, I understand the outsized role image plays in public perception. It's the *entirety* of the role. And as someone who pinned her dreams on a network television show, in Los goddamn Angeles of all places, I should have known what an important role my image would play in achieving that dream.

I'm not embarrassed about having a sex life, but having one with Ryan was always going to be objectionable. I knew that. I thought about the risk to his job, thought we'd be in the clear so long as nobody found out (womp). But it was shortsighted not to think about the risk to my own future if it were to get out.

A future that's feeling more and more like a mirage, hazy and indistinct, fading away on the horizon.

Fantasies that have taken shape in my mind since I formulated the talk show plan begin to dissolve. Revealing the news to Mom by showing up on her doorstep with moving boxes. Her delight at the prospect of living in L.A., of living in the same city as me again. My delight in finally bringing her happiness, gratification. Her shouting from the rooftops that her daughter is going to be on television. *Ana was right to choose this path—she's made it. Everyone can see she's made it. There's no gray area, generational or cultural divide, no doubt whatsoever. She is a success.*

Her father would be proud.

I use my sleeve to swipe away the moisture gathering in my eyes, my breathing too loud in my ears.

Thankfully Maral has taken over the conversation with Nadia, wrapping up the call. I mutter a half-hearted thank-you and goodbye, forcing my mind to regain some composure.

Mar hangs up, casting sorrowful eyes on me. "I'm so sorry, Ayn."

This angel. Here I am, having ruined our mutual future because I couldn't keep my grabby hands to myself, and she's apologizing to me. "No, Mar, *I'm* sorry. I'm sorry I squashed our dream."

I wrap her in a hug, but she's stiff for a moment. I don't blame her—of course she's mad. But then she relents, putting her arms around me.

"I'll make it up to you," I whisper into her hair. "I'll fix this."

I feel her shaking her head in the crook of my neck, and she pulls back. "No, you don't have to fix anything."

"I do, and I will," I say firmly. "I'm not giving up. L.A.'s crawling with producers—we'll find someone else."

She looks concerned, but doesn't say anything more.

"Our flight leaves in a few hours," I say, clearing my throat. "I'll meet you downstairs in time for the airport shuttle."

Mar hesitates for a moment before rising quietly from the bed. "I'll be right down the hall if you need me."

Shanthi's head swivels from me, to her, to me. "Are you sure? Maybe it would be better not to be alone."

Maral gently cups her elbow, leading her to the door, knowing it's a losing battle. Knowing I'd rather be alone than have anyone bear witness when I'm in any state other than (jazz hands) *Ana Movilian*.

After they've left, I start packing. Anything to keep me moving, keep me focused on something other than the thing prying at my mind, seeking a fissure so the darkness can get in. Or, worse, out.

But it's no use. Just as I'm tucking my running shoes into a suitcase, a torrent climbs up my body, unleashing in a whoosh that's somewhere between an exhale and a sob. I crumple onto the bed, helpless against it, turning to drown the sound in the wrinkled bedding.

Mom. I'm sorry.

I picture her face, beatific in the imagined happiness I've been chasing for what feels like my entire life. The vision waves, scuzzes, her smile morphing into a grimace, a cry. She's curled, broken by the weight of all she's lost throughout her life. I reach for her, but she changes once more, her delicate features turning masculine, a beard sprouting and nose hooking. Kind black eyes under bushy brows and a barrel chest that smells like khoung and that I wish so badly I could hug again. Disappear into. Seek some measure of solace in, even if I can't let all this darkness out. Even if that's never been an option.

At the sound of a knock on the door, I sit up too quickly, my head dizzy.

I consider ignoring it, pretty sure it's Ryan and very sure he cannot see me this way.

"Ana," he says softly from the other side. "It's me."

It's me. Like there's only one person who could show up at my door in my bleakest hour and declare himself *me*. Like there's only one *me* for me.

That's exactly who Ryan has become, isn't it? The person I most look forward to seeing every day. The person who listens to what I have to say without dismissing it in any way. Who helps me feel less alone. Who takes care of things. Who takes care of me.

Before I even know what my body is doing, it has teleported to the door, opening it wide to reveal his broad form filling the frame. His green eyes magnificent as he assesses me with concern.

"Are you still employed?" I ask, the vibrato in my voice betraying the emotion that's threatening to burst the dam.

He can tell immediately. His brow furrows further as he steps into the room, closing the door behind him and enveloping me in a hug.

Damn, it feels good. Too good.

I melt into him, telling myself it'll just be for a moment. Just a moment, until I can organize my heart, and have a conversation like a normal human. His arms feel so solid, unwavering, as they wrap around me. Like if he had the choice, he'd keep me in them forever.

The thought snaps me to, and I pry myself away.

"How did it go?" I ask.

He still looks troubled, but he doesn't reach for me again. "They won't pull me mid-tour, but I have a meeting with my boss and HR first thing on Monday when I'm back in New York."

I breathe, some of my tension easing. "Is it a good sign that they're keeping you on through the tour?"

He does a half-hearted shrug. "Who knows," he says.

My shoulders curl in. "I'm sorry I put you in the position to risk your job. I know it's why you kept . . . resisting when I pushed. I shouldn't have pushed. I need to stop doing that—steamrolling. Mar's been telling me for years."

He takes a step forward, moving me back against the dresser. "Ana, I love that you're tenacious. It's one of your hottest qualities— and there are a lot of them. Obviously I could have done without this shitstorm, but . . . I'm glad you pushed. I mean, *glad* is a weak word for how I feel about having the best sex of my life. Elated, maybe."

Something warm, satisfying, spreads through my chest. Like the first sip of strong coffee in the morning. My eyes drop to his lips, and he gathers me up once more, kissing me gently. My body softens in response, half sitting on the dresser as he presses into the cradle of my splayed legs.

"How are you feeling?" he says, tucking a strand of hair behind my ear. "I hated seeing those ugly things said about you."

That sting reappears in my nose, and I bite the inside of my cheek to suppress it. "I'm fine," I say, hoping to convince us both.

His intense gaze never leaves my face. "You say that a lot."

My pulse beats loud in my ears. "I'm fine a lot." I'm trying for breezy, but it's coming out cat-on-a-running-dryer. "The key is to not think about it. Focus on something else. Like packing, tidying." I gesture limply to the room, which is only slightly less of a disaster than it was before.

He grimaces at the disheveled bed, the clothes still strewn on every surface. "I don't think you know what *tidy* means."

I point a finger at him. "That's the last time I invite you into my room."

A beat passes before he says, "I hope not."

This brings a smile to my face, which seems to ease his frown a little bit.

"It's okay to not feel fine," he says softly, the earnestness in his face doing its best to crack my defenses. Too bad those things are ironclad.

Because I know better than to believe him.

"And it's okay to think about your own needs for once," I say, turning the tables.

He regards me thoughtfully. "Yeah?"

"Yeah."

"Well," he says slowly, "there is one option."

"What's that?"

"We could do this for real."

"Real," I repeat.

Pink sweeps across his face as he nods. "A relationship."

My stomach drops. His pulse beats a drumline in his throat, his gaze unwavering on mine.

"You . . . want to be my boyfriend?" I ask dumbly, before I can think better of it. God help me, I'm at such a loss for how to navigate this land mine of a conversation—with him, and in this fraught moment—that my brain isn't working properly.

Between my legs, where he remains pressed against me, I feel an unmistakable stiffening. I raise an eyebrow at him.

"The heart wants what it wants?" he says faintly.

"That is not your heart," I say.

His eyes are all sincerity—he's shot his shot and is waiting to see if it hit its target. But I can't give it the space to land.

"It's no wonder your dick wants me after the things I've done to it these past couple days," I say, steering the ship away from the iceberg.

"You don't have to tell me. Those memories will visit me on my deathbed," he says. "But, Ana. I'm serious. What if we—"

"You're hanging on to your job by a thread," I interject. My mind kicks into gear, grasping at ways to deflect. "Don't go saying things that could set fire to it."

His face shutters at that. *Good.* I don't want to hurt him, but I can't have him going down this path any further. This is not open for discussion. I press ahead. "And it won't help me, either—Craig Waters has already dumped me."

The dismay that clouds his eyes would be darkly comical if I were in any laughing mood. "Who is Craig Waters?" His voice is sandpaper.

"A producer. I was being considered to host a talk show, kind of like the podcast but on TV. Was supposed to meet with Waters tomorrow in L.A., but he canceled because I no longer fit the *wholesome image* they want to project."

He seems to be processing everything I just said. To be fair, there's a lot to unpack there. "A TV show?" is what he goes with first.

"Yeah," I say. "Probably won't work out with this producer, but hopefully Nadia can get something else on the books."

He's watching my lips as I speak, the flush on his neck deepening. "In L.A.?"

"That's the goal." A goal I have to keep in my sights at all costs.

"You want to move to L.A.," he says stiffly, as if he's learning each word for the first time.

I nod. "If I get the show, I'll move my mom out there with Maral and me. It's the biggest Armenian community in the country. Maral's parents already live there, and my mom would love living near them again. Our parents would all be over the moon to have Mar and me close by again. It would make them so happy."

"What about you?"

"What about me?" I ask.

"What would make you happy?"

His eyes are intense on mine, like he genuinely, desperately wants to know. Like it's the most important answer in the world, despite the question bordering on ridiculous—a senseless, meaningless question I've never been asked before. But he's looking at me like the sky could fall outside and he wouldn't even glance toward the window if it meant breaking eye contact for one second.

What would make me happy?

I picture my mother's smile, a flame only I have any hope of igniting. A flame that's been extinguished for years, since my father's death. Longer . . . since she had to give up everything she's ever known to build a whole new life on the other side of the planet, so her daughter could have opportunities she never did.

For the first time, another image overlays it—advanced reader copies next to a maniacally preset alarm on a nightstand. Twin laptops side by side on a coffee table. The scent of a fresh pot of dark roast and pancakes as snow falls outside, dusting skyscrapers. Warm fingers kneading tired feet. A hand reaching for mine under a blanket. Strong arms wrapping me up tight, holding me close.

Forever, baby.

The picture is more ridiculous than the question that inspired it. The ache so profound it's unfathomable. As in, I can't fathom it—I won't.

"Moving to L.A.," I answer. "That's what would make me happy."

This time, my voice doesn't falter at all.

Chapter 16

"Nobody," I repeat for the third time. "You're telling me *nobody* is interested?"

Nadia is holding on to her patience, I can tell. I picture her in a canary-yellow suit at her giant old-world mahogany desk in the Verity offices, pinching the bridge of her nose as she deals with her distraught *talent*.

"It's not that nobody is interested," she says, impressively calm, "it's that I don't think it's the right time to be booking you meetings."

"But we can meet in person tomorrow," I say, pacing the terminal for the fiftieth time. If the other travelers can't see the earbud in my ear, I 100 percent look like I should have my meds recalibrated. "Trust me, if people think I'm good on-screen, just wait till they get a load of me in person."

"You're the freaking sun," she coos. "It's not about that, Ana. You don't want the kind of interest you'd get right now, not given the first thing people will see if they look up your socials. It's too fresh."

I envision myself on the set of some frothy, gossipy reality TV show, all tarted up in low-cut necklines and tacky lashes. I look pretty hot, if I'm honest. But I get her point.

"I know you're anxious," Nadia says. "But trust me. Lay low for a few days, then we can put out feelers."

Feelers doesn't feel particularly encouraging. "Or maybe you can do a bit of in-person feeling—wait, that sounds—you know what I mean. When you're in L.A. tomorrow? We can meet for lunch and discuss which of the producers you scouted on previous rounds seemed most promising."

The line is silent. All I can hear is the airport announcement system above my head, the call for mispronounced passenger names to check in at gate B19.

"Did I lose you?" I ask, checking the screen of my phone.

"No," she rushes to say. "Ana . . . I canceled my flight. I'm not coming to L.A."

The muscles in my face, my shoulders, my whole body droop. She canceled her trip? She canceled her trip because there's no point in coming out here, trying to sell something nobody wants.

"It's all about timing," she assures me. "We'll regroup after the tour."

"Right," I say, my voice sounding faint, even to me.

Thankfully, Kissgate remains contained to socials, and comments have died down by the following day. Still, after spending Friday morning carefully pretending nothing is amiss during my L.A. media tour, and despite every interview serving dark roast coffee (silver linings), I'm so depleted by the afternoon that I beg Maral to go to Glendale without me. I have zero appetite for the homemade pastries I'd normally be eager for my horkoor Sosi to forcefeed me. I just want to hole up in my hotel room until someone has to drag me to the airport. But Mar insists that neither of us will be able to live down the intensity of her parents' scorn if I am anywhere in their vicinity and don't visit. As always, she is correct.

At least my horkoor and horyekhpayr seem to have no idea their niece has recently been defamed in the online world they are so staunchly unplugged from. In fact, true to form, they seem completely oblivious to the fact that we're in L.A. for work at all, treating us to a delightful plethora of backhanded (and front-handed) criticisms about the shortness of our visit.

"Vay, thank you for making time for us, janikner," Sosi gripes as she gives us each a double-kiss in the entryway. Despite her passive-aggression, being gathered close in her maternal embrace, even if it's somewhat infantilizing, feels so good in this moment.

She holds Mar at arm's length to survey her. "You're looking too thin," she says in Armenian. "I'll send you home with some basturma."

"Mom, we're traveling through the weekend," Mar answers in Armenian. "I'm not taking basturma on the road with me."

I suppress a laugh at the image of Maral carrying a bundle of cured meat among the delicates in her tiny carry-on.

"Soos," Sosi shushes her. "You're going home tomorrow"—like Mom, she refers to Boston as *home*, no matter that we haven't lived there in years—"so you'll take enough for Vartouhi too. She likes the one from Sevan's shop."

Maral turns to me, pleading wordlessly for backup, but I just nod. "It *is* her favorite."

She doesn't break her glare as she says to her mom, "I'm glad I can be your own personal FedEx."

We remove our shoes and follow Sosi into the kitchen, from which mouthwatering scents of sour-creamy dough and spiced meats and herbs waft. We could smell it from outside when we stepped out of our Uber. The orange trees on the neighbors' crunchy green lawns are no match for the aromatic food—though the aromas could be coming from any house in the all-Armenian neighborhood. It smells like home in the best possible way.

Mar drapes an apron over her sundress to protect the silk from inevitable grease splatters. Without being asked, she picks up the tongs from the red, blue, and orange–striped spoon rest beside the stove and starts turning the zhingalov hats sizzling on the stove. The expectation to assume domestic duties the moment we cross our parents' thresholds remains immovable, no matter how long it's been since we lived with them.

Sosi never lets me help with the cooking, because let's get real, but micromanages as I set out miniature cups and saucers for Armenian coffee.

Mar's dad—my horyekhpayr, Hrag—sits at the table reading an actual honest-to-god newspaper. He greets us with a smile and double-kiss without ever getting out of his chair, while the three of us set the table around him like flittering birds.

After coffee, accompanied by numerous varieties of dried fruits and nuts, fresh pomegranate, nazook, and gata, Sosi serves a meal fit for a dozen guests. I wish I had the appetite to tuck in as I otherwise would, and my inadequate portion doesn't escape her notice.

"You haven't eaten anything!" Sosi cries, even though I've forced down a lahmejoun and some sjookh and zhingalov hats.

"Don't worry, I'll eat some of the basturma Maral transports across the country." I wink at my cousin, trying for a levity I don't feel. She is not amused.

The conversation, if you can call it that, is mostly Sosi telling us which of their friends' kids have recently had or are expecting children, watching us for our reactions and casting pointed looks at an oblivious Hrag when we give her nothing. Her "subtlety" wears off quick, and soon she's moved on to full-on grumbles.

"Not that it would matter if I were so lucky to have grandchildren. They'd live across the country and I would only see them on the FaceLook!" she says. It's unclear whether she's butchering FaceTime or Facebook.

"Hamperoutioun," Mar says, imploring her to have patience. "I'm only thirty-one."

"How are you going to become a mother before your uterus dries out if you only date these unserious man-children? I told you I would set you up with Vachik's son. He is almost finished at the seminary. He will have a good job while you raise the babies."

She rolls her eyes. "You're really selling this imagined future."

"He lives in Queens!" she cries, as if that's an argument clincher.

"Any eligible bachelors here in L.A.?" I ask, and Mar glares at me. I'm not so wrapped up in my own drama that I've forgotten how she's been sneaking her phone around this past week. She may already be seeing someone, but this is what she gets for keeping it secret from me.

"Plenty. But what's the point when you live so far away?" Sosi bemoans. Something about the way her brow gathers—the shape it gives her dark eyes—resembles my father so uncannily in that moment that the hair on my arms stands straight up. He was her brother, so it stands to reason, but the effect is jarring. Suddenly my throat feels full of something thick, solid. I try to swallow it down.

"We may not for very long," I manage to say.

Disbelief and frustration intertwine like a caduceus on Maral's face. She hates when I jump the gun, impulsively spilling the beans before something is set in stone. And, yeah, we've had a major setback in the plan to move here anytime soon. But hell, if I can salvage anything right now, our parents' happiness might as well be it. The look of elation on Sosi's face—a smile so bright and beautiful and familiar and beloved—goes down like cold lemonade in a heat wave, and is worth Mar's temporary ire.

Because it is temporary. Mar will come around well before our move to L.A. is fail-safe—which it will be. I'll make sure of it.

When I explain that I'm working on something that may bring

us here permanently in the near future, their first question is whether I've gotten a job at a nearby hospital. Sosi and Hrag speak over each other—"Adventist is excellent"; "Armen's daughter works at Dignity Health, you'll have friends there!"—and I have to remind them that I'm not a practicing doctor. They tsk and ask more questions, which I try to circumvent as much as I can. Without going into detail, I tide them over with the promise of good news to come.

They cheer and hug us, and Hrag breaks out the Ararat brandy for a toast. Though premature, the celebration feels vitalizing. A foreshadowing of what's to come—happy, easy camaraderie with parents who no longer view us with disappointment, but with pride. *This is how it can be. This is how it* will *be.*

Maral is silent and reserved, not willing to corroborate my insinuations. When Sosi turns the conversation to which of their local friends' sons are still single, Mar twirls her wrap-it-up finger and I know it's time to go.

In the Uber back to our downtown hotel, I nudge her. She doesn't respond, staring resolutely out the car window at the lit-up billboards along the freeway.

"Don't be mad," I cajole. "Did you see how happy they were?"

She shakes her head, still not over it. "I don't care about that," she says.

I jiggle her knee. "They're your parents."

"So what?" she says, her voice clipped. "Should our lives revolve around pleasing our families?"

Whoa. She's really pissed—I haven't seen her like this in a long time. Mar is the chill one, eternally unflappable even in the face of crises.

"Where is this coming from?" I ask. "We've been planning to move here for the show all along. Why are you freaking out?"

She's silent for a long beat, worrying her fingers. "Things have changed." I wait for her to elaborate, but she doesn't.

My sigh is weary. "I know, I fucked up. I'm sorry." I bite the inside of my cheek, the smell of the leftovers Sosi packed in yogurt containers too strong in the small back seat. My stomach churns. "I'm going to figure something out," I assure her. "We'll still move here. Don't worry."

I reach for her hand, which remains tense in mine. She keeps her eyes trained out the car window, watching the freeway lights zip by in a blur.

I vow to fix this. If it's the last thing I do, I'll put a smile back on Mar's face. I'll make sure she's happy, *and* that our parents are happy. I'll take care of them—I always do.

Chapter 17

After the late-summer smog of Southern California, the temperate East Coast climate of Boston is a welcome relief. People here complain endlessly about cold winters, but I've always liked the changing seasons. How can you enjoy summer if you don't struggle through the browbeating of an East Coast winter? Dad had an oft-repeated line on those blustery below-zero days: *If you didn't already know you're alive, now you do.*

Winter in New York takes my love of the season to a whole other level—the way a fresh dusting of snow makes the streets, parks, and buildings feel clean and even more picturesque than they already are, temporarily muting the eternal high-frequency commotion before the filth and noise regain their upper hand. It's magical.

As the shuttle zips us into the city from Logan airport, I text Mom that we've arrived safely, and that I'm looking forward to seeing her at the event this evening. The ellipses that indicate she's writing back appear and disappear a few times before the gray text box finally pops up: Arent you coming to the house?

My teeth clench. We talked about this—there isn't time to get from the airport to her place and back to the South End bookstore in time for the event. Mar booked a car to bring Mom to the bookstore and everything—surely she remembers this, given the earful she gave me about it (*A car! Is it the Oscars? Do I need to make an appointment to hug my own daughter?*). But I know she just misses me and this is her way of expressing her discontent with the plans, whether she knew them in advance or not.

I force my jaw to relax and type back: I'm sorry, Mayrik, there isn't time. I'll see you at the event. We'll go to the house together after.

Sleeping at my parents' bungalow in Dorchester, where we moved when I was twelve, is not exactly enticing. To me, it still carries the pall of my last year there. *It's just two nights,* I remind myself.

Never mind that the thought of two more nights without Ryan makes me restless. As if by some unspoken agreement, neither of us has made a move toward the other since Kissgate and its fallout, and the sexual frustration rattling through me is a living thing. Now I have to go two more agitated, sleepless nights without him.

And then . . . we're heading back to New York. Where hopefully he'll still be employed.

And this . . . *thing* between us will be over.

We can't bring it home with us. Ryan needs to hold on to his job, if it's still his. Even if there wasn't a conflict of interest, Ryan won't be content with a no-strings kind of arrangement—that's becoming as clear as smog-free air. And I don't do any other kind of arrangement. So . . . end of story.

The car feels too small suddenly, my perfume too strong. In the seat ahead of me, Ryan's hair curls a little at the nape of his neck. I know how that part of his body smells. I know what those dark strands feel like between my fingers. I don't know if my senses will ever forget.

I find myself searching through my messages for the familiar names from my in-phone Rolodex that used to give me a little spark of excitement—Evan, Malcolm, Jacob—hoping that just seeing them, the promise of the sexual delights they have to offer, will settle this gnawing creature in my esophagus. But no dice. Their names seem distant, as though they belong in another life.

It's just travel, I tell myself. A lot has happened in the past couple of weeks—it makes sense that people from home would feel far away. Even if they never have before. As soon as I'm back in my apartment, back to my daily routines, I'm sure hitting them up will feel just the same as it always did.

Perfectly satisfying.

The drive from the airport to More than Words Bookstore is mercifully short, because too much time staring out at the cityscape and harbor will not help me put on my event face. Every corner of this city is chockablock with memories, many of which used to be sweet, but have since become tinged with bitterness. The seafood restaurant I took my parents to as a celebration when I scored in the ninety-ninth percentile on the MCAT. The Lawn on D, where Nathan and I attended a concert on one of our first dates. All the streets I've run, working out the stresses of school, of work . . . of home. Long walks along the waterfront when I needed space from my parents' house, or the apartment Nathan and I shared, or when I moved back in with Mom after Dad passed, outside being the only safe place to let the waves crash over me. Alone.

My knee feels warm and I notice Maral's small hand there. She squeezes gently, acknowledging that there may be capital-F Feelings happening. She knows I won't talk about them, but she's offering me bare-minimum support—the only kind I'll accept. I place my hand on hers and squeeze back.

When we pull up to the store, Ryan opens the back door for us before helping the driver unload our bags from the trunk. The brief touch of his hand on my waist as I emerge from the car sends a frisson of want through me, and I wonder how bad it would be to kiss him publicly again.

Bad, Ana. Don't jump back into the hole you just climbed out of.

Especially after I spent the morning before our flight running damage control on all fronts. Given that we're no longer the scandal-du-jour, I sent Nadia a screenshot of my squeaky-clean mentions with the text time to re-up? She replied with a thumbs-up and a promise to get in touch as soon as she had anything to share.

Next I sent an email to the marketing VP at Woodsworth. I know Ryan didn't want to put me in the position of having to explain myself to his boss, but I've never been one to sit idly by. So I detailed in writing that Ryan did nothing untoward at all. He was a perfect, professional gentleman, and I the architect of his demise, so please don't make him pay for my bad behavior. Whether it will save his hide is yet to be seen, but here's hoping it makes a difference.

The bookstore staff greet us warmly, stow our bags behind the counter, and lead us to the event area, which is all decked out with creative displays of the book on breakout tables. There's about an hour till showtime, and the first order of business is to sign some of the store's stock. I set to work while Shanthi and Maral do lighting tests and Ryan confirms the run of show with the manager. It's a reading followed by an onstage interview with a bookstore rep who's apparently a big fan.

The room is beginning to fill with attendees when my mom arrives, the sight of her filling my heart with competing emotions—nostalgia, trepidation, profound love. She looks adorable but out of place in the crowd of young, hip urbanites. I can tell she's made an effort—she's wearing her houndstooth jacket and low navy heels, and she's styled her dark bob. When I greet her with a hug and a double-kiss, the scent of her hairspray catapults me back in time. It's been so long since I've seen Mom put thought into her appearance—since Dad was alive. Her depression was too dark, too all-consuming in the year that followed his passing for something as inconsequential as her looks to even occur to her. Understandably. And then I was gone, fleeing to New York and not bearing daily witness to her gradual ascent out of the darkest part of her grief.

My visits in the intervening years have been spent at the house, where there was no need to doll up. But now, given the opportunity, here she is—a picture of who she was prior to the version of her in my rearview mirror. Close, anyway. The picture is slightly weathered, a filter applied that dulls its original colors.

"It's so busy in here, Anahid jan," she says in Armenian as people continue streaming in through the doors, squeezing past to get to the rows of chairs. "Maybe you should have planned this at a different store?"

"All these people are here to see me, Mayrik," I say.

Her eyes widen with surprise. "To buy your book?" She waves at the displays lining the perimeter of the event area, my face smiling back at us three hundred–fold.

"That, and to hear me speak," I say quickly, as though it's insignificant. "How are you? How was the drive here?"

She shrugs, heaving a sigh. "Too much traffic in the evenings."

I nod, sympathetic. "Rush hour. By the time we leave it will have cleared. Thanks for making the trip to be here."

"It would have been nice to see you alone for a little while before"—she gestures vaguely to the crowd in distaste—"this."

"You're right," I say. "The timing was tough, with the flight and the event. I could have planned it better." I don't know why I say this—I didn't do any of the planning myself. "But we'll have all day together tomorrow."

Her brows meet in the middle of her forehead. "Just tomorrow? Aren't you staying longer?"

Breathe. Just breathe. "No, remember, we have to get the train to New York Monday morning."

"When will you be back?"

"Soon," I promise, unwilling to commit to returning anytime in the near future.

She smiles, reaching up to cup my cheek. "I just miss you so much, janikus."

I swallow thickly, my eyes burning. "I miss you too."

Maral joins us, giving my mom kisses and getting an earful about the store being too crowded when an attendee accidentally bumps her handbag as they pass by.

"What's this Sosi said about moving to Los Angeles?" Mom asks suddenly. I bet my horkoor called her as soon as we left Maral's parents' house last night. Seeing Maral must have jogged her memory.

Mar shoots me a censuring look, unimpressed. "We are considering possibilities," she says vaguely, then pats my back a little too roughly. "Ana can tell you all about it later."

Mercifully, Ryan appears at my side then. "This must be Mrs. Movilian," he says.

My mother takes his proffered hand as I complete the introduction. "Mom, this is Ryan Grant. He's the publicist who's been helping with the tour."

He gives me a funny look, like he's waiting for me to say something more. What, I'm not sure. Does he expect me to tell my mother that he's also made her only child orgasm to within an inch of her life?

Maral pipes up. "He planned this whole event," she adds. Never mind that Meredith actually did the planning—giving Ryan the glory right now serves the greater good.

Mom waggles her head. "Maybe a bigger place next time," she suggests, switching to English.

So much for glory. The store is quite large, not to mention lovely, with lofty ceilings and a dedicated event space that fits enough chairs to accommodate the attendees we were able to pull. But stating facts won't change her mind.

To his credit, Ryan still offers her a smile that would soften butter straight out of the fridge. "With the number of tickets Ana's able to sell, we'd have to book a stadium in every city."

She doesn't seem to register his compliment. "Why aren't any of your friends here?" she asks me.

Unsure which *friends* she's referring to, I come up short. I haven't really kept in touch with anyone from Boston since moving five years ago. High school was such a blur of studying, extracurriculars, and student government that anyone I befriended was more of an acquaintance than a long-term friend. Harvard was all competition, all the time—nobody was that interested in making friends with the top student they'd just have to elbow aside on their way to the most prestigious residency positions. That left Nathan, and we are certainly not friends anymore. Last I heard, he was married to a periodontist, with one baby almost out of diapers and another on the way. (Mom is still Facebook friends with him and gives me updates from time to time, which is when I tend to tune out of the conversation.)

Maral—the only friend from Boston who matters—helps me out. "We only advertised on the brand platforms, so unless people follow those, or her publisher's socials, or any affiliates, they wouldn't have heard about it."

Mom fans a hand at Mar. "All this internet stuff is too complicated. You wouldn't have to *advertise* yourself to attract patients—anyone with an ache or pain would 'follow' you."

Ryan, still standing at my side, tenses. It's slight, but my body is attuned to his every movement.

I try to laugh it off. "Talk about a dour account, though."

"At least you would be giving people something they need," Mom says.

Okay. That one stings. I repeat the same refrain in my mind, the one I've leaned on countless times in the past: *Just because she doesn't understand what I do doesn't mean it's not worth doing.* If I say it enough times, I might eventually believe it.

I feel Maral's hand slip into mine and squeeze, our positions making it undetectable by my mom.

"She is." The words are spoken quietly but firmly, in a deep voice. Ryan's.

"She is what?" Mom asks.

"Ana *is* giving people something they need," he says. His tone doesn't sound defensive or angry but gentle, coaxing. "Many people feel alone with their experiences, their emotions. With this book, she's giving voice to people's stories, offering readers solidarity and empowerment they may never have felt before. That's extremely valuable."

The look on Mom's face is almost comical in its incomprehension. These are words she has zero reference for, ideas she's never so much as considered. And even as a knot seems to loosen inside my chest at the way Ryan has stood up for me in the face of derision—again—habit and loyalty rear their heads.

"It all sounds a lot more complicated than it is," I say. "It's just a book."

Ryan turns to me. "It's an important book, Ana." Something in his eyes implores me to agree, to accept his words as true. He's professed how deeply *So Proud of You* spoke to him—my diminishing its significance is akin to dismissing what it's meant to him. And not only that, but dismissing what it is to so many people. Not least, me. This thing I've poured my heart and soul into for close to six years, this community I've built that has felt like home in a way my actual home hasn't for so long—maybe ever.

And while I don't want to shrink it down, while I want to accept Ryan's support—his praise for this thing Mom doesn't understand—the lifelong dynamic between my mother and me is not easily overcome.

Maral's hand still holds tight to mine, its comfort helping me in the effort to keep my tone light. "Speaking of which, we don't want to lose these fine people's interest in said book," I say, gesturing to the attendees around the room. "Shall we get started?"

The burn of Ryan's continued attention rises up my neck. But

Mar checks her phone, confirming that it is indeed time to begin, and I feel swift relief at being able to step away from this conversation. I wish I could escape into a back room for a few minutes, take a few solitary breaths, but I pull myself together and slip into my well-worn public persona.

I'm on autopilot throughout the introduction, the reading, the interview. We didn't plan an audience Q and A or a signing for this store, the manager having cited time constraints when Meredith booked the event, and I feel a rare gratitude not to have to chitchat with anyone beyond the moderator. Something I tend to love would be torture at this moment when all I want to do is retreat, knowing that I won't be able to do so once we get back to the house—that my limited time here will have to be spent with Mom. Even though she's the last person whose company I want to be in right now, may heaven forgive me.

A few people come by the podium afterward to ask questions, and I keep my responses friendly but brief. Maral—ninja that she is—infers that I need a respite and keeps Mom occupied with conversation. I take the opportunity to slip out a side door into the gathering dusk.

I'm greeted by a short alleyway that runs off the main street and leads to a parking lot behind the building, the nearby freeway offering some grounding noise. Breathing deep, I focus on the interview I just gave, trying to remember the questions the bookstore rep asked me and what my answers even were, concentrating on concrete thoughts so there's no room for the amorphous but powerful ones that loom just below the surface. Hoping that if I don't give them any headspace, they may dissolve into the evening air.

Over my years of doing the podcast, I've met people with such a range of experiences, the worst of which involved pressure, abuse, even disownment by their families because of the choices they've made. Older generations are often under unimaginable pressure themselves and, whether they're aware they're doing it or not, some pass it down the line. I'm so grateful I never had to experience such worst-case scenarios. *Do you know how lucky you are?* How lucky that my parents never took out their stresses on me. That my aunt and uncle were always within arm's reach when my father worked sixteen-hour days to pay our half of the rent, or when my mother retreated into the bedroom for weeks or months at a time, barely registering the straight A's or awards I brought home in the hopes of offering her a glimpse of happiness. If the worst thing I face is disappointment that I didn't continue to pursue medicine, I'm sitting about as pretty as possible. What right do I have to complain? None whatsoever.

I repeat this to myself, over and over, seeking comfort in the assurance. I'm overreacting—I have no reason to feel anything but grateful for the bounty I've been awarded in this life. I take a deep breath but it goes in shaky, a little wet. I force it down, down.

Do you know how lucky you are? So lucky. So. Lucky.

Just when the right amount of air seems to be filling my lungs, I hear the heavy crunch of a door opening, followed by footsteps. Ryan emerges in the beam of a streetlamp.

"Ana," he starts, but doesn't go on. Because the way he says my name, the concern in his eyes, catapults my heart right into my throat, causing a wobbly breath to rush out before I can stop it.

He clears the space between us in three long strides, and before I know it, I'm in his arms.

Chapter 18

Ryan rubs slow circles on my back, his palm soothing chills I didn't realize I was feeling. He doesn't say anything for many long moments, and neither do I, content to be held even though there's nothing legitimately wrong. Sometimes it's just nice to feel someone's body against yours, right?

Finally, he pulls back. "I'm sorry," he says.

"For what?" I ask.

"That you had to . . . perform. When you're feeling like this."

"I feel great," I say.

"Right. People always flee into dirty alleys when they're feeling great."

"The dumpster aroma boosts serotonin."

A beat passes. "Ana." His voice is gentle, a soft boop right in the center of my chest.

"I'm f—"

"Please don't say you're fine when we both know you're not."

The directness of his words catches me off guard. But I *am* fine—I'm safe; I'm healthy; I'm in my hometown in a free country on the last leg of a successful tour for a bestselling book, reunited with the person who loves me the most in this world. On paper, life can't get any better.

"I just needed a few minutes to myself," I reassure him. "To recharge."

"Recharge? Or gird yourself?"

"Gird myself for what? The event is over."

"But the battle begins," he says.

Before I can refute him, he continues. "That was out of line. I didn't mean—but you should know . . ." He takes a breath. "Your book, your podcast, *So Proud of You* as a concept. You're casting a light into a lot of people's lives. Maybe you're not saving lives in an immediate way as a doctor, but you're making lives a lot more livable. It's important—it's dire—to feel understood. And that's what you're giving people. Don't let anyone tell you that's not worth the immense effort you put into your work."

His words are like a balm over scalded skin, soothing the worst of the burn. *The path you chose was right, or at least okay. You're okay.*

Legs suddenly weak, I sink onto the cement parking block at my feet. He sits too, his thigh grazing mine. Solid, rooted, at my side.

"My dad died a few months before I dropped out of my residency," I say. My voice sounds far away, snatched up by a passing car on the freeway.

Ryan is tuned in to me with his whole body. But he remains quiet, waits for me to continue. Patient. He's so patient—my complete opposite, yet it's something I'm appreciating more every day. He doesn't insist or impose. He just lays open a path before me, inviting me to walk it if I so choose. Making it so easy to take the first step.

That must be why I keep talking, why I tell him—aloud—something I've never shared with anyone.

"When I got into med school, it was the first time I ever saw him cry. He was always stoic, taught from birth that strength means holding it together no matter the circumstances. Even when we immigrated here, even as they lost the only life they'd ever known, he weathered the storm like a lighthouse. My mom . . ." I pause, feeling guilty for revealing a piece of someone's story that isn't mine to tell, but knowing it's necessary to explain my own. "Didn't."

Ryan's warm hand settles between my shoulder blades, but he remains quiet.

"Grief overtook Mom. For a long time. Having to leave behind everything and everyone they knew, build a new life in a place that felt totally alien to them. It was hard on them both. But if my dad felt it, he never let it show. He got out of bed every morning, went to work, put food on the table. Provided. He may not have done it with a smile on his face, but he certainly never shed a tear. Until I got my acceptance letter from Harvard Med. He read it with glistening eyes and wrapped me up in the biggest hug I can remember."

My nose prickles at the memory of his barrel chest, solid as a house. His khoungy scent, potent in the hairs poking out from the collar of his sweater. His beating heart against my ear. Alive.

"He never said it in words, but I know it made him proud. That his child was going to be a doctor." An image of his dark eyes shining in the glow of the kitchen light assails me, and my stomach folds in on itself. "I'd always been self-motivated, but it drove me even harder knowing that I was giving him this . . . gift, after everything he'd given me. That I hadn't squandered it—his sacrifice was worth it, I was delivering on the promise of 'better' for the next generation. An American Dream come true."

Ryan rubs circles on my back again, the movement coaxing me on.

"I was halfway through my residency when he died. It was so sudden, his heart attack. So unexpected. His loss carved this . . . canyon into our lives. Mom needed me so much. I moved back home with her. I still went to work every day. I thought maybe the association with my dad would be a good thing—a way to stay connected to him—but it went the opposite way. I just couldn't hold it together."

Every corner I turned in the hospital reminded me of him. Every chart I examined blurred before my eyes, every code on the PA system echoed in my ears, the smell of disinfectant stung my throat and threatened tears. He'd come to me in images so sharp I could barely breathe through them. There was no safe space. Not at work, and not at home. Mom needed me to be strong, sinking deeper and deeper into a Mom-shaped hole. Sized to hold her and only her.

Nathan and I had been living in a small apartment together for a couple of years by then. When it was clear how lost Mom was, living alone in the house she used to share with her family but that now felt hollow and haunted, I couldn't leave her hanging. She was my mother, I loved her, and she was suffering. I needed to be there for her. *There* being a relative term. I moved back in, took care of everything that needed taking care of, and kept my clouds at bay to spare her. But part of me was operating on a different plane altogether. One that hovered somewhere in midair, muted and bare. By myself.

Nathan was supportive at first, on the surface. Until it became too much to bear for me, the holding it together. Until I thought he might provide a safe space for me to fall apart a little. But Dad's death took a toll on our relationship—the ultimate toll, as it turned out.

"When I saw the response to that first video I made . . . it was like a stone chipped away from the wall around me, letting in a tiny pinprick of sunlight. I felt a kind of good I hadn't for months, since Dad passed. The more time I spent making videos, then starting the podcast and doing speaking events, the better I felt. These things didn't carry the taint that medicine now did. They were fresh and different and mine. And even though it would have broken my dad's heart to know I jumped ship before I ever became a doctor, and my mom is clearly still not thrilled about it, and I don't even know if it was the right thing to do . . ." I trail off, not sure how to put into words this aching need to follow what my heart was desperately screaming for.

"You couldn't not," he says softly, his palm vibrating against my back.

Leave it to Ryan to sum up something so complicated in three simple words. My eyes trace the line of his jaw and the hint of five-o'clock shadow whose exact texture my skin knows intimately. He was beautiful enough without being so empathetic, so supportive, so . . . *Ryan*. His wonderfulness only enhances his looks a hundredfold.

"Have you ever told your mother about this?" he asks.

"I've never told anyone about this," I say.

Maybe it's how much time has passed, the wounds dulled and scabbed over, or maybe it's just that I was ripe for oversharing after what my mom said. But part of me knows there's more to it. That the reason I feel comfortable telling Ryan things that I've never told anyone, that I've never quite admitted to myself in so many words, is that he listens to me in a way nobody ever has. He gets it, or at least tries to with every ounce of himself. Makes it okay, somehow. Like he's taken a heavy backpack off my shoulders, carrying it for me so I can be blissfully unencumbered for a little while.

"Maybe you should tell her," he says. "It could help her understand, or at least lay off the passive-aggressive remarks. So you don't crave space after five minutes of conversation."

"Or move to New York to escape." The words jump from my mouth, unbidden. I clench my jaw, damming any other confessions from leaking out.

But Ryan just nods. He takes my hand, threads our fingers together. The contact seems to stop the guilt from cinching around my throat.

"I thought Celine was going to go to NYU," he says, his deep voice breaking the heavy silence. "She didn't even tell me she'd applied to Berkeley. Didn't want to open a can of worms when she didn't know if she'd get in or not. And when she got her acceptance, she sat on it for weeks. Thought there was no chance I'd let her move across the country and didn't want to confirm her fears, I guess."

My mind is brimming with questions, but I try to take a page out of the Ryan playbook, staying silent and (semi-)patiently waiting for him to go on.

"I didn't consider myself overbearing," he says. "Protective, sure. Raising a child in the biggest city in the country, you have to be. She was so precious to me . . . Every decision I made was to keep her safe. But it read differently to her. She felt trapped. Suffocated.

"When she told me she wanted to move to San Francisco, she led with her arguments against all the reasons she assumed I'd refuse. It was eye-opening. Here she was, just trying to do the best thing for herself, for the future I'd worked so hard to safeguard for her, but overcome with the fear that I'd impede her." He grimaces. "I felt like shit after that conversation, but I'm glad it happened. I needed the push to look inward, to take steps to change the way I related to her. To be what she needed me to be for her."

I squeeze his hand, a small show of gratitude that he shared this with me. "You're a good dad. Brother. Dad-bro." I groan inwardly at myself. "She's lucky that you listen. That you're tuned in to her feelings and open to change. It says a lot about you."

"There were—are—a lot of bumps along the way. *Chill* doesn't exactly come naturally to me."

I hum. "I can relate."

"No kidding," he says, then winks at my faux-affronted gasp. "But if Celine hadn't talked to me about it, I wouldn't have had the chance to at least *try* to step up that way."

Subtext: *Give your mom a chance. Tell her how her actions affect you.* I sigh. "It's not that simple in my case," I say.

"I didn't say it was simple."

How would I even approach talking to Mom about my needs when our dynamic has never made space for them? Not beyond the immediate, base-of-Maslow's-hierarchy ones, at least, and it's been decades since those were on her plate. Would she hear me? What would I even say?

I've been relying on the TV show as the thing that would finally neutralize Mom's issues with my career choice and resolve this problem once and for all. But there are times when I question whether this is even a problem to be resolved. She's just expressing her thoughts and feelings—it's not her job to manage my reactions. Isn't it just a matter of me being less sensitive? Letting it wash off my back? I was always so good at that until . . . Dad. His death stripped the buffer from my head, from my heart, and I could no longer absorb the blows.

But that was years ago. It seems ridiculous for me to hide from someone I love just because she says a few words that make me feel icky. It's time I put on my armor, like the boss I am.

I should get back to her. Maral can only hold her over so long, and she has plans to meet up with friends from college—*she* actually kept in touch with people—which is why she opted to stay in the city instead of Dorchester. Can't say I blame her.

But I don't move. Although I'm in no rush to get started on the next thirty-six hours with Mom, I'm in even less of a hurry to say goodbye to Ryan. Unwilling to examine why his hand feels so good in mine, so right, I opt instead to do something very out of character: Simply stay still. In this moment. With him.

As if he can sense what I'm thinking, he says, "You have my number. Call me anytime you want to talk."

Anytime. Meaning if I need an understanding ear, a shoulder to lean on, a hand to hold. Someone to help carry the heaviness.

"Careful what you offer—I may be blowing up your phone all day," I say.

His eyes shine with a smile that doesn't quite reach his lips. "You can blow it up every day," he says.

Heat prickles up my neck.

Forever, baby.

I swallow around an obstruction in my throat. "Don't worry. Lucky for you, you're officially off the hook."

I don't let him voice the question radiating off his expression, rambling on. "Tonight was the last tour event. You're heading home tomorrow. Hopefully to a job you need to keep on the straight and narrow for. And the Bryant Park event on Tuesday isn't even Woodsworth-related, so, you know." I shrug, like, *that's all she wrote.*

"I'll be at the Bryant Park event on Tuesday," he says.

My stomach flips. "I thought you were just doing publicist duties for the tour. I didn't expect you'd attend the local events after we get back." Assuming he's still employed.

His gaze is steady. "If you're there, I want to be there."

His image blurs before me. My eyes are wet, my fingers trembling as they loosen around his. I stand up, forcing steel into my spine to stop it from turning to goo. My throat feels too tight, constricted. I offer what I hope looks like a smile but may well look like evidence of a neurological disorder.

"Then, I guess . . . I'll see you there. Safe travels home," I say shakily and head toward the door, the clop of my heels on the pavement echoing in the alleyway.

Pushing back through the door, I barely register the lingering patrons; the picked-over displays of my book; the polite goodbyes between Mom, Maral, and Shanthi as we don our jackets and gather our bags at the front of the store. I tap at my Uber app as if in a trance, shuffling Mom into the car on autopilot and participating only in rote conversation on the drive home.

It's not until my phone pings with a message from Nadia as we're speeding down Morrissey Boulevard that I'm jostled from my inertia.

Interest from Scope!

My stomach leaps at the name of the popular L.A.-based TV network, whose bright logo was splattered on more than a few billboards we passed on our way to Glendale just yesterday. A tartness settles in my belly, but that's just how hope feels when it comes as a pleasant surprise.

Yay! I make my fingers type, despite the tension in my shoulders. Already left L.A. tho?

Her response comes a few seconds later. NP, can do zoom mtg next Friday

I take a deep breath, screenshotting the text chain and sending it to Maral. Mom's profile is silhouetted against the moonlight as she talks about the nazook she baked for us to enjoy with coffee tomorrow. This is good. It's good. I exhale slowly.

I'm back in the game.

Chapter 19

The nazook is delicious. So is the Armenian coffee, the dolma, the lahmejoun, the kofte, and every other delicacy Mom toiled over in the days leading up to my arrival. You'd think I was staying for a week with the sheer volume of food she's prepared, so I do my due diligence and stuff myself. The food brings back treasured flashes in time—Maral and I stealing bites off each other's plates at the table and giggling over the yeasty crumbs stuck in our dads' beards; our moms affectionately stroking our heads, gratified to fill our bellies, murmuring *anoush, anoush,* which translates directly to *sweet* but is used to mean *I hope you're enjoying it.* Mom does the same now as I bite into a flaky boreg, her eyes shining with tenderness as she whispers, "Anoush, anoush," and it makes me want to stay in this moment forever. In the love she bestows so freely, the best way she knows how, filling my stomach and my heart.

If only it could always be like this—I would move us to L.A. together right now, to hell with the show. But it isn't long before conversation inevitably veers into unwanted territory again.

Like when Reese Witherspoon's team gets in touch asking me to record a short video for their socials, and I set up in the garden (a scenic backdrop), and Mom watches on confoundedly.

"What's all that for?" She nods at the portable ring light/tripod combo before me.

"It holds the camera and improves the lighting quality for the video."

Her brows rise. "To think you could be traveling with a medical bag. Instead you cart this"—she waves at the setup on the grass—"*equipment* around to make your little videos."

I swallow hard. Count to five, this time with Ryan's suggestion hanging in the back of my mind: to share my needs with her, ask her to stop with the disparaging remarks. Whether she hears me or cares or changes her behavior is up to her, but I could put the ball in her court. I give it a shot.

"Mayrik, that commentary isn't going to help me get this done any faster."

Okay, as far as shots go, it's a weak one. It doesn't exactly convey my needs, but at least it succeeds at stopping the diatribe for now, as she heads inside to set the table for afternoon coffee. Somehow the idea of being any firmer feels more like an intrusive thought than anything—uncharacteristically aggressive, and its likely result needlessly disruptive.

Handily, my visit is short enough that unwelcome conversation is curbed by the various projects she's saved for me to do—packing away the outdoor furniture for the season, clearing the acorn husks from the oak tree out of the gutter, removing unused programs from the ancient desktop computer in the kitchen so it doesn't take ten full minutes to load a single web page. Typical adult–child tasks she won't let me outsource between visits.

I'm lugging a box of extra dishware to the basement (*Why do I need so many plates and cups if I'm the only one here to use them?* she asked wistfully) when my eye catches on a cable-knit sweater vest slung over a brown faux-leather suitcase from the previous century. I set the box on a shelf and pick up the garment, its wool coarse and springy against my fingers. I bring it to my nose.

It's been too long for his scent to remain, but I swear I detect a whisper of it in the fibers. Smoky khoung, warm and homey. Memories—his broad smile, crooked teeth shining bright against his dark beard, soulful eyes glittering under thick brows—rush over me with such potency that my nose burns, the broad gray cables blurring before me. I bury my face in the sweater, breathing him in for long moments, sinking into the feeling, until I hear Mom's footsteps heavy on the basement stairs and drop it like a teenager caught with a joint.

She pauses halfway down the staircase, eyes lingering on the fabric swinging on the edge of the suitcase. Time seems to slow, the basement air heavy, like we're underwater. Movements lethargic, strenuous.

I swipe at my eyes, arrange my face into a smile. "Done down here," I chirp.

She's silent for a long moment, not noticing—whether by true or willful ignorance—anything untoward in my demeanor. "Good. Almost time for dinner."

When my Uber arrives on Monday morning, Mom's wringing her hands by the door, griping about how short my visit was until I hug her, offering assurances that we'll see each other again soon. She hands me a travel cooler full of leftovers, insisting that I share some with Mar, Shanthi, and Ryan on the train back to New York. I promise I will, even though Ryan flew out yesterday so he could be back at work this morning. Today is his potentially consequential meeting that was delayed till the tour ended. I cringe, thinking of Ryan facing a firing squad made up of Woodsworth's top brass and HR, hoping against hope that my email made a dent, and count the minutes until I can text him to see how it went.

There's probably a German word for the feeling of missing something you rejected. Or at least never accepted.

There's probably also a word for climbing out of your skin from missing the touch of someone no longer in your reach. Even my little purple friend hasn't been cutting it. Sex with Ryan has ruined me for masturbation—wouldn't have predicted that. In all the time I've been sexually active, no partner has had that effect. When I was with Nathan and getting it regular—one of the things he praised about me was my ridiculously high libido—I was still insatiable enough to need to auto-stimulate once in a while if he had class or a shift when I was raring to go. It always did the trick, calming my buzzing nerves and settling the tingle in my belly for at least a short while. I've never felt even *hornier* afterward . . . like it was only an amuse-bouche before a favorite main course.

Uncannily, my phone chirrups as the car whizzes up the 93 with a message from Jacob, of ye olde NYC roster. You home yet, gorgeous? Missing you. My bottom lip burns and I realize belatedly that I'm chewing on it. What should be a welcome invitation from a tried-and-true hookup somehow doesn't feel as satisfying as it should. It's probably just because it's been a while. I'll feel differently once I'm back home. I lock my screen without responding just as the car pulls up to South Station.

The three of us agreed to meet at the Starbucks kiosk inside, but Shanthi is alone when I arrive. She nods a hello and hands me a grande cup from the tray she's holding.

"Bless you," I say, the first sip like electricity powering through my veins. "How was your day yesterday? Did you get to see everything you wanted to?"

When Shanthi said she wanted to stay in Boston an extra day and return on Monday with us, Mar and I each invited her to join our respective plans. But Shanthi was quick to decline—this was her first time in Boston and she wanted to explore. Hard to believe she'd rather hit up the many cool neighborhoods, museums, and restaurants than watch me do chores at my mother's house in the suburbs or listen to Maral reminisce about college with strangers. Kids these days.

"It was awesome," she says. "I walked through Beacon Hill and the Charles River Esplanade then to the Back Bay Fens." Mar and I had suggested the parks to her—some of the most beautiful Boston has to offer. Their foliage is at its lushest now, at the tail end of summer, just before it starts to morph into a spectacular kaleidoscope of fall colors. "I wanted to hit up the museums but there wasn't enough time. When are we coming back?"

"Tomorrow, if my mom has anything to say about it. Where's Mar?"

"She texted that she's running late," she says, sipping her own coffee.

"Weren't you staying at the same hotel? Why didn't you come together?"

Shanthi shrugs. "I haven't seen her since Saturday. She just said she had something to do this morning."

"What thing?" I ask, surprised.

"I don't know," she says, tapping her phone to check the time. 10:25 A.M. Ten minutes till boarding.

Weird. We may be out of our routine, but usually I know Maral's plans right down to buying gum at the bodega. What could she have to do that was pressing enough to be squeezed into the few morning hours before our train departs?

It hits me like a defibrillator shock. Checking her phone more frequently and surreptitiously than usual. Evading my questions about it. My suspicion was right—she's seeing someone. Someone in Boston, it appears. They must have spent the night together and couldn't tear themselves away, enjoying each other's *company* one last time before she has to leave.

My heart swells with happiness for her, my goddess of a cousin who deserves for every man in the world to fall at her feet in worship.

Something niggles beneath the surface, though. Maral is seeing someone and she's kept it from me. The concern I had over her evasiveness at the bar last week rises like magma.

Why would she keep this from me?

We've always been totally open with each other about our love lives. Sure, I've only ever had one serious boyfriend, but she had the honor of being privy to every single detail of Nathan's and my relationship—from my budding crush on a fellow student to our first kiss to every date to moving in together to falling apart. I met every boyfriend of hers through high school and college, dutifully on my best behavior when she warned me not to put them off by, quote, *going all Ana*. I even helped her write her profile for dating apps (she wasn't being as effusive about her positive attributes as she should have been, and it's criminal to undersell the wonder that is Maral). What changed?

The coffee turns in my belly. When Maral strolls into the station, bag slung over the shoulder of her lucky emerald-green wrap dress, long black hair flowing behind her like that of a siren calling from the sea, my eyes sting just looking at her.

She's so happy, she's practically radiating with it.

"Sorry I'm late." She's slightly out of breath from her brisk walk. "You look . . . weird," she says, spying my wretched grimace.

"You look spectacular," I say, voice hitching on the last syllable.

"Whoa, what's the matter?" She steps toward me, concerned. "How were things with your mom?" she asks knowingly.

I sniff. "Filling. There's two weeks' worth of dinner for you in this cooler."

She takes in the travel cooler at my feet, then raises worried eyes to me. "Ryan?"

I swallow. "Long gone."

"Have you heard how his meeting went?"

"Not yet," I say. "It started at ten—I'll text him after."

Shanthi waves her phone at us. "Speaking of which, we need to get boarding."

We make our way to the platform, questions cropping up in my mind like moles I keep whacking down, fighting my instinct to hammer Maral with them. She's being secretive for a reason. Badgering her will only cause her to clam up more, probably. So I aim for breezy.

"Where were you?" I ask. It comes out less breeze, more howling gale.

"Just met someone for breakfast." She keeps her gaze averted, busying herself with opening doors, fussing with one of my suitcases.

"Who?"

"Simone James. We did our master's together."

She climbs aboard the train and we're distracted by finding seats, stowing bags, and getting settled. I decide not to press. (Someone give me an award.) Maybe she did meet Simone for breakfast. Maybe she's really wearing her lucky dress for no reason at all—or at least not to impress her secret lover. Hell, maybe Simone's her secret lover and she's not ready to come out yet. What kind of cousin would I be if I pushed that?

Shanthi promptly puts on her noise-canceling headphones, effectively pulling a curtain between us. Maral and I sit side by side across from her, Mar suddenly quite taken with her phone. I check my own. Ryan's meeting is probably almost over. I start to draft a message, erase it, try again, erase that too. Every attempt is either too flirty or too cold. I bite the inside of my cheek, unsure what tone to hit because I'm unsure what we even are at this point. He remains an employee of my publisher—if he hasn't been fired—and we remain . . . friendly. Do I just ignore the undercurrent of what else we've been?

I have to.

I decide on something simple. Hey, hope you got home safe. How did the meeting go?

Easy enough. Sounds like something I'd text to Meredith. That's a good barometer.

I watch the screen, expecting ellipses on his side of the text chain, but nothing comes up. Maybe he's still in the meeting, even though it took me so long to actually write that stupid message that it's well past eleven now, our train chugging toward home. Meetings go long all the time. Would that be a good thing or bad?

Or maybe his lack of response is deliberate. Maybe Woodsworth did let him go and he doesn't want to tell me for fear that I'll feel guilty (accurate). If he's out of a job, he has way bigger fish to worry about than telling me.

"You okay?" Maral asks, making me jump.

"Fine," I say, my tight voice sounding anything but.

Her lashes dip as she glances at the phone in my hand. "Any news?" she asks.

I shake my head.

She reaches for my hand, but I flinch away, and she drops hers.

"Sorry," I mumble.

"As soon as there's anything to share, you'll be the first person he tells."

A sound escapes my mouth, something between *puh* and a choke. "I don't know about that."

"I do," she says.

Something about her tone, its conclusiveness, irks me. "Now you're a Ryan expert?"

To her credit, she takes my impertinence in stride. "I'd have to have spent the past two weeks *buried underground* not to notice that he's got feelings for you beyond just sexual ones."

The very mention of his sexual feelings has my thighs sneaking together. It feels like it's been a month since Ryan touched me, instead of just a few days. How will I go on without it?

"Do you know he called ahead to every daytime event to make sure they served your favorite coffee?" Maral goes on. "You're not a diva, you don't have a rider. But he did it. What about what he said to that dickwad at the Chicago event? And how about the way he stood up to your mom? Vartouhi may not have loved that, but I sure did. And I know you did too."

My chin quivers as visions play on a loop in my mind. Ryan at my side, coming to my defense at the Chicago Q and A. Standing in my doorway that night, asking if I was okay, nobly averting his gaze from my braless breasts. Valuing my work, validating my choices. Sitting with me on cold cement in an alleyway as I reeled from my mother's criticism. Listening with every ounce of his attention. Understanding, empathizing. Rubbing my back. Weaving his fingers through mine.

"It doesn't matter," I say. So defeated it aches. "The tour is over, and he's out of my life now. My personal one, anyway. Maybe also my professional one." The phone—as yet responseless—feels like a lead weight in my hand.

"He doesn't have to be. If he's no longer at Woodsworth, nothing is actually standing in your way. Except you."

"Are you forgetting our plan to move across the country?" Nothing is certain yet, but Nadia and I are meeting with Scope this Friday. Wheels are in motion. And they're going to take me far, far away from Ryan. Which, all the better. Or at least not worse. Right?

She rolls her eyes, muttering, "How could I forget."

"What's that supposed to mean?" I ask. Her lackluster responses to anything L.A.-related lately are beginning to irritate me.

She presses her lips together, hesitates. "Nothing," she says finally. "Just—who knows how long that could take? There's plenty of time to see where things might go with Ryan in the meantime."

"You mean to watch things crash and burn."

Her eyes soften. She tucks her hand through the crook of my elbow, wraps her slender fingers around my biceps. "Ryan isn't Nathan."

"No," I say. "But I'm still me."

And there's the rub. No matter how well things may go at first, there is a side of me that—if revealed—causes the whole house of cards to come tumbling down. It happened with Nathan, and that was hard enough. I couldn't face that with Ryan. He got enough of a peek behind the curtain in Boston, and I'd rather chew on stemware than let him see any more. Would much rather he remain a fond memory than a present heartache.

My phone buzzes, saving Mar from having to muddle through a response to that mic drop. Butterflies take flight in my stomach when I see Ryan's name on the screen. *Finally.*

All is well.

Relief whips through me like a whirlpool, despite the hint of an undertow beneath its surface. The implication of his continued employment at Woodsworth is that there is officially no chance for anything more between us.

Which was always the case, anyway. So, pulse, you can stop your arrhythmic beating now, thank you.

I share the news with Mar and ignore the disheartened look in her eye that indicates she's also connected those dots. I'm starting to respond when I get another buzz.

How are you? How'd it go with your mom?

I slump back in my seat. Of course. Even as he's facing what is surely an intensely stressful day back at work, he asks after me.

Fine, I start to type, then erase it, remembering the way he scolded my oft-used refrain. But I clam up at the idea of answering with something too real, feeling like I'd be giving too much credence to what we shared in that alleyway two nights ago. Not only to him, but to myself.

At the same time, it feels wrong to brush him off. After everything.

Could have been worse, I finally write.

True, he responds. You could have been camping.

A laugh bubbles out of me. I send a skull-and-crossbones emoji, follow up with Food was amazing, at least.

His response comes back. But how was the coffee?

A smile spreads across my face like watercolor paint. I send him a drooling emoji in response. Consider whether I should write that I'll see him tomorrow. He did say he'd come to my keynote at the Lead Tomorrow conference on Tuesday, and I assume he's still planning to. Though . . . who knows. It's not strictly a book event. No reason for anyone from Woodsworth to be there, least of all the head of publicity who was only assigned to my tour at the last minute due to a staffing change. One who was caught in flagrante delicto with an author on camera, no less, and almost got fired for it. Surely they've reassigned him now—maybe even warned him to keep his distance, for optics' sake. Which . . . all the better. Ryan will move on, work on other books, sleep with other women, and maybe find one whose heart is a cozy refuge rather than a haunted house.

My shoulders feel heavy. I sink into the worn upholstered seat, closing out of the text chain.

Before I swipe out of the app, another message catches my eye. The one Jacob sent this morning.

My thumb hovers over it for a moment before I give in, tapping it open. I type—Heading back now; hit you up soon—and before I let myself think about it, I press Send.

Chapter 20

The Lead Tomorrow conference is held at the public library in Bryant Park, aka the most magical location in all of New York.

They've rented one of the bigger event spaces this year, since their attendance is much higher than it was the last time I was invited. So high that I can't pick out faces in the crowd. The spotlight shining in my eyes doesn't help. Still, I can't help scanning the silhouetted heads in the glorious salon, hoping but failing to see one specific one.

I guess he changed his mind after all. Which is fine. He has every right, doesn't owe me anything. It would be *weird* for him to show up here. Right?

Intermittently, my eyes land on their true north: Maral. Seated at a table near the front and to the left of the stage, a sweating glass of water standing untouched beside her conference packet. Her dark eyes as grounding as the hardwood floor beneath our feet.

Shanthi's not here—I gave her a few days off in exchange for being on 24/7 for almost two full weeks, plus the overtime she racked up fielding notifications during Kissgate. Girl has earned a vacation. (And she'll get one: I booked her a spa day tomorrow, the gift card tucked into a delivery of a case of her favorite red wine.)

When I wrap up my keynote and step down from the stage amid a chorus of applause, people rush the small staircase before I even descend, questions and kind words and entreaties for selfies and endorsements ricocheting off me like pellets. They speak over each other with no regard for others doing the same. Ah, New York. It's good to be home.

After the crowd thins, I inch toward Maral, who's chatting with someone with brilliant red hair pulled into an artful chignon who gestures animatedly as she speaks.

Meredith!

I gallop at them and practically knock her down with the force of my embrace, her puff of laughter blowing back strands of my hair.

"It's you, it's really you!" I pull back and hold her by the shoulders. "What are you doing here?"

"As if I would miss the one event I could actually make it to!" she gushes.

"But you're not my publicist anymore," I say. "You're not even at Woodsworth anymore as of this week."

"What does that have to do with anything? I'm still your number one fan."

I crush her to me in another hug, Mar beaming at us over Meredith's shoulder.

"How's the new job?" I ask.

"Great so far—thank you for the flowers, by the way. That was so sweet of you."

I wave her off. "Those were a Trojan horse. Keep your enemies closer and all that."

She laughs, her blue eyes sparkling. "Oh, I've missed you."

Her arms give under my squeeze. "Tell us everything."

"Well," she says, "today was only my second day, but the people are really nice, I inherited some exciting projects, and I have an *office*. With a *window*!"

I gasp, knowing what a coup this is. The cubicle farm that was the PR department at Woodsworth left much to be desired.

"Coming off a fresh *New York Times* placement didn't hurt," she says with a wink. "Speaking of which, *bestselling author*, how was the tour?"

"Not as good without you there."

"I know, I wish I could have gone. But seems like Ryan did a great job?"

There is not a hint of solicitousness in her tone, even though she would obviously have seen the photo and knows things weren't strictly professional between Ryan and me on the trip.

"He was excellent," Mar puts in, saving me from having to navigate any potential awkwardness. "Except for the last-minute reorg in Chicago, every event went off without a hitch. If you couldn't be there, he really was the next best thing."

"Oh *yay*," Meredith says. "I mean, I knew he'd kill it—he's a friggin' rock star. Woodsworth will be sorry to lose him."

My eyes shoot wide. "What do you mean, lose him?"

She looks from me to Maral, then back to me. "Shit. My big mouth. Sorry, I thought he would have told you. Don't worry—your book is still in good hands. Alison knows the whole campaign, and some *excellent* candidates are interviewing for my position—"

I shake my head. "Meredith, relax, that's the last thing I'm thinking about. I trust the team."

She's visibly relieved. "Oh. Phew."

"But," I say, my stomach hollow, "I thought his job was safe. That . . . what happened . . . didn't endanger it."

Her hand darts out. "Oh my god, he didn't get fired. From what I heard, they were willing to forgive the transgression because, well . . . they were told there wasn't any coercion," she says, confirming that my email had something to do with their assessment, "and *SPOY* was going to be reassigned to my replacement after the tour anyway."

"If he didn't get fired, why are they losing him?" Maral asks.

Meredith's head swivels between my cousin and me. "He resigned."

A boulder, heavy and cragged, lands in my stomach. "*What?*"

"Yesterday," she says. "Alison told me."

So when he texted me that *all is well* yesterday, he didn't mean he was still employed, but that he *resigned*?

"But . . . *why?*" I ask, completely dumbfounded.

She shrugs. "That I don't know."

I aced advanced calculus, yet my mind grasps at the pieces of this equation like so many wet eels, slipping and sliding out of its grasp.

Why would Ryan leave Woodsworth? He was in the end zone—his position safe. At a company that matches Celine's sizable tuition fees and would save them from years and years of debt. Why would he walk away from that?

The photo. He must have resigned because of that. I consider the scandal of it and a cringe creeps up in me like a weed through cracked paving stones. Even though Woodsworth didn't fire him over it, the very fact that he was caught kissing an author would scar his reputation. How can he face his colleagues if they know what he's done? How can he work alongside them when a twelve-thousand-pound elephant is trampling everything in the room?

A hurricane brews in my gut. He didn't want to put me in an uncomfortable position, but turns out I put him in one. I crossed his professional boundaries, and Ryan, a man of immeasurable honor, *had* to step down from his post. Fuck. *Fuck*.

My pulse roars in my ears, my legs suddenly weak. I steady myself against a chair, clutching it as though it's a lifesaving device in a swirling ocean storm.

Meredith gathers her bag from where she perched it on the banquet table. She and Maral are wrapping up their conversation, and I shake myself back to the moment.

"Don't be a stranger, okay?" I say to Meredith. "Let's grab lunch soon."

"I'd love that," she says. "And drinks too! We need to celebrate *this one's* big news." She pinches Mar's arm.

My cousin freezes, pure petrification overtaking her face.

"Big news?" I ask. I'm still reeling from the Ryan news—have I been so distracted by my own shit that I've somehow missed something? Or is this related to Maral's mysterious recent caginess? No, there's no chance Meredith would know whatever it is that Maral is not even willing to tell me.

Still, Mar's expression tells me that Meredith has let slip yet another juicy piece of gossip. One that she specifically does *not* want me to know about.

Meredith looks caught out, appropriately sheepish. "Shit," she says. "I thought you knew . . ."

Maral glares at her, like, *Are you fucking kidding me? Shut! Up!* Knowing that she's stuck, that I won't let her get away with an excuse this time, she turns to me. "I was going to tell you. I was just working up the nerve."

Oh god. Is her secret boyfriend really a secret fiancé? Secret baby daddy? She has been looking extra glowy lately—

"I've been offered a job as a consultant at the Metropolitan Planning Agency. In Boston," she says quickly. Ripping off a Band-Aid. "And I've accepted."

Chapter 21

"I'm sorry," I say. "I thought I just heard you say you've taken a *job*? In *Boston*?"

Maral shoots a *save me* look at Meredith, who excuses herself, says she'll talk to us soon, I believe apologizes a few more times—I don't know, the thunder in my brain is so loud it's drowning her voice out—and books it.

My head feels stuffed with cotton, or steel wool. Barbed wire.

This can't be happening. Maral—my Maral.

"I was going to tell you," she says.

"*When?*" I ask. "After you told my *ex–book publicist?*"

"Ayn, please calm down."

I try my very best to obey the command. Try to breathe, to find some chill in the roiling volcano that is my mind. But it's no use.

What is *happening*? Does nobody keep their goddamn jobs anymore?

I collapse into a chair, leaning over, head in my hands. Mar sits in the one next to me, gingerly, as though it's a land mine.

"I'm sorry," she says. "This is not how I wanted you to find out. It's not personal. I just . . . I've been feeling like maybe *So Proud of*

You has . . . run its course for me. I really want to contribute to climate action, put my degrees to use." Her voice is small when she says, "I never stopped wanting to."

My insides crumble like a sandcastle in the rain. The shock is so overwhelming that I have to remind myself to keep breathing.

How could Maral leave behind what we've built? The people whose lives we touch every day? Me?

How will I go on without her? I've never done a single podcast episode without her by my side.

Now I understand why she's been so weird about L.A. every time it's come up recently. But we've been pursuing that for ages. What about all our plans? She's moving to the literal opposite side of the country, even farther away than we've been from her parents all this time. And for what? To follow her freaking *dreams*?

Okay, that's a good reason.

Through the betrayal and shock, I can't help the pride that seeps through. The happiness I feel for her. The gratitude that she's stuck with *SPOY*, with me, for so long while secretly wishing she could be somewhere else. The guilt over limiting her in what she wanted to do with her life. This angel, this queen, worthy of every good thing the world has to offer.

Questions pile up and snake through my mind, bottlenecking and becoming trapped before they reach my mouth. I want to scream and rail. I'm in a place too public to feel this much hurt.

I stand up, test the ground beneath my feet, make sure it's solid and not the quicksand it feels like.

"I need some space," I say weakly. Then, with a bit more strength, I add, "Congratulations."

"Ayn," she says. A plea.

Her look of dejection tugs on my sympathy. My beautiful Maral. I reach out and clasp her hand, the most reassurance I can muster in this moment, before walking out of the salon and into the vast darkness beyond.

The doors leading to Fifth Avenue crunch loudly as I push through them and outside, inhaling the humid late-summer air in gasping breaths.

Hold it together. Get home, get alone. Then you can let yourself feel it.

At the base of the wide stairs, someone is racing toward the entrance. Someone so familiar now, so welcome, that I feel I may split in half at the sight of him.

Ryan.

He came.

He reaches me halfway up the broad staircase, breathing heavily from running. "Shit," he says. "Did I miss it?"

Miss my life falling apart? I nod weakly.

"Are you okay?" he asks, stepping closer. "I'm sorry, I had a thing and didn't expect it to go so long, and then there was traffic and my cab got stuck—I wanted to be here for it. I feel awful, I'm so sorry I missed it."

He looks wretched with guilt. This man who owes me nothing yet gives me everything. I can't stop myself, stepping onto the stair just above the one he's standing on, walking directly into him, and burying my face in the concentrated scent of him at the base of his neck. Breathing deep for the first time since the ground collapsed beneath my feet and stole all the oxygen from my lungs.

His arms go around me so quick it's as if they don't obey the laws of physics. And I'm cocooned, comforted, coveted. His touch is a snake charmer's song, stoking the emotions in my belly, manipulating them to rise. They crowd up my throat, threatening to spill out, and I swallow hard, push them down again. Step back, breaking contact.

"What happened?" he asks.

I want to tell him. Want to share the heaviness so he might hold some of it for me, ease its weight with his understanding, his care. His Ryanness.

But I can't. I'm too raw—the walls around my heart papyrus-thin and ready to crumble. And if they do, that's it. There's no protection left.

I know from brutal experience that the price for that level of intimacy is too high. And I'm less equipped to pay it right now than ever.

"You resigned," I say.

His face falls.

"Meredith has a mouth like the Grand Canyon, apparently," I say.

He sighs, rubbing his jaw. "I didn't want to worry you. Your book is in good hands there, my leaving won't impact—"

"My book is the least of my worries," I say. "Ryan, did you resign because of me? Because of what happened between us?"

"No," he rushes to say, reaching for me but then thinking better of it, dropping his hands to his sides. "I mean, yes, but—"

"*Fuck.* I'm sorry," I say, my voice cracking. "I'm so sorry I crossed boundaries. I put you in an impossible position."

"Ana, that's not . . ." He swallows. "I wanted you more than I've ever wanted anything."

"Even more than keeping your job?"

"Yes," he says faintly.

Butterflies are staging a mutiny in my belly. "You said Woodsworth served your greatest needs."

"It did. Before. I've . . . reevaluated."

"Reevaluated how?" I ask.

"I just signed on with Merit. As director of publicity."

My heartbeat is erratic. That was fast. The kiss photo went out just last Thursday, and he had a new job by Monday morning? "Wait, Merit, the entertainment company? You want to leave publishing altogether?"

He waggles his head. "Not necessarily, but they're staffed to the gills there, which means that at my level it's a lot of strategy and oversight but not as much hands-on work. It'll mean fewer hours spent putting out fires. More time to myself. More opportunities to pursue things I want."

A single ray of relief peeks through the dark clouds of dread. "Like writing?" I ask, voice so hopeful I could be a wide-eyed Disney princess.

"Yeah. For one thing." His gaze dips for a moment. "Someone wisely told me I should put my own needs first for once."

A shaky smile reaches my lips, gratification tugging behind my rib cage. If nothing else, at least our acquaintance has given him this—the impetus to follow his own path.

But I know life isn't that simple. Prioritizing himself necessarily means letting down the person he cares about most. "What about Celine's tuition?"

"The pay is good, but it won't cover the difference entirely." His shoulder lifts in a half shrug. "So we'll have a bit more debt. No different than anyone else in this country."

While that part is certainly bittersweet, my heart swells knowing that, after a lifetime of taking care of everyone else, Ryan is finally taking care of himself. He said that writing is who he is. What could be more important than serving your true self?

"I'm happy for you," I say. "I didn't know Merit even had offices in New York."

He nods, not meeting my eyes. "In Tribeca—that's where I'm coming from. Met the team for a celebratory drink." His Adam's apple works on a swallow. His chest expands as he takes a deep breath. "They also have offices in L.A."

The air feels thin, the ambient street noise going quiet. *Breathe*, I tell myself. "L.A.?"

"Good to have options," he says quietly. Slowly, so slowly, his gaze lifts to mine. "If you're there, I want to be there."

Something unfurls in my chest, a rosebud's petals unsticking in a slow, radiant bloom. Tears rise up my throat, the emotions that Maral's revelation brought forth making themselves known. I bite my lip to stem them, Ryan watching the movement with concern etched on his face.

His hands fly up in surrender. "I heard you when you said you only want something casual . . ."

He pauses, and for a fleeting, heart-fluttering moment, I wonder if he'll offer to keep this going on my terms. Take what he can get—fuck me when I want him and not expect anything more. My heart is beating double-time as I try to figure out if I'd take him up on it. It'd be win-win, right?

So why does it feel like lose-lose?

"I went with it, because . . . because I just wanted you so fucking bad, I'd take you any way I could get you." He shakes his head. "But I'm sure you've figured out that I'm not exactly a casual type of person, and I *definitely* don't feel casual about you. I never have." His throat works. "So I'm going to honor my needs once and for all and tell you that I want something real with you, Ana."

That brittle wall in my chest cracks and crumbles away, a sinkhole behind it that grasps and claws to pull him inside. To swallow up his heart, this gift he keeps trying to give me but that I, ingrate that I am, keep refusing to take.

But sinkholes don't target what they swallow up. They consume indiscriminately. The good along with the bad. A dark, yawning mouth hungry not only for the good that is Ryan, but for the dangers—the utter devastation—inherent in giving my whole self to him. Those fracture lines in my heart, hastily superglued so many years ago against any further pain, won't be able to withstand the test. This knowledge is fossilized, deep within the cavernous pit.

"Ryan," I say, my voice cracking, "I can't be what you need."

His eyes are so soft. "Hard to believe. Since you already are."

"You don't know me. Not really. If you did, you wouldn't want me."

He frowns, taking a step up. Closer to me. "I know that you're strong. And smart. And caring, and thoughtful. That when you love someone, like your cousin or your mom or even your content manager, you give them every ounce of yourself. I know being with you makes me feel more like myself than I ever have in my life. No matter the circumstance—listening to audiobooks on trains, or feeding you orgasms in bed, or crying in alleyways—I never don't want to be in your presence."

My insides feel as though they're filling with helium. Any moment, I'll float away.

"I know that the only time you stop fidgeting is when you're unconscious." He leans closer. "I know how breathtakingly beautiful you are when you sleep, and how your hand reaches for mine under the covers like it doesn't even realize it."

My breathing is shallow. *My* hand reaches for *his*?

"I know enough," he says. "I know enough to want to know everything."

I'm trembling so hard that he finally makes contact, gently holding me by my arms. "I know you've been hurt. I may not know all the details of your past, and you don't have to share them with me if you don't want to, but Anahid . . ." His thumbs rub back and forth on my biceps, spreading that unmistakable Ryan warmth through the fabric of my blazer. "I'll never be callous with your heart. I promise, I'll keep it safe. Protect it. Cherish the privilege of having it in my care."

Tears spill over my lash lines, sending wet spots onto the silk of my white camisole. My heart, its sutures holding together so tenuously, knows it can trust his words. Knows that Ryan would treat it with utmost tenderness. That it would be safer than it's ever been, sealed away from peril in the lockbox of his love.

But even if my ruined heart could figure out how to trust, my brain has a longer memory. Nothing lasts. Not romantic love, nor any love. Nobody stays by your side forever, not even the people who are unconditionally tied to you.

I take a breath, razor blades in my airways. "Ryan," I whisper. My face is damp, downcast. "If I could, I would. But . . ." I worry my lip, not meeting his eyes. Not having the courage, the resolve. Sure that the moment I do, I'll snatch it back, fall at his feet, and offer him everything. Damn the consequences.

"Can you seriously tell me you don't feel anything for me?" he asks. No edge, all earnestness.

"It's not that simple—"

"I didn't say it was." His voice is so gentle. "But admitting that would be a good first step."

Toward what? Being *known*? I've already been through that fire and lived to drag the scorched wreckage in my wake.

"I can't do that," I say.

"Can't?" he asks. "Or won't?"

I don't answer, and he doesn't push me to. He simply drops his hands, my arms suddenly cold at the absence of his touch, and nods.

He's quiet for a long moment. Jaw working. Wheels turning behind his eyes. "I wish there was a way I could be in your orbit and not feel . . ." He gestures broadly with his hands. "It's been hard enough to deny it all this time—it would be impossible now. I can't do that to myself."

As far as goodbyes go, it's devastating. *Final.* "Ryan," I say. Whimpering.

"Good luck with your TV show." His voice is thick, strained. "And with everything."

I reach for his hand, and he doesn't snatch it away. In fact, he grips mine tight, uses it to pull me close. Guiding me into his chest, wrapping his arms around me, burying his face in my neck, my hair, breathing deep. One last time. He whispers into my skin, but I can't hear the words over the reverberation in my ears. I turn my face, my lips finding his like a homing beacon. He kisses me gently, his heart hammering against my chest, my face wetting his.

I clench my eyes shut against the tears that continue to spill out, dripping on the shoulder of his jacket. When he presses his lips to my forehead, I dissolve out of his embrace more than I pull away. Legs numb, I take one step, then two. Down the staircase, away from Ryan, my descent feeling like a tumble down the side of a mountain.

Chapter 22

I spend the next day in a daze. When I finally draw open the blackout curtains, the sun is already high in the sky. I slept later than I have in ages. My body feels like it got hit by a semi, so I forgo a workout and crawl back into bed.

I scoffed when Maral insisted we not schedule anything into our calendar for today or tomorrow—she'd reasoned that we'd be bushed from the tour and back-to-back events—but now I'm grateful. Well, grateful that I don't have to figure out how to put on the public persona today. Not grateful for yet another reminder that Maral is brilliant and regularly saves me from myself.

My apartment is a maze of Maral triggers—the den where we record podcasts, the kitchen where she and only she ever cooks anything, the closet filled with clothes that are at least a third hers. She's come here practically every day for the past five years. And she was no stranger before that.

How on earth am I going to survive without her?

Beyond the heartache, I can't face the fact that I'll have to find a new brand manager. That someone other than Maral will run the *SPOY* brand, handle my entire calendar, have access to my whole life, be my right-hand woman. It's laughable that anyone could measure even halfway up. She gets it. She gets me. We grew up in the same house—in the same *room*. She knows how to talk me down when I'm spiraling. And, more importantly, she knows when to leave me alone.

Except now, when her name is blowing up my texts like it's the end times. Which, hell, it is.

I slump out of bed and to the kitchen, find my stash of edibles, and pop a gummy into my mouth. It takes effect pretty quickly on my empty stomach, softening the edges on my emotions, dulling my racing mind, and allowing me to doze for the rest of the morning.

When the door buzzer sounds, I snap awake, disoriented. I shuffle toward the entryway, expecting Maral on the threshold, but instead find the doorman, Henry, holding an elaborate bouquet of autumnal flowers.

"Afternoon, Ms. Movilian." *Afternoon?* I feel like a teenager—sulkiness and all. "These came for you. Shall I bring them inside?"

I take the vase from his hands, vaguely aware that I haven't showered or even brushed my teeth yet today. "I can take them, Henry, thanks."

I bid him a good day and carry the arrangement to the kitchen island, where I pluck out the card.

> Congratulations on week 2 on the NYT list! xx, Nadia

Well, shit. The things you miss when you ignore your phone for an entire day.

I can't help the pang at how differently the news hits compared to last week, when Ryan showed me the email from Meredith. When both of them were still at Woodsworth. When I felt like I was on top of the world—on tour for a successful book and savoring the best sex of my life.

It feels like another era. Has it really only been a week?

I dig my phone out to text a quick thank-you to Nadia, and the number of notifications makes my eyes water. Normally I'd hand this machine of overwhelm to Maral and have her triage the situation. But that's no longer an option. And further, she's added to the stress with a dozen texts of her own.

can I come over?

ayn, talk to me.

i'm sorry. please understand.

boyid mernem.

I navigate back to the messages menu, chest pinching when I see Ryan's name, unbolded and way down the list, our last exchange from two days ago when I was on the train home from Boston.

Jacob's name, by contrast, is bolded with an unread message whose preview shows a series of emojis that would make me blush if I were anywhere near the mood. I can't imagine touching another man again. Except the one crowding my mind like he owns the joint.

I turn off the screen, leave the device on the counter, and crawl back into bed.

By Thursday morning, I'm sick of my bed, my apartment, my own maudlin company. I am not built to be alone for long periods of time, and a full day of self-imposed solitary confinement feels like a month.

I pull on my running clothes and venture into the muggy late-September air. My usual route—east to the park and then a loop around the reservoir—doesn't feel like enough today, so I add some miles through the North Meadow. I set a punishing pace, my loud breaths overpowering the comfort read I plugged into my ears. Still, Michelle Obama's voice as she recounts her college counselor telling her she wasn't fit for Princeton, even half heard, is a better companion than my own unfiltered thoughts. I've had quite enough of those.

I wind my way back through the park toward home, panting, my legs weak and wobbly.

Henry opens the door as I approach, a broad smile on his face. "You have a visitor," he tells me. "I been wonderin' where she's been! Usually see her every day."

On the bench near the elevator bank, settled in like she's been waiting for hours, sits Maral.

Even though seeing her face feels like slipping into fleece pajamas right out of the dryer on a cold day, and even though some part of me wants so deeply to forget the past few days and rejoice in her company, I'm still deep in some feelings, and I can't be letting them run me ragged with her here.

She stands, raising the strap of her purse to her shoulder. "Hi."

I nod. "Hi."

Henry's head swivels between us before he gets the hint and steps back outside.

"Maral, I don't think I'm ready to talk about it yet. I'm still processing—"

"I've given you enough space. Too much, I think." She sounds... angry? Or something.

I thought you wanted to give me all the space in the world. Or the country, at least. I can't control the thought but kick myself for my petulance.

Her tone softens. "Please don't shut me out."

At the shine in her eyes, the plea in her voice, my heart turns to mush. I relent, pressing the call button on the elevator.

Inside my apartment, Mar takes in the bouquet on the kitchen counter. "Congratulations on the *New York Times*. I called but you didn't answer. Just like you didn't respond to any of my texts."

I pour myself a glass of water. "I kinda unplugged yesterday."

She watches me take a sip. "I know. People have been calling me to ask where you are."

"People?" I ask, knowing better than to hope that includes one specific person. Knowing better but hoping anyway.

"Nadia, Alison, Grayson from the Infinitude Symposium."

Right. The conference I'm booked to speak at tomorrow evening. I'm grateful for my cousin handling work-related correspondence when I clearly haven't been up for it. Who will run interference for me once Maral's no longer here? My eyes prick again, and I crumple onto a stool.

"Does Shanthi know?" I ask.

She shakes her head. "I didn't want to tell her before talking to you."

I make a face. "You told Meredith."

She winces. "I'm sorry about that. She was raving about her new job, and how much happier she is working in educational publishing—how it was fulfilling this dream she'd forced into dormancy for so long. I've been . . ." Her shoulders sag. "I've been feeling that myself, and I guess I just couldn't hold it in."

"So you pulled an Ana?" I say.

She seems encouraged by my joke. "Blurters gonna blurt."

I sigh. "I wish you'd told me."

"Because you'd have been so receptive," she says.

Her statement settles on my chest like a heavy stone. Sweet Mar. She's denied herself for so long, for my sake. And the one person she should have been able to talk to wasn't there for her. My petulance retreats like the tide, replaced by guilt. "I wish you'd felt comfortable enough to confide in me. I'm sorry I wasn't a safe place for you."

Her eyes dart up to mine, and there's so much in them—

hesitancy, anticipation . . . hope. "I should have told you anyway." She shakes her head. "I don't think I realized how much it was calling me until I forced myself to stop and, like, listen to it. When I met with Kamila, she told me about this role they were looking to fill at the MPA, and it made it all seem so . . . possible."

She met her grad school friend, Kamila, for lunch a month ago when she was here for some urban planning conference. Now that I remember, Mar was particularly pensive afterward, less talkative on the podcast episode we recorded that afternoon.

"You've been pursuing this for a month?" I ask. This has all been happening under my nose and I've been so oblivious. So self-involved that my favorite person in the world has been struggling with this life-changing decision without my support.

"The conversation started a month ago," she says. "I had an introductory call with her team. But it's been ramping up over the past couple weeks, lots of emails, defining the role, and then I met everyone in person when we were in Boston." She looks appropriately contrite saying this last part.

And it all clicks into place. Keeping her phone close to her chest, being late for the train in Boston the other morning, wearing her lucky dress—not sex-lucky but interview-lucky.

Air judders out of my lungs, and my nose burns. Everything—all of this—without my even knowing. I should have been in her corner, cheering her on, wishing the best for her. She deserved *at least* that much from me.

I can't go back in time and fix that. But I can do the next best thing—I can be here in this present moment. And in every moment after.

I round the counter and pull her into a hug. At first she remains still, in shock, then her arms come around me with such speed it's as if she thinks I'll disappear if she doesn't clutch me to her.

"I'm so happy for you," I say into her hair, my voice shaky with tears.

"Yeah," she says slowly. "You sound *real* happy."

"This is happy crying," I wail.

She squeezes me, not letting go. "You don't have to be happy," she says. "I'll settle for acceptance."

"You've got both. And don't worry," I qualify, "I'm still very sad for me."

She laughs wetly and then pulls away from me. "Sad and smelly," she says, looking down at her dress, wrinkled now from embracing my sweaty body. "How long since you showered?"

"Hey, I've been wallowing."

"Well, wallow yourself into some soap, please." She waves a hand in front of her nose. "Because ew."

I grumble, pointing at her face. "Don't push it."

She follows me to the bathroom in a routine as old as *SPOY*. I undress and step into the stream of water as she tells me more about the job, the things she's excited about and the things making her nervous. I listen and tell her in various ways that she's the smartest and most valuable employee anyone could ever hire, that the Metropolitan Planning Agency is lucky to have her, and that if they don't realize it, they'll have me to answer to.

As I dress, I feel marginally more human, due less to the cleanliness and more to the normalcy of having Maral in our shared space again. Then I remember that soon this won't happen anymore, and my chin starts wobbling again.

Mar tries to bolster me. "Nadia says Scope is excited to see your talk tomorrow night."

My stomach drops. I have been avoiding facing reality for two days, and part of that was ignoring the fact that I have to go up onstage at the Infinitude Symposium tomorrow and be jazz-hands Ana for the two thousand people attending, not to mention the thousands more who will tune in to the Instagram Live that Shanthi will be streaming of the event. Nadia emailed me over the weekend to let me know that Scope, with whom I'm meeting in the morning, will also be tuning in. So they can see my screen charisma in action, I guess.

Reading my reaction, Mar says, "I'll be there with you. It's going to go great—you can do this talk from memory at this point. I'll bet they sign you immediately. You're going to get everything you want."

I blow out a breath. "Not everything. Not you. Not—" I stop myself, not sure how I almost slipped and said his name when he wasn't on my mind for once.

Or wasn't he? Isn't he always right below the surface, simmering like a riptide, ready to draw me under?

Maral presses her lips together, reading the subtext. I'm wearing sweats and one of her MIT T-shirts—represent—but feel exposed under her gaze.

"Your parents are gonna be *pissed*," I say, pushing through the moment. "Just when we dangled the carrot of you moving closer to them."

"*We?*" she asks pointedly. Then she sighs. "I honestly don't think I care. I mean, not that I don't care. I'm just . . . making a concerted effort to care less. I don't want to be guilted into a life I don't really want."

My stomach knots. Have I been doing that to her? Guilting her into staying on with *SPOY* when she would have rather been somewhere else? I feel dizzy again and sit on the edge of my rumpled bed.

"I don't think you should be, either," she adds.

I lift my chin. "I'm not being guilted. I'm the one who's pushing the move to L.A."

"Yeah, but is that what you really want?"

"Why does everyone keep asking me that?"

"Because it matters," she says. "What you want matters, Ana. What you feel matters. Your mom doesn't think so, but it does."

Whoa. What's this, now, Throw Our Parents Under the Bus Day? "That's not fair."

She scoffs. "You know what's not fair? Putting all your shit on your child."

"She doesn't do that—"

"No?" Her voice is strident now—like she's had this conversation locked and loaded and is finally getting to pull the trigger. "What about when Vahag died?"

My breath catches, sticks. "What about it?"

"It was all about her. She didn't let anyone else grieve him."

"She'd just lost her husband! She was broken."

"You'd just lost your dad," she says. "So were you."

I shake my head but it feels stiff, uncooperative.

"You needed space to grieve just as much as she did," Mar says. "But she sucked all the air out of the house, didn't let you share the pain. Didn't let you even feel it—keeping you running all the time."

She's not being fair. I *wanted* to keep busy, do the arrangements, the paperwork, the upkeep. I wanted to run, needed to hustle. Mom may have benefited, but it was my choice. It was my choice.

"And then that fair-weather fucker wouldn't let you grieve, either," she says, and it doesn't take a leap to know who she's referring to.

Nathan had never seen that side of me—a side I'd never let into the light of day, because some part of me knew it was unwelcome. I'd never needed to, until then. I'd always been able to be the bright, sparkling Ana everyone loved, because the Persian rug had never been yanked out from beneath her feet before. Because she had never lost everything before.

And he didn't know what to do with it. Suddenly his girlfriend was a completely different person, one he didn't recognize. One who didn't provide a reliable escape. Who was once always smiling and energetic and ready for a good time, for a hot fuck, for a boost before a tough exam or entertaining small talk at parties. The girlfriend he signed up for was gone, and in her place was a hollow chasm with smoke billowing out of its center.

No wonder he didn't want me anymore.

"I wish I'd been there more," Maral says. "I should have been."

I shake my head. "You were in the middle of a grueling master's program. And anyway, I didn't need someone there with me. I was fine."

"Fine!" she cries, and it's loud. Loud enough that I wonder if Henry will come up here and ask what's going on. "You were not *fine*, Ana. You were playing a part for your mom and for Nathan, but that's not the same as being fine. That's toxic positivity talking."

What the actual fuck? "What are you talking about?"

She huffs. "Do you ever think about how we were never, like, *allowed* to feel anything other than happiness? Gratitude? Subservience?"

My brows draw together. "Maral, if you're mad at our parents over something—"

"I'm not *mad* at our parents. I'm just seeing things a lot more clearly than I have before. Their way of thinking. How it's affected us, and not for the better."

I'm trying to follow what she's saying, but I'm not sure I'm ready for where it leads. Still, she presses on.

"They went through some tough shit, I'm not negating that," she says. "Starting life all over again here, raising us, and trying to integrate into a foreign culture." She watches me carefully, making sure I'm listening. "But they used that against us. Anytime we were upset about anything, from a scraped knee to a B on a report card to a mean kid at school, it was always 'That's nothing' or 'You should be so lucky' or 'Do you know what other people have to live through?'"

"That was just their way of helping us get over things."

"Did it help you get over things?" she asks.

"I mean, I never got a B," I say, buffing my nails on my T-shirt.

Her eyes narrow. "Did it help you feel less shitty when you were feeling shitty?"

I search our surroundings blindly. "There's nothing anyone can do to help you stop feeling shitty."

"Yes, there is," she says. "There are a lot of things. Listening, for one. But they never did, and we stopped telling them. We stopped ever showing any negative emotions around them, because we were only ever berated for it. But we were rewarded for being good, grateful, deferential daughters, so we assumed those roles full-time."

"Great! So they raised us to be good, grateful people. I'm not seeing the problem here."

"The problem," she says, "is that you bury any emotions that aren't one-hundred-percent positive all the time. Not only with family, but with *everyone*."

"Did you ever consider that I'm just a positive person?" I paste on my winningest smile.

"You aren't. You're fucking miserable sometimes, and you think you're hiding it but you're not. And you shouldn't." Her eyes are glistening now.

Something viscous spreads in my throat. At her words, but also at her tears. "Hey," I say, stepping toward her.

She swipes at a drop that escapes her long lashes. "You've always been the rock. For me, for your parents. We've relied on you so much. Too much. I'm guilty of it too. I let things go. Let you retreat. I enable it."

I'm at a loss. She gives me what I need in those moments and thinks she's doing something wrong? No, no, she has it all backward. "You're not enabling anything. That's what I need sometimes."

Her eyes meet mine, the sadness in them so big that I wish I could spin her a cocoon and protect her against it forever.

"I don't think that's what you need," she says. "I think you need someone to listen, to tell you it sucks, to validate you. To take the shame out of those feelings. Because there is no shame in those feelings, Ana."

My breathing is funny, requiring too much concentration. I want to end this conversation. "Let's just drop it."

"No," she says, her gaze steady, holding mine. "I'm not letting you steamroll me on this anymore. Not when there's so much at stake."

"What is at stake? You're already leaving!" I cry.

"Not me," she says. "You'll always have me, no matter where we live or what work we do." She takes a breath. "I'm talking about your life."

"My life is great! Well, not at this very second, I have this fucking annoying cousin—"

"Do you even want to move to L.A.?" she blares over me.

A sound comes from my throat, unsure what it's trying to be. Maybe I don't want to live in L.A. specifically, but it's not about the location—it's about what L.A. will fulfill. I can't stop wishing to make my family happy. I can't just extricate a piece of myself that's been a driving force my entire life. "It's not that simple," I say. Words I may as well emblazon on my forehead for the number of times I've said them recently.

Her head bobs. "It kind of is. I want to be an environmental engineer. I'm doing what I want, and it's the right thing, even though it's inconvenient for people I love. Think about what you actually want, Ana. Because that matters." Her voice is soft, coaxing. "It matters what you want. And it matters how you feel, whatever those feelings may be."

Why or how my bones become liquid, I don't know, but I collapse onto the bed, legs unable to hold me up any longer. My breaths are coming too fast. Tears rush up my throat and down my face, as though Maral's words have turned a faucet.

She sits beside me, pulling me close, and my body droops against hers like crumpling fabric. The sound of great, heaving sobs fills the room. They're coming from me.

My chest aches, like my heart is skidding on asphalt, scraped up and raw. I'm not sure how long I cry, but as my sobs recede, my pulse normalizing and breaths coming at a non-alarming rate, I feel lighter. Like I've handed half the burden to Maral, and she's taken it without even a thought, as trusted and dependable as she's always been. It aches to realize how long I could have had this but denied it.

"Why haven't you brought this up before?" I ask, my voice breaking on the last word.

"'Cause you're so receptive," she deadpans, and we both chuckle softly.

I sober quickly, though. I'm a long way from living a new truth. I may never be able to get where I want to be—I may have thrown away the opportunity one too many times.

"I fucked up," I say. I know she knows what—who—I'm referring to.

She swipes at my tears with her thumbs. "You can fix it."

I nod automatically. But . . . "What if I can't?"

She tsks. "You're too smart to say something that stupid." She smiles. "You can do anything."

Chapter 23

"And it would be more interactive than typical talk shows. Think Jimmy Fallon, with games and challenges and stuff in addition to the interviews." Mike Logan, Scope's blond Gen X exec, is animated on the wall-mounted screen. "But obviously you'd be bringing your own brand's spin to it. We want it to appeal to a diverse viewership, so guests would be people from all communities."

Nadia's nod from across the table prompts me to follow suit. She asks questions about the network's key demographics, showrunners, timing, and other things I don't quite register because I'm distracted by the cup of weak coffee before me.

I arrived at the Verity offices just before the meet and greet with Scope was set to begin, and Nadia's assistant, Quinn, offered me refreshments as they herded us into a boardroom with a sleek virtual conferencing setup. One sip of the brew and I left the rest untouched. It wasn't Quinn's fault—they weren't responsible for serving my specific tastes.

But I can't help remembering that dark roast was served everywhere I went on tour. All because Ryan made sure of it.

I shouldn't be thinking about coffee right now. I should be focused on this meeting, given how hard I've been gunning for it. And yet, my outsides fly on autopilot while my insides tie themselves in knots.

"We'll stay in touch," Logan says, wrapping up. "Oh, and our studios are in L.A. I assume you'd be cool to move here—nothing keeping you in New York?"

I open my mouth to answer but nothing comes out. The words seem stuck in my throat. As if by divine intervention, a cacophony of cab horns blasts from Madison Avenue below.

Nadia pipes up. "Ana can't *stop* talking about moving to L.A. Year-round sunshine—what's not to love, am I right?"

"Great," he says. "Looking forward to seeing you in action tonight. Our network head will be tuning in to the livestream too. He's the one who green-lights new shows, so . . . no pressure, but y'know."

I finally find my voice. "I thrive under pressure," I say, smile immovable.

We end the call and Nadia leads me back to her office, where I roost on a mint-green guest chair across from her incongruously old-fashioned desk.

"I didn't want to distract you with this while you were on tour, and I know things are a bit fragile now with Maral's exodus," she says, "but I've been getting tons of interest from publishers sniffing about a potential second book. It went into overdrive when you hit the *NYT*."

My instinctive response at the prospect of writing again is excitement. Ever since the talk with Maral yesterday, I've been brimming with ideas for a follow-up. Maybe as a way of processing the host of new thoughts and feelings she stoked in me. I can't help but feel like writing again will be good for me—help me connect with myself in a way I never really have.

"We have an option clause with Woodsworth," Nadia says, "so they'd get the first look. Laura has shown some of the loudest interest. I know you've had a good experience with her, but would you rather I shop your proposal to other publishers given the whole Ryan situation?"

"What do you mean—are they soured on me after the photo?"

"Not at all. I mean more the conflict-of-interest bit. Aren't you guys a thing now?"

I swallow hard, shake my head once. It's all I can manage.

She frowns sympathetically. "Damn shame. Wouldn't have taken Grant for a commitment-phobe, but he *is* a male from New York, so." She rolls her eyes and sighs, like, *c'est la vie*.

"He got another job, anyway," I croak.

"Seriously?" she asks, suitably shocked.

I nod. "He's leaving Woodsworth."

She shakes her head. "Everyone's flying the coop," she says. "But hell, that's handy, isn't it? Out of your life and out of your mind. All the better to unstick that stickiness if we do sign with them. Shall we book a meeting?" She opens her laptop. "Another book *and* a show. Think of the tie-in opportunities."

When I open the door for Maral later that afternoon for our usual pre-event glow-up routine, tears spring immediately to my eyes. Seeing her on the threshold calls to mind that this is one of the last times we'll do this together. She's moving next month, and we only have a handful of events before then.

"This is your fault," I say, pointing to my blubbering face. "Both for leaving and for telling me to feel my feelings."

She winces. "Think of the endogenous opioids?"

A laugh warbles out as I step aside to usher her in.

She wraps her arms around my neck. "The flowers were beautiful. You didn't have to do that."

I squeeze her tight. "I should have done it right away."

A strand of her hair sticks to my wet face as she pulls back. "How did the meeting go with Scope?" she asks.

She'd offered to come, but I thought it would be better to appear as we mean to go on, should Scope want to move forward. Since Mar won't be a part of the show, it wouldn't be right to present ourselves as a team. "Good," I say. "Our visions are aligned, and they sound more than passingly interested. The head of the network will be watching tonight. He's the final decision-maker."

"You're gonna kill it," she says.

I nod, but it feels mechanical.

We talk about tonight, bounce around ideas about the podcast and how we'll manage the transition from duo hosts to solo, and I walk her through the four pages of ideas I've already jotted down for a second book. When I give a seven-minute monologue about some of the potential new content I'm toying with including, she beams at me. "I haven't seen you this excited about something in a while."

She's right. I'm a pretty excitable person, but this hits different, deeper. I can't wait to start writing.

She recounts her parents' reactions when she told them about Boston this morning—they were understandably unhappy about her not moving to L.A., but that was tempered by their delight that she'll be working as an engineer at last, and living close to her aunt, at least at first.

It's getting harder to envision myself in L.A. An image that only a short while ago seemed so crystal clear in my mind is becoming hazy, undefined. Maybe because Maral's been removed from it.

It occurs to me that nothing's logistically stopping me from moving back to Boston too. What is home if not with family? The people you love? I could find a new brand manager, hire a producer, continue the podcast solo, write my next book, do speaking events. Figure out some way to deal with Mom's passive-aggression every day . . . find a padded, soundproofed room to stifle my screams.

My shoulders droop.

Even if Boston didn't sit so heavy in my memories, it's a skin I've shed and that won't fit anymore. I don't want it to.

I can't deny that the strongest call of all emanates from the center of this bustling island. Yet staying alone in New York feels . . . disgraceful. Like a selfish deed, a choice I can't justify in any familiar terms.

What do you want?

The question has been plaguing me since Maral raised it. My fingers itching to pick up my phone, to contact Ryan, beg him to give me another chance. But the fear of putting myself out there—of rupturing the thick membrane around my heart and leaving it exposed—keeps winning out. I don't know how to overcome it. I wish there was some resource that could guide me. It may be time to look into therapy. (Long past time, but who's counting.)

As though reading my mind, Maral asks if I've heard from Ryan. After I fill her in on what happened on the steps outside the Bryant Park library, she whistles, low and slow. It sounds like a bomb dropping. But the surprise I expected to see on her face is markedly absent.

"What's with this lack of reaction?" I ask.

She shrugs. "I mean . . . I knew he was all in."

She did. And I just threw it away. "He told me how he felt, and I turned him down."

Her shoulders rise to her ears. "That doesn't mean you're out of the game."

"He said he can't be around me anymore."

"Only if you don't want a relationship with him. Pretty sure he'd be all up *in* you if you do." She applies setting powder to her forehead, the bridge of her nose. "Have you been with anyone else since we got home?"

"No." I sent Jacob a kind but firm brush-off this morning. It felt wrong to lead him on, to make him think I'd be DTF anytime soon when the prospect of being with someone, anyone, other than Ryan feels wrong on a cellular level. Unimaginable. Not when I can still feel his touch electrifying my skin, despite having gone over a week without it now. I wonder if it will ever fade. I wonder if I want it to.

"Then what are you worried about?" she says.

I bite my lip so fresh tears won't streak my makeup. "I think... that part of me is broken."

She rolls her eyes. "I thought the elderly were supposed to be wise." She hands me a tissue. "You're not broken—you're recovering. You've just been burying shit for so long that your recovery is protracted. There's not a person on this earth who works harder than you. So work on yourself. Open yourself up, invite him in. Let yourself be happy." She watches me to see if her words are resonating.

First things first, I need to get this waterworks situation under control. Because the death grip my teeth have on my lip is not damming the tears. I cannot get up in front of thousands of people, under unforgiving lighting, with puffy eyes. Unacceptable.

As I reapply concealer, Maral excuses herself, tapping on her phone as she leaves the bathroom. She comes back a few minutes later and says she needs some privacy. "I had a burrito for lunch," she says.

"I don't know why you insist on doing that to yourself," I say. "Or to me."

"They need to stop being so delicious."

As I leave her to desecrate my bathroom, I hear my phone ringing from the living room. I rush to see who it is, hoping dumbly against hope, but it's not even my phone ringing—it's Maral's. The name scrolling across the top reads *Celine Grant*.

I knew they'd been in touch since San Francisco—Mar mentioned something about introducing her to people at the Boston MPA so she could network for potential national internship opportunities—but didn't realize they were on regular-calls terms. Although maybe this isn't so regular. Maybe something happened?

Quickly, I swipe to answer. "Celine, hi," I say. "It's Ana."

"Ana!" she squeals on the other end. "How are you?"

This ray of sunshine. Is it possible to miss someone you barely know?

"Getting through," I say, surprising myself by not saying my rote line of *I'm fine*. Is this what they call progress? "Maral's indisposed for the moment. Is everything okay?"

"Totally!" she says. "Well, actually. Y'know, depends on what you call *okay*. I'm in kind of a bind."

Something pinches in my chest. *Shit*. In all my own drama, Celine's tuition predicament got back-burnered in my mind. Ryan's leaving the cash cow behind.

"I'm so sorry," I rush out. "About your tuition."

"Ugh," she says. "Yeah, that's a bummer. But at least my brother can finally be happy for once in his life. Worth the debt!"

I chuckle at her dramatics. "To be fair, I don't think working at Woodsworth made him *that* unhappy."

"But it was always an obstacle standing in his way with you. And now it's gone! I saw that picture of you guys kissing—which, gross, by the way. But also, like, *finally*."

I'm at a loss, not quite following. "Finally," I say, it coming out as more of a hesitant statement than a question.

"Yeah! He's had a crush on you *forever*. All I've heard about for years is how amazing you are. I kept telling him, leave Woodsworth so you can ask her out! But he talked all this nonsense about the tuition-matching program and *maintaining professional boundaries*," she says, dropping her voice to emulate him. "He always does that. Denies himself, puts himself last. Meanwhile, I'm pretty sure he thought he didn't stand a chance with you. I mean, the way he talked about you, it was as if you lit the sun. But then you guys kissed and it was like, *Woodsworth who?*"

I try to form words, but they're trapped in tar somewhere behind my sternum. *Had a crush on you forever* keeps whirling like a dervish in my mind.

"I just want him to be happy!" Celine goes on. "Merit's been trying to recruit him for ages—since he did some tie-in thingy with their team or something? He kept refusing to take it seriously. But, boom, one kiss and he's blowing up their phone the next day."

I'm desperately trying to catch up to what she's saying. Merit's wanted Ryan for a while—that must be why he was able to make the new gig happen so fast after Kissgate. "I mean, that kiss *did* threaten his job at Woodsworth. It was smart of him—necessary, even—to line something else up."

"Oh, he didn't call them after that photo went viral—it was after your *first* kiss. In Seattle, I think it was?"

What? He planned on switching jobs because we kissed *one time*? My pulse is running a marathon as I think of Ryan's strict adherence to professional boundaries—until I plowed right through them. Did he reach out to Merit out of guilt? Because he'd behaved inappropriately?

Or was he trying to eliminate the obstacle in the way of something happening between us? Not knowing I'd be a whole other, insurmountable one . . .

It was just a kiss, though. We hadn't even slept together yet . . . I hadn't explained yet that I didn't want anything serious. Did he, even then?

I definitely don't feel casual about you. I never have.

He's had a crush on you forever.

My heart is banging against my rib cage like a wrongfully convicted prisoner as I try to make sense of it all. I know I'm fooling myself if I think that kiss was just a kiss, when really it was like opening the fucking gates of heaven. Even I felt the promise in it . . . even if I told myself I didn't.

"But he kept his distance," I say, my voice strangled. "Like when we were with you in San Francisco—he was still toeing the company line."

"Well, he hadn't secured the new job yet by then. He was still in talks with them—I know because he took meetings from my apartment and bored me half to death talking about *strategic management*." She makes a fart sound through her lips. "Plus he was worried about making you uncomfortable—he was still your publicist at that point."

As the haze begins to clear, Ryan's concern about my discomfort drifts to the surface. I sigh inwardly at his chivalry. "I guess it wasn't secure yet by the time that photo spread online, either. He was so worried about getting fired."

"Oh yeah, I mean, it's never a good look to be caught kissing a client. He didn't know if the photo would affect the new job, either, and we can't afford for him to have *no* job. But he told Merit it wasn't tawdry, and they'd already talked to some of the authors he's worked with as references, who all praised him for being super professional. So I guess he got a pass."

I throw up a silent thank-you to the universe that Kissgate didn't rain shit on his reputation. Chalk it up to the patriarchy that men can get away with something like that as long as they have strong character references otherwise. At least in Ryan's case, he's earned that honor.

"I thought he took the new job because it would give him more time to write." I was so gratified, thinking our acquaintance had given him the push he needed. He didn't deny it, or tell me any of the things Celine's telling me now. But then, he wouldn't have. He knew I was skittish as a squirrel, that any pressure would send me sprinting for the highest tree. Knew I'd perceive his leaving Woodsworth to clear the path for something real with me as level-ten pressure. He would have been right.

But I don't think he'd be right anymore.

Celine makes a sympathetic sound on the other end of the line. "I'm not saying that's not part of it, but it's all wrapped up together. Ana, he never would have taken that plunge to prioritize his writing if not for you. He's just never given space to what he wants, you know? But it's like he's seeing everything differently now. Because of you."

My spine gives out, and I crumple back into the couch cushions.

"Which, *yay*," she says. "Because now you guys can finally be together!"

My head is swimming, drowning, gasping for air as it tries to stay afloat in the churning waters of all this new information. All the bits and pieces coming together to form the larger picture, this beautiful, sweeping watercolor, bright and vivid in the light. Ryan had feelings for me, but didn't act on them. Kept them under strict lock and key, just as he did his creative dreams. Centered his sister's needs, like the responsible father figure he's always been to her.

There's no help for my makeup, it's a lost cause. I'll be puff pastry tonight. I can't stop the tears that stream down my face, my running mascara making Rorschach splotches on my skin.

He always does that. Denies himself, puts himself last.

The words are sharp, acute, a scalpel slitting a vital organ. He denied himself for my sake too. Wanted a relationship but settled for just (the best-ever) sex. Put my needs first. Even when my needs hurt him.

He may be his own worst enemy, but I'm no better.

And poor Celine thinks we're a couple. Doesn't know about the fallout. Ryan hasn't told her. I feel guilty revealing something he maybe didn't want to share with her yet, but I also feel guilty lying to her.

At last, I relent. Let the chips fall where they may.

"We're . . . not together," I say.

There's a long pause. Then: "Why not?" she asks, such innocence in the question that I have an instinct to tuck her away in a nest and keep her safe from the world.

"I . . . I couldn't," I croak.

She's silent for a moment. "Oh." Then, knowingly, "Is it 'cause he's such a dork?"

My laugh, if you can call it that, sounds pained. "He's not a dork."

"Is it 'cause you're way out of his league?"

"Does he really think that?" I ask, disbelieving.

"Any sane person would think that."

"Then they should check their sanity."

"Is it 'cause you're moving to L.A.?" she asks. "He would move there, you know. I'm pretty sure he'd move to the middle of the woods if you were going to be there. And he *hates* the woods."

A tear, warm and salty, breaches my lips. "So do I."

Another pause. "Then . . . why?"

I shake my head, though she can't see me. "I have . . ." Unsure how to say it, I settle on, "Some issues. Someone hurt me, a long time ago, and I haven't quite figured out how to get past it."

"Oh," she says sagely. "Well, you know, there's therapy for that."

"Never thought I needed it. I have Taylor Swift's entire catalog." I sigh. "But you're right. I'm going to book an appointment." I mean it. I have work to do, and I'm determined to do it. I've never stood to lose so much.

She exhales loudly. "Good. 'Cause I was so freaking excited about you being my sister-in-law, you have no idea."

I laugh, charmed by this woman I'd be honored to be related to. "Don't get ahead of yourself."

"Can't help it."

That, I understand. "About your tuition . . ."

"We'll make it work. I've already applied for student loans. Plus, if I keep my GPA above a certain level, I can apply for scholarships. And Maral's a hot connection—I'm already in talks about a job next summer that'll help pay down the loans and look great on my résumé."

There Mar goes, being a guardian angel for yet another go-getter. The relief I feel about the Grants' financial situation is tangible. "You said you were in a bind, though."

"I am!" she wails. "My fluid mechanics class assignment is sucking my will to live."

I smile, relieved to hear of a problem that, while it may not be small, feels manageable. Solvable. "Do you want me to make you a video? Remind you how capable you are?"

She gasps. "You would do that for me?"

"Call it an equal exchange. Maybe you could put in a good word with your brother."

She laughs, a bell chiming from three thousand miles away. "Deal."

We sign off after I give her my own number and make her promise to stay in touch with me, no matter what happens. She says I'll be sorry for inviting that into my life, and I tell her she'll be even sorrier, which summons another darling giggle from her.

When I press the End button, the screen reverts to the last app that was open on Maral's phone—her text chain with Celine. The last few messages were sent only fifteen minutes ago.

Maral: hey, are you free right now? can you call me?

Celine: sure! everything okay??

Maral: yeah. ana could use some talking to. about you-know-who. from someone other than me

I squint at the screen, then up at the bathroom door, behind which lies suspicious silence. No burrito evidence to be heard.

Pretty sneaky, cuz.

Chapter 24

Half an hour later, I'm lying on the couch with cold packs on my eyes, mind reeling, while Mar riffles through my closet for clothes she wants to take to Boston. Which is not helping my de-puffing situation, but I don't tell her that.

My phone rings and I reach for it blindly, peeking around a cold pack to see who's calling. Mom. I swipe to answer.

"Is it true?" she asks, voice full of hope. "Maral got a job back home?"

Part of me is surprised that it's taken this long to hear from her, given that Maral told her parents hours ago and Sosi must have spent every moment since screaming it from the rooftops.

"She's moving to Boston, yes," I say.

"Park kez, der astvatz," she says, blessing the Lord. "When is the move scheduled? Have you found an apartment yet? You can stay here as long as you need—or you can just live here."

I sit up, the cold packs falling off my face. My heart aches at the desperation in her voice. "Mayrik, Maral is moving back, not me."

"What?" she asks.

"*She* got a job in Boston. I didn't."

She tsks, frustrated. "Surely you won't stay there all by yourself. Take this as a sign, janikus. You had a fun time and got it out of your system. Now you can come home and get back on track."

"I am on track," I say. "There are a lot of balls in the air, but none of them involve moving back to Boston."

"What could matter more than being with your family?"

It's not that I don't agree with her on some level. After all, that's why I've been chasing L.A.—to bring the family back together, because what *could* matter more? But not having Maral there with us has changed the shape of this prospect so much that I can't see it quite as clearly anymore.

I'd be deluding myself if I professed that's the only thing that's changed.

I've never been geographically far from my cousin for more than a few days. Even when we were in college or at our pre-*SPOY* jobs, we lived in the same city. I could always hop on a bus and be with her in a matter of minutes. And I did that—often—when my ruthless residency schedule wasn't kicking my ass. Sometimes especially when it was. We'd settle in together on the scratchy couch she and her roommates had "thrifted" (read: found on the side of the road) and talk about school or work or gossip or read books or study or blast music and have impromptu dance parties in the kitchen. Whatever—as long as we were in each other's company.

I don't know how living without her is going to look. How it'll feel. If I'll be so lonely that she'll seem farther away than she actually is. Maybe she will. But I can't follow her to Boston just because I'm scared of loneliness. I've run away from loneliness before—I can't keep repeating my old patterns. Pretty sure any therapist, TayTay included, would tell me as much. I need to try to do better. It may take a while to figure out what that means, but I know it doesn't mean basing my decisions on hers. Or basing them on what I think—what I *hope*—will appease Mom. I have to decide for myself.

"I need to figure out what will make me happy," I say.

She makes a disbelieving sound. "God only knows how you expect to find happiness when you throw away every chance at it. Your career, your boyfriend. And now your family."

"I didn't throw any of that away," I say, trying to find my patience.

"Even if you didn't want to be a doctor, you could still be married to one. Surely that would make you happy."

"Nathan and I were not a good match, Mom. He didn't even want to really know me."

"He wanted to *marry you*!" she cries. "He wanted you to have his children! Now some spitak woman has all that with him, and I have no grandchildren!"

I lean forward, resting my head in my free hand. I've never been totally honest with Mom about why Nathan and I split up—I've just vaguely referred to discovering things that made it clear we weren't right for each other. I knew she wouldn't get it, knew she'd say . . . well, everything she's saying now. That I should be so lucky to be with someone like Nathan. That I should appreciate what I had and do whatever it took to hold on to it.

Everything Maral said about our parents was true. I don't doubt they love us, but they've never cared to understand our more complex emotions, sweeping away our grievances like so much dust. Insignificant nuisances, incomparable to the much larger problems that exist in the world.

But I've also played into it. I haven't tried to break through that wall. I shut down that part of myself because I believed my feelings were immaterial in the grand scheme of things. In some way they are, but in another they're not—they're everything. My whole inner world. That has to mean something, doesn't it?

I didn't want to aggravate them, though, these people who had sacrificed everything to give me this privileged life. Especially my mom, who'd suffered so much already. It wasn't her fault she was depressed—inasmuch as external factors play a part in depression, she had them in spades. It wasn't her fault that she was emotionally unavailable. Who would have taught her to be anything else? Her mother, who died when she was just a child? Her father, widowed and overwhelmed with needing to provide the bare necessities of life for multiple children?

While she may not understand my emotional needs, she also doesn't deserve the blame for that—I didn't give her any opportunity to understand. I told myself I was just being oversensitive, that it wasn't her job to manage my feelings. I kept them hidden. From her. From everyone. Even myself.

Maybe, if I give her the opportunity at last—like Celine did for Ryan—she'll surprise me. Not like the pathetic attempt I made in Boston last weekend, but a real college try. If she doesn't take it, how much worse off can I possibly be? And if she does . . . it could mean a paradigm shift in our relationship.

I take a breath. "Mom, I was really struggling after Dad died." It feels strange to say it aloud, for her to hear it. I've never talked about my grief with her before. But I have to start somewhere. "Working at the hospital became too triggering, and I couldn't hold myself together anymore. I'm sorry it upsets you that I left medicine, but I needed to do it. And I need you to accept that."

"We were all grieving," she says after a short pause. "If you could have gotten through that time, things would have been better on the other side. You had Nathan—"

"I didn't. Not really." Shaky air leaves me. "He couldn't handle my grief. He only wanted me when I was happy."

"Doesn't everyone want to be happy?"

The question seems absurd coming from her. "Yeah, but a person can't be happy all the time. Especially right after their dad dies." I crack on the last two words, and they come out broken.

There's another, longer pause on the other end of the line. "Men are simple creatures," she says finally. "They want simple lives, no complications."

"But life isn't simple. Terrible things happen, and we need support through them. Like how Dad supported you in the tough times after you immigrated. Or how I supported you when we lost Dad." She's quiet, not acknowledging what I said—maybe not knowing how to. I finger the cold pack in my lap. "I may not be an expert, but I don't think relationships are meant to make you feel lonely."

"But you wouldn't be alone—you'd have him."

"But he made me *feel* alone," I say.

"You wouldn't *be* alone, though," she says emphatically. "Anything is better than being alone, Anahid jan. I promise you."

My stomach contracts. I picture her, by herself, in the bungalow's small kitchen, the yellowed wallpaper behind her dotted with cheerful pomegranate vines. The recliner in the living room notably empty. The cable-knit sweater vest lying limply on a box in the basement, his scent dissipating more from it every day. The person meant to fill the house, to fill her heart, absent.

Maybe being alone is worse for her. Maybe her relationship with Dad made her feel understood, accepted, beloved, and she can't imagine anything worse than being without him. My heart aches for her, because if anybody understands the pain of losing Vahag Movilian, it's me.

But our experiences of partnership and romantic love are not the same. Nathan didn't want to know all of me, and I didn't want to let him. I guess I felt it would herald the end, because nobody had ever accepted all of me. And that subconscious instinct was right. When my grief could no longer be contained, he retreated.

It's deeply painful to be in the presence of the people who are supposed to love you the most and feel alone.

As opposed to being with a relative stranger—a colleague, then a friend, then a lover—and feeling less lonely than you ever have in your life.

Maybe self-awareness or emotional acuity are too much to expect from Mom. She may never get it. But that's okay. My feelings are valid, whether or not she understands them. I'll continue to give her the chance, and maybe one day we'll connect emotionally. Or maybe we won't. I can't change her, but I don't have to. I can still heal, move forward, regardless.

It won't be easy, I know that. But if the many people I've met while running *So Proud of You* are any indication, I'll figure it out. I have a whole community behind me.

And I have me behind me.

Chapter 25

Grayson, the mustachioed Infinitude Symposium coordinator, leads Maral and me through throngs of attendees to the main ballroom of the gargantuan Marriott Marquis in Midtown. Navigating the many escalators and corridors is practically a workout.

We're seated at a speakers' table near the front, where Shanthi is already set up to record the livestream of my speech. Grayson says he'll cue me a few minutes before I'm set to go up and races away, presumably to deal with some emergency or other.

I sit quietly through the first couple of speakers, flanked by Shanthi and Maral, only barely registering that this may be the last time the three of us attend an event together. Which is good, because my makeup can't stand another water feature so close to showtime.

"Are you okay?" Maral whispers as the MC takes the stage again. "You're really . . . chill."

"I'm always chill," I say.

She rolls her eyes before getting distracted by the woman to her right asking her to pass the water jug.

She's not wrong, though. My legs are motionless under the table and I haven't been fiddling with the conference packet or my water glass or my phone. Which is all very weird. Maybe it's that my emotional stores have been depleted, but I'm actually feeling . . . fine. At peace. Like something has settled into place inside my chest. Something new, but honest and real. And while I don't fully understand it yet, it feels good.

To my left, Shanthi is examining the angle of the camera on her phone, set up on a small tabletop tripod. I lean closer to her. "Hey, you can check if specific accounts are logged in to the Live, right?"

"Yeah," she says. "You want to know if the Scope people are watching? Do you know their handles?"

I bite the inside of my cheek. I know it's stupid to hope, but after my call with Celine earlier . . . "Search *aintlovegrant*."

Her eyes dart to mine. She remembers our conversation with Ryan about Instagram—the revelation of his ridiculous username. "Sure, I'll look out for him."

"Cool. I owe you one."

She makes a face. "I work for you."

"A raise, then," I say, just as Grayson signals me to join him at stage left. I rise from my seat, leaning down to Shanthi. "Or better yet—want to be my new brand manager?"

I wink at her slack-jawed expression, gratified by finally getting a reaction out of her, and walk toward the stage.

The ballroom looks even bigger from the elevated platform than it does from the floor, but the lights pointing at the podium are bright enough to obscure the faces in the crowd. I smile and wave as the audience welcomes me with applause and camera flashes, a familiar rush of adrenaline coursing through me.

"Thank you," I say into the mic. "Give it up for the organizers of the symposium, who have done a colossal amount of work behind the scenes for the event to feel so seamless to those of us attending. And thank you all for giving me such a warm welcome this evening."

The uproar gradually dies down and I glance at the notes I brought. I prepared today's speech a while back. It combines pieces of my regular keynote with anecdotes from my book and the odd joke thrown in for good measure. It'd be easy to deliver it as planned, to lean on the stories I've been culling and telling over the past several years. I know from experience which ones are the most crowd-pleasing, and I could deliver them in a way that will paint me in the best light for the Scope execs and make me seem like a shoo-in to host an interview show.

I scan the room, my gaze automatically landing on Maral. I'm a heliotropic plant and she the sun. As she's always been—the center of my universe. Casting light when I've needed it most. And now that she's illuminated certain truths, allowing me to see them clearly for the first time, nothing about the Before feels right anymore.

So I go off script.

"I have something to confess," I say, inhaling. "I am a disappointment."

Silence turns to confounded murmurings throughout the room.

"One of the questions I get asked the most is some variation of *How do you reconcile your own happiness with your family's expectations?*" I continue. "People look to me as some kind of authority on the subject, as though I've mastered a self-actualized life—successful, fulfilled, with parents who are satisfied with where I am professionally and personally. I haven't exactly dispelled this image, mostly because I avoid talking about myself in any real way.

"Sure, people know details about my life. Tidbits about my parents and my family. That my beloved cousin Maral is my right-hand woman, that I went to med school, that I look forward to my morning coffee when I go to bed every night—which is somehow the most notable of those items, given how much I talk about it." Mild laughter ripples across the audience. "I've never delved deeper, partly because it hasn't been necessary, but more truthfully because I didn't want to expose myself that way."

I take a deep breath, the lights shining bright in my eyes.

"I haven't told anyone that I dropped out of my residency because every moment of it was such an unbearable reminder of my late father that entering through the hospital doors felt like being pierced through the heart. I haven't shared that my father would likely have been deeply disappointed in my choice, just as my mother is, but that it was a choice I had to make if I didn't want to risk a complete breakdown."

A tremor courses through me. I hold on to the sides of the podium, steadying myself.

"How did I reconcile my own happiness with my family's expectations? I didn't. And I won't." Air rushes into the microphone from my exhale. "This is my life. If I could have it all, of course I'd want to meet their expectations. But if that means veering off the path to my own happiness, I'm not willing to do that. Even if that means disappointing them."

A few people applaud.

"I don't want to be a doctor. I want to work on *So Proud of You*, because nothing has brought me more fulfillment than building its community. I want to write more books, because I enjoy the creative process and I have so much more to share. I want to live in New York, because I enjoy its hustle and energy and seasons. I've never liked the idea of year-round sunshine."

Maral's eyes are wide, but not as wide as her smile.

"Sorry to the Scope execs watching—I'm not moving to L.A.," I say to Shanthi's tripod. Confused murmurings rise from the audience. "Oh, yeah, I was pursuing an opportunity there, but I know now that I was chasing it for all the wrong reasons. I'm not leaving New York. I love it here. And . . . there's someone here I really don't want to say goodbye to."

Mar's jaw drops. I catch Shanthi's eye, raising my brows in a question she understands immediately. She'll make a good Maral 2.0 (though let's get real, there is no better version of Maral than Maral. Shanthi will make an excellent Shanthi, just as she always has).

She taps at the screen quickly, and her face falls as she shakes her head.

Ryan's not logged in. He's not watching.

I wait for the pain to slice me open, but it's not quite as sharp as I expected. Instead, it's a soft ache, strangely satisfying in its familiarity. Like a contusion being pressed.

It's okay. It's good, in fact. He's doing what's right for him—serving his needs. Which happens to mean keeping his distance from me. I can't fault him for that. I can only respect him for it.

Regardless of whether Ryan's watching, it's worth sharing this. Because it's the truth—and I've spent far too long running from it.

"For a long time, I've believed that holding myself in is the only way to safeguard my heart and protect myself from getting hurt. But the joke was on me, because turns out denying your true feelings is more painful than feeling them has ever been."

My vision blurs, casting halos around the spotlights beaming down at me.

"And I wasn't the only one hurt by that denial. Someone so special to me was brave enough to put himself out there and I wasn't. Even though I felt the same things, I paid my pain forward to him. Hurt him just as I was hurting. But as soon as I'm done here, I'm going to find him, apologize a hundred times, and hope with my whole heart that he'll . . ."

My voice trails off as a silhouetted figure enters at the back of the room. Even from this distance, I recognize the set of his shoulders. Their proportion to his neck. The line of his jaw. That posture, the grace in his steps.

My heart rises slow and steady from my chest to my throat, bringing with it a wash of tears.

Ryan.

He didn't tune in because he's *here*.

And I could just about melt into the stage at the sight of him.

"You're here," I say, my broken voice cast loud into the room by the mic. If anyone in the audience wasn't paying attention before, they are now.

I step around the podium, my legs finding their way to the stairs and down the center aisle of their own volition. I make my way toward him, his face coming into clearer view as I swipe at the moisture clouding my vision. God, he looks good. Wary, maybe, a little beaten down, but fucking gorgeous. A sight for cried-out eyes.

The silence is so absolute that, despite my having left the mic back on the stage, my voice rings out, clear as day.

"Did Celine call you?" I ask.

"She did." His tone is hesitant, his gaze darting around the room as everyone's attention turns on him. Having just arrived, he has no idea why I've interrupted my speech to approach him, or why the whole ballroom is rapt by this moment.

"Ryan . . . I'm so sorry." The words feel small, insignificant. "For everything."

His eyes land on mine, surprise registering in them. "Hey, we can talk about this later—"

"No, it's too important. I didn't treat you the way you deserved."

"Ana, you don't owe me—"

"I was lying. All along."

A groove etches itself between his eyebrows as a gasp rises from the audience members nearest where we stand. "What do you mean?" he asks.

"I lied to you and to myself. I said it was casual. Insisted on it, because I thought that would be safe. If I kept my heart out of it, it couldn't be hurt. I could keep you at a distance, not let you know me deeply enough to be turned off when you see I'm not always the sparkly, charismatic woman you were drawn to."

The lines melt off his forehead, his expression softening. "That's not—"

"And I tried," I say wetly. "I tried not to feel anything for you. Told myself those tugs in my heart were just because you're an attentive publicist and a thoughtful friend, taking care of me in ways nobody ever has. Defending my work, standing up in my honor at every turn, listening and understanding and supporting me when I opened up to you about things I've never told anyone. Or maybe it was because you're hands-down the best sex I've ever had in my life." Even though I dropped my voice for that part, for his ears only, pink flushes up his neck as heat flares in his eyes. "I swore to myself that I wasn't feeling the things I was feeling."

He swallows. "What were you feeling?"

"Besides terrified?" I take his hands in mine and notice the tremble in his fingers. "I haven't ever felt . . . safe, being my full self. Showing any hint of the dullness behind the shine has only ever resulted in people pulling away. But it wasn't fair of me to put that baggage on you. Not when you've proven yourself different at every turn. And not when . . ." I steady my voice. "Not when I feel so, so much for you."

His shoulders drop from up around his ears. "Don't toy with me, Ana, I can't take it. Not after the hell I've been through these past few days."

From the corner of my vision I see audience members clutching their chests, their mouths. You could hear a pin drop on carpeting in here.

"I'm not toying with you," I say. "I'm finally being honest. I'm sorry I wasn't until now. I want something real with you, Ryan. Not just for a night, or the length of a tour. I want you for as long as you'll have me."

His eyes are glistening silver pools in the morning sun. "You're serious."

I nod, flash a hopeful smile. "You want to be my boyfriend?"

He exhales shakily. "Watch your mouth or I'll commit public indecency."

My cheeks hurt from the size of my grin. "I like you indecent," I say.

"Good," he says, leaning in to whisper in my ear. "Because as soon as this is over, I'm going to get you alone and make you call me that again and again."

I wrap my arms around his neck and kiss him fiercely. The crowd rises to their feet, applauding and howling at top volume.

"Will you make me pancakes in the morning?" I murmur into his ear.

"I'll make you pancakes every morning."

"Good, 'cause that's kind of a deal-breaker."

He feigns stern daddy, but the trembling quirk in his lips gives him away. "Coming from someone who can't make a pancake herself."

"That's irrelevant."

His chest expands. There are diamonds in his eyes and I feel like my bones are no longer solid. But if I sink to the ground, I know he's here to hold me up. I trust he always will be—as long as I'll let him.

"Will you go up there and finish your goddamn speech so I can take you home?" he says.

"I thought you'd never ask," I say.

Reluctantly, I tear myself away to head back to the stage, but not before he leans in to kiss me again—god, I've missed his kiss—and the room erupts in applause so loud you'd think it would drown out Ryan's professions of devotion against my lips. But it doesn't. I'd hear them anywhere. I'll hear them forever.

Epilogue

Two years later

"Gray or blue?" Ryan asks, holding up two identical shirts.

"Which is which?" I ask.

He makes a face. "Come on." He holds out the hangers, as if bringing them nearer will help me differentiate the colors. If I squint, one is *maybe* a slightly cooler gray than the other, but that could be a trick of the light. The sun is starting to set outside our bedroom windows.

"Are you playing a joke on me?" I ask. "They look the exact same. Just pack both, who cares?"

"I don't want to be lugging three suitcases to Germany."

I shrug. "It's not so bad. You just need a handsome publicist to help you carry them."

He throws the shirts down on the bed and hooks an arm around my waist. This kind of easy, sensual touch has become so commonplace you'd think my body would no longer respond so viscerally, but it does. I wonder if it'll ever get old—Ryan's natural, carnal knowledge of my physical responses. Hard to imagine it ever will.

"I'd carry a thousand of *your* suitcases," he says in a low rumble as he backs me toward the bed. "Open them up, go hunting for the delicious surprises inside."

He sucks at the base of my throat and I whimper, both at the sensation and at the memory of the last trip we took together, to Toronto for a speaking event a few weeks ago—when he discovered the vibrator I'd packed. Not the travel one, but one made specifically for couples. The one we put to such thorough use that my thighs tingled for days afterward.

"Now I wish I was coming with you," I say.

"Oh, I'll make sure you come with me," he growls into my skin.

My low laugh turns into moans, then cries, then sighs, as Ryan works his reliable magic on my body. On my heart.

Both shirts become crumpled beneath our bodies and he doesn't wind up packing either of them. It's fine—he's packed plenty of gray shirts already, and he'll only be in Frankfurt for four days. Just enough time for his agent to introduce him to foreign publishers as the face behind the hottest upcoming release on her list: the multiverse love story that's been deemed the most-anticipated book for the winter season here in the U.S. His agent, Gwen, says the foreign rights will sell so fast that four days at the international book fair will be overkill.

Ryan's debut novel is getting so much buzz that Gwen could sell the rights herself. She doesn't need to parade him around to get bites. But her argument is that meeting him will sway publishers to pay double. I can't say I disagree. Even if he weren't a vision and didn't have deep connections within the industry, his book—about a man pining for the love of his life across dimensions until they're united at last—is so heart-wrenchingly amazing that the attention is absolutely warranted.

Anyway, it's not like Ryan needs convincing to accompany Gwen to Frankfurt—not when his dreams are coming true. Starting with a multibook offer with an advance so robust he was able to quit Merit after a year and still cover the remainder of Celine's tuition until she graduated last June. It also helped that we'd moved in together by that point, cutting down the cost of rent. But the real prize is living with me. Now my kitchen actually gets used! I get to eat homemade food every day. His pancakes are indeed to die for, and for an odar, he's doing a commendable job learning some of my mom's best Armenian recipes. My favorite part is waking up to spectacular dark roast pour-overs every morning, served by Ryan in the drool-inducing gray sweats I got him for our first Christmas together. And he gets to grumble about living with the hottest chaos goblin in the world. Win-win.

After Germany, Ryan will meet me in Boston, where I'm heading tomorrow to visit Maral for the second time this month alone. Mom warmed to him early in our relationship when she saw how readily he showcased his love for me. Not only in the way he says *I love you* twenty times a day, but in the way he devotedly listens to everything I say, understanding, validating, empathizing. Acts that are wholly foreign to her. He accompanies me roughly half the time I visit, begrudgingly staying home the other half at my insistence. He'd lose too much writing time only to spend days doing Mom's bidding while we're at the house. He still requires reminders to put his needs first sometimes—we're working on it.

But he will be joining me more frequently now that Celine is in Boston too, starting her paid internship at the MPA with the team Maral has built. Our girls are killing it.

Mom definitely enjoys the increased frequency with which she's gotten to see me these past couple years. Happily, it has cut down her entreaties for me to move back. Plus, having Maral there acts as a welcome buffer during my visits. Win-win-win.

The only non-win is Maral living in a different city from me. That is still taking some getting used to.

Through the wonders of modern technology, we've been able to keep our daily morning routine largely intact—only instead of her coming over, we FaceTime. She says she prefers it, because she's no longer subjected to me post-workout, but I know better. She misses me, sweat stink and all.

Woodsworth is publishing my second book next spring. I'm not sure yet if I'll do as elaborate a tour for it as I did for the first one.

Alison, now my primary publicist, suggested we do a pared-back version, only hitting a few major bookstores in cities where book one sold particularly well. Shanthi said we can pepper in a handful of bigger speaking events if they make sense timing-wise. While I'm happy to publicize the book on the podcast and my ever-growing socials, part of me is less interested in shouting my message from rooftops across the country this time around. Probably because this book is a lot more personal than the first one, and I feel . . . protective, maybe, of my story.

Shanthi is being an excellent Shanthi 2.0 by convincing me that it doesn't matter either way. There will be good reviews, there will be bad ones. Lovers gonna love and haters gonna hate. It's the way of the world. And I'm coming to terms with it.

I've started talking more openly about myself—my experiences, my feelings—on the podcast since I started therapy a couple years back. I know intellectually that there's no shame in being open about things that aren't always sunshine. But I'm still coming to terms with the feeling of exposure. Sima, my therapist, says that's normal—that it's a lifelong process, and I'm only in the beginning stages. And being a public figure who trades on stories of personal experiences means sharing my vulnerabilities farther and wider than most people do. So it's okay to hold some of it back—to only share what I feel comfortable sharing as I continue to heal.

I talk more about Dad with Mom now too, rather than treating his memory like some taboo subject. It's helped me to finally grieve his loss, even if Mom isn't ever going to be super open to me expressing my feelings. She still clams up or reverts to tried-and-true methods like changing the subject or dismissing it altogether. I try not to take it personally and keep chipping away, one visit at a time. I may never get the emotional support I'd like from her, but at least I can stay true to myself by trying to meet her halfway.

And when I need someone to listen, and care, and provide support, I need look no further than home.

If I'd known a relationship could be like this—full of understanding and acceptance and love—I wouldn't have shunned them for so long. Though, let's be honest, no relationship could be as perfect for me as the one I have with Ryan. Who loves me at my best and my worst. Who doesn't even consider my worst my worst. It's just another part of my whole self, all of which is worthy of love.

We lie in bed for a while, sweat cooling on our skin, Ryan pulling a blanket over us. The bustle of the city outside is a soothing soundtrack as my hand reaches for his under the covers.

The fall foliage has started to turn, reds and oranges burning bright throughout the Northeast. Ryan and I walked through the Public Garden last year around this time when we were visiting Boston, and he declared it the perfect spot to revel in the colors. I suggest we do it again when we're there later this week.

"We can go with Celine and Maral before our *yay-you-have-an-internship* celebration dinner," I say.

"I don't know," Ryan says, absently stroking my hair. "Top-tier fall foliage *and* you? That might be beauty overload. Don't know if my brain can handle it."

"All the more reason. I like when you lose your cool a little—get that wild look in your eyes."

"Yeah?" he rumbles.

"Mmm-hmm. It's a turn-on."

"You just said your cousin and my sister will be there with us."

I roll my eyes. "Contrary to what you might think, I can keep it in my pants."

He purses his lips, disappointed. "Well, that's no fun."

I roll onto his chest. "Is that a no on the garden, then?"

"It's never a no." His indulgent smile still does all kinds of things to me.

I lean down to press a kiss to his lips. "Good. Because if I'm there, I want you to be there."

Acknowledgments

When I resigned from my publishing job, I expected to become a freelance editor, but I truly never expected also to become an author. I never would have anticipated that, for the first time in my life, a character would poke at the back of my mind over and over, day and night, demanding for me to step out of my comfort zone of editing and into the terror dome of writing. But Ana is nothing if not relentless.

While I may have taken the leap to write her story, it's because of so many other people that you're holding it in your hands today (or listening to it in your earbuds, or however you enjoy your stories).

Thank you to my agent, Sharon Pelletier, for believing in this book and in me. To my editors, Sarah St. Pierre and Wendy Wong, whose enthusiasm for and dedication to this project from the very beginning remain unmatched. Thank you for seeing the promise in Ana and Ryan and working so hard to make them shine as bright as you knew they could. Thank you to my publishing teams in Canada and the United States. In my home country, Kristin Cochrane, Sue Kuruvilla, Charidy Johnston, Evan Klein, Karen Ma, Polly Beel, Megan Costa, Deirdre Molina, Trina Kehoe, Madison Hendricks, Malaika Eyoh, and everyone at Random

House Canada who make magic happen every day. In the United States, Kara Welsh, Kim Hovey, Jennifer Hershey, Kara Cesare, Shauna Summers, Luke Epplin, Alexis Flynn, Saige Francis, Sophia Chunn, Taylor McGowan, Caitlin Sacks, Samuel Wetzler, Emily Siegmund, Hope Hathcock, and everyone at Ballantine Bantam Dell who has helped bring *The Book Tour* to readers.

To my parents, who moved to Canada and gave me the opportunity to live this privileged life. Thank you for teaching me to be capable and letting me define success for myself. For being a trusted safety net, always. I know how lucky I am.

To Noelle, my first reader. Thank you for being so gracious, kind, and effusive with your feedback. You gave me a precious gift and inspired me to step out of my shell. I'm so grateful that you've trusted me with your work and that you are so trustworthy with mine.

Thank you to my friends. The Breakfast Club, for your loving support on long drives and chill weekends. The Fancy Pals, for cheering me from the group chat. The Echo Beach crew, for your enthusiastic reads and generous cheerleading when publishing possibilities started taking shape. Margo, for your help with the pitch. Jamee, for your insights into the schooling-to-climate-action-careers pipeline for environmental engineers. Izzo, for turning your birthday party into a celebration for me after I got a publishing deal. Matt, for hailing this endeavor from the start and being such a dependable, caring support throughout our lives.

Thank you to Spring, without whose push I would never have upended my life in such a way that I had the bandwidth to write a whole book.

To my love, Don, for teaching me that it's okay to not always be fine. For understanding story so well, providing excellent sounding board for outlines, and giving me tough love when I veer into the *I am shit* phase of the creative process. You are the hardest-working author I know, and your commitment to the growth mindset is second to none. Walking and talking with you is the best. Thank you for your good heart and for your belief in this book.

To Isla, who trolled me by claiming that "writing isn't that hard once you learn where all the letters are on the keyboard," you amaze me every day and light up my world. I love you so much.

Finally, to the romance community. Authors, for giving of yourselves to create such wonderful, escapist stories. I cannot convey in words what your work has meant to me as a reader, how much more enjoyable my life is because romance novels are a part of it. Booksellers, reviewers, bloggers, bookstagrammers, booktokers, and everyone who loves the genre loudly and vitalizes it so widely. And to romance readers: Thank you for screaming your favorite books from the rooftops, thank you for your voracious appetite that allows our beloved genre to thrive, and—most of all—thank you for reading. ♥

The Book Tour

EMILY OHANJANIANS

A BOOK CLUB GUIDE

Behind the Book

To be dramatic for a moment, *The Book Tour* is kind of like a phoenix that rose from the ashes of the previous era of my life.

In early 2022, I'd been working in publishing for fifteen years. Editing books was my dream job, that rare mix of challenging and fulfilling and fun. Anytime someone found out what I did, they sighed wistfully, noting that it sounded like a "romance job"—one that FMCs in romance novels or rom-com movies might have. I agreed. I couldn't believe I got to do it for a living.

But also: I was completely burned out.

Being an editor in a publishing house is different from what most people imagine. Yes, you get to edit books and work with inspiring authors, but you also project-manage those books through their entire life cycle. The day is filled with answering emails and going to meetings, liaising with various departments, writing pitches and copy, updating metadata and triaging your submissions inbox, and and and. The job is ten jobs. And my *favorite* part—the editing—got squeezed into the midnight hours and weekends. The pace wasn't sustainable. I worried that I wouldn't be able to give my all to my work. And when you love books with all your heart and your job is bringing them into the world, you care *so much* about your work. I didn't want to let anybody down, including myself.

Grasping for relief, I thought that if I could just detach a little, I might be able to reduce the stress. The question was: How to detach?

In late January, I outsourced that question to my therapist, asking her for tools to take my heart out of the work a little more (y'know, easy peasy). In response, she asked me why on earth I would want to reduce my love for a job that clearly meant so much to me instead of figuring out how to do it on my own terms.

"Don't editors work freelance?" she asked. "Aren't they their own bosses?"

"Yeah . . ." I said warily. "But I could never do that."

"Why not?"

"Because . . ." In this economy? I knew editors who'd gone freelance and were making great money, but still. Me? "Because I've never considered it? Because working for yourself is risky, scary, so much pressure. I don't know if I have it in me—"

She interrupted me: "Emily, I work with a lot of women. And I will tell you, not a single one *doesn't have it in them*. Women are capable af—you can do anything."

It was like she flipped a switch. All at once, the truth in her statement glared brightly in my face.

A colleague had just recently told me how she sanded, stained, and sealed the concrete floors in her basement because she couldn't find a suitable contractor and figured, *How hard can it be?* (They look professionally done, btw.)

A few years ago, my friend had her third child. With two toddlers and a newborn baby now at home, I imagined that her maternity leave would be spent simply trying not to perish, but what did she do instead—in addition to caring for *three human lives*? She got her MBA.

Last year, another friend mentioned in passing that she got a new job. Like, *oh yeah, by the way, no big deal*. Turns out her new job was directing the entire northeast division of a consulting firm whose clients are Fortune 100 companies. Decidedly a big deal.

Pretty much without exception, every woman I know is a freaking *boss*.

Including, according to my therapist: me.

A few short weeks later, I resigned from my dream job and started a new dream job, as a freelance editor.

In the months that followed my resignation, as I established my business, I quickly emerged from the anxiety part of upending my career and began reaping its rewards. Not only editing books during daytime hours and having free time to read for pleasure again, but also a surge of confidence in myself, not to mention increased mental bandwidth. My brain could finally breathe again, and with my therapist's inspiring message hovering in the back of my mind—that's when Ana appeared.

Ana's character burst into my mind like the Kool-Aid Man, almost fully formed. A highly capable, confident woman—one who works hard and knows she can achieve anything she sets her mind to, whether it's graduating top of her class at Harvard Med, running an online empire, or writing a bestselling book. All while doing her best Elle Woods impression: "What, like it's hard?" Ana felt so real, so wholly human to me because she epitomizes so many women I know in real life.

I'd never considered writing a book (see: editor was my dream job, and I was truly loving freelance). But Ana being Ana, she was relentless. She wouldn't leave me alone. *C'mooon, write me, write me, write me,* she pestered. So I did what any capable woman would do—I reminded myself I had it in me, and I did the thing.

In Ryan, I wanted to create a love interest who is not only attracted to Ana's capability but reveres her for it. Pines for her fiercely *because* of her confidence and tenacity. And wants to give her the freedom to not *have* to be so capable all the time, to boot. (*Swoon,* amirite?)

One of the many things I love about romance is that, by and large, in most subgenres, it celebrates women. Our thoughts and feelings, our desires and conflicts, our journeys, our ultimate happiness. Sometimes we need reminders to celebrate ourselves. To think of ourselves with as much fondness and admiration as we do our FMCs. If Ana and Ryan's story can be anything more than a fun, joyful, romantic read, I hope that it serves as a reminder that you are capable af—and you can do anything. ♥

XO,
Emily

Questions and Topics for Discussion

1. *The Book Tour* touches on several romance tropes, like forced proximity, grumpy/sunshine, forbidden romance, etc. What are your favorite romance tropes and why?

2. A key relationship in the novel is the one between Ana and her beloved cousin, Maral. If you have cousins, how would you describe your relationship with them?

3. Ana's initial purpose with *So Proud of You* was to deliver encouragement and support to people who may not have heard such messaging from their own families. What kind of messaging did you receive growing up, and how do you feel it affected you?

4. Ana describes the experience of being the child of immigrants as having one's foot in two worlds, belonging to both and to neither. Is this an experience that you can relate to, and how?

5. Ana faces criticism for her decision to leave medicine to pursue an influencer career. Have you ever been criticized for a career decision you made, especially by loved ones?

6. Ryan is the steady calm to Ana's whirlwind. What do you think attracts these two types of personalities to each other? How do they meet each other's needs?

7. Ana's biggest lesson is learning to accept her emotions—even the negative ones. Is this something you are comfortable doing in your own life?

8. Ryan assumes responsibility for Celine at a young age, almost inhabiting the role of a father figure despite being her brother. Have you ever been in a similar situation? If not, what would you have done in his shoes?

9. By the end, Ana's and Maral's paths diverge, something Ana previously couldn't have fathomed since Maral is her *person*. Have you ever experienced a similar separation from someone important to you?

10. Which city along Ana's book tour would you most want to visit? Were there any other stops that you would have added along the route?

11. If you were casting a movie version of *The Book Tour*, who would you choose to play the characters?

EMILY OHANJANIANS lives with her family in Toronto, Canada, where she works as a professional book editor. After many years on the other side of the desk, she decided to parlay a lifelong love of joyous, escapist, romantic stories into her own writing. *The Book Tour* is her first novel.

emilyohanjanians.com
Instagram: @emily.ohanjanians

About the Type

This book was set in Caslon, a typeface first designed in 1722 by William Caslon (1692–1766). Its widespread use by most English printers in the early eighteenth century soon supplanted the Dutch typefaces that had formerly prevailed. The roman is considered a "workhorse" typeface due to its pleasant, open appearance, while the italic is exceedingly decorative.

RANDOM HOUSE BOOK CLUB

Because Stories Are Better Shared

Discover
Exciting new books that spark conversation every week.

Connect
With authors on tour—or in your living room. (Request an Author Chat for your book club!)

Discuss
Stories that move you with fellow book lovers on Facebook, on Goodreads, or at in-person meet-ups.

Enhance
Your reading experience with discussion prompts, digital book club kits, and more, available on our website.

Join our online book club community!
randomhousebookclub.com

Penguin Random House collects and processes your personal information. See our Notice at Collection and Privacy Policy at prh.com/notice.

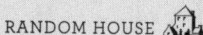